**RIMRUNNER**

So they knew her face: that meant they'd gotten her picture off the card-on-file, the same one that she'd filled out when she'd gone through Thule immigration and gotten her temp card. They had her prints, they had themselves a spacer with a black eye and a lot of scratches, and had themselves a very dead body in a room where, eventually, they were going to find a lot more of her prints –

That would take time. The question, the first question was whether they were going to break in there; whether they'd ever made the Ritter-man connection; whether they had enough right this moment to get the station legal department to swear out a warrant to take her to hospital and start asking questions under trank.

After that, two dead men were a minor problem.

**Also by the same author,
and available from NEL:**

Cyteen

**About the author**

C. J. Cherryh is a well-respected voice in the
science fiction field. She has written such
masterpieces as *Downbelow Station, Merchanter's Luck* and *40,000 in Gehenna*.

# Rimrunners

## C. J. Cherryh

**NEW ENGLISH LIBRARY**
Hodder and Stoughton

Copyright © 1989 by C. J. Cherryh

First published in Great Britain in 1990 by New English Library

*New English Library edition 1991*

**British Library C.I.P.**

Cherryh, C. J.
    Rimrunners.
    I. Title
    813'.54[F]

ISBN 0 450 54981 X

Printed and bound in Great Britain for Hodder and Stoughton Paperbacks, a division of Hodder and Stoughton Ltd., Mill Road, Dunton Green, Sevenoaks, Kent TN13 2YA (Editorial Office: 47 Bedford Square, London WC1B 3DP) by Clays Ltd., St Ives plc.

# RIMRUNNERS

# The Post-War Period

From: **The Company Wars** by Judith Nye
2534: University of Cyteen Press, Novgorod, U.T.
Bureau of Information ref. # 9795 89 8759

*In 2353, when the Earth Company Fleet fled Pell under the command of Conrad Mazian, the overriding fear of both Union and Alliance was that Mazian would retreat to Earth and draw on its vast material and human resources. So the immediate strategic consideration was to deny the Fleet that refuge.*

*It was rapidly clear that the Sol Station megacorporations which had built the Fleet did not support Mazian in his bringing the War to Sol system; and the arrival of Union warships before the Mazianni could so much as effect repairs drove Mazian into a second retreat.*

*Alliance ships, dropping into Sol system close behind the Union fleet, entered into immediate negotiations to enlist Earth in the Alliance. Union ships, returning from the battle, offered similar terms. The governments of Earth saw in this rivalry a situation which did not demand their capitulation to either side; and in effect, while it may have been Earth's fragmented politics that led to the Company Wars in the first place, it was that long Terran experience in diplomacy which enabled a reasonable peace and assured the survival of the Alliance.*

*In fact it can be argued that without Earth's independence, the Alliance could not have maintained itself as a political entity, and without the Alliance, Earth could never have remained independent. Alliance, consisting at the time only of one star-system, Pell, immediately laid claim to the abandoned Hinder Stars – a bridge of close-lying points of mass which, linking Pell to Earth, promised economic growth for the newborn Alliance.*

*Union, which had come through the war with its industry intact, laid claim to the war-ravaged nearer star-stations of Mariner and Pan-paris, simply because it was the only government capable of the huge cost of rebuilding. Further, it offered repatriation, free transportation and a full station-share to certain refugees from those*

*stations who had been evacuated to Pell — specifically to refugees
who could demonstrate technical skill and who had no record of the
kind of criminal profiteering that had arisen in Pell's quarantine
zone. This program of repatriation, the work of Union Chairman
Bogdanovitch and Defense Councillor Azov, drew a large number
of skilled and educated refugees back into Union and, according to
some speculations, purposely left the Alliance a troublesome remnant
of those whom Union considered undesirables.*

*Nor was Pell Station able to absorb such a number of unskilled
and destitute.*

*The Alliance solution was to offer similar station-shares and
free transport to the seven mothballed stations it had claimed in
the Hinder stars.*

*Meanwhile the allies had hoped that the Company Fleet had
exhausted itself with no possibility of return from deep space; but
Mazian's escape from Sol had evidently been toward some secret
supply dump, at precisely what point of mass still remains a mystery.
The Mazianni made a sudden return to Sol, but, thanks to the allied
forces who had remained on guard there, they were driven a second
time into deep space.*

*After this skirmish Union strategy was to deprive the Mazianni of
supply by driving them into deep space on the far side of Sol. Union
viewed the re-opening of the Hinder Stars and the resumption of trade
with Earth as extending a potential supply line to Mazian, who
had regularly provisioned his ships by raiding commercial shipping
throughout the latter stages of the War; but the newborn Alliance,
with only the Hinder Stars and its proximity to Earth as assets,
determined to take the risk over Union's protests.*

*It was a strangely assorted group of volunteers who went out to
re-open those abandoned stations, some adventurers, some survivors
of the riot-wracked quarantine zone at Pell, and some few certainly
with dreams of a new Great Circle trade. . . .*

*Alliance offered inducements to small, marginal freighters to take
those dangerous routes, an opportunity which promised survival for
such ships in a burgeoning post-war trade; but it reckoned without
the discovery of a point of mass off Bryant's Star that bypassed four
of the newly reopened stations, and most of all it reckoned without
the competition of Union-built super-freighters like Dublin Again
which soon moved in off Union's long-jump routes — ships which
could, via tiny Gaia Point, hitherto unreachable by any freighter,
bypass the Hinder Stars altogether. . . .*

# Chapter 1

Every day she came into the Registry, and he began to watch her – tall, thin woman, unremarkable among others who came looking for jobs, men and women beached at Thule, men and women at the end of the line and hoping for a new beginning somewhere, on some further station or aboard some ship that came to dock and trade in the days of Thule's second fading.

The jumpsuit had grown threadbare, once a definite blue, no longer crisp lately, but still clean. Her fair hair was haggled up the back and sides, a ragged mop of straight hair on top, crackling with fresh-washed static. Each day she walked into the Registry and signed the application sheet: *Elizabeth Yeager, spacer, machinist, temp*; and sat down, hands folded, at a table at the back. Mostly she sat alone, turned talk away, stared right through any hardy soul who tried her company. At 1700 each mainday the Registry closed and she would go away until the next sign-in, at mainday 0800.

Day after day. She went out to interviews and sometimes she took a temp job and dropped out for a day or two, but she always came back again, regular as Thule's course around its dim, trade-barren star, and she took her seat and she waited, with no expression on her face. The rest of the clients came and went, to jobs, to working berths or paid-passage on the rare ships that called here. But not Elizabeth Yeager.

So the jumpsuit – it looked like the same one day after day – lost its brightness, hung loose on her body; and she walked more slowly than she had, still straight, but lately with a feebleness in her step. She took the same seat at the same table, sat as she had always sat, and these last few days Don Ely had begun to look at her, and truly to add up how long she had been coming here, between her spates of temp and fill-in employment.

He watched her leave one mainday evening; he watched

her come in and sign the next morning, one of forty-seven other applicants. It was week-end, there was nothing in dock, little trade on the dockside, nothing in Thule's dying economy this week to offer even a temporary employment. There was a perpetual sense of despair all around Thule in these last months, of diminishing hopes, an approaching long night, longer than her first, when the advent of FTL technology had shut her down once: there was talk now of another imminent shut-down, maybe putting Thule Station into a trajectory sunward, to vaporize even her metal, because it was uneconomical to push it on for salvage, and because the most that anybody hoped for Thule now was that she would not suffer a third rebirth as a Mazianni base.

Nothing in port, no jobs on station except the ones station would allot for minimum maintenance.

And he watched the woman go to her accustomed table, her accustomed seat, with a view of the news monitor, the clock, and the counter.

He went to the vacant workstation behind the counter, sat down and keyed up the record: *Yeager, Elizabeth A., Machinist, freighter. 20 yrs.*

*More?* comp asked. He keyed for it.

Born to a hired-spacer on the freighter *Candide*, citizenship Alliance, age 37, education level 10, no relatives, previous employment: various ships, insystemer maintenance, Pell.

He recalled other applicants in the same category, as the records of hires floated across his desk. They were either employed at Thule on the insystemers – keeping Thule's few skimmers running took constant maintenance – and stacking up respectable credit; or they had shipped out to Pell or on to Venture. But Yeager got sweep-up jobs, subbed in for this and that unskilled labor when somebody got sick. Waiting all this time, evidently, for something to turn up. And nothing did, lately.

He watched her sit there til afternoon, when the Registry closed, watched her get up and walk to the door, wandering in her balance. Drunk, he would have thought, if he did not know that she had hardly stirred from that chair all day. It was that kind of stiff-backed stagger. On drugs, maybe. But he had never noticed her look spaced before.

He leaned on the counter. "Yeager," he said.

She stopped in the doorway and turned. Her face, against the general dim lighting of the docks outside, was haggard, tired, older than the thirty-seven the record showed.

"Yeager, I want to talk to you."

She came walking back, less stagger, but with that kind of nowhere look that said she was expecting nothing but trouble. Close up, across the counter, she had scars — two, star-shaped, above her left eye; a long one on the right side, one on the chin. And eyes —

He'd had a notion of a woman in trouble; and found the trouble on his own side, having gotten this close. Eyes like bruises. Eyes without any trust or hope in them. "I want to talk with you," he said. She looked him over twice and nodded listlessly; and he led her back into the inner, glass-walled hall, toward his office. He put the lights back on.

She might think about her safety. He certainly thought about his, the danger to his career, such as it was, bringing her back here after hours. He punched the com on his desk, waved Yeager to a chair as he sat down behind its defending breadth, hoping the other Registrar had not gotten out the front door yet. "Nan, Nan, you still out there?"

"Yes."

That was a relief. "I need two cups of coca, Nan, heavy on the sugar. Favor-points for this. You mind?"

A delay. "In both?"

He always drank his unsweetened. "Just bring it. Got any wafers, Nan?"

Another pause. A dry, put-upon: "I'll look."

"Thanks." He leaned back in his chair, looked at Yeager's grim face. "Where are you from?"

"This about a job?"

Hoarse. She smelled strongly of soap, of restroom disinfectant soap, a scent he had to think awhile to place. Under the overhead lighting her cheeks showed hollow and sweat glistened unhealthily on her upper lip.

"What was your last berth?" he asked.

"Machinist. On the freighter *Ernestine*."

"Why'd you leave her?"

"I worked my passage. Hard times. They couldn't keep me."

"They dumped you?" At Thule, that was a damned rough thing for a ship's crew to do to a hire-on, or she had deserved it by things she had done, one or the other.

She shrugged. "Economics, I guess."

"What are you looking for?"

"Freighter if I can get it. Insystemer's all right."

A little hope enlivened her face. It made him guilty, being in the least responsible for that illusion. "You've been here a long time," he said, and said, to be blunt and quick, "I haven't got anything. But there's station work. You know you can go station-work. Get basics that way, shelter, food, get an automatic no-debt ticket out of here if there's a fold-up. It's pretty empty here. Food's awful but the accommodations are take-your-pick all over station. A machinist – could damn sure get more than that, if she was good."

She shook her head.

"Reason?"

"Spacer," she said

He never quite understood that. He had heard it a hundred times before – the ones who had rather starve than go stationside, take a job, draw the ration: the ones who would go by drugs or outright suicide, rather than lose their priority on the Registry hire-list, that little edge that meant who went to the interviews first.

"Papers?" he asked, because there had been none on the record, comp-glitch, he reckoned, nothing unusual in Thule's frequently screwed-up systems.

She touched her pocket, not offering to show them.

"Let's see," he said.

She took them out then, offered them in a hand that shook like an old woman's.

"My name's Don Ely," he said conversationally, since it occurred to him he had not. He looked at the folder – not the official paper it ought to have been, just a letter.

*To any captain*, it said.

*This is to attest the good character and work record of Bet Yeager, who shipped with us from '55 to '56 and who paid passage with honest work at watch and guard, at galley and small mechanics, general maintenance, in which she has many skills which she has gained under supervision of able spacers and which she performed with zeal and care. She leaves this ship with the regret of me personally and all the crew. She earned her passage and had credit in the comp at her leaving.*

*Bet Yeager boarded without papers under emergency conditions and this ship testifies that they know her to be the person Elizabeth Yeager whose thumbprint and likeness are hereto affixed, who served honourably on this ship, and hereby, by my authority, this stands in lieu of lost identification and swears her to be this person Elizabeth Yeager according to the Pell Convention, article 10.*

*Signed and Sworn to by: T. M. Kato, senior captain, AM* Ernestine, *lately based at Pell.*

*E. Kato, a/d captain.*

*Q. Jennet Kato, chief engineer, IS pilot.*

*Y. Kato, purser.*

*G. B. Kato, supercargo, IS pilot.*

*R. Kato; W. Kato; E. M. Tabriz;*

*K. Kato. . . .*

He looked at the back. The signatures went on. The paper was wearing through at the folds. There was no other sheet in the papers-folder, nothing official but *Ernestine*'s embossed seal and the date.

"That's it?" he asked.

"War," she said, flat and quick.

"Refugee?"

"Yes, sir."

"Where from?"

"*Ernestine*," she said. "Sir."

Cold turn-down. Go to hell. Sir.

He saw Nan behind the glass wall, coming down the hall with the tray. She caught his eye discreetly, got his nod and came inside with it.

Yeager took the cup Nan offered. Her hand shook. She ignored the wafers and set the cup down untasted on the table beside her.

"Set it there," Ely told Nan, meaning the tray with the wafers, indicating the same table. He took his own cup and sipped at the sweet stuff as Nan set the rest by Yeager. "Have a wafer," he said to Yeager.

Yeager took one, picked up the cup and sipped at it.

Hell with you, that look still said. I'll take hospitality, you better not think this is charity.

"Thanks," he said to Nan. "Hang around, will you?"

Nan gave him a look, added zero up, and left in irritated, worried patience. Nan had her own problems, probably had dinner going cold in the oven if this dragged on, maybe had a date to keep. He owed her for this one: and Nan clearly thought he was a fool. Nan, being a veteran of the Registry at Pell, had probably seen hundreds of Yeagers while he had sat in insulated splendor in Mariner's shipping offices. Certainly they dealt with odd types in this office. All of them had troubles. Some of them *were* trouble.

He laid Yeager's paper on the desk in front of him. Her eyes followed that, the first hint of nervousness, now that Nan was gone, up again, to meet his. "How long," he asked, "have you been here?"

"Year. About."

"How many jobs?"

"I don't know. Maybe two, three."

"Lately?"

A shake of the head.

"Maybe I could find something for you."

"What?" she asked, instant suspicion.

"Look," he said, "Yeager, this is straight. I've seen you around – a long time. This – " He flicked a finger at the paper from *Ernestine*. "This says you know how to work. You show that to the people on interviews?"

A nod of her head. Expressionless.

"But you won't take station work."

A shake of the head.

"Those papers don't say anything about a license. Or a rating."

"War," she said. "Lost everything."

"What ship?"

"Freighters."

"Where?"

"Mariner. Pan-paris."

"Name." Mariner was his native territory. Home. He knew the names there.

"I worked on a lot of them. The Fleet came through

there, blew us to hell. I was stationside." No passion in the voice, just a recital, hoarse and distant, that jarred his nerves. It was too vivid for a moment, too much memory, the refugee ships, the stink and the dying.

"What ship'd you transport on?"

"*Sita.*"

That was a right name.

"No records, no registry papers." She set the cup down, hardly tasted, pocketed the wafer. "They got stolen. So'd everything else. Thanks all the same."

"Wait," he said as she was getting up. "Sit down. Listen to me, Yeager."

She stood there staring down at him. A light sweat glistened on her face, against the dark outside, the lone desk light in the next glass-walled cubicle that was Nan's backroom office.

"I was there," he said. "I was on *Pearl*. I know what you're talking about. I was in Q just the same as you. Where are you living? On what? What pay?"

"I get along. Sir."

He took a breath, picked up the paper, offered it back, and she took it in a shaking hand. "So it's none of my business. So you don't take handouts. I watch you day after day coming here. It's a long wait, Yeager."

"Long wait," she said. "But I don't take any station job."

"And you'd rather starve. Have people *offered* you other jobs?"

"No, sir."

"You turn them down?"

"No, sir."

It would have been in the record. Illegal to turn them down, if she was indigent.

"So you fail the interviews. All of them. Why?"

"I don't know, sir. Not what they're looking for, I guess."

"I tell you what, Yeager, you do the scut around this office for a few weeks, you keep the place swept and the secs happy. A cred a day worth it?"

"I stay on the Registry."

"You stay on the Registry."

She stood there a moment. Then nodded. "Cash," she said.

It had to be. He nodded. She said all right, and she was his liability, a problem not easy to cure; and his wife was going to look at him and ask him what the hell he was doing handing out seven cred a week to a stranger. A Registry post on Thule was no luxury berth, and if Blue Section questioned it he had no answer. Probably it broke regulations. He could think of three or four.

Like unauthorized hire-ons in a station office.

Like failing to notify security of a probable free-consumer. No way in hell that Bet Yeager afforded a sleepover room. Damned right she was an illegal, taking Station supplies and returning nothing.

Day after day in the Registry. With the smell of restroom soap.

He fished in his pocket. What came out was a twenty-chit. He found no smaller change. He offered it, regretfully.

"No, sir," Yeager said. "Can't say where I'll be twenty days from now. Ship's due."

"So pay me back if you get a berth. You'll have it then."

"Don't like debts. Sir."

"Won't fill the gut, Yeager. You don't eat, you can't work."

"No, sir. But I'll manage. Your leave, sir."

"Don't be — " — *a damn fool*, was in his mouth. But she was like as not to walk out then. He said: "I want you here in the morning. With a full stomach. Take it. Please."

"No, sir." The lip trembled. She didn't even look at the money he was holding out. "No charity." She touched the pocket, where the papers were. "Got what I need. Thanks. See you tomorrow."

"Tomorrow," he said.

She gave a scant nod, turned and left.

*Military*, he thought, putting it together. And then he was worried, because there was nothing like that in the letter, very few freighters were that spit-and-polish, and military meant station militia, or it might just as easily mean Fleet or Union, if it was more than a few years back.

That scared him — because big, armed merchanters were rare, because *Norway*, the only real force the Alliance had, was God-knew-where at any given time: the Earth Company Fleet was God-knew-where too, and every unidentified blip that showed up on station longscan sent cold chills through Thule.

Call security, was the impulse that went through Ely's bones. An investigation was not an arrest. They could do a background check, ask around, see if there was anyone else of the three thousand souls on Thule who remembered Bet Yeager on *Sita* or in Pell's infamous Q-zone.

But Security *would* arrest the woman if she came at them with that none-of-your-business attitude, Thule's very nervous Security would certainly haul her in and question her . . . *feed* her, that much was true . . . but they would go on to ask unanswerable questions like Where are you living? and How are you living? And maybe Bet Yeager was everything she said, and had never committed any crime in her life but to starve on Thule docks, but if they got the wrong answers to those questions about finances, they would put Bet Yeager on station rolls and charge her with her debt, and Bet Yeager would end up a felon.

A spacer – would end up shut up in a little cell in White Section. A spacer – who would suffer anything to keep to dockside and the chance of ships – would end up working for a fading station til they turned the lights out.

That was what his inquiry could do to Bet Yeager.

He walked out into the front office, behind the counter, saw Yeager open the outside door.

He had no idea where Yeager might go for main-night; tucked up in some cold corner of dockside, he guessed, wherever she had been spending her nights. *Wait*, he could say, right now. He could take her home, feed her supper, let her sleep in the front room. But he thought of his wife, he thought of their own safety, and the chance Bet Yeager was more than a little crazy.

The word never left his mouth, and Yeager went out the door, out into the actinic glare and deep shadow of dockside.

"Huh," he said, recalled to the office, to Nan standing by her desk looking at him.

He motioned toward the door. "You know that one?"

"Here every day," Nan said.

"Know anything about her?"

Nan shook her head. They shut down the last lights,

walked to the door themselves. The door sealed and they walked down the docks together, under the cold, merciless glare of the floods high in the overhead, in the chill and the smells of cold machinery and stale liquor.

"I offered her a five once," Nan said. "She wouldn't take it. You think she's all right in the head? Think we – maybe – ought to notify security? That woman's in trouble."

"Is it crazy to want out of here?"

"Crazy to keep trying," Nan said. "She can sit still. Another year, they'll shut us down, pack us up, move us on to somewhere. She could get a berth from there, likely as here. Maybe more likely than here."

"She won't live that long," Ely said. "But you can't tell her that."

"I don't like her around," Nan said.

He wished he could do something. He wished he knew if they ought to contact security.

But the woman had done nothing but go hungry. He had worked a year in the Registry System, helped administer the hiring system that was supposed to be humane, that was supposed to give highest priority and first interviews to the longest-listed. But it ended up encouraging cases like Bet Yeager, it ended up making people hang on, suffer anything rather than step out of line and let somebody get in ahead of them, God knew where another spacer was going to come from now who could threaten Yeager's seniority on the roll, if it was not the incoming *Mary Gold* that let him off – but tell that to Yeager, who was down now to scrabbling for the little temp jobs that made the difference in how long she could hold on, and *those* had become nonexistent. Another few days and it was the station bare-subsistence roll: the station judiciary always reckoned free-consumers at ten cred for every day they could not prove they had been solvent. In Bet Yeager's case, that money had probably run out a year ago. And she had tried so damned long.

Next week, she said. Maybe next week. A ship was due in.

But none of the other ships had taken her.

# Chapter 2

**B**et walked carefully, having refuge in sight, the women's restroom on Green dock, a closet of a facility, an afterthought the way the whole dock was an afterthought, the bars and the sleepovers, the cheap restaurants, in a station designed for the old sublights and now trying, in a second youth, to serve the FTLs and their entirely different needs.

And there was this restroom. It was graffitied and it stank and there was one dim light in the foyer and one no better in the restroom, with four stalls and two sinks, where spacers in the early heyday of the place had engraved shipnames and salutations for ships to come:

Meg Gomez of *Polaris*, one said. Hello, *Golden Hind*.

Legendary ships. Ships from the days when stations were lucky to get a shipcall every two years or so. Something like that, station maintenance had painted over.

Damn fools.

It was home, this little hole, a safe place. She found the dingy restroom deserted as it usually was, washed her face and drank from the cold trickle the better of the two sinks afforded –

Her legs failed her. She caught herself against the sink, stumbled and sank down against the wall beside it. For a moment she thought she was going to pass out, and the room swam crazily for a while.

Not used to food, no. She'd wanted the coca for the sugar in it, but the little that she had drunk had almost come back up right in Ely's office and now the half a wafer threatened to, while her eyes watered and she fought, with even breathing and repeated swallows, to keep from the heaves.

Eventually she could take a broken bit of wafer from her pocket and nibble on it, not because it tasted good, nothing did, now, and eating scared her, because the last had made her sick and she couldn't afford to lose the little food that was in her stomach. But she tried, crumb at a time, she let it dissolve on her tongue and she swallowed it despite the cloying sweetness.

Smart. Real smart, Bet.

Got yourself into a good mess this time.

Time was on Pell she'd hid like this. Time was on Pell she'd been almost this desperate. Hard to remember one day from the other when it got that bad. Somehow you lived, that was all.

Somehow you stuck it out, in this dingy place, sitting on an icy floor in the loo trying to keep your gut together. But bite at a time, you kept it down and it kept you alive, even when you got down to a pocket full of wafers and the hope of a cred-a-day job. A cred got a cheese sandwich. A cred got a fishcake and a cup of synth orange. You could live on that and you had to survive this night to get it, that was all.

She'd stopped believing yesterday, had really stopped believing. She'd gone in to the Registry today only because maintenance checked out the holes now and again, because going to the Registry was a way to stay warm, and showing up there proved she was still looking, the one proof an uncarded resident could use to maintain legal status. And most of all it kept her priority with any available job on that incoming freighter. Hoping for that was an all-right way to die, doing what she chose to do, looking forward to what she insisted was the only thing worth having. A good way to die. She'd seen the bad ones.

And if it got too bad there was a way to check out; and if the law caught her there were ways to keep from going to hospital. She carried one in her pocket. She'd gotten down to thinking about when, but she hadn't gotten to that yet, except to know if she passed out and people were calling the meds she might; or if they convicted her and slapped a station-debt on her – she could always do it then. Just check right out, screw the lawyers.

And now there was a little more chance. So she'd been right about sticking it out so far. She could turn out to be right in everything she'd done so far. She could win. That ship next week could come in short-handed. It could still happen.

So she sat there in the shadow of the sink awhile til one whole wafer had hit bottom, and then she knew she had to move because her legs and her backside were going numb, so she pulled herself up by the sink and got some more of the metal-tasting water on her stomach and went into one of the stalls to sit down, arms on knees and head on arms, and to try to rest and sleep a little, because that was the warmest place, the walls of the stall cut off the draft that got everywhere else, and manners kept people from asking questions.

Two women came in, way late, probably dock maintenance: she heard the murmur of voices, the curses, the discussion about some man in the crew they had their eye on. They sounded drunk. They went away. That was the only traffic, and Bet drowsed, catnapping, thinking that tomorrow evening, she could go to a vending machine and put that one cred in a slot and have a hot can of soup . . . start with that. She'd had experience with hunger. Keep to the liquids when you came off starvation, do a little at a time, nothing greasy. Her stomach was working on the dissolved wafer and the third of a cup of coca, not sure how to cope with what it had.

The docks outside entered a quiet time then, less noise of machinery and transports moving outside. Alterday on Thule was hardly worth the wake-time. Hardly any of the offices stayed open on that shift, no ship traffic was in to make it necessary, the few bars were mostly empty. Early on, when she'd had a few chits left, she'd gone into bars to keep warm. Docks were always cold, every dock ever built would freeze your ass off. Thule-alterday shut down just like some old Earth town going into night, and the general lack of machinery working all over Thule during that off-shift, she reckoned, and the demand of all the people back in their apartments for heat, meant a fierce chill-down in the dockside air. Which meant stationers were even less likely to be down here during main-night, and station scheduling didn't care to do anything about it.

So nothing got loaded out there, nothing got signed, moved, done, anywhere on the docks until maindawn brought the lights up. Thule was dying. The Earth trade opened up again after the War, but Thule had turned out to be superfluous, the run had drawn a few big new super-freighters like *Dublin Again*, that could short-cut right past the Hinder Stars, and the discovery of a new dark mass further on from Bryant's meant a bypass for Thule, Venture, Glory and Beta, which was over half the re-opened stations at one stroke.

A route straight to Earth via Bryant's, straight past the place *Ernestine* had left her, the Old Man apologetic, saying, "Don't be a fool, Bet. We've got to go back to Pell, is all. We'll be short, but we can make it. It's no good here and further on is worse."

*Hope you made it*, she thought to old Kato. But she knew *Ernestine*'s chances, a little ship, running mostly empty, trying to get back to Pell against the tide of economics, luck, and the onus of her own mass, because the Hinder Stars were heartbreak, the Hinder Stars had drunk down more than one small ship, and *Ernestine*'s last hope, after losing all her cargo credit in a major mechanical, was Pell, just getting there, even stripped down, carrying a few passengers whose fares would get her a little credit in Pell's banks.

But Pell wasn't where Bet Yeager wanted to go.

"Not me," she'd said, "not me."

*Ernestine*'s crew had argued with her, they'd known her chances too. The free-hands other ships let off found berths here and went on. Jim Belloni had tried to give her a third of his sign-up money when he left on the *Polly Freas*. He'd gotten her royally drunk. He'd left it in her bed.

So she'd gotten drunk again. She still didn't regret that extravagance. Not even when her belly cramped up. It was the times like that kept you warm on nights like these.

She catnapped a while more, waked hearing the sound of the outside door.

Her heart jumped. It was unusual, alterday, main-night, for somebody to be in this particular nook to need this particular restroom. Maintenance, maybe. Plumber or something, to fix that sink.

She tucked her knees up in her arms, just stayed where she was, shivering a little in the cold. It was a man's step that came on in. Rude bastard. No advisement to any possible occupant.

She heard the door close. Heard him breathing. Smelled the alcohol. So it wasn't a plumber.

*You got the wrong door, mate. Go on. Figure it out.*

She heard the steps go the little distance to the door
and stop.

*Go on, mate. G'way. Please.*

She heard the door close, She dropped her head against
her knees.

And still heard the breathing.

*Oh God.*

She shivered. She did not move otherwise.

The steps came back to the stall. She saw black boots, blue
coveralls.

He tried the door. Rattled it.

"Get the hell out of here!" she said.

"Security," he said. "Come on out of there."

*Oh, hell.*

"Out!"

It was wrong. It was damned indelicate. And he stank of
alcohol.

"Hell if you're security," she said. "I'm spacer, on layover.
You get your ass out of this restroom, stationer, before you
get more than you bargained for."

"No ship in, skuz." He bent down. She saw an unshaven,
bent-nosed face. "C'mon. C'mon out of there."

She sighed. Looked at him wearily. Waved a hand. "Look,
station-man. You want it, you owe me a drink and a sleepover,
then you got it all night, otherwise I ain't buying any."

A toothy grin. "Sure. Sure I'll give you a good time. You
come out of there."

"All right." She took a deep breath. She put her feet
down.

She saw it coming. She knew it, she tried to clear the
sudden grab after her ankle, but the knees wobbled, she
staggered and he tried again, under the door.

She smashed a foot down, bashed his head into the tiles,
but he twisted over and got a hold on her ankle and twisted,
and there was no place to step but him, and he was pulling.
She staggered against the stall, felt his fingers close, tried to
keep from falling and went down against the toilet seat, a
crack of pain on one side, pain in her cheek as she rebounded
and hit the wall and then the floor beside the toilet. His hands
were all over her, he was crawling under the stall door onto
her, arms wrapping around her, and everything was a blur of

lights and his face. He hit her, cracked her head back against the tiles once and twice, and for a while it was exploding color, alcoholic breath, his weight, his hands tearing at her clothes.

*Damn mess*, she thought, and tried to stay limp, just plain limp, while he ripped her jumpsuit open and pawed her, which she couldn't stop: he had her pinned between the toilet and the stall wall.

Just a little more breath. Just a little time for the stars to stop exploding.

He started choking her then. And there was damned little she could do except struggle. Except get her right hand to her pocket, while his stubbly mouth was on hers and he was choking the sense out of her.

She got the razorblade. She kept her fingers clenched despite the pain and the fog in her brain and she got it out and slashed him down the leg. He reared up, howling, his back against the stall door. She nailed him dead-on with her boot-heel and he gasped and fell down onto her, so she got him with the razor again.

Then he was mostly trying to slither out of the stall, and she let him. She got an elbow over the toilet and heaved herself up and got the stall unlatched while he was throwing up outside.

He was on his knees. She caught her balance against the row of stalls and kicked him up under the jaw. When he hit the sink and went down on his back with his leg under him, she waited until he tried to get up again and then kicked him in the throat.

After that he was a dead man. She could finish it, while he lay there choking to death, but she just stared at him with her skull pounding and her vision going gray – she came to with the water running and water in her hands and splashing up into her face. Which was stupid. She could be wrong about how hard she'd hit him. He could have a knife, he could get up and kill her. But she looked to see where he was with the water dripping off her face and her hands and running down her collar and he was lying there with his eyes open.

So he was dead. A dizzy wave came over her. She threw cold water on him to be sure he wasn't shamming, but there was no blink or twitch.

Another wave. She remembered he'd yelled. Somebody could have heard the shouting outside. She looked herself over for marks. There were scratches all down her chest and on her throat. There was blood on her jumpsuit, blood soaked one knee. So she peeled down and washed that leg of the jumpsuit in the sink until the water ran pale pink and the jumpsuit was mostly clean; and she almost blacked out, so she leaned her elbows against the sink to scrub, and she wrung out the jumpsuit and got it on again, one leg and a lot of spots all over it icy cold. So she used the blower to dry them. It was dangerous while the docks were this quiet. Security might hear.

But she wanted to go on leaning there in the warm air, wanted to stay there the rest of the night. She pushed the blower switch again and again, legs braced, staring at the man on the floor, while the gray and the red came and went in her vision. There was a trail of blood from the stall to where he'd died. She remembered the razor, but she had that in her pocket again, she found it there. Along with two cred chits.

She was walking outside on the docks. She couldn't remember how she had gotten there. She remembered the restroom, that was all. She remembered the man on the floor. Remembered going through his pockets, stopped, and turned and looked around to find out where she was.

You could get caught from evidence too. Station bank had her prints. But a woman could use the damn restroom. So she had. So a lot of people had. So he was where he had no business being. She walked further, thought about the law getting a genetyping off his fingernails: but they had to catch her first, they had all those cards, all those prints they did have, all those women to question.

Another dark spot. She felt wobbly-hungry. She kept walking, eating a very few soggy crumbs of wafers she scraped out of her pocket, and finally, steadier than she had been, with two cred in her pocket, she went to a bar and had a plastic cup of watery chowder she could even manage to eat.

The barman was lonely, she sat and talked. It turned out he wanted more than that. "All right," she said. Her head hurt and she was sick and she was tired. She'd done it to pay off a bet, never done it just to pay a tab, but he was quiet, he was lonely, she didn't even care what his name was, he had something to offer her and she was down to that finally, if it got her a warm spot and away from the law. "Place to sleep," she said. "What the hell."

"I got that," he said.

So she went back in the storeroom with him, he made a pallet down, she lay down with him and he did what he wanted to while she lay there and thought about Pell and old shipmates.

His name was Terry. He found out she was hurt, she gave him a story about a dockworker getting rough in a sleepover and her walking out on him. He got her something for her headache and he was careful with her, he excused himself to go take care of a customer and he came back and started in with her again, while she was half asleep.

So that was all right too. He was gentle about it. He was soft, sweaty and nervous, she let him do whatever he wanted, he waked her up a couple of times, but she was too weak to do anything. "I'll come back tomorrow night," she said. "I'll be better. Do what you want. You buy me breakfast."

He didn't say anything. He was busy at the time. She went out like that, just back into the dark. A couple of times she felt him. In the morning he bought her breakfast. She sat at a table in the bar and she ate plain toast while she watched the morning news, about how a woman had found a dead man in a restroom on Green dock.

Terry was busy doing his checkout with the owner. He was hangdog, slightly overweight, nothing to look at and nothing too clean. He never looked the owner in the eye. The owner looked at her once, a long stare. But Terry Whoever was smart enough to pay cash for her breakfast, so she could have been a chance customer and the owner had nothing on him.

The dead man was a dockworker, two years resident on Thule, recently laid off his job. The company he'd worked for had folded. He'd been on station work. His supervisor had docked him three days' work yesterday for drinking on the job.

They said his windpipe was crushed.

They said they were checking fingerprints. Naturally. And

when they got down to hers, she could say she'd been here, Terry might say she'd been a customer all night, Terry might even say they'd had a fight, if she could keep him interested.

She took careful spoonfuls. Her head hurt. Her whole body hurt. She had never done what she'd done just to get a bed and a meal, not even on Pell.

But there was a ship next week. After weeks since the last, there was a ship named *Mary Gold*, and damn, she meant to be on it.

Anything. Anything, now, to get off Thule.

# Chapter 3

The woman Ely called Nan looked up from her desk in the outer office, took one look at her and came abruptly to her feet.

"Fell," Bet said, because the eye was going to go black, she'd had a look at it in the bar's restroom. She looked like hell, she had her collar zipped up high to cover the scratches on her throat, she was still wobbly, and she smelled of sweat and God knew what. But she was on time. She signed in at the desk and she ignored the stare a moment doing that. Then she looked up.

"Ma'am, I got faint and I fell. I'm sorry. I got breakfast this morning. Kind man gave it to me. I'll be better."

"O dear God," the woman said, in a shocked, bewildered way, and just stood there, so that Bet found herself staring eye-to-eye with this stationer woman, this upright, respectable stationer woman who could kill her with a phone call to the authorities. "God. Sit down."

"I'm here to work," Bet said. "Mr. Ely said he'd pay me."

"Just sit," Nan said sharply, pointing to a chair behind the counter. And when she did that, Nan brought her coca and wafers.

She took them. "Thank you," she said meekly, figuring she was in no place now to quarrel. "Ma'am, I really want the job."

It was begging. But she was out of choices.

"I'll call the infirmary," Nan said.

"No." Her heart thudded. She almost spilled the cup over. "No. Don't."

"You didn't fall," Nan said darkly.

Bet looked up, met more straight sense than she'd looked for in this dry, plain woman. Not accusing. Just knowing damn well a fall didn't do what had happened to her face. "I got shoved up a wall. Rough night. Please. I don't want any trouble. It's just bruises. Give me a chance. I'll work back in the offices. Won't frighten the clients."

"Let me talk to Mr. Ely. We'll fix something up."

"No meds. Please. *Please*, ma'am."

"Stay here."

Nan left. Bet sat and sipped the coca. It hurt her cut mouth; the sugar made a loose tooth ache. She held the cup in both hands, trying not to panic, watching toward the glass-walled corridor where the back offices were, trying not to think about phones and security and the restroom last night.

But her heart was beating in hard, painful beats, enough to make her dizzy when Ely came back with Nan and looked down at her. "Wall, huh? You look like hell, Yeager."

"Yes, sir."

He looked at her a long while. Arms folded. He said, "I want to talk to you in my office."

"Yes, sir," she said. She put the cup down on the counter. "Thank you," she said to Nan, but, "Bring it," Ely said. So she did, as she followed him down the corridor and into his office.

He sat. She sat, the cup warming her hands.

"You all right?" he asked.

She nodded.

"You report it?"

She shook her head.

"You get robbed?"

"Nothing to steal," she said.

"Are you all right?" he asked again, which she guessed finally in a stationer's delicate way meant had she been raped.

"I'm fine," she said. "Just a disagreement. Damn drunk and I crossed paths." God, if he or Nan put it together with the morning news – "I just wasn't walking very steady last night. He shoved me. I cussed him. I hit the wall. I went out. He apologized. Bought me breakfast."

Ely looked as if he doubted her. He looked at her a long time. Then: "Where are you staying?"

She thought, desperately. A year since anyone had asked that. She remembered the name of the bar. "Rico's. Good an address as any."

"You staying there?"

"I get my mail there."

"Who writes to you?"

She shrugged. The heartbeat was doing doubletime. But Ely didn't have to help. Ely didn't have to hand out a cred-chit to a down-and-gone spacer. He didn't have to call a woman friend in when he talked to her, all proper, so she could read his signals, that it wasn't her he was after, that he was trying to do a good deed. That kind was scarce on station docks. "Nobody," she said. "But if someone did, it'd be there. If something came in."

He just looked at her. Finally: "You do the trash-sorts. You run errands. You sign in every morning and you make sure you look like a client otherwise, if somebody's here besides Nan and me. I don't want Personnel to see you. If somebody comes in and you get caught in the back hall, just make like you were going to the restroom."

She nodded. She sat back in the back room and sorted the trash for recycling. She weighed it out and she noted the weight on each bundle because sometimes the cyclers cheated you. She'd heard that about Thule the first day she was onstation.

Mainday noon she got her cred-chit from Ely and she went to a sit-down restaurant and had another bowl of soup.

That night she went back to Rico's and Terry, his last name was Ritterman, bought her a beer and a cup of chowder.

He took her into the back then. She undressed, she said she had to wash her clothes, so he got her a bucket and she scrubbed her jumpsuit and her underwear and hung them to dry over the heat-vent. He came up behind her while she was doing that and put his hands on her. Without saying anything. She let him. She let him pull her down on the floor and he still wanted to touch her, that was all, while she shut her eyes or stared at the ceiling, and finally somebody came in out front, so he swore and went out to see about that.

She turned over and wrapped up in the rug and went to sleep for a while before he came back and woke her up, turning her over again and starting in.

Customers came in. He was gone awhile. He came back and he got down again and she thought he must've been a long time without, he'd wear out finally and maybe go to sleep or let her sleep the rest of the night. But he never did.

She got dressed in the morning, he bought her breakfast. He wanted her to come to his apartment. "I got to work," she said.

She earned her chit. She thought about finding somewhere else to spend the night, she was recovered enough to be more fastidious, and Terry gave her the chills, but that meant no supper and no breakfast.

So she went back to Rico's.

It was that way every day. Every day she got the single chit. Every main-night she went back. Terry got stranger. He wanted her to come to his apartment. He wanted to show her his place, he said.

He got to doing weird things, like wanting to tie her up. "Hell if you do," she said. "I don't play those games."

He acted embarrassed. But she was worried about the drinks he gave her after that. She was worried about going to sleep with him. He kept fingering her scars and asking how she'd gotten this one and that one and being weird, just weird, the way he went at sex while he was doing that. "Quit it," she said, finally, and shrugged him off. He slammed her back again, her bruised skull hitting the tiles and sparking color through her vision. She lay still, because she'd told her subconscious she was in trouble, — *don't react, don't react, he's a fool, is all —*

"That night you came here," he said. "That black eye and all."

He hurt her. She got a hand free and clouted his ear. "Hurts, dammit!" He pawed after a hold on that arm and she gave him the knee. He yelled. She got away, off the blanket, over where her shoulders hit the corner and the shelves.

"You damn bitch," he said.

"Just back off." She levered herself up and sat down on a beer keg. It was cold. The air was. The whole place stank. "Back off, friend."

"Come on back."

"Hell. Just let me alone. I'm tired. This is my night-time, man. I work mainday. Just back off."

"You and that black eye. That man you say grabbed you — "

"Just leave me the hell alone. You got your supper's worth."

The front door chimed. He sat there, ignoring it, breathing hard.

"You got customers, Terry-lad."

"Security's looking for some woman, off in Green, same night, same night you came here, all marked up. You got no card, no ID, come in here beat up – Don't call the meds, you say. Don't want anything to do with the meds – I bet you don't, sugar."

Someone came into the hall. Shouted for service.

"Get out there, dammit," she hissed. "You want the law in here?"

"You're the one don't want the law, sugar." He put his hand on her leg. "I do what I want. Got that? I know where you hang out at the Registry. I followed you. Hear? If I call the law I can tell 'em where to look, even if you aren't in the comp, like I bet you aren't, sugar. . . ."

"You want the law dammit, get out there and wait on those guys before they call security!"

He stroked her skin. "You be here. You better be here. I got you for a long time. You better know I do."

More shouting. "Just a minute," he yelled. He got up and limped around putting his clothes together, staggered out the door fastening his belt.

She sat there on the beer keg with her arms clenched around her knees. She wanted to throw up.

She thought it through, what her choices were. She listened to the voices in the bar and she got up and got her clothes from over the heat-vent, she dressed and she walked out into the bar where he was waiting on a rowdy tableful of dockworkers.

He gave her a stark, mad look. She went over to the bar and got a drink for herself and listened to the rude comments from the four dockworkers, the invitation to have a drink, go to a sleepover with them and do this and that exotic number.

Attractive notion, considering. But the thought that kept coming through cold and clear was how fast Terry Ritterwhoever would be on the com to Central.

And with her fingerprints at the scene, the law just needed

to get a look at her black eye and those scratches and to know that she was a transient and an illegal to get a judge to give a writ for real close questions.

Under trank.

She gave a scowl toward the dockworkers. Loaders. Lousy lot. But cleaner than Terry Ritterman. Maybe even decent types, sober and solo. Terry came up and put his hand on her hip.

She took it. She leaned on the bar and drank her vodka sip by sip, she stared at the dockworkers with the thought that any one of them would be a hell and away better pick.

She walked over and got a bottle, she went over and poured their glasses full while they protested they hadn't ordered it.

"It's on me," she said, and played a scenario through in her mind, stirring up a ruckus where a soft little man could get his neck broken by some dockworker. But that still meant the law. It still meant questions.

So they drank, she played up to them and enjoyed Terry squirming and worrying, played it all the way and hoped to keep them there til maindawn, when the owner came.

Terry rang up her charges on his own card, Terry glowered at her and beckoned her over, but she ignored it until he picked up the phone.

Then she came over to him.

"You go home with me," he said, cutting the phone off then. "You're going to pay for this."

She said nothing. He pinched her hip. Hard. She stared at the mirrored room and when he demanded a response from her, nodded.

The dockworkers left, fifteen minutes before maindawn. She poured herself synth orange while they walked out.

"My place," Terry said. "Understand?"

She nodded again. He rubbed her shoulder. She flinched away and went to sit down and drink her breakfast, while the owner came and checked out the accounts. The owner gave her the eye and gave her a laconic good morning.

"'Morning," she said. Probably he was more than suspicious why an orange juice and toast always turned up on Terry's card. It was that kind of look.

Probably that look followed them when Terry came and told her to come with him, they were leaving.

"You'll learn," he said, linking his arm through hers. They walked like lovers as far as the lift. He had to behave himself: there were other passengers in the car. But he trapped her arm again when he got her off on his floor, over in Green. He radiated heat like a furnace. He kept squeezing her hand in his soft, sweating fist. He started telling her in a half-whisper that she'd like him, he really had to teach her not to misbehave, but they could get along, she could stay in his apartment and as long as she did the things he wanted he'd keep her safe from the law.

She said nothing, except when he squeezed down on her hand and insisted she say yes. So she said yes.

He got his keycard out of his pocket. He led her to a dingy door in the dingy miniature hall that could have been the bowels of some ship, instead of a station residency. He opened the door and he turned on the lights with a manual switch and he shut the door again.

It was an ugly place. It was all clutter. It stank of bad plumbing, unwashed dishes and old laundry. She watched him take his coat off and throw it down on the table. His hands were shaking.

She watched. She waited til he turned around and reached for her. She took his hand and twisted around, and he hit the floor. Hard.

"I want to tell you something," she said in that instant of shock. "My ship name's *Africa*."

His eyes got wide. He scrambled to get up. She let him. He staggered over against the wall. There was a phone around somewhere in the filth, she was sure of that. She gave him a chance to make a dive for it. She leaned on a chair back, just waiting. But he froze, gone white.

"You're lying," he said, standing there with his hair on end. "You damned whore, you're lying to me."

"Got separated from my ship when the Fleet pulled out. Just mixed with the refugees, worked docks awhile, talked my way aboard a freighter." She patted her breast pocket. "Even got myself an Alliance testimonial. Said I lost my papers. Not too hard to get this far. I was born spacer, friend, that's a fact. But I was *trained* marine."

"Go away," he said, waving a fluttering hand. "Get the hell out of here. You got nothing to gain here. I got no percentage in saying anything."

She shook her head slowly. "Oh, no, friend, you know I'm going to kill you. And in your case I'm going to take my time."

# Chapter 4

"'Morning, Nan," she said, at the door of the Registry, and Nan looked at her oddly and tilted her head as she unlocked.

"You're right cheerful," Nan said.

She nodded. And went and had her morning cup of coca, in the back, out of view of the couple of clients that were coming in the door — that being an employee privilege.

Rico was going to wonder for maybe an hour this mainday evening, when Terry failed to show. And maybe he'd call up the apartment and maybe leave a message, but Terry's kind was cheap, Terry's kind was the sort that showed up to work a stretch and then got his life in a mess and just dropped out of sight. Rico might have a new alterday man by mainday next, that was all Rico was likely to do. Meanwhile Terry's card still had credit in the bank, it worked in the vending machines — she wasn't fool enough to walk into some restaurant and claim to be Terrence Ritterman; she just used the machines, just cheap stuff, just to tell anybody who happened to check the card-use records that Terry Ritterman was still walking around, no reason for alarm unless someone had specific reason to be alarmed.

And was it unusual if alterday help in a skutty bar walked out one shift-change with some piece of ass that might have more money than he did, and just not bother to tell the owner he wasn't coming back?

She could live off stuff in the apartment, but she wanted to keep the card active. So she'd had this morning's breakfast out of the dockside vending machines. You didn't need an access code check for that, you just slipped it in and out came breakfast. Or lunch. Or dinner. There'd been a little cash in Ritterman's pocket. Eight cred. She knew where that could turn to a cheap duffle: she could use that, for when the ship came; that and a few other necessaries off Ely's cred a day, that she could save now.

She'd left the body in the bedroom, she'd turned the heat off in there, she had stuffed the vents and cracks under the door and sealed everything up with tape. It could get real unpleasant in a week or so, but there were no neighbors close and if people noticed a scruffy spacer coming and going out of Terry Ritterman's apartment, all they could figure was, she was crazy as he was for hanging around with him. And nobody much bothered a crazy woman.

She'd washed the jumpsuit, she'd had herself a shower, she'd scrubbed with perfumed soap and she'd given herself a haircut; and Ely gave her a second look when he came in. Looked pleasantly surprised to see her scrubbed-up and cheerful, as if he'd really done something spectacularly good with his charity.

"Looking good, Yeager."

"Adds up," she said back, and grinned. "Few meals don't hurt, stationer-man."

She had a real warm feeling for people like Nan and Ely. They were probably real happy doing good. And it was really too bad, they were probably going to shake their heads and have long second thoughts about their helping strangers when station-law found what was in that apartment bedroom and linked everything up.

Damn mess was what. Get herself a ship out of here, get clear back to Sol if she had to, change ships where she could, just keep moving far enough and long enough and stay alive.

The Old Man was operating hell and gone away from here. *Africa* was still alive, and maybe she could be lucky enough, sometime, somehow, to match up her course and the Fleet's. Meanwhile she just hoped to hell to avoid Alliance law and Mallory's attention. *That* was the thing gave her the chills, that turncoat Mallory was out hunting her old friends, and *Norway* made these ports from time to time, Mallory being respectable now. The rest of them had come up on the losing side, that was all, and Mallory was smart, Mallory had gotten herself on the outs with Mazian, then luck happened and here was Mallory, shiny-new loyalties and all. Smart captain. Damn good, Bet gave her that. If luck had been on her own side she'd have gotten snagged up in *Norway*'s company instead of *Africa*'s and have herself a clear record right now – have credit in her pocket, have a snug spot and a rack to sleep in, rich as a skut could get. No matter *Norway*'s captain was a hardnosed bastard who'd gunned down her own troops and tried to blow *Africa* to hell – no love lost at all between Mallory and Porey. They'd fought in space, fought on dockside, Mallory had arrested three of *Africa*'s marines and *Africa* troops had sniped at *Norway*'s on the docks of Pell before they got to open space. Not to ask what *Norway*'s skuts would do to one of *Africa*'s if they got her aboard.

Long, long way to die, she knew that.

And if station law caught her they'd hold her for Mallory, who would take a direct, even personal interest in her.

She shivered. She did her work, she thought about that ship that was coming and how long they were going to be in port – some three, four days from now. Another three, four days to fill *Mary Gold*'s tanks –

While the contents of that bedroom got more noticeable, long enough for an inquiry into that business in the restroom to get damned close.

They said they were going to close down Thule, they were going to blow it and shove the pieces into the sun so there was no way the Fleet could even mine the place for metal – so there wasn't going to be a Thule Station for a ship to come back to, the people were going to be scattered across a dozen lightyears and maybe they wouldn't even bother about the records, just junk everything, maybe forget all the old records as useless and she could go on and never worry about the business on Thule catching up with her someday, if she could just keep it quiet for a week, keep on using Ritterman's card in places Ritterman might go, and convince the computers he was still alive. Thule wasn't like Pell, where there might be relatives to ask questions: the types that had come out to this armpit of the universe were all loose-footed, the dregs of Pell, mostly; the sweepings out of Q-section, refugees and nobodies hoping for a break that might have come but wouldn't, now. And Ritterman wasn't the sort to have a lot of friends.

Just get the supplies she needed, look respectable enough to impress *Mary Gold*, work to the next port, and just try

to make herself useful enough to stay on – anywhere, any
port but Pell – that being *Norway*'s port.

That was why she'd told old Kato she was staying, because
*Ernestine* was going back. And Kato had believed the crap
about her wanting to take her chances on the Rim, but Kato
had desperate business to do at Pell and a ship in debt and
Kato left her for a fool, good luck, mate, stay out of trouble,
hope you find your luck.

Hell.

She went back to Ritterman's apartment, she read the messages on the comp, which was only a notice from station
library that tapes were overdue. She found the ones the
library wanted back, she laid them on the table, to take
out and dump in the return the next morning, she looked
the address up in the station directory to be able to find it.

And she kept the vid tuned to station traffic ops, always
hoping, while she made down a comfortable bed on the
couch and drank Ritterman's vodka, ate Ritterman's chips
and candy and read Ritterman's skutty picture-books til
bedtime.

Back to the docks the next morning, down to the row of
vending machines spinward of the lift. She had her mouth full
of cheese puffs when the bell rang, that loud long burst that
meant a ship had just dropped into system; and she gulped
it down with a mouthful of soda and took a breath.

So she made her leisurely stroll toward the corner where
the public monitor was, because it was just the longscan had
gotten the info from the zenith buoy, and that was an hour
and a half light away.

Thule was a dim double star, hardly more than a mod-
erately treacherous jump point, no traffic: the buoy was
close-in, and that ship, if it was *Mary Gold*, a day and a
half early, had probably just shaved a quick lighthour or
so off that distance in the *V*-dumps since that information
had started on its way to Thule Central. Which still put her
some hours out at realspace *V* and a long, long burn to go,
plus another hour on docking once she got close-in.

A cold-hauler, *Mary Gold*, just the regular supply run out
from Pell. And on from here to Bryant's, that was the

schedule. Moving less mass than expected, she reckoned: that could speed a ship up a day, easy. Thank God.

But when she got to the corner where the monitor gave its tired, gray cycles of information, the shipname was *A S Loki*.

Her heart ticked, just a single bewildered jolt.

Who in hell is *Loki*?

She stopped, ate a couple of cheese puffs, washed them down and stared at the progress marker on the vid. She wasn't the only one. Dockworkers gathered around to wonder.

It was coming in smartly enough. It was an Alliance ship designation.

Her stomach felt upset. She heard somebody speculate it was a Unionside merchanter, just come into the Alliance.

Not unless it was some damn tiny ship, she thought, something come in from some godforsaken arm like Wyatt's Star, clear on Union's backside: she knew every shipname that was worth knowing, knew the Family name, the cargo-class, — and the armament class. Down in *Africa*'s 'tween-decks, shipnames and capabilities were a running topic. The skuts in the 'decks might not be able to do a thing in a ship-fight, but if you were down there strapped into your rack and your ship was going into a firefight, what the cap was on the other ship was a real important topic; and if you were going to have to board after that, go onto some merchanter's deck into twisty little corridors full of ambushes, you liked to know those little details. Damn right.

She ate her cheese puffs, she watched the data unfold — then suddenly she remembered the time and she ducked out of the crowd and hurried on down to the Registry.

"I wondered if you were coming in today," Nan said, at her desk as she slipped in the door.

"Sorry." There was a reg about eating and drinking in the front office. "Breakfast. I'll dump this in the can. 'Scuse."

"You know what ship that is?" Nan asked.

She shook her head. "Thought I knew 'em all. Spooks."

Trooper word. It was getting to be common, since the War, but she wished she hadn't said that. She oozed past Nan and into the back hall, where Ely met her and asked, "You know that ship?"

"Just saying: no, sir. New one."

Ely looked worried. Well he should. She went on into the back-office work area, tipped the last of the puff-crumbs into her mouth and washed them down with the dregs of the soda, chucked the foil and the can into the cycle-bin before she walked out where the vid was.

Where everybody was: Ely, Nan, the three other clients looking for jobs this morning, all standing, all watching the vid and not saying a thing, except she got looks from the three stationers that maybe added her up as an honest-to-God spacer and maybe a source of information.

"Do you know – ?" one started to ask her.

She shook her head. "New to me, mate. No idea." She folded her arms and looked at the numbers, heard one of the stationers say that looked like an all-right approach, the numbers didn't look like a strike-run.

*Depends, station-woman. Depends on the mass. Entry vector. Lot of things, damnfool. Sometimes you got to maneuver. And we lied to those buoys, damn if we didn't.*

She watched, standing there with her arms folded, thinking, the way the stationers around her had to be thinking, that it could be one of the Fleet; feeling, the way the stationers certainly weren't, a little stomach-unsettling hope that it was one of Mazian's ships.

Hope like hell it wasn't a Fleet ship going to pull a strike for some reason, and hole the station.

And hope while she was at it that any minute that single blip was going to start shedding other blips, that that screen was going to go red and start flashing a take-cover, and *Africa* itself, with its riderships deployed, was going to be on station com, old Junker Phillips himself telling a panicked Thule Station that a Fleet ship was going to dock, like it or not.

She watched. She bit her lip and shook her head when one of the stationers asked her about the numbers. She listened while the com-flow from station intersected the com-flow from the incomer, all cool ops, station asking the intruder for further ID and a statement of intent, the intruder within a few minutes light, now, but going much, much slower.

Decel continuing, the numbers said.

"Huh," she said finally, figuring there was nothing much going to happen for a while, so she went over and sat down, which got a momentary attention from the stationers, who looked at her as if they hoped that meant something good.

So she relaxed. Watching on vid, waiting to see, was hell and away more comfortable than they'd gotten between-decks, just the audio, the com telling them what they absolutely needed to know, while the ship pulled G and racks and paneling groaned like the pinnings were going and somebody's gear that had been loose when the takehold rang became a flock of missiles.

Nan and Ely drifted back to work. One of the job-seekers went over to the counter to finish an application, but the other two just stood there looking up at the vid.

"*This is* Loki *command*," the vid said finally, amid the muted, static-ridden comflow that had been coming through. "*Clear on your instructions, Thule Station. We're a fifteen tank, running way down.*"

God. No small tank on that thing.

"*This is Thule Stationmaster. We've got a scheduled shipcall,* Loki, *we can do a partial.*"

Bet sat there with her feet in a scarred plastic chair and listened, with her heart picking up its beats, brain racing with the figures while the timelag of ship and station narrowed, but not enough.

An unknown and a tank that size. Claiming Alliance registry.

Thule Control reported the incomer had done the scheduled burn.

"*Thule Stationmaster,*" the same voice came over the com, finally, "*this is* Loki *command. We're carrying a priority on that fill. Request you route us to your main berth.*"

The stationers finally figured out *priority*. There was a sudden tension in them. Bet sat there with her feet up, arms folded, knowing it was still going to be a while, with her heart thumping away in leaden, before-the-strike calm.

Priority. There was only one berth on Thule with a pump fitting that was going to accommodate a starship. The pump was two hundred years old and it managed, but it was slow, and the station tanks were nowhere near capable of turning two large-cap ships in the same week — it took *time* for Thule's three skimmers and the mass-driver to bring in a ship-tank load of ice.

If that ship was priority and if it was Alliance, then it was official, something recommissioned, something Mallory herself might have sent, if it was telling the truth and it wasn't just talking itself into dock to blow them all to hell.

And if it was official, and if it was sitting there for the five days it was likely to take drinking Thule's tanks down to the dregs, there was no way in hell a freighter like *Mary Gold* was going to get into that single useable berth and out again for another week.

Or two or three.

Information trickled out of Station Central. Central got a vid image. "God," Nan said when that came up, and Bet just sat there with her arms crossed on a nervous stomach.

Small crew-quarters, a bare, lean spine, and an engine-pack larger than need be.

"What in hell?" Bet said, to a handful of nervous civ stationers, and put a foot on the floor suddenly. "Damn, what class is that thing?"

Ely was out of his office again, coming out to look at the vid in this room, which showed the same thing as the vid in the office. People tended to cluster when they thought they might be blown away.

"Oh, God, oh, God," one of the clients kept saying.

Bet got up while the comflow ran on the audio, business-as-ordinary, with an apparent warship coming in to dock.

"Bet," Nan said. "What is it?"

"Dunno," she said. "Dunno." Her eyes desperately worked over the shadowy detail, the midships area, the huge vanes. "She's some kind of re-fit."

"Whose?" a civ asked.

Bet shook her head. "Dunno that. It's a re-fit, could be anything."

"Whose side?" someone asked.

"Could be anything," she said again. "Never seen her. Never see ships in deep space. Just hear them. Just talk to 'em in the dark." She hugged her arms around herself and made herself calm down and sit down on the table edge, thinking that there was in fact no telling. It was whatever it wanted to be. Spook was a breed, not a loyalty.

But there was no likelihood it was going to open fire and blow the station. Not if it wanted those tanks filled. Not if its tanks were really that far down. Either it was hauling mass that didn't show or it'd been a long, long run out there.

The comflow kept up. The stationer-folk huddled in front of the vid, remembering whatever stationers remembered, who'd been through too much hell, too many shifts, too much war.

Not fools. Not cowards. Just people who'd been targets once too often, on stations that had no defense at all.

Bet kept her arms clenched, her heart beating in a panic of her own that had nothing to do with stationer reasons.

# Chapter 5

I t took time to get anything into dock at Thule – minimum assists, a small station. The process dragged on, a
long series of arcane, quiet communications between the
incomer and Station Central, long silences while the station
computers and the incomer's talked and sorted things out.
That was normal. That relieved the stationers of their worst
fears, seeing that the incomer was actually coming in instead
of shooting.

So things moved out on the docks, people began to separate
themselves a little from available vids: Bet went out for her
lunch, down to the vending machines by the lifts.

She got looks from the office types – as if suddenly anybody
who looked like a spacer was significant, whether or not
she could possibly come from that ship. She ignored the
looks, got her chips and her sandwich and her soda, tucked
the chips into her pocket and walked out on Thule's little
number one dock, where a cluster of lights blazed white on
the gantry, spotting the area where dockworkers went about
their prep, Thule's usual muddled, seldom-flexed system of
operations.

She gave a disgusted twitch of her shoulders, looked at
that port, swallowed bites of sandwich and washed them
down with soda.

Damn, that ship was a problem, it was a major Problem,
it bid fair to cost her neck. It was probably Alliance, all right,
her luck had been like that for two years, but her heart was
beating faster, her blood was moving in a way it hadn't in
a long time. Damn thing could kill her. Damn thing could
be the reason the law finally hauled her in and went over
her and got her held for Mallory, but it was like she could
stand here, and part of her was already on the other side of
that wall, already with that ship – and if it killed her it still
gave her that feeling awhile.

"Shit," she muttered, because it was a damnfool thing to feel, and it muddled up her thinking, so that she could smell the smells and feel the slam of G when the ship moved and hear the sounds again –

She swallowed down the sandwich, she looked at that dock and she was *there*, that was all, and scared of dying and less scared, she wasn't sure why.

But she went back to Nan and stood by her desk with her back to the locals the other side of the counter and said, "Nan, I got to try for this one."

"Bet, it's a rimrunner. We got a freighter coming in – it's going to *be* here. This thing – "

Like she was talking to some drugger with a high in sight –

But: "I got to," she said. "I got to, Nan."

For reasons that made her a little crazy, for certain; but crazy enough to have the nerve – like the Bet Yeager that Nan and Ely had been dealing with and the Bet Yeager who was talking now were two different things, but she was sane enough to go back to friends, sane enough to know she didn't want to alienate the only help she had if things went sour.

"You turn 'em in my request?" Bet asked. "Nan?"

"Yeah," Nan said under her breath, looking truly worried over her, the way not many ever had in her life.

So she left.

The dockside swarmed with activity, the dull machinery gleaming under the floods, crews working to complete the connections, in Thule's jury-rigged accommodation for a modern starship. It wasn't a place for spectators. There were few of them. Thule's inhabitants remembered sorties, remembered bodies lying on the decking, shots lighting the smoke, and there were no idle onlookers – just the crews who had work finally, and the usual customs agent, and no more than that.

Excepting herself, who kept to the shadows of the girders, hands in pockets, and watched things proceeding. She inhaled the icy, oil-scented air, watched the pale gray monitor up on top of the pump control box ticking away the numbers, and felt alive for a while.

The whole dock thundered to the sound of the grapples

going out, hydraulics screamed and squealed, the boom groaned, and finally the crash of contact carried back down the arms, right through the deck plating and up into an onlooker's bones.

Soft dock, considering the tiny size of the Thule docking cone and the tinsel thinness of little Thule's outer wall: damn ticklish maneuver, another reason the dock was generally vacant. There *was* the remote chance of a bump breaching the wall. But there was equally well a chance of a pump blowing under the load or God knew what else, a dozen ways to get blown to hell and gone anywhere on Thule. Today it failed to matter. She thought that she could, perhaps, a major perhaps, go the round of vending machines and buy up food enough and stash it here and there in the crannies of Thule docks, maybe go to cover if somebody got onto what was in Ritterman's bedroom. She could just ignore this ship, wait it out and hope to talk her way onto *Mary Gold* when and if she came. That was the hole card she kept for herself, if *Loki* was what she was afraid it was.

But *Mary Gold* had become a small chance, a nothing chance with too many risks of its own.

She waited, she waited two hours until little Thule got its seal problem corrected and got *Loki* snugged in and safe. She stood there very glad of Ritterman's castoffs under the jumpsuit, made as it had been for dockside chill: breath still frosted and exposed skin went numb, and she kept her hands in her pockets. Ice patched the corrugated decking, and the leaky seal that was dripping water at the gantry-top was going to breed one helluva icicle in five days' dock time.

Finally the tube went into place, the hatch whined and boomed open, letting out a light touch of warmer, different air, a little pressure release; and of course it was the customs man first up the ramp.

She found a place to sit in the vee of a girder, cold as it was, she sat and she watched, and finally the customs man came out again.

She shivered, she felt – God, a sense of belonging to something again, just being perched out here freezing her backside, like a dozen other sit-and-waits she remembered. And it was damn foolish even to start thinking that way. It was suicidal.

But she wasn't scared, not beyond a flutter in the gut which was her common sense and the uncertainty of the situation; she wasn't scared, she was just waiting to risk her neck, that was all, she thought about where she'd been and where she could go, and it was all still remote from here.

She heard the inside lock open again, heard someone coming. Two of the crew this time, in nondescript, *not* military. Her heart beat faster and faster as she watched them meet with the dock-chief, all the slow talk that usually went on.

More crew came down. More nondescript, nothing like a uniform, no family resemblance either. She worked cold hands, got up from her wedged-in perch between the girders and shook the feeling back into her legs, then put her hands in her pockets and walked up to the latest couple off the ramp.

"You!" a dockworker called out.

But she ignored that. She walked up, nodded a friendly hello – it was a man on rejuv and a woman headed there, both in brown coveralls, nothing flashy. Work stuff. "'Day," she said. "Welcome in. I'm looking. Got any chance?"

Not particularly friendly faces. "No passengers," the man said.

She touched her pocket where the letter was. "Machinist. Stuck here. Who do I talk to?"

A long slow look, from a cold, deeply creased face; from a hollow-cheeked female face with a burn scar on the side.

"Talk to me," the man said. "Name's Fitch. First officer."

"Yes, *sir*." She took a breath and slipped her hands back into her pockets, a twitch away from parade rest. Damn. Relax. Civ. Dammit. "Name's Yeager. Off *Ernestine*. Juniormost and they had to trim crew. Others got hire, but it's been slim for about six months."

"Not particularly hiring," Fitch said.

"I'm desperate." She kept a tight jaw, breathing shallow. "I'll take scut. I don't ask a share."

A slow, analyzing stare, head to foot and back again – like he was figuring goods and bads in what he was looking at.

"Dunno," Fitch said then, and hooked a quick gesture toward the ramp. "Talk to the Man."

She was half-numb from standing in the airlock, in the kind of dry cold that froze up any water vapor into a white rime on the surfaces and left the knees locking up and refusing to work when she stepped over the threshold into *Loki*'s dim gut. The knees had gotten to the shaking stage when she got through into the ring (there looked to be only one corridor) and did a drunken walk down the tiled main-deck. There was one light showing, one door standing open, besides the hatches that were probably the downside stowage.

She reached it, saw the blond, smallish man at the desk. Plain brown jumpsuit. The gimbaled floor made a knee-high step-up. She stood in the corridor and called up, "Looking for the captain."

"You got him," the Man said, and looked down at her from the desk, so she stepped up by the toehold in the rim of the deck and ducked to clear the door.

"Bet Yeager, sir." Fitch's name had gotten her inside. Now she was shivering, her teeth trying to chatter, not entirely from the cold. "Machinist. Freighter experience. Looking for a berth, sir."

"Any good?"

"Yes, sir."

A long silence. Pale eyes raked her over. A thin hand turned palm up.

She reached to her pocket and pulled out her papers, trying not to let her hand shake when she put the folder in his hand.

He opened it, unfolded the paper, read it without expression, looked on the back – everyone did, the last few signatures. And folded it again and gave it back.

"We're not a freighter," he said.

"Yes, sir."

"But maybe you're not spacer."

"I am, sir."

"You know what we are?"

"I think I do, sir."

A long silence. Thin fingers turned the stylus over and over. "What rating?"

"Third, sir."

More silence. The stylus kept turning. "We don't pay standard. You get a hundred a day on leave. Period. Board-call goes out ten hours before undock. My name's Wolfe. Any questions?"

"No, sir."

"That's the right answer. Remember that. Anything else?"

"No, sir."

"See you, Yeager."

"Yes, sir," she said. And ducked her head and got out, off the deck, down the corridor, out of the ship, still numb.

She thought about going to the Registry. She *wanted* a drink, she *wanted* to go out on the docks with a little in her pocket and hit the bars and get a little of the cold out of her bones, but she was a stranger to *Loki* crew and she could not use Ritterman's card.

So she went back to the apartment and made herself a stiff one.

*Loki* was no freighter. The captain told that one right. She was still shaken, the old nerves still answered. *Loki* wasn't a name she knew, but the name might not have been *Loki* six months ago, or the same as that a year ago. The frame was one of the old, old ones by the look of its guts, a small can-hauler with oversized tanks where the cans ought to be, something naturally oversized in its engine pack – tanks easy come by, easy to cobble on even for a half-assed shipyard like Viking, which had built three such ships the Fleet knew about – ships to lie out and lurk in the dark of various jump-points, to run again with information.

Except the Line was shady, and the spooks went this side and that of it, and the Fleet had trusted them no more than Union had: if you pulled into a point where a spook was, you took it out and asked no questions.

So this particular spook was all official in the Alliance. The free-merchanters had put themselves a boycott together, the merchanters had taken over Pell, and now the spooks the stations had built to keep themselves informed came out in the open, government papers and everything.

Damned right the captain wasn't going to quibble about her papers. When somebody shiny bright and proper came in there looking for a berth, that was the time *Loki* might ask real close questions.

She sipped Ritterman's whiskey. And tried not to think that, spook or not, it was about as good as joining up with Mallory. She had to stop the little twitches, like the one that said stand square, like the *sir* and the *ma'am*, like the little orderly habits with her gear that said military –

So they were Mallory's spies, most probably – but not *with* Mallory, not *too* legitimate, since spooks had regularly sold information to any bidder. And going onto that ship was a case of hiding in plain sight. If she could learn the moves, learn the accent, learn a spook's ways – then she could get along on a spook ship, damn sure she could.

Dangerous. But in some ways less dangerous a hire than on some merchanter on the up and up, with a crew that expected a merchanter brat to know a lot of things, things about posts she'd never touched, especially about cargo regs and station law, things that never had been her business.

She had stood real close to *Africa*'s Old Man once or twice. A couple of thousand troops in *Africa*'s gut, and Porey rarely put his nose down there, except he went with them when they went out onto some other deck, Porey was always right in the middle of it; and being close to him that couple of times – she'd gotten the force of him, gotten right fast the idea *why* he was the Old Man, and why everybody jumped when Porey said move. Porey was the damn-coldest man she had ever stood next to; and maybe it was only how desperate she was and how *Loki* was the hope she'd thrown double or nothing on, but this Wolfe, the way he moved, the way he talked – said competent, said no-nonsense, said he was a real bastard and you didn't get any room with him. And that touched old nerves. She knew exactly where she was with him, cut your throat for a bet, but show him you were good and you just might do all right with a captain like that.

Spook captain. That Fitch, that Fitch was no easy man, either. That woman with him you didn't push. That told you something about the captain too.

She poured herself another glass. Maybe, she thought, she was crazy. She wasn't sure whether she ought not just drop out of sight now until the board-call rang, stay mostly in the apartment, not go back to the Registry at all except she wanted to keep that card of Ritterman's active and she didn't want any chance of getting an inquiry going into Ritterman's inactivity.

Five days, at least, for *Loki*'s tanks to fill. Maybe closer to four til boarding, counting the ten hour boarding-call. If she could just keep things quiet that long, do the daily run to the vending machines, back to the apartment, and stay put, then everything would work out.

All she had to do was stick it out and check the comp for things like overdue tapes, things that could require Ritterman's intervention.

Meanwhile she got out Ritterman's collection of fiches and started sorting. That kind of trade goods was low-mass, it would pack real easy, Thule customs only worried about guns and power-packs and knives and razor-wire and explosives, that kind of thing, it had no duty on anything, and there were no regs on Thule about liquor.

She started packing, at least the sorting part.

She bedded down, the way she had been doing, on Ritterman's couch, she watched a vid, she drank herself stupid and she woke up with a headache and the absolutely true memory that she had a berth.

Best damn night she'd had in half a year.

# Chapter 6

She made the morning trip to the vending machines, she lived off chips and soda and cheese sandwiches she heated and added Ritterman's pickles and sauce to. That was the second day down. She stayed in the apartment otherwise and she went through everything in the cluttered front rooms, to see what was worth leaving with.

She checked the comp, she drank, she had another cheese sandwich for supper, she looked at skuz pictures and she made a hook and fixed up the one of Ritterman's useable sweaters that was really snagged – like ship, a lot. You tinkered with stuff, you mended, you washed, you did the drill, you scrubbed anything that didn't fight back, but hell if she was going to give Ritterman a good rep by cleaning up this pit: she just kicked his stuff out of her way and washed what she was going to drink out of.

But that night sleep came harder, and the level in the vodka bottle went down markedly before she could rest.

She kept thinking about immigration and the one formality there was, that she was going to have to log out of station records to get by that customs man. Right now she might be hard to find, on Ritterman's card, in Ritterman's apartment, with not even the Registry knowing where she was right now and only Nan and Ely able to connect her name to her face – but all of that changed the moment she had to hand dockside customs that temporary ID card of hers and that customs man sent the information back through the station computers, right from a terminal on dockside, to be sure she was who she said.

The one thing Alliance was touchy about besides weapons was people, because Mariner and Pan-paris had learned the hard way that people were much more dangerous – the kind of people who came and went under wrong names and false

IDs, at the orders of people parsecs away. Customs insisted on checking crew IDs: they'd checked her onto Thule off *Ernestine* and they'd check her off and onto *Loki*.

And that check, if anyone was looking for her, if they had any questions about her fingerprints among a hundred others, if the customs man himself had any interest in why her face showed marks –

She tried to think of a way to dodge that check, like maybe going down to Thule's few bars, finding *Loki*'s crew, maybe sleeping over with somebody and maybe talking her way into an early boarding that might miss customs altogether, if *Loki* would cooperate –

But doing anything that might make *Loki* back off taking her on, that scared her more than the check-out did.

Besides, getting in with the crew during liberty took money she didn't have, and a body was expected to stand her own bar-bill.

She had certainly fallen asleep with worse prospects on her mind, but solitude was a new affliction. Her mind kept going back to old shipmates on *Africa*, wondering if they were still alive, wondering whether the major was, and who Bieji Hager was sleeping with now.

Teo was dead. Blown to cold space. So was Joey Schmidt and Yung Kim and a thousand more, at least.

*Damn* Mallory.

So here she was, taking a berth on a spook ship, one that might be on Mallory's orders to boot. So maybe it was fair pay to old debts, if they ended up saving her neck. She imagined Teo shaking his head about what she was doing, but Teo would say, Shit, Bet, dead don't count. And Teo would never blame her.

She tossed over onto her belly and tried to not to think, period, just tried to go away, just go nothing, nowhere, like when the G-stress was going to hit soon and the missiles were going to fly and if you were a skut in a carrier's between-decks, you just rode it out and let the tekkies keep the ship from getting hit.

Damn right.

Fourth day. She got up, stumbled across the clutter in the apartment and checked the public ops channel on Ritterman's vid to see when the board-call was posted. M/D 2100, it said. Fill 97% complete.

Thank God, thank God. *Mary Gold* was in, now, *Mary Gold* had made it into Thule system during the night; and the vid said: Condition hold, which meant that *Mary Gold* was taking a slow approach, lazing along and probably damn mad and desperate, figuring on a fast turn-around and instead finding out they could be weeks down on their schedule – the same way that Bryant's Star Station, next on *Mary Gold*'s route, was going to find its essential supplies a month late; and so was everybody else down the line. A little schedule-slip at a place like Pell, a huge, modern station – that was nothing. But here . . .

It was a question, what the reason was on that priority of *Loki*'s, whether it was just using it, hell with the stations and the trouble it caused. Or whether there was an urgency about its getting outbound.

And urgency with that kind of ship meant . . .

She thought about *Africa*, she thought about the chance of finding herself on the wrong side of things in a firefight.

Of getting blown to hell with a spook, that was what would happen. By her own ship, her own old shipmates.

She shoved thoughts like that out of her mind, she had her breakfast of chips and sat and read, and checked the comp for messages.

Ads, all ads, like always. Not one call for Ritterman, nothing but those overdue tapes, in all the time she'd been here.

Popular man.

She got down to serious packing finally. She'd made herself wait for that, the way she always made herself wait for things she wanted too much. She had another bag of chips, she had a shower, she trimmed her hair, and finally she started putting her personal kit together, the last thing, the very last to go into the duffle.

The door buzzer sounded.

She stopped still. She stood there in the bathroom just breathing, that was all, afraid it was somebody with a key. So – so if it was, Rico could vouch for her, she'd been with Ritterman, she'd come in here when she knew she was shipping out – had her stuff in stowage here, hadn't seen

Ritterman in days, never asked where he was, he'd always said just walk in –

Second push at the buzzer.

Third.

But they went away.

She let go her breath. And brought her little bag of personal things out into the living room and finished packing, watching the time.

1527.

The phone beeped.

God. She held her breath again until whoever it was gave up.

She stood there, thinking about how to move, where to move: *fast* was the only way, fast and direct and if somebody was waiting outside in the hall or down by the lift, just to see who came out –

Oh, God, she'd given Rico's as an address for the Registry.

If somebody had asked for her at Rico's, if Rico had told them some woman with a black eye had gone off with Ritterman, they could be looking for *her*, instead of Ritterman –

And they were going to find Ritterman once they got in here.

She checked her pockets to be sure of the card, she grabbed up the duffle and she left, down the dingy metal hall, heart pounding, down to the lift.

Nobody. Thank God.

She ditched the card behind a loose base-moulding, there by the lift, a place where it was out of her possession if she got searched, and available if she needed it – she'd spotted that two days ago; she took the lift down to dockside, she walked out, she just kept all her movements normal. If they hadn't followed the trail as far as *Loki* yet, if she could just get down the dock and get aboard, counting on Thule's usual inefficiency –

Crew came and went all the time til board-call, a body forgot things, somebody had to go back and check with the ship's purser: and a ship had no particular wish to have anybody but crew coming and going through its hatch, especially in a skuz place like this, so customs habitually reckoned a ship had a strong motive to police its own entries, and customs didn't watch that until the last moment, at least Thule didn't. There was just that log-off formality if they were taking passengers.

And ships didn't ordinarily let new-hires on til board-call, when there was crew aboard to keep track of them and make sure they behaved.

So it was 1600. She was five hours early.

She walked toward that berth and toward the lights, and she kept thinking all the while that, even if the station mofs were tracing her the long way around, and they had gotten to Rico's via Nan and Ely, and tracked her all the way to Ritterman, they *knew* she was spacer, and they didn't need to go that far. She was on the Registry list, Nan and Ely couldn't cover that fact even if they would lie for her and even if Nan didn't tell half as much as she knew: once they were looking for her, the authorities needed only one functional neuron to think about that ship in port and to know where she was going to go.

Dammit, they *couldn't* get you for having fingerprints in a damn restroom.

*All right*, she thought, approaching that ship-ramp, that dark skein of lines and gantry-braces and the maze of pump-housings and buttresses, *all right, Bet Yeager, so something goes sour, no good breaking heads, there's enough of them to do what they like. If they grab you, you go with it, you do the innocent act, you get them to call Nan, that's what, Nan's got good sense – Nan might, could nudge the situation on your behalf –*

She walked up to the working area. She had her foot on the ramp when the voice yelled, "You there!" and she did a moment's flash between running up that ramp and risking a shot in the back and sanely realizing *Loki*'s hatch was going to be shut up there, even if she got that far, no way they left it wide open to dockside cold.

"I'm crew," she said to the men who walked up to her – no dockers, for sure, very definitely upstairs types. "I'm *Loki* crew. Got a load to take aboard. What's the trouble?"

"Elizabeth Yeager," one said, and showed her an ID. "We'd like to ask you some questions, upstairs."

"For what? I got a board-call going in a couple of hours!"

"You'll make your board-call, if you can satisfy the legal office. We have some questions, that's all."

"About what?"

"Come with us, Ms. Yeager."

"Hell – I got a call to make, then. Just a minute."

"No calls, Ms. Yeager. You can notify anyone you want upstairs."

She looked at the two of them, had this momentary irrational impulse to try her luck making a break for it and losing herself on dockside, to try to get to crew, but what she'd already decided weighed heaviest in crisis-thinking, always did. You had your plan, and especially when things went absolutely worst-case you stuck to it, you most of all didn't get rattled and do something stupid. "All right," she said, and waved a hand toward the lifts, distant across the dock. "All right. Let's get this settled."

But she was close to panic. She wasn't sure what she'd decided to do was right, now. She distrusted knee-jerk decisions, *always* wanted to think, always wanted to be sure, as long as it was something she'd had a chance to plan out, but God, she was in a mess, she knew she was; and that mess involved stationers, who did things by rules that made no sense, every station eccentric and unpredictable in what it allowed and the way it worked.

So they knew her face: that meant they'd gotten her picture off the card-on-file, the same one that she'd filled out when she'd gone through Thule immigration and gotten her temp card. They had her prints, they had themselves a spacer with a black eye and a lot of scratches, and had themselves a very dead body in a room where, eventually, they were going to find a lot more of her prints –

That would take time. The question, the first question was whether they were going to break in there; whether they'd ever made the Ritterman connection; whether they had enough right this moment to get the station legal department to swear out a warrant to take her to hospital and start asking questions under trank.

After that, two dead men were a minor problem.

They walked her far across the docks and down, they got her into an official-use lift, and they shot straight up to Thule's little blue-section – a single level up, then, and down a corridor to grim little offices.

"ID," the officer at the desk asked, and she handed over the temp card. "Papers," the man asked next, which scared her as much as anything else in the proceedings. That was everything, that little folder. But they had a right to ask and they had a right to hold it until they were satisfied. They said they would put her duffle off behind the desk and it would be safe. They had her sit down and fill out a form that asked questions like: *Present address* and *Current Employment* and *Most Recent Prior Employment: Date.*

Deeper and deeper. They wanted to know things she couldn't answer – like what her credit balance was and where receipts were that proved she'd been spending cash since she left *Ernestine.*

They wanted to know stationer references. She gave Nan and Ely.

Desperately she said she'd been living with Nan. Nan might cover for her. It was the only thing she could think of.

God, if they asked her the specific address. . . . Nan lived in Green, she remembered Nan and Ely talking once. She could remember that.

*Estimated income this month,* they asked. She counted. She wrote, *25 cred.*

Counting what she'd gotten off Ritterman, off the dock-worker, off Ely. She was going to lie, but she'd spotted the next question, with a possible out, a possible escape from all the traps.

*Other source of support,* it asked.

*Nan Jodree,* she wrote. *Room and board, even exchange, for cleaning and errands.*

She looked at the time. *1710.* She sweated. The last answer put her legal, she knew it had to – if Nan backed her, and she had some belief that Nan would, then they couldn't hold her on the likeliest charge, free-consuming, which was what they'd want to use to keep her here while they checked the other things.

If it was legal on Thule to do private work.

If Nan wouldn't panic or just answer some trick question and hang her, never knowing.

They took the form, they looked at it, and then they asked her to step into an interview room – "To answer a few questions," they said.

"I answered!"

"Ms. Yeager," the men said, holding the door.

So they had her sit down at a table, they sat on the other side and they asked her questions, like What happened to your face, Ms. Yeager?

Fight with a drunk, she said, the same as she'd told Terry Ritterman.

Where?

Green dock, she said.

When?

She had to be honest about that: the eye made it clear, and it was possible Rico might remember the date she'd shown up. She said, "Last week, I don't know what day."

"Wednesday?"

"I dunno. Could have been. – Look, I got to call my ship. I got a right to call my ship. . . ."

They said, "What's Nan Jodree's address?"

And she said, suddenly thinking like a merchanter, "I got a right to call my captain."

"What's his name?" they asked.

"Wolfe!" she said, the first answer she'd had absolutely no doubt of.

But then they went back to the first questions.

"I don't have to answer you," she said. "I answered you once. Call my captain."

"Do you want to go before the judge?"

Civil law. Alliance law. Stations and civil rights and judges and hospitals where they could get the truth out of you. Where *nobody* could keep from spilling everything they'd ever done or thought about doing. "I don't have to talk to you without my captain knowing."

"Come on," they said, "you're not crew yet, you aren't logged out of station records."

"I'm *Loki* crew, I've got a right to notify my captain!"

"No, you don't," they said. "You can call in a lawyer, that's the only thing you're allowed."

"Then I'm calling *Loki*'s legal staff."

That stopped them. They went outside and consulted,

maybe what to do next, maybe what their choices were or whether they had to do that: she had no idea.

They kept arguing about something; then three of them walked off and left her there, in that cubbyhole of a room with one large window. One stayed standing by the door.

She didn't know what they were up to now. Maybe checking with Nan.

Maybe finally making that call to Wolfe, who could not be happy about getting a call like that from a new hire-on.

They had never searched her. That meant, she supposed, she wasn't quite under arrest yet. That meant she still had the little razor. She thought about it while she sat there. She thought that Wolfe was about one jump away from Mallory herself, if Wolfe got onto her case – if they got a court order to question her under trank and found out what she was; but there was no chance of that, no chance unless maybe they rushed an indictment through at the last moment, between the board-call and the undock, when *Loki* had to be away, on whatever business was so urgent they'd prioritied out an honest freighter and created hardship on stations down the line.

She could see the outside clock through the window. She saw the time pass 1745, and 1800 and 1830, and she got up finally and tried the door, to talk to the man outside, but it was locked. She bashed its metal face with her fist.

"I got a board-call to answer!" she yelled; then, with no answer at all, not even any interest on the man's part, she walked back to the chair and sat down, raked a hand through her hair, and came the closest yet to complete panic.

She hoped – hoped if nothing else, they'd called Nan, and Nan or Ely had backed her, and Nan or Ely was going to come through that door and take her side, do something clever, get her clear. At least they could call Wolfe for her, if no one else would.

But it wasn't Nan or Ely who stood there when they unlocked the door. It was uniformed Security.

"Bet Yeager," one said, "you're under arrest."

"For what?" she asked, all indignation.

"For the murder of one Eddie Benham, the murder of one Terrence Ritterman . . ."

"Terry isn't dead!" she yelled back. She'd primed herself

for that one while she'd been sitting here. "I picked up my stuff at his place this afternoon! I don't even know any Eddie Benham!"

"You picked up your belongings there. The duffle out front? You said you were staying with a Ms. Jodree."

"I was. I was staying there. I left my stuff with Ritterman, I borrowed a fifty from him, I was trying to pay it back!"

"Mr. Ritterman's dead. You didn't go in the bedroom?"

"No, I didn't go in the bedroom! What call would I have to go in somebody's bedroom?"

"That's one of the questions we want to ask you, Ms. Yeager."

"I want my lawyer!"

"Turn out your pockets on the table, please."

She thought about refusing, she thought about taking out a couple of security men, which came down to the same thing it had on the docks. She emptied her pockets, and it came down to a one cred chit and the razor. She laid them on the table.

They took her down the hall and put her in Detention. She did not argue.

She sat there staring at the door, making up her mind that Nan was going to come after her at any minute, they would surely have talked to Nan by now, and Nan was going to come down here and handle the station legal people the way a stationer knew how to do.

And she'd tell Nan it wasn't the way it looked, she'd tell Nan everything, – at least the part about Ritterman and the other man, and Nan would understand that, Nan would back her story about not being a free-consumer – And the Thule stationmaster would give her a personal apology and a thousand cred too, of course he would, that was the way station justice worked, every one in the Fleet knew that, the way they knew there was thanks from stationers for favors done or a memorial to the Fleet's dead or a shred of support from the merchanters who had persistently smuggled war supplies and intelligence either side of the Line, then cried piracy because the Fleet supplied itself the only way it could – with no damn help from the stations, none from the merchanters, none, at the last, from Earth.

She could always ask Mallory for a posting on *Norway*. Apply for a commission in the Alliance while she was at it.

Oh, *God*!

Past 1900 now, past 2000 hours. She paced and she studied the calluses on her hands and the tiles on the floor. She was aware of pain in her stomach that would have been hunger, except she couldn't have kept anything down.

Finally they unlocked the door and it was security again.

And Fitch, God, it was Mr. Fitch.

"That's her," Fitch said, to Security. "Let's go sign the papers."

Bet stared at him. Security beckoned her and she came, and Fitch, as she passed him in the doorway, caught her arm a second and said, "You're in *deep* trouble, Yeager."

But she knew nowhere else to go, when a Station lawyer showed up to tell her she had a two-way choice: she could stay on station or accept extradition by *Loki*, which was claiming Alliance military jurisdiction over her case.

She thought about that little room back there, she thought about the dockside and that ship and being off Thule; she thought a long, long few breaths about Mallory and about what could happen if she'd slipped somehow with Wolfe and Wolfe knew what she really was.

But it was all the same, sooner or later, if the stationers started in with their questions under trank; and *Loki* was the only way she saw that had a chance in it.

"Give me the paper."

"You realize," the station lawyer said, "if you sign this, you're giving up all right to civil process. That includes appeal. And military law has a death penalty."

She nodded. Her stomach had cramped up. She was stark scared. She signed her name, *Elizabeth A. Yeager*, and she gave the station-man the paper.

So Fitch took her by the arm. "I got my duffle," she said, and Fitch called another *Loki* crewman out of the outside office, before they cuffed her hands in front of her and Fitch and the crewman took her out into the corridor of Blue section and down to the lift.

All cool and quiet then, Fitch not saying a word; and she figured silence was a good idea, under the circumstances.

She stared at the door during the ride down to dockside. She walked on her own between Fitch and the crewman, out across the docks, over to *Loki*'s berth – the customs man'd had the word evidently, and there was no objection as they walked up the ramp and into the tube.

They reached the airlock and Fitch opened it up, Fitch took her by the arm and brought her inside.

"Stow that," Fitch told the crewman with the duffle. And shoved her back against the wall. "You got anything to tell me?" Fitch asked.

"Thank you, sir."

Fitch slammed her back a second time. "You're a damned problem, Yeager. You're already a problem to this ship. Hear me?"

"Yes, sir," she said, and halfway expected a punch in the gut then. Or a crack of her head against the wall.

But Fitch said: "So you know." And snatched her around by the arm and marched her along to the first latch-door along the corridor.

Stowage compartment, dark series of zigs and zags going God knew how far back.

*Oh, shit!* she thought. And Fitch shoved her inside, and shut the door.

She searched beside it with her hands, found a number of switches. None of them worked. No com in here that she could feel. No power to anything, not even ventilation, so far as she could hear. The master switch had to be cut off from ops.

She leaned back against the wall of lockers facing the entry, did a fast mental sort, in the total dark, what the orientation was, where the ship-axis was.

What Fitch had said – a problem. She was a problem.

Like Fitch was damn pissed about her, but Fitch didn't seem to be onto her as one of Mazian's. Fitch *might* not know anything beyond the fact of a new-hire the captain wanted hauled out of the station brig and dumped into a secure place aboard.

Wolfe himself might not know.

God, *if*, if there was any chance of getting out of here, if there was any chance a spook ship was that desperate for crew –

She braced one boot tentatively against the door opposite to see if there was the right amount of room. Just about.

After a long time she heard the take-hold.

And there was no going back from here, live or die. She knew that, knew that better than the station lawyer could ever say it.

You held on, that was all, just held on, braced the best way you could, fair chance — fair chance that son of a bitch had given her, the kind of a safe-hole you used if you got caught by a take-hold in a long corridor, narrow space, a place to wedge in: and after the shocks of *Loki*'s oversized engines firing and after the slam of force that tried to float your kidneys through your stomach and a second one that bashed a sore skull against a metal locker, you just clenched your teeth and tried to stay braced and keep from slipping, because if you got pushed off center you could spend a real uncomfortable ride; and if you slipped off to the left you could fall a long, long way.

And when *Loki* finally smoothed out into a steady one G plus push, you just lay on the face of the lockers that were going to be the deck for a while and kept your foot braced, in case, in case of God-knew-what.

Eventually Fitch would get somebody down here. Eventually somebody would get around to it before the ship went jump. *Somebody* would get the drugs you had to have in hyperspace, without which you were good as dead.

Without which you had no grip on where you were and you had no way back again, no way to process what the mind and the senses had no way to get hold of.

It was one way to get rid of a problem. All it took was a little screw-up in orders. And there was no com in here.

Somebody remember I'm down here, dammit!

She risked her skull to try the switches again, overhead this time. Nothing. The acceleration dragged at her arms, made her dizzy, made her knees weak. She lay down and braced one foot up against the door again.

Calm, she told herself. They'd get around to it. A ship heading for jump was damned busy, that was all. Matter of priorities. Somebody like Fitch didn't trek all the way up to station ops to get a skut out of the brig only to scramble her brain for good and all in some fucking official screw-up.

Couldn't do that.

God – *get somebody down here!*

# Chapter 7

She heard the latch give, and she moved, rolled across the uneven surface of the lockers and staggered for her knees as the hatch opened and light flooded in – a man was standing astride the doorway, which was the way the stowage was oriented since the sort-out, a pit of unguessed depth in its zig-zag contours.

It wasn't Fitch. "Up," the man said, and she pulled herself to her feet, tried to use the door-edges beside her for a ladder up to the deck level, but the edges were shallow and her own weight dragged at her.

He reached down and grabbed her chained hands, she climbed and he pulled, and landed her over the rim onto the floor. She would have been happy just to lie there and breathe a moment, but he grabbed her by the collar and hauled her to her feet. "Come on, come on," he said. "We got a narrow window here."

"I'm walking," she protested, trying to, on the narrow plastic mat along the edge of the burn-deck, – doors to the right, the main-deck a wall at their left, lights on the right-hand wall. The hard push they were under kept buckling her knees and making her vision come and go. Well more than one, maybe most of two G's, she thought. That was most of the problem with her head and her legs. Or the bashing against the wall had rattled her brain more than she'd thought. "God, – "

Black skeins of webbing hung in front of them, around the curve. Crew safety-area, hammocks up and down it, empty black-mesh bundles strung vertically along the left-hand wall. She limped ahead, walking more on her own now, just sore from the G-stress and the cold, through the safety-area, curtain of hammocks giving way into a rec-hall, crew members sitting on a low main-deck/burn-deck bench along the wall, where the walkway mat spread out wide, clear up to the swing-section galley. Sandwiches and drinks. Food-smell hit her stomach hard, she wasn't sure whether it was good or bad.

A handful of crew stood up to look at her, not in any wise friendly.

"This is Yeager," the man holding her said, and turned her loose and said, "Good luck, Yeager."

She stood there, just managed to stay on her feet for a few breaths, dizzy in the G-stress, dizzy in the sudden realization they *were* turning her loose, that they had bought the story, everything –

She had a chance, then – fair chance, exactly that, exactly the way you got when you got swept up into the Fleet, volunteer or otherwise. You were the new skut in the 'decks, you got the rough side of things, and you learned the way to live or you died, end of it, right there.

*Good luck, Yeager.*

"What ship?" a woman asked from the bench, while she stood there in front of everybody, maybe thirty, forty crew, varied as the Fleet was varied, a dozen shades, most of them looking at her as if she was on the menu.

"*Ernestine.*"

"Why'd you leave her?"

"I was a hire-on. They got a mechanical, couldn't take me further."

"You any good?" a man asked, one of the ones standing.

"Damn good."

*Any way you want to take it, man.*

Long silence, then. While her knees shook. She set her jaw and stared at them with sweat cold on her face.

"You about missed board-call," a second man said.

"Had a problem."

Another long pause. "Makings on the counter," another man said, from further down the bench, and made an offhand gesture toward the galley. "You want anything you better get it now."

"Thanks," she said.

Permission to help herself, then. Handcuffs and all. She walked on to the counter, did an instant soup out of the hot-water tap, got a packet of crackers; she came and sat down at the end of the bench where there was a little room, and drank her soup, deciding finally she was hungry and that food was what her upset stomach needed. Her hands were still shaking. The salt stung where her teeth had cracked shut on the inside of her cheek. The man next to her seemed less than glad of her being there; he was no temptation to conversation, which was all right, she had no interest in talking right now: the soup was uncertain enough on her stomach; and she phased out, staring at the detail of the tiles, not interested in advance planning at all. Her situation could be hell and away worse. And all the planning she could do now had the shape of memories she had just as soon keep far, far to the back of her mind.

A fool kid had volunteered herself onto *Africa*'s deck, volunteered because *Africa* was going to take what they wanted from that refinery ship at Pan-paris, anyway, which was always the young ones, and that was her. Better choose, she had thought then, because that way you were a volunteer and that was points on your record; and because she hated her life and hated the mines and she wanted starships more than she wanted anything.

And the fool kid had found herself in something she'd never remotely imagined, and the fool kid had figured out damn fast how not to be a fool. The Fleet taught you that straight-off, or it broke you, and she was still alive.

The fool kid had gotten part of what she'd wanted. She still reckoned that had to be worth the rest of it . . . and still must be, since she'd just had her chance at station-life, and here she was back again. If it killed her, she thought, right now it was like something in her was back in connection again and a part of her was alive that wasn't, on station.

And you couldn't make sense of that, but it was true.

She drank her soup, she kept her mouth shut except when a man two places down the row asked her questions, like her side of the business on Thule.

Like it was behind her already; and that was a breath of clean air too.

"I killed a couple bastards," she said quietly. "They picked it. Me or them."

Fitch walked in. Her pulse picked up. She looked up very carefully while Fitch made himself a cup of tea at the counter.

Fitch stood there to drink it and look at her, and after a moment he tossed a key down three or four places down the row. It lay there a moment.

Finally one of them, older man, picked it up and tossed it down toward her.

The man next to her, the unfriendly one, picked it up and gave it to her.

"Thanks," she said. She fumbled around and got the cuffs off.

No one said anything. She certainly didn't expect a You're Welcome from Fitch. She just pocketed the cuffs and the key. You didn't leave junk on the deck, and nobody asked for it.

"Hour til," Fitch said. "Yeager?"

She looked up, fought the twitch that said stand up, reminding herself this was a civ ship. "Yes, sir?"

"You like this ship?"

"Yes, sir."

"Like what you see?"

"Fine, sir."

Long silence.

"You being smart with me, Yeager?"

"No, sir. I'm glad to get off that station."

Fitch sipped his tea. And ignored her after that, thank God. Fitch left, and some of the rest did.

"Is there a place I'm supposed to pick up a trank-pack?" Bet asked the man next.

The man shrugged, pointed with a forefinger and his cup. "Galley. Right there by the hot, should be."

She got up and went and opened the cabinet, found the plastic-wrapped packs and found the c-pack in a clip beside it. "Thanks," she said, coming back to sit.

"Name's Masad," the man said, and indicated the man on his left. "Joe. Johnny." The one past that.

"Bet," she said.

Other crew came through the section. And the jump-warning sounded.

"Better get hammocked-in," Masad said. Olive skin. Fortyish. Shaved head. "You got any problems?"

"No," she said, and got up and offered a hand for other cups — hard to do, a let's-be-friends move; but she was smarter than she'd grown up: the surly brat who'd signed onto *Africa* had gotten hell and away smarter nowadays. And a little friendly move won things with strangers, sometimes. So they handed theirs over, she chucked them all in the galley bin, then walked with them down-ring, found herself a vacant hammock, stepped in, wrapped up and snugged the tabs closed. Then she carefully put the c-pack in her breast-pocket and took her trank-dose.

Going out of here, she told herself, while the bell kept ringing and the ship drove toward jump. She had no idea where they were going. It could even be Pell. But she felt the trank take hold and felt herself drifting, old familiar feeling, live or die, you never knew how or if you'd come out when the ship made transit.

The burn stopped. They went weightless for a few seconds, inertial. And slowly the G started pulling her down horizontally instead of vertically. Main-deck orientation, now. The light that had been shining in her eyes was clearly, by body-sense, truly in the overhead, and her back was to the deck.

Going out of here.

Goodbye, Thule. Goodbye, Nan and Ely. You give stationers a good name.

Blow the rest of you to hell.

# Chapter 8

The fog cleared, the bell that signalled system-drop was ringing, but that was for the tekkies to handle, they were making their dumps.

Dark spot again. The bell had stopped, the mind kept trying to make it into *Africa*'s crowded lowerdeck, tried to smell the same smells and hear the same sounds and hear the major cussing them awake: not the same, with the black mesh in front of her face, the glare of light in her eyes, not *Ernestine*, either, with its cubbyhole cabins –

No doubt it was shipboard, everything told you that, sounds, smells, the muzzy feeling of trank downbound now, knocked her for a long, deep one, it had. She found her mental place again, remembered when and where she was, remembered –

*V*-dump, then. Another half-nightmare. She heard the wake-call ringing, at least she thought it was, she fumbled after her c-pack and got the foil torn. Fingernails broke doing that, three of them on the same hand, a bad sign – she lost the rest of them pulling the tube out, and sucked down the citrusy stuff in the pack bit by bit, fighting nausea, trying to get her head clear.

"Move, move, move!" someone was yelling and you never argued with a voice like that. She gulped the last, stuffed the foil in her pocket and fumbled the catch open, rolled out and held on, with the jumpsuit hanging on her and her hands like claws clutching the black netting. Steady one G main-deck. *Loki* was inertial now. If the bridge expected maneuvers, they wouldn't order crew up and about.

Undo the floor clip, the one that held at your butt, undo the end clips and furl the hammock in its elastic lines, into the latch-bins that were the mess-hall bench while specific crew-calls pealed out over the general com, but none of them said Yeager.

Thank God, one part of her said; and another part said: *This is odd. We're star-to-star on this track, did those dumps feel light? Was I that far out, or are we still carrying that much V in a station-zone?*

*And no take-hold?*

*Spook ship. We've short-jumped, we're nowhere near the star, and we've dumped and we must be doing a real quiet run-in, that's what we're doing.*

*Where in hell are we?*

There was a dizzying quiet, ship-quiet, full of pumps and fans and systems cycling, heartbeat of a healthy ship. Crew passed her in a business-like hurry, some probably on call, other crew on private emergencies, things like finding the head, like getting to the galley, on a priority of duty and off-duty crew. Her lower gut told her what her own priorities were, and she followed crew members into the first door down the corridor.

Not like *Ernestine*'s cabin-style cubbies, but not damn bad either, she thought, looking around: plastic sheeting tight-stretched between the bunks, downside and loft with a buffer-net up there for safety – but you got the view.

And toilets downside, that was what she was interested in, fast as she could get there. She fell in the nearest, shortest line and stood there rubbery-legged with her back against the wall, and distracted herself by cracking the rest of her fingernails off.

Every one of them brittle, breaking down to the quick. Gums were sore. Hair came out when she raked a hand through it, a web of blond hairs in her fingers.

Short rations too damn long, and the time in jump took it out of you, used up nutrients, made your knees pop and your joints brittle. She'd seen it happen. It had never happened to her. Not like this – and it scared her. The thought that a spook was prone to far, fast moves, that they might kite out of here again – that also scared her. You lost more than fingernails if you got worn down like that.

Hit the galley, pour down the c-rations if she could get them, anything to get her weight back up.

Her gut kept cramping. Another crew member came up behind her and didn't bump her out of line on privilege, which could happen to a new skut on *Africa*, damn likely. You didn't get favors. You didn't get anything but hell.

All right, she decided about that man – Muller, G., was the name on him – and asked, while they were waiting: "Where are we? Venture? Bryant's? – 'Dorado?"

Muller looked at her like that was some kind of privileged information, like asking made him wonder about her.

So she shut up, she ducked her head and she waited and gritted her teeth until she made it through the line.

Back up to the galley, then. She waited her turn, picked up the sandwich and hot tea the cook was handing out, and she sat down along the wall where a squat-level ell between main-deck and burn-deck made one long galley bench, sat and sipped her tea and ate the best sandwich she'd had in half a year.

Better than the vending machines on Thule, damn sure.

She sat there, no idea where she was assigned; no real hurry about matters, she figured, the ship must be on some kind of sit-and-wait, spook-like, maybe at Venture, maybe at Bryant's, wherever. She left the whereabouts of the ship as a whole to the mofs and just wished she knew if she dared go back to the lockers and see where her duffle was; she wished she knew if she had a bunk or whatever, and if she let herself think as far as the other prospects of settling in, her stomach got upset. But she figured she was on somebody's list, sooner or later, and somebody was going to tell her. Muller's reaction told her it was a nervous ship and experience told her staying low and quiet was the best thing to do for the time being.

Especially if it got her fed and got her a sit-down, long enough to get the wobbles out, before some mof showed up with a duty list.

Damn sure.

Damn near a med case, with teeth sore and the bones showing in her hands til she hardly recognized them for hers – but she was afraid to go to the meds and complain, afraid to start out her sign-up on this ship with a med report, afraid to go anywhere near officers and people who might take a close look at her and then start watching her more than they needed to.

But a man came by, stopped and stood in front of her.

"Yeager."

She looked up, did a fast scan from the boots to the faded collar with the three black bands of a civ ship's officer and the circle-and-circuit of Engineering on the sleeve.

"Sir," she said, "Bet Yeager, sir." She would have gotten up, but the man was in the way.

"Been a problem, have you?"

"*Had* a problem, sir. Don't want one here."

The man stared at her a long moment like she was a contamination. Finally he put his hands on his hips. "What's your experience?"

"Freighters, sir. Machine-shop. Injection molding. Small-scale hydraulics, electronics. General maintenance. Twenty years."

"We aren't real specialized."

"Yes, sir."

"Means you do any damn thing that needs doing, at any hour around the clock. Means you do it *right*, Yeager, or you tell somebody you can't, you don't fuck it up."

"Yessir. No problem with that, sir."

"Name's Bernstein. Chief of Engineering, Alterday. Hear it?"

"Yessir."

"What in hell are you doing here on your butt?"

"No assignment yet, sir."

"Got a mainday crew of thirteen, alterday's down to two. We're a re-fit. That's special problems. And they give me a damn small-hydraulics mechanic." Bernstein drew breath. "With no papers."

Long silence, then.

"You screw anything up," Bernstein said, "I'll break your fingers one at a time."

"Yessir."

Another long silence. "You got a trial run on my shift, Yeager. We got a few areas you keep your nose out of, we got a few cranky systems I'm real particular about. You got a piece of property in stowage one, you get that, you get yourself checked into quarters. Somebody show you around?"

"Nossir."

"Why's it my job?"

"I dunno sir. Sorry, sir."

"You got any bunk that isn't claimed, ring's got ten
sections, front number's your section-number, ten-four's a
stowage, eight-four's crew quarters, section five's bridge,
one-one's engineering; you see a white line on the deck you
don't cross it, *you* don't cross it, without a direct order:
sections four, five, and six are all white-lined, you got to
walk the long way around. You steal, Yeager?"

"No, sir!"

"You see this deck?"

"Yessir."

"You got a job. You get your supplies from ten-four, you
get on it, get it done. Crew-wise, on your shift, I'll tell you
right now, Musa's all right, you're all right with him. NG,
you don't mess with. That do, Yeager?"

"Yessir."

"Anything I need to know?"

"Nossir."

Bernstein stared at her long and steady. "Regulations are
posted in quarters, you take a look. It's coming up 0600
right now, alterday. You get that deck clean before you go
to sleep, I don't care whose shift it is. Got any problems
with me, Yeager?"

"Nossir," she said.

"Good," Bernstein said. And walked off.

Put an armor-rig in working-order, take it apart and put
it together again, right down to the circuitry, same with
weapons, sir, probably any fire-system a spook might carry,
damn right, sir.

Twenty years' seniority on *Africa.*

Sir.


First thing, you consulted the reg-u-la-tions.

And the reg-u-la-tions Bernstein named were official print
with the Alliance seal behind them, shiny-new, behind plastic, mounted right on the wall, all about the captain's authority and how you had a right to station-law if you wanted
to appeal a case off your ship; and another sheet that was
Alliance military law, that said they could shoot you out of
hand for mutiny or sabotage or obstructing the execution of
proper orders while the ship was in a power-up condition or

in an emergency; but there was another list taped on at the bottom, and those were the ones you wanted to know, the ones peculiar to this ship – like you could get on report for going onto the bridge without a permission from an exec, and if you were working with tools you damn well better have an adequate belt clip or a wall clip on every one of them and never have but one outsized number clipped to *you*.

That meant a ship that tended to move in a hurry. No surprise there.

So, first thing, you got around to the stowage directory and you got yourself a belt and some clips and then you got into the supply locker Bernstein had said and got to it, wiping down the burn-deck, mindless scut. You could drift and do it, you could shut your eyes and halfway sleep sometimes and just feel the tread with your fingers to know you were on, and check sometimes with your eyes to make sure the strokes didn't miss any dust.

Effin' scrub-duty.

But you got to hear a bit, like the couple saying the ship was on a sit-and-watch, like the three bitching about somebody named Orsini, somebody saying Fitch had put somebody named Simmons on report for a slow answer to a page, and Simmons was asking for a transfer to alterday, but Orsini wouldn't take him: you got a feel for the way things drifted on board.

But then the back started to ache and the arms ached, and the kneecaps got to feeling every shift of weight.

And you knew every damn doorway and every crack and crevice in the burn-deck, and you damned every foot that stepped off the mat. You got to know those prints that did it often and what size they were, and thought if you ever found that son of a bitch he was meat.

Up to the galley by noon, for tea and a Keis-roll, the hard way, quiet there, because mainday was sleeping.

All the way around through the galley and past sickbay – right next to each other; and right around to the white-line and the bridge by a/d 1800. The bridge was a swing-segment like the galley, thank God, no burn-deck to scrub at all, its cylinder-segments oriented itself whichever way the G might want to be –

And hell if she wanted to ask Fitch or the captain permission to trek through the bridge to the burn-deck on around the ring, so she gathered up her supplies and stowed them, and went on back down-ring to the galley for a sit-down supper and a plate of real food and cup of hot tea with mainday's breakfast – and she didn't want trouble with Fitch, she didn't want trouble with anybody, so she avoided looking at people, especially looking them in the eye or starting up a conversation, just stared blankly at the main-deck and all those possible footprints people were making walking back and forth – footprints had occupied her mind all day, still occupied it, in her condition, – and she mentally numbed out, tasting the food and the tea down to its molecules, it was so good, and finding her hands so sore holding a fork hurt.

People stared at her. She knew they did. A few talked about her, out of earshot, masked by *Loki*'s constant white noise. She could get scared if she let herself. So she just finished her dinner and got up without getting involved with anybody, chucked the recyclables, and went down and got the supplies out again.

That was halfway around *Loki*'s ring.

Up the other way around the ring, this time, past downside ops and the purser's office, and Engineering, where mainday crew was getting to work and alterday had gone to rec.

Arms and knees were beyond simple hurting now. She sat to work, she inched her way along, changing hands every time she changed position to keep the shoulders and hands from cramping up, and by now it hurt so much all over she just shut the pain out as irrelevant to any one place.

Past Engineering and up toward the shop and the machine storage.

Past 2000 hours a/d, and people walked by, crew evidently on errands, occasional officers. People minded their own business, mostly. Occasional laughter grated on her nerves, maybe not even her they were talking about, but she figured it likely was: she was the new item, she was getting it from Bernstein, she'd already had it from Fitch, and probably it satisfied their souls to see somebody else sweating on a duty maybe five or six of them in some other department would be doing, otherwise. At least they were quiet enough. And no one interfered with her and nobody messed with her clean deck.

She gave the occasional kibitz-squad the eye, just enough to know who the sum-bitches were. Just enough to let them know it was war if they messed with her or put a foot near that mat. No one tried her. And she went on. Could stop for a cup of tea, she thought. Could go and put the stuff away and get a tea or a soft drink – hell, it was past mess, supposed to be her rec-time, they might let her have a soft drink on credit, and tea might be free. Bernstein hadn't said no break, the regs in galley had said there was beer for a cred, honest-to-God cold beer you could buy during your own supper hours, if you weren't on call, regs let you have that. There was that vodka in her duffle if it hadn't been stolen: regs didn't object to that either, on your own time.

But she had mof territory yet to go, she didn't want to go and plead cases with anybody tonight and her knees and her under-padded right hip were halfway numb now. She had no desire to let the bruises rest and stiffen up and start hurting all over again.

*Just* a quarter of the ring or less to go, not so trafficked as the crew-quarters side. Maybe she could get finished before midnight. Maybe get that cup of tea. Even a sandwich. Knees wouldn't bruise so easy, arms wouldn't shake if she got a few regular meals. Please God.

Feet strolled up. Stopped. Stood there.

No stripe. Nothing but a hash-mark and an Engineering insignia. Just the two of them in this line-of-sight in the dim systems and shop area, and her trouble-sense started going off, little alarm, a larger and larger one, as the man kept standing there.

She edged forward on her track. Another arm's-reach.

"One of Bernie's ship-tours, huh?"

"Yeah," she said. "Go to hell."

He didn't go anywhere. She kept wiping, edged forward another hitch.

"Real clean job," he said.

She said nothing, just kept her head down. It could start like this, you could get killed. And if you killed the bastard you could end up taking a long cold walk. The bastard, of course, knew it.

"Name's Ramey," the bastard said.

"Yeah. Fine."

"Friendly."

"Yeah. Real. You want to stand out of my light?"

The bastard moved around behind her. "View ain't bad."

"Thanks."

"A little skinny."

"Go to hell."

"Now, I was going to offer you a beer."

She looked around at the pair of feet, looked up at a not-at-all bad face. Younger than herself, ragged black hair, not-at-all bad rest of him. *What in hell*? she thought, squinted to unfuzz her tired eyes, and recollected Bernstein talking about an all-right type on her shift, name of Musa.

So she got painfully to her feet, trailing clip-lines, wiped her hands on her legs and gave him a good look-over. "Beer, I could stand, but the way I'm going, doesn't look likely tonight."

"I can wait." He leaned his hand up against the wall, up real close. She had this defense-twitch, a gut-deep he-could-use-a-knee twitch, but it wasn't the way he was going, shift of his body that put her up against the wall – Oh, good God, she thought with a little wilting sigh and an urge to put her knee up, hard. She was disgusted, annoyed he was going to be a son of a bitch, and stood there a breath or two thinking really hard about doing something about it, except that being In with somebody was safer than trying to lone-it, except, point two, that he was too good-looking for a move like this and he was probably trying to have a laugh at her expense. So she leaned up against him, soapy hands and sweat and all and still felt little jolts where his hands touched, damn difficult to ignore.

He got warm real fast. Breathing a little heavy. So it wasn't all a set-up: he was really interested. And he asked: "You want that beer tonight?"

"Anything come with it?"

"Yeah," he said. "No one's in the shop stowage right now."

Mmmn. There was the set-up. Nice little trap to catch

her breaking a dozen regs and start off real fine, that was. She made a little move of her hip. "Nice, but I don't see my beer. You let me get finished. Hear?"

She figured that would cool it down, whoever put him up to this was going to be disappointed. But the man was downright having trouble with that no-go, hell if he wasn't. It was enough to make a woman feel a little better-looking than she knew she was – or feel like she was hallucinating.

Man's weird, she thought when he backed off and muttered something about getting her the beer, about meeting her in crew-quarters. Man's real weird.

Another Ritterman, that's what I got. Don't tell me *that* face can't get a come-ahead any time he wants it.

She wiped her neck when he walked off. Hell if she wasn't a lot warmer herself than she had been.

Hell if she wasn't thinking about him and that beer all the way down the corridor, right through the mofs' section, all the pretty little officer-quarters, so much that she ran right up on Fitch himself – bright, *shiny* pair of boots standing there for a full second before she looked up.

"Yessir," she said, and started to get up, but he waved a permission and stood there scowling.

And Fitch walked off without finding anything to bitch about. Which from Fitch, she reckoned, was some kind of compliment.

Damn *prig*, she thought. Mainday, middle of his morning. *Her* watch-officer was that Orsini the skuts had been cussing, she'd heard enough so far to figure that. She hadn't seen Orsini. Didn't expect to see him out supervising a deck-scrub. Didn't expect him to come 'round and introduce himself. Fitch seemed to be definitely, worrisomely curious about her.

She leaned into it and scrubbed that burn-deck all the way to the bridge again, swearing that it was a basic law, officers had dustier feet than the skuts who knew they were going to have to scrub it up.

But she lived to get to the white line on the other side of the bridge, after which she got up on her feet again, straightened her aching back and walked down to stowage, put up the scrub-gear exactly the way she'd found it, coiled and put up all the clip-lines, exactly so, and got her duffle out of the stowage locker where Bernstein had told her it was. Then she hiked up-ring, with a major thirst for that promised beer by now, and telling herself all the while that pretty-boy wasn't going to be waiting, or *if* he was, it was going to be some damn bit of trouble, maybe a damn *lot* of trouble: on *Africa* you got hazed and it got rough, it got to be real rough, and if that was the way it was going to be, then smart and cool was the only way you lived through it.

She walked into the dark crew-quarters, where a vid was playing. Lot of noise that direction. She looked around in the dim light trying to figure what bunk might really be vacant on this shift, and where people might just be sharing-up. Pick the wrong one and you could get hell; and she wasn't entirely convinced she was going to get through the first night without getting jumped by somebody in one sense or the other. *Some* sum-bitch in the lot had to have a sense of humor, and maybe half a dozen of them. Maybe the whole damn lot. Her stomach was upset. Memories again. Twenty years on *Africa* and she'd gotten seniority enough so she could hand it out instead of taking it. It wasn't the case here.

Somebody came down the aisle to intercept her, a single dark-haired somebody who said: "Want that beer?"

"Yeah," she said, once her heart had settled. She still didn't trust it entirely, but it was a scary kind of night and she was fuzzy-tired enough to hope she was being alarmist, that it was a civ ship even if it was a spook, and the whole thing was just a good-looking younger man who for some fool reason thought skinny, sweaty and almost forty was attractive. Or who was just appointed to find out what she was and report on her to the rest of the crew.

So she snubbed the safety-tie of her duffle to a tempring by the door, and they went out to crew rec, up by the galley: he logged himself a double tag on the keyboard there on the counter, drew a couple beers from the tap, and handed her one.

"How d'you earn extras?" she asked.

"You get fifteen cred a week, shipboard," he said. "Use 'em on beer, use 'em on food, save 'em for liberty, they don't care."

"Thanks, then," she said, figuring to buy him one on her tab, if she liked him, which looked likely, except she still couldn't figure him. He put his hand on her back. She twitched it off, because it was bad business if any mofs walked through here and caught you hands-on. She stood there like a kid with her first boy-interest and drank her beer while he drank his.

"You're Engineering," she commented, for an opener.

He nodded.

"Guess you know that's my assignment."

Another nod.

Spooky man, she thought. Talks about as much as everybody else on this ship.

So she tried again, on something you couldn't answer without talking. "How long've you been on this ship?"

"Three years."

"You mind to say where from?"

"Hire-on. General. What about you?"

Not a question *she* wanted, that one. She shrugged. "Same thing. Last hire was *Ernestine*."

"Kato," he said.

She nodded. But she didn't want to talk down that line either.

"Bernstein easy to work for?" she asked.

"He's all right."

"Fitch?"

"Bastard."

"Guessed that," she said, and saw him toss off the rest of his beer.

"Come on," he said.

Nervous man. Real nervous. Steps were echoing in the corridor, somebody walking in from down-ring. "I dunno," she said, annoyed, a little anxious herself with that sudden hurry-up he wanted. "Minute. I'm still drinking."

"Come *on*."

"Hell. You can wait a damn minute!"

The steps got closer. It was Muller – who gave them both a frown, a halfway pleasant nod to her, and a second frown at her company while he logged himself a beer.

"'Evening, NG," Muller said.

She took another look at the man she was with.

"'Evening," her company said, not friendly, and laid a hand on her shoulder to steer her out.

NG. The one Bernstein had included on his watch-it list.

"I'm not through yet," she said, with a swallow left in the bottom of her cup, and NG dropped his hand.

"You been introduced?" Muller asked, and NG said: "Shut up, Gypsy."

"No, I haven't," Bet said. "Man introduced himself."

Muller gave her a thinking-look. NG stood there outside her vision, a shadow whose reactions she couldn't see.

"You watch this one," Muller said, dead grim, and turned to the counter again, got a cup and drew his beer.

Trouble. She felt her heart thumping, instinctively backed up a step between her company and this Gypsy, touched NG's arm to distract him and saw very clearly nobody was joking.

"Come on," she said, and he came away with her, put an arm around her and she let him for a few steps, no matter it could get them on report.

"Let's get out of here," he said.

She stopped a step. "No way," she said. What he wanted was trouble, damn sure. You didn't need long on a ship with Fitch on it to figure that out.

He stopped. He shoved her hard. "Hell with you," he said, and walked off, just headed down-ring and kept going.

Something in his voice that wasn't right, she thought, with her shoulder still stinging and her knees a little wobbly-tired. *Hell* with you!

"Yeager," Muller said from behind her, not hostile, not trouble, himself. She looked back at him. "Yeager, let that go."

She wasn't sure she liked advice from Muller. She wasn't sure what it was worth or whether it was right or whether it was friendly to her.

"What in hell was that?"

Muller shrugged. "A lot of trouble. Not my business, understand, but I figured you might not know about him."

"What about him?"

"Name's NG. Ramey, sometimes. Mostly NG. Crew gave him that name, you figure it? Short for No Damn Good."

NDG. Like you painted on something you were going to junk. Like with a spoiled can, a piece too skuz even for the cyclers.

She looked around where NG had headed. She looked back at Muller.

"What'd he do?"

Muller made a face, shook his head.

"What'd he do?"

"Question is, what he hasn't. Man's a foul-up. *Damn* good at what he does, or Fitch'd have spaced him, twice, three times over. You let him alone, you let him do what he does, you don't have anything to do with NG you can help. Man's got a way of paying back every favor you try to do him."

She didn't get the feeling Muller was anything but serious. She didn't particularly get the feeling Muller was actively after NG's hide. It was more a set-up for an eventual I-told-you-so.

But something upset her stomach and put a twitch between her shoulders.

"Muller," she said, polite, very polite, "Muller, I got to thank you for fair warning: may be so and I'm not doubting it, but I got a problem not at least asking the other side of it."

"You got the right," Muller said. "I don't say it's not smart, on principle. But you got a rep to make in this crew. *Don't* start it with him. More'n one in this crew's got station-problems, a few've got other-ship problems, but NG's in a whole different class."

"I take everything you say," she said. "Thanks. But I got to make up my own mind on a man. Maybe you're right. But I'm just that way."

Muller nodded, not offended, not offensive, just an I-did-my-best.

So she wiped her aching hands on her pockets and she walked off, wobbly-tired as she was, because, dammit, she'd gotten into the middle of something and it bothered her, it bothered her a whole lot the way the man had been, the on-the-edge way he acted. That made her think Muller might be right.

But most, it bothered her that a whole crew hung a tag on a man like that, just wrote him off like he was garbage.

Maybe he was. Maybe she was crazy. Maybe it was because she was more than a little strung-out that she even gave a damn. She hurt, she was staggering-tired, she could do a lot more for herself, just to go find some vacant bunk and fall in it and let a grown man handle whatever problems he'd made for himself.

But she thought she knew where to find him.

# Chapter 9

"Ramey?" She let the door shut. Shop area wasn't a place she felt secure wandering around, a real warren of a machine-shop, a narrow aisle, the lights down to a dim glow, place cold as hell. She left the lights alone. She stayed where she was, not precisely scared, just careful. "You here, man?"

Silence. Maybe she was wrong. Maybe she was a fool talking to an empty room. Maybe somebody on mainday shift was going to walk out of Engineering next door and find her here off-shift and she was going to catch hell.

"Ramey?"

A slight movement, from back in the aisles of drills and lifts and presses.

He was there, all right. It occurred to her that he could be crazy – but that wasn't what Muller had said, precisely.

But he wasn't being cooperative, either.

"All right," she said, "all right, I can take a hint. I'm going to bed, I've had better times, Ramey, but thanks for the beer."

She heard the move, she saw the shadow at the end of the aisle.

Man *is* crazy, she thought. On drugs, maybe.

And I'm stark crazy for being here.

Ought to go for the door, but that could set him off, like as anything else. *Talk* to the man.

"You want to come on back," she asked him, "maybe have another beer? Can't say I'm up to too much deep thinking, but I owe you the beer. Except you'll have to put it on your tab, haven't got my week here."

The shadow stood there a moment, finally made an abrupt throwaway gesture and sauntered up the aisle into the light – man in a faded jumpsuit, the light making hollows of his eyes, under his cheeks. He stopped there, put his hands on his hips, then came walking up to her, closer and closer.

Careful, man, she thought. Trying to scare me. Trying to put the fear in me. I'm a damn fool to be here in the first place, but this fool can break your neck, man.

"You looking for trouble?" he asked.

"Looking for another beer," she said, hands on hips herself, making up her mind to keep the whole situation cool: damned if he was going to think he had his bluff in and start any petty, hands-on stuff in the dark corners during duty hours when Bernstein could put her on report. "Dunno what else. I'm blind tired, Fitch gave me a hard time, Bernstein gave me a hard time, man buys me a beer and shoves me off – right now I got nothing particular in mind, except yours was the bed I was headed for and I got no notion where to put my duffle without waking somebody up. Got *no* desire to pick the wrong bed, don't want to get some sum-bitch mad at me, I don't want some damn skuz next to me either; and I ain't awake enough right now to make critical judgments, so I want to go back down there – " She hooked a thumb toward the door. " – and get me another cold beer and a shower and I ain't up to deep philosophy after that. You interested?"

He was close now, not nice, *trying* to spook her. But maybe he had sensed she could be trouble. He backed up against the counter and leaned there with his arms folded, just looking down at the deck.

"Get out of here."

Probably it was good advice. She started to take it, legs all ready to walk. But he kept staring down like that, tight muscle across his jaw. So she stayed, folded her arms, just stood there looking at him, and he stood up and looked at her with pure venom.

"Get," he said.

"Hell," she said. "I do get the idea why you're not too popular."

He jerked away toward the door and went out it. She crossed the same space in about as many steps and walked after him, down the corridor, him walking as fast as he could like a damn kid on a tantrum, herself trailing, because his legs were that much longer and she refused to run to catch him up.

They passed a couple of crew on some errand, maybe getting a couple of looks from behind them. She didn't look. He didn't. He stopped, just past that line-of-sight, about the time they reached the general stowage area, and glared at her. "You're damn persistent."

She glared back. "So were you. You give me the whole come-ahead. Wasn't my idea. And if I got a lunatic on my shift, I want to know it, mister."

He gave her a killing kind of look. But not quite. The not-quite became a saner, thinking-something-over kind of scowl. "Name's NG. NDG."

She stuck out her hand. "Mine's Bet."

He looked at her like she was crazed. She kept the hand out. A long time.

"What're you after?" he asked.

"Fuckin' beer. Maybe both of 'em. Is that some big deal? Ain't to me."

He drew a shaky breath, took the hand, not handshake-like: hooked his cold fingers on hers and closed, like, she thought, pulling somebody out of a pit. *All chilled down,* she thought, *man totally out of the mood, looking for something else for a while.*

But he didn't let go of her fingers, either. He pulled her up against him, body against body, which she hadn't expected, backed her against the inside wall, and stared at her, all the while she was thinking how her knees ached and her butt ached and her back and her arms ached and her skull kept echoing the sounds back, she was so tired.

Crazy man, she thought. Ought I to do something about this? What's he do then? What's Fitch do, what's crew do, if I break his arm?

And NG was saying, up against her ear: "Do it the other way around, don't go back there, go on back up to the shop, then a beer, if you want, you want to do that?"

She was mostly numb. But what she felt so far, felt all right. He wasn't bad, she thought, not bad at all, oh, really, not bad! – which was a relief to her, she hadn't been sure there was feeling left anymore, since Thule. And what part of her brain was working said a crazy man was trying to get her off somewhere there weren't any witnesses, dangerous, dangerous as hell, he could very likely be some kind of real major trouble, he could have kinks God only knew.

"Locker right here is real private," he said, breathing against her neck, with his hand inside her collar.

I'm a fool! she thought. What do I even want 'im for? I don't want to get tangled up in bed with some damn spacecase, don't want to sleep with this man, don't even want his damn beer, I sure don't want to go in any locker with him.

But I don't want any trouble with him, either. I can take care of myself. I seen crazier. On *Africa*, I seen crazier.

He opened the stowage beside them, shoved her in, pulled the door to and that was the end of the light, black after that. She hoped to hell he wasn't fool enough or rattled enough to let it lock: she was still worrying about that when he pushed her back deeper into the zig-zagged recess, pressed her up against the lockers and started unfastening her jumpsuit and running his hands over her. – Hell, she thought, then, not thinking terribly clearly past the echoing in her skull and the things he was doing: she unfastened his and they did a little warm-up, real gentle, real polite, she thought, now that he'd calmed down a little; but things came on him a little sudden then and they ended up sorting it out on the stowage deck in the dark, rough, a few more bruises on her backside and real pain, so she was thinking whether it was safe to say anything about the way he was going, crazy as he was; criticism didn't help a man and it might set a real lunatic off good and all.

But "I'm sorry," he said, then, between breaths, when he'd suddenly finished, and sounded mortally earnest and embarrassed. "'S all right," she said, and fussed with his hair while he just lay on top of her breathing hard and sweating, for a long time.

"Hope to hell nobody needs in here," she said finally, when his breathing had calmed down, but he hadn't moved, and she wasn't sure he was collected enough to think of practicalities. "You all right?"

He didn't say anything. He just started making love to her then, really making love, nice and gentle a touch as could be, best man she'd had since Bieji, except he was already done and he was doing it, she thought, just for politeness, just a thank-you.

"Damn!" she said finally, not as exhausted for a moment as she'd thought; "Damn . . ." and several other things. She held onto him awhile then, and he held her, and when she'd gotten her breath back she said, "Thanks, mate. I appreciate that. I really do."

He didn't answer. He just held her and rubbed her shoulder. And finally, after she'd been comfortable a few breaths: "I got to get to bed," she said, not wanting to talk, not wanting to think about moving. "I'm going to go to sleep here if I don't."

So he politely helped her up and helped pull her clothes together, all in the absolute dark. Then he put his own self in order, went and felt around after the latch, and cracked the door carefully. She leaned on his shoulder, looked out and listened too, and the two of them slunk out into the corridor and shut the locker door.

"Better go on ahead," he said, then, tight-mouthed, the only words but two he'd said during the whole business. "Find yourself a bunk. There's two vacant midway up the loft."

She looked at him with a real clear idea now at least what part of his spookiness was, and why he had no inclination to do anything in crew-quarters. A man living in with everybody, where everything went on all the time without any privacy, that bothered a lot of people who hadn't grown up with it: bothered her, at first, on *Africa*. It bothered a man a lot worse, if he was inclined to freeze up real easy, if he *was* on the outs, and people gave him a hard time, and especially if he was straight off some family ship like *Ernestine*, where he wasn't used to that. Merchanter. The war killed ships and scattered their people. She knew that for sure, knew it the way she knew the breed when *Africa* jerked some scared kid in off a merchanter deck and put him through the Initiation, same as she'd gotten, same as everyone got.

But some of that breed cracked. Some suicided. Some just died.

"Muller make a habit of giving you a hard time?" she asked.

He drew a breath, hesitated as if words cost by the gram, and looked skittish at the sound of somebody coming further around the curve. "Get. I'm doing you a favor."

"Oddest damn favor I ever had." She stayed, he started walking, so she walked and caught up with him, stride for stride, keeping ahead of whoever it was back there.

"They'll give you hell," he said without looking at her. "They'll give you real hell if you get caught with me, think it's real damn funny. Take your stuff topside, 'bout third, fourth bunk up-ring." He reached over, gripped her shoulder, friend-like, let it go with a sexy little brush at her arm that left a tingle behind it.

Oddest man she'd ever had, she thought, except Ritterman. *Two in one couple of months. What'd I do to deserve this?*

*Blind tired, I'm going to screw up tomorrow, sure, hell of an impression I'm going to make with Bernstein.*

But she got inside, slipped up the ladder with her duffle and tied it to the end of the second vacant bunk, fell down on top of the mattress, cover and all, fumbled the safety-net across her and snapped it, and just went numb, out, gone, til the alterdawn bell rang.

"I got to talk to you a minute, Yeager," Bernstein said when she reported into Engineering, and then, beckoning her over into a corner: "We got a complaint, Yeager, we got cleanliness standards on this ship, don't care how tired you are, you don't fall into a bunk that isn't dressed and you be careful and shower after duty, Yeager."

"Yessir," she whispered, feeling her face burning. "Not my habit, sir, I apologize, sir. Just couldn't find everything right off, I didn't want to wake people up."

"Not putting you on report," Bernstein said. "First and only warning."

"Yessir, I appreciate that, sir."

He looked at her odd, then, real strange for a minute, so she thought maybe she'd reacted wrong, or spoken wrong, or something, and that made her nervous.

God, maybe somebody had spread the word about her and her associate.

"You just remember," Bernstein said, then took her the tour himself, what was where, where the jury-rigs were, the special problems, told her what had to be done, what had to be checked on what schedule.

Thank God, she thought, she'd done a lot the same for

*Ernestine*, even to the point Jennet let her sit alterday watch alone toward the end, taught her the read-outs and told her in Jennet's sane, easy way what was critical and what was an as-you-can. Walk the rounds with Musa, Bernstein said, and introduced her to a small, dark man.

And introduced her to NG, who looked at her cool, smartass, and just inside Bernstein calling him down. She felt the tension in the air.

So she gave NG Ramey a raised eyebrow and a cold stare for Bernstein's and Musa's benefit, as if she'd just met somebody she had no trust of at all.

Which might be the case.

Musa had nine fingers. He was one of those people you'd never ask how that was. Something had hit his nose once, broken it and scarred it right across, and that same something, probably, had made a burn-scar across his temple and right on into his cotton-wool hair, where there was a gray bit right at that temple: you didn't ask him about that either. He looked about fifty, his skin was pale brown, that shade really dark skin did when you went on rejuv, not a bad-looking man at all, but his real age might be fifty or ninety-five or a hundred fifteen for all she could tell.

But Bernstein was right: Musa was all right, Musa knew what he was doing with any system on this ship, you could tell that right off, and Musa kept saying, "Ask questions, I don't mind."

Musa truly didn't, she found out, and that was a relief. Musa said Bernstein had put her on maintenance, plain scut to start with, and job one was a simple matter of a dead pump that needed fixing as a backup.

She was positively cheerful then. It was mindless work, it was something she understood backward and forward and it was sit-down work, at a bench alone in the machine-shop — no matter that her arms hurt and her hands hurt and it was all she could do to hold a wrench.

So a simple plastic diaphragm was shot. "We got one," she went back to Engineering to ask, and it was NG she ran into, on the check-rounds, "or do we make one?"

NG showed her the parts-inventory access on comp, turned up a backup in storage. "Show you where to get it," he said, and showed her on the computer-schematic of the storeroom.

Bernstein being in a briefing and Musa being on a check-see call in ops, they were alone. He put his hand on her hip, not smartass, just kind of trying to see what she'd do, she thought. She twitched it off.

"Not on duty, friend."

He glanced off at the comp then and scowled. Not a word.

"Didn't say never," she said, and frowned. "You make me damn nervous."

Not a word to that, either.

"Trade you," she said. "You tell me where the hell we are and what we're doing out here, and we do a little private rec-time tonight."

"Don't need to do that," he said sullenly, without looking at her. "We're lying off by Venture."

"What in hell for?"

"Hunting. Just hunting."

"Hunting what?"

"Mazian's lot," he said.

No hard work to guess that much – as long as you could guess which side a spook ship was on.

"They got any notion who?" she asked.

He shrugged. "*Australia*, maybe. Not real sure right now."

*Africa*, she thought. Her heart beat higher. Thinking about her ship made a little lump in her throat. "Watch-see, huh?"

"We just spot 'em," NG said. "Cripple 'em if we can. Run like hell in any case. This ship hasn't got a big lot of armament."

"Wouldn't think," she said under her breath, thinking – thinking that she was on the wrong side of everything. She was desperate to get home to *Africa* again, to *Australia*, *Europe*, any ship that might be operating in the Hinder Stars: and she had no chance, no chance at all of living through an encounter like that, except if *Loki* got disabled and boarded.

Chance of arranging that, a little sabotage –

You could get spaced for thinking about it.

And to do that without blowing yourself to glory, you had to know more than she knew about ship systems.

She looked back at NG, saw him sitting there at the

console, mop of black hair, always a brooding look, like he was never happy, like he expected nothing good out of anyone or anything.

Crazy man, she thought. Maybe no fault of his how he'd gotten there, and he might be a damn good lover as far as that went, but a man that nervous could go crazy someday, it had happened a couple of times on *Africa*, even to seasoned troops, and you could tell the look, day by day, just quieter and crazier. One had got hold of an AP, shot right down the main downside corridor, blew six skuts to hell before somebody got him; one ten year vet had just spattered pieces of herself all over barracks three one main-night when she was sleeping just four spots over, – nobody could account for how she'd gotten the grenade.

NG wasn't damn happy on this ship, with this crew.

And NG – the thought gave her a queasy stomach – was in Engineering.

# Chapter 10

S he got settled in – she figured who the skuz was who had complained, figured it for one Mel Jason, who had the bunk next, and whose stuff was all over the walls, pictures of flowers and souvenirs of bars and stations and pictures of naked, nice-looking men, all of which told you not much about Mel Jason except you supposed by that, that Mel Jason was a she.

As for the other, the downside ladder was down-ring from her, Jason was up-ring from her, she had no neighbor on the left, and the plastic privacy sheet and all prevented most neighbors *seeing* that she hadn't put a sheet down last night, except one up-ring that might be passing by the foot of the bed headed for the ladder – always possible it was somebody else, but the one next was the likeliest, the way she figured it.

So she put one Mel Jason on her tentative shit-list, and still made up her mind not to be too mad, all things considered: *nice* quarters on this ship, she thought, with the privacy screens and all, real fine airy feeling and safe at the same time, with the safety net there to prevent anybody going flying onto the downside skuts in any sudden maneuver.

Best of all, in her figuring, you got your own rack to yourself, and your own storage underneath for all your stuff: the ship wasn't crewed even half to quarters capacity and you didn't have to share with mainday.

So, seeing how clean things were and how people expected to live, she didn't much blame Jason, if it had been Jason who had complained, although Jason had been a little quick on the trigger. *Africa* had had standards, crowded as they had been, and if she'd gotten some skuz neo moved in next to her who broke the sanitation regs, she'd have bitched too.

Life had just made her a little more willing to give a body room, that was what she detected in herself.

So she was pleasant to Jason, walked around the privacy screen, and said: "Sorry about last night. No excuses; but it's not habitual."

Jason looked around from her sewing, bit off a thread, nodded then, once and definitely. That was all the comment Jason was going to make. Jason didn't even ask what she was talking about, and that was all the answer she wanted out of Jason right now. She figured time would kill or cure, and she went on down to supper.

NG was there. NG gave her hardly more than a look, and she didn't walk past empty spots to sit with him, considering he'd warned her keep clear of him in public, for what might be good reasons of not wanting a ruckus. So she just sat down at the first convenient vacant place on the bench and paid all her attention to her food. He left. She didn't know where.

But afterward, when a lot of the crew gathered back in the darkened quarters to watch a very tired pre-War vid, a man came up close beside her at the back of the crowd, while she was standing with her arms folded and thinking she'd seen this one twenty times at least.

The man touched her shoulder, made a nod toward the door, and said: "Yeager?"

Not NG. She'd thought that it was at first.

But it was an approach, she knew the dance. His name was Gabe, he said, he wanted to buy her a beer, he was polite and interested, and he wanted to sit and talk awhile, with intentions for the rest of the night by no means hard to figure.

She wasn't altogether enthusiastic about the invitation, she'd been looking for NG with the hope of straightening some signals out with him, but if NG had been in the quarters she couldn't spot him and if he'd gone off somewhere else he damn well hadn't signaled her a come-ahead. So she found no immediate excuse, she had the beer, she had two, and Gabe – the name on his pocket was McKenzie – asked her questions she told the usual lies to: merchanter swept up in the Pan-paris rout, dumped at Thule, desperate, – what about himself?

McKenzie was sympathetic. McKenzie said he was ten years on *Loki*. McKenzie was clearly more interested in making his move than in answering detailed questions. Then another couple of crew came wandering up from down-ring, both male, friends of McKenzie's, just to look over the neo, do a little safe shopping and neo-baiting – get her rattled if they could, have a little fun if they couldn't. An all-right couple of guys, she decided: Park and Figi. They didn't sit down, they just hovered, asking how was it going, checking out her disposition toward McKenzie with an eye to a more personal check-out later if she was amenable.

– McKenzie, Park, Figi, obviously a buddy-system, all three of them scan-techs, McKenzie the good-looking one, Park and Figi a little shyer, a little less comfortable with a stranger, under the smartass facade.

You could bet who ran that trio, she thought, and she laughed at their fun-poking. It was kind of cute, actually, that McKenzie actually blushed – they nailed him with a tag about getting wrong bunks in the dark and he told them go away.

But McKenzie was just trying to get friendly again when another couple of male crew showed up in the rec area, and *they* had to walk over and introduce themselves – Rossi and Wilson, by the tags, Dan and Meech, by name; not bad, either, certainly Rossi wasn't, but you didn't get picky when you were new: not good business, and you didn't start with one man and go off with another either, not unless you wanted a rep as a trouble-maker. "Hey," McKenzie said, finally, slipping a protective arm around her, "it's my beer. Get out of here. – Kate, *get* these guys." – to a woman getting herself a beer.

"Do I get a favor-point?" Kate yelled back, which got a friendly rec-riot started, just comfortable stuff over at the counter between Kate and Rossi and Wilson: McKenzie took his chance to get familiar, a little squeeze. "Don't take 'em serious. How're you doing? Quarters is pretty private right now, everybody's watching the vid. I got a private bottle. What do you think?"

"Fine," she said.

Except when she got up to go with McKenzie, she saw NG over against the wall by the quarters, just standing there looking at them.

Her gut tightened up. She remembered about that rec-time promise she'd tossed off to him this afternoon, and he'd tossed

it off the other way, a kind of a don't-bother she'd decided
was his opinion on the matter.

But that look he was giving her didn't say don't-bother.
Her heart started pounding and she didn't want eye-contact
with him, but it happened, once, fast, direct, while she was
walking toward the door.

Then he turned his face the other direction, just leaned
there with his hands in his pockets while she walked through
the door and into the quarters with McKenzie.

McKenzie had a downside bunk, back in the far end from
where the vid was still going on. They weren't the only
couple back in the dark end, very likely not everybody in
their proper bunks this evening, because of the vid occupying
the other end of the quarters. McKenzie got out a bottle and
took a drink and passed it to her while he was undressing. She
took a couple or three big ones, then passed the bottle back
and stripped down. They got in bed, got under the sheet,
while the end of the room erupted in a cheer for that damned
tired vid, about the time the good guys' ship showed; she
remembered the plot. But the cold air got her, or the straight
vodka did, and she tucked down against McKenzie, her teeth
all but chattering.

"What's the matter?" he asked, rubbing her shoulders, and
was real careful with her, real concerned about her maybe
being scared of him. "Just a little cold out there," she said.
"I'm fine."

So they had another couple of swallows off the bottle. Hell, she thought, there was nothing *wrong* with Gabe
McKenzie. He was polite, he was sane, he was worried
about her, he did everything right and he appreciated her
the same – but it was like her skin was dead all of a
sudden, the way it had been with Ritterman – like she
was just too tired or the hormones weren't working or
something.

It scared her, and then she flashed just for a second on NG
and his hand on her arm and it tingled, it tingled just thinking
about that, all the while nothing that McKenzie did was even
getting past the surface.

*That's crazy*, she thought, and thought suddenly about NG
out there in the rec area, NG knowing what was going on

right about now, and probably mad and upset about her skipping out on him –

No, dammit, she hadn't skipped out, he hadn't taken up on her, he'd put her off this afternoon when she flatly propositioned him, he'd had a chance at dinner to at least look her direction and cue her.

She wished to God he wasn't a crazy man, wished he wasn't out there right now being a damn lunatic, hanging around like that. She wanted to kick him down the corridor.

She wanted –

Damn, she wanted him touching her instead of McKenzie, so she kept flashing deliberately to him last night in the rec area and back to what McKenzie was doing, trying to get some kind of feeling back – damn, dammitall! She reckoned what kind of a buzz she was getting off NG Ramey, and when somebody ever got to doing that . . . anytime you ever got to confusing sex with risking your neck, you had a problem. She'd seen that kind in the Fleet, – seen them take a few bystanders with them, too, when they screwed up for the last time. Damn stupid, that was what it was. . . .

Except there was something else about NG, there was that wounded look of his, that was no expression McKenzie could have caught if McKenzie had been looking straight at him: she was the only one who knew *why* NG was standing there – and she couldn't forget he was there, couldn't stop, even while McKenzie ought to have her attention, thinking that nobody had ever affected her the way NG had.

No, dammit, that was a lie, too, that was an absolute lie, the man had shoved her off in a dark locker, gone near the limit of her patience with any man, no matter what his excuse – nothing had been that damn spectacular in the first place –

Except her mind kept getting the business in the locker all confused with the way he'd touched her in the corridor and gotten that crazy jolt out of her nerves that she'd never in her life had even in sex, that feeling that, if she could get it twice and turn it over and figure it out –

Damn, you flat couldn't go on getting it, it was a cheat, a first-time-in-two-years adrenaline buzz, that was all it was, it wasn't going to repeat, she was just stressed out and NG was the first man along. She certainly wasn't crazy enough to get a high like that off a man who could just likely go off the edge some night – and she damn sure wasn't crazy enough to get a high only *because* he could go off the edge some night.

No. The risk wasn't what was nagging at her, it was that look he'd given her out there, that look that said he was doing something *his* common sense told him not to do.

And it was two different people, the man who had smart-assed his way into a beer with her – and the one who was out there, scared to come in here . . . and still refusing to walk off and leave it at that. – God, it could look to everybody else like he was just being his usual spook self, but that wasn't what was going on out there, she knew it, she was sure of it. NG was pushing it tonight, his standing outside that door was a kind of fighting back, even if McKenzie wouldn't even notice it.

*That* was what got to her, deep down. He wasn't out there to start a fight, not to embarrass her, either – risking, she thought, a whole lot of his pride with that one moment of eye-contact, before he just turned his face the other way. *That* was the thing that kept bothering her while she was in McKenzie's bunk. She had no idea where NG's bunk was, she had no idea, finally, as people came and went by that corridor doorway, whether NG had come on into quarters or not. She might have passed out awhile, she woke up and another vid was on and McKenzie was snoring, so she got out of bed and went on up to the loft.

Somebody accosted her up there in the dark of the walkway past the bunks, big man, a little rude, drunk and offering her a drink if she'd stop at his bunk, so, what the hell, she did it with him, she didn't know why, she just wasn't sleepy, and she wanted somebody to touch off what NG had last night and blow holes in all her careful analysis.

He didn't. He didn't care, either, he was far too lost in his own space, but he shared his bottle, she got herself wobbly-drunk,, still found her bunk, got undressed and went to bed in good order, out soon after her head hit the mattress.

But she woke up part of the way through the night, disgusted and scared by what she'd done, dropped off and woke up a second time with the alterdawn bell ringing and people getting up to go to work.

Damn, she had no idea who the second man had been or what bunk she'd been in.

She wanted a shower. She wanted not to have done what she'd done, at least the second one, for God's sake. *That* piece of gossip would make the rounds, damn sure it would.

Fool stunt – no name, nothing – get blind drunk in a strange place, let herself get talked into a bunk with some skuz as drunk as she was, God, she couldn't even remember if one was all there had been, or how she'd gotten back to her own bunk. She could've ended up a med case, no knowing what could have happened, they were no shipmates of hers, not yet, not by a long way.

Only hope was, the drunk she'd slept with might be wondering who *she* was.

Damn, damn, damn! she was mad at NG Ramey, that was what, damn spook, damn lunatic, she was crazy if she had to have *him* to set her off, it was a piece of nonsense, a feeling bred of too many drinks and too many loose ends around her, that was all, it was insecurity, and it was easier to worry about an effin' spacecase than it was to worry about where the ship was and what kind of game she was into and what she was going to do when Bernstein tried her on some complicated something she *couldn't* fix.

She got her shower, she ate her breakfast, a few quick gulps of synth orange and some salt to get her blood back in balance, piece of cracker, enough to cushion her stomach and buffer a couple of pills for a sick hangover.

But she showed up in Engineering, first to sign in this time, clean sweater, clean pants, never mind the red in her eyes and the pounding in her skull.

There was check to do, she grabbed the checklist off the wall-clip, and got right to it, all enthusiastic efficiency, exactly the way Bernstein had said first-in was expected to do.

NG showed up, walked over and took the board out of her hand.

"Good morning," she said.

"I'd better check it over," he said, and then started re-running all the checks, everything she'd just done, from the top.

"I'm right," she said indignantly, at his elbow, trying to keep it all quiet from the mainday crew members that were still finishing up. "Dammit, I can write down a damn number, Ramey!"

He nodded, and didn't even look at her, just walked on his rounds.

She couldn't do anything about him just then. The mainday chief was still there, within earshot, and then Bernstein walked in with Musa. So she choked it down and waited for Bernstein to put her on something.

Bernstein put her on a core-crawl with Musa, *that* was how the rest of the day went – suited up and still freezing her ass off, a long, long misery of checking joints and looking for leaks and all the while knowing, as Musa put it –

"I like to move a little fast on this. Different from any merchanter, – if *Loki* had to move right now, mate, . . . we'd be in for one hell of a ride."

"How are we so lucky?" she asked, meaning alterday shift. They drifted, zero-G, in the dark dizzy perspective of pipes a quarter kilometer long, half swing up and over the pipes, half swing down under, like lacing, helmet-lamps and hand-held spots throwing close pipe into light, losing itself down the long, long fall Musa was talking about.

"Bernstein lost a bet," Musa said.

"You serious?"

"Crazier stuff goes on." A moment of silence, while the sniffer-lights ticked away, blink-blink, blink-blink.

You had a tether you kept moving and clipping on as you moved. You hoped to hell you never had to trust it. You never let yourself think up or down in a place like this, or they might have to pry you loose from the girders.

Anybody in the Fleet knew all about long corridors and sudden moves. A carrier's ring wasn't a ring, it was a cylinder with a few long, long corridors fore to aft, and corridors zigged, precisely to break falls like that, but even those could be a long, long drop if the engines cut in. You ran like hell when the take-hold sounded, you set yourself into a nook, hoped you had a ringbolt close you could clip your safety-belt to, you held onto the handholds as long as your hands could stand and sometimes the push was too hard for that, you just hoped it quit soon and concentrated on breathing. One time there'd been only a three-second split between the take-hold siren and a push that became a whole lot too much, a hundred twenty dead, that time, just couldn't get the clips on, – God, she remembered that, she dreamed about it sometimes, remembered bodies falling right past her – and herself just lucky enough to have her back to a solid wall.

You didn't look at a perspective like the core as *down*, no way, or you could heave everything in your stomach.

Especially with a hangover.

Damn him.

"Musa."

"Yeah."

"You mind to tell me something? – Is anybody going to monitor us?"

"Not real likely. Can. What d'you want?"

"What's the story on NG?"

"Who you been talking to?"

"Muller."

Long silence, just the hiss of the airflow and the ping of the sniffer-readout. Then: "What'd Muller say?"

"Just he was on the outs. That he had some bad shit with the crew, didn't say what."

Another long silence. "He give you trouble?"

"No. What's his problem?"

"At-ti-tude, mate. I told him. – I tell him that now and again. What he did, he killed a man."

"Law didn't get him?"

"Wasn't like that. Just wasn't where he was supposed to be, wasn't watching what he was supposed to be watching. Damn pipe blew, killed a man, name of Cassel. Good man. NG – just had that habit of ducking out when he wanted to, Cassel tried to cover for him. That's how he paid Cassel."

"Hell of a tag."

"Not only the one thing that won it for him. I'm fair with him, I don't pick any fights, I don't make trouble, and Bernstein's his last chance. Fitch had him up on charges, last time he ducked out. Fitch was going to space him, no shit. Those rules and rights in quarters?"

"Yeah?"

"Don't you believe 'em. . . . And NG, he was done, but Bernstein got him off, Bernstein threw a fit with the captain and said put him on alterday crew, and move this other chap, *he'd* take him. Or NG'd have gone the walk, damn sure."

*Lot* to think about in that, she thought.

"He thank Bernstein?"

"I dunno. Maybe. Maybe not. — I tell you, I tell you something. That man's not altogether here. But he never run out on duty again. Never gives Bernstein any trouble, never gives me any. You just don't cross him." Another long silence, Musa rising above the level of the pipe, arcing over toward her. Musa grabbed her hand and pulled her close until their helmets touched. He cut his com off. She understood that game and cut hers. "I tell you something else, Yeager." Musa's voice came strange and distant. She could see his face inside the helmet, underlit in the readout-glows. "I think one time this ship went jump and NG was in the brig, — I'm not real sure Fitch saw he got his trank. I'm not sure, understand, but that time Bernstein got him off — maybe it was just one time too often in the brig, maybe it was just that jump and looking that spacewalk in the face — but I'm not real sure that didn't happen, just the way I said: Fitch hates his guts, we had an emergency, we had to go for jump, NG was dead, the way Fitch had to figure. But once Bernstein got him reprieved, the other side of jump — no way was Fitch going to tell the captain what he'd done. Can't prove it. NG don't talk. I'm not real sure all of him came back from that trip."

"God . . ."

"Not saying it's so, understand. No way to prove it. Don't even think about it. We're *legitimate* now. We're Alliance. There's *rights* and there's *laws*, and the captain's signed to 'em. But they aren't on this ship, woman, and you don't get off this ship, no way you ever get a discharge from this crew, I hope you figured that when you signed your name. You skip on a dockside, Fitch'll find you, you go complain to station law, Fitch'll lie and get you back, and you'll go a cold walk, that's sure. Fitch tell you that?"

"No. But I'm not real surprised."

"You got the right of it, then."

"NG a volunteer?"

"Dunno. Fitch gets 'em. NG never has said. Unless he

told Cassel. Doesn't matter. He's on this ship, he'll die on this ship, and so will all of us." Musa pushed her adrift and turned his com back on. She flipped the switch on hers.

"Let's make a little time," Musa said, motioning along the ship spine with a shine of his lamp. "I hate this effin' core-crawl, damn if I don't."

# Chapter 11

She peeled the suit, she checked back with Bernstein along with Musa, a long, long day, a chill set deep in the bones. "Just go on," Bernstein said. "Quiet day, only an hour til shift end, NG's on and you're off, get."

She was willing to swear, then, that Bernstein was human. But she hung around reading the duty sheet while Musa was already checking out, and she dropped by NG's work-station on her way, while Musa was leaving and Bernstein was busy with his back turned.

NG didn't turn his head, NG kept on with his keyboard and his readouts, and she came up close and brushed her fingers across the back of NG's neck. "Want to see you," she said. He swatted at the nuisance, and looked around at her with an expression –

Mad, maybe; disturbed, confused, scared – all of that in a second's blink, then a scowl and a furious set of his jaw.

She said, "Where?"

He kept scowling at her.

"Front of the lockers?" she said cheerfully. "'Bout 2100?"

"Shop-stowage," he said with no change of expression.

"You'll get us – " – spaced, she almost said, but that wasn't a good idea.

He didn't say anything. He didn't look happier, either.

"All right," she said, and walked on out before Bernstein could turn around and notice anything.

So she picked up her laundry from Services, walked on up-ring to rec, sat down on the bench and had a cup of tea with Musa during mainday shift's breakfast, waiting on mainday crew to clear the showers, then very purposefully dawdled through cleanup and through dinner –

Because McKenzie had more notions. She saw the look he gave her when he spotted her, and she was dodging him.

She took a seat close between two women, nodded a pleasant hello to two stony silences, then paid absolute attention to the stew; but McKenzie walked over and asked her how she was doing.

"Oh, fine," she said, thinking fast, "except I got to get Services straightened out, damn screw-up with my laundry – "

"What about tonight?"

"I dunno," she said, in the friendliest possible way. She saw NG walk in, down at the down-ring end of rec, – dammit! And McKenzie could properly feel insulted if a woman turned cold after a first-time sleepover . . . especially if man number two from last night was going around telling how she'd left McKenzie and come up to his bunk because McKenzie had given out. God!

So she smiled at McKenzie, wrinkled her nose in a sweet expression. "I tell you, I really want to take you up on that." She got up with her tray in hand, tried just to shake him, but at least the retreat moved McKenzie over where she could talk to him without the two women in earshot. "I owe you the truth, Gabe. Fact is, I got an appointment tonight, – well, actually a couple of nights ahead, right now, and I don't think I ought to do any different, – but you're on my good-list, you really are. I'm just not ready to go single, first off. Never been my policy."

Damn man was entirely out of line, coming on her twice in a row like that, putting her to it in public, making her defend herself when there was no wrong on her side. Damn! she could pick them.

"After that," he said.

"Hey," she said, "I *got* to be politic, Gabe."

"Nothing you don't want," he said.

"Did you hear *don't want*? I didn't hear that. But I just got this bad feeling about singularity first and right-off. Bad business. But I do make my favorites after the new wears off." She patted him on the arm, chucked the dishes and the tray, turned around and winked at him. "See you, luv."

She escaped. She didn't know how McKenzie felt about it, but he looked at least a little mollified. She got back to quarters, she ducked into the head for a bit in the case McKenzie was following her or one of his friends was, then

ducked out again and escaped out the door of the quarters
in the other direction without even turning her head, well
down the corridor before she slowed down.

Damn! she thought, her heart pounding. McKenzie gave
her the shakes. The appointment she was going to gave her
the same.

*Damn,* she thought, *why are you doing this, Bet Yeager?*

No good answer for that one, besides hormones – and
besides a real disgust with the skuz who was back there
trying to buy her along with a beer, and disgust with
the women's surly silence, and a disgust for what she
was picking up for morals on this crew. There were
a lot of peculiar things on this ship, she thought, and
only one crazy man gave her anything like a healthy
feeling.

Hormones, maybe. But there was her own experience with
Fitch. There was what Musa had said. And Gypsy Muller's
ambiguous signal.

She headed on around past Ops and Engineering, past
ordinary traffic, and ducked into the shop-stowage, quite
business-like.

The lights inside were on power-save. The place was three
long aisles of bins; and all around the edge, barrels of plassy
for the injection-mold and pieces of the press, and pieces
for the extrusion-mold, and hoses and rods and wire and
insulation-bales that made the whole huge compartment a
maze. She leaned against the door, looked left and right and
listened for sound above the general white-noise that masked
everything on a little ship.

"NG?" she called out, enough to carry in the place, in
case he had gotten here ahead of her and just hadn't heard
the manual-latch door.

Not a sound. But with him that was nothing unusual.

She had a sudden, bad case of the willies, felt the chill in
the place, her breath frosting in the dim light. She chafed
her arms and folded them, wishing she had a sweater under
the jumpsuit.

*God, the man wants to make love in a damn freezer.*

*If that's actually what he wants,* she thought then, with a
little upset at her stomach, thinking that a man on the edge
could just be crazier than anybody thought, could be waiting

somewhere in here with a knife or something, in some notion
that she was pushing him –

*What in hell am I doing in this hole? I got more sense than this,
I always had more sense than this.*

*So I can take care of myself. Taking care of myself means getting
the hell out of here, back to quarters, just tell him later I couldn't
find him –*

*And, sure, he'll believe that. And then I got trouble with him.*

*You focus a crazy on you, you got trouble forever, that's what
you've done, Bet Yeager. You know better, you known better since
you were eight years old. . . .*

She ought to get back to quarters, just go to bed, *not* with
McKenzie, not with anybody tonight, not for a lot of nights,
maybe, – just get her thinking straightened out and maybe
figure out some things. She already had two problems on
this crew, three, counting Fitch, and the smart thing to do
now, the smart thing to have gone for in the first place, was
to shed all connection with NG Ramey, and get in with a
compatible crowd well on the Ins with everybody, some
group with a woman in it, dammit, she wanted buddies
as well as bedmates, and the female crew was being more
than stand-off right now. She was getting hostile signals out
of certain people, all women, like she was doing something
entirely wrong, or like she was crossing lines she didn't
know existed – and she was less and less sure she was doing
anything *right*.

She was about two jumps from scared about this crew,
considering the confused signals she was getting out of
McKenzie – scared of what she was picking up from the
women the way she was scared with stationers, scared the
way she'd been scared sometimes on *Ernestine*, like she walked
around making wrong move after wrong move and people
were putting their heads together and whispering at her back
– look at her: look at the way she did that – that's not civ.

She *tried* to remember civ manners. She tried to act right.
She'd been sixteen when she'd volunteered aboard *Africa*, but
she remembered very little about home before that, couldn't
even clearly remember her mama's face, just the apartment
where you had to let down the bunks to sleep every night and
put them up to move around, everything was so crowded;
and mama's clothes hanging all along one wall and lying all

over the deck – just the dingy metal corridors of Pan-paris
number two refinery-ship, and the places she used to hang
out, the holes there were – her mama trying to handle a kid
who never did take to civ rules, who was always in trouble,
people always making up their minds two and three times
what they wanted, rules they never posted, exceptions they
never told you –

But then, mama could have done a better job of telling her
the regs in the first place. And mama never had a real grip on
things. Mama would break something, mama would slap her
for it, mama would come in mad and you just ducked out,
didn't matter whether it was your fault or not.

Never could figure mama out, let alone mama's friends.
Never could trust what one said, never dared get alone with
them.

Because she never was In with civs. But when you got In
on a ship, you could trust people. Like Bieji Hager, and Teo
– the five of them – the times they had –

Damn!

She got a lump in her throat, suddenly felt like it was the
refinery-ship around her again, felt herself strangled and had
to get out, get a breath of air, get herself back to bright light
and sanity –

She opened the door and ran straight into NG, inbound.

"I – " she said, face to face with him. She didn't want to
upset him or act the fool, and then it was too late, she'd let
him back her up inside and shove the latch down on the
door. So there she was, in the middle of it.

She shoved her hands into her pockets and said: "Wasn't
sure you were coming."

She felt like she was sixteen again. Or twelve. Only it
wasn't mama they were dodging. It was *Fitch*.

"I wanted to talk to you," she said. He tried to take hold
of her right off and she flinched back a couple of steps, fast,
not even what she wanted to do, she was that spooked.

He turned his move into a throwaway gesture, a hell with
*you* kind of shrug, and, God, her hands were shaking. She
balled them into fists and stuck them back into her pockets
where they were safe.

*I like you*, she wanted to start with, but that was stupid,
there was no knowing what NG was capable of: he could

go off the edge, do something violent later if he got the idea there was some kind of claim he had on her. She said: "Are we safe here?"

He just stared at her, talkative as he always was when he was crossed.

"Aren't," she concluded, and her skin crawled. Then she thought about Fitch, thought about NG getting on report about one more time.

*Last chance for him*, Musa had said.

"I don't want to get you in trouble," she said. "Ramey, dammit, – "

*Hell, I can't even get my own shit straight on this ship. What can I do for him?*

She shook her head and raked a hand through her hair, and looked at him again. "Look, I got caught up with a guy last night, didn't really want that. I wanted to go over and ask you up to my bunk, that was what I wanted, I wanted to get things straight, but you said it'd make trouble. So I didn't come over and talk to you, I don't know what you're mad at."

Not a word, hardly a blink from him.

"Ramey, give me some help here."

Long silence. Then: "You can get in a lot of trouble," he said, so quietly she could hardly hear him above the ship-noise. "More than crew. Better not to be here. Better not to talk to me."

That miffed her. "Is that what you wanted, night before last?"

NG just shrugged.

She screwed up her courage to have it out, then, her whole body going on alert to move if she had to. "I talked to Musa," she said, and expected some blow-up, but all he did was breathe a little faster, no change of expression. "He's half on your side, Ramey."

"Musa's all right," NG said, so little moving of his jaw it hardly showed. "McKenzie's all right, far as that goes. I do my job, crew lets me alone, don't screw it up."

He was going to leave. He reached for the door latch.

"Ramey."

"Forget it."

"Hell if I will." She put her arm in his way, heart-thumping scared, knowing he could break it in that position. "I go back down there and McKenzie's all over me. I don't want McKenzie."

He stood still, just stopped with his hand on the door, not looking at her.

"Ramey, don't walk out on me. Dammit, don't you walk out on me! I got some answers coming!"

He dropped his hand, turned around of a sudden and hauled her up against him, nothing she couldn't stop, but she went entirely null-state then, scared – God, getting body to body with him was so damned stupid. He could do anything, he could break her neck, she ought to make him back up and work this through slow and sane, but she was having real trouble putting two thoughts in a row right now, not on-course with anything that had to do with him.

"Out of the damned doorway," she gasped when she got her mouth free and had a breath, "dammit, NG, – "

She hadn't meant to call him that. He didn't even seem to notice. "Come on," he said, and pulled her off with him into the dark, into a gap between the wall and the cans, where the track they rode on turned a corner.

There was an old cushion and a couple of blankets back there in the dark, about enough room between the track and the outside wall for a body to fit; or two, one on top of another, if they arranged things. Cold, God, it was cold, but his hands weren't, and he wasn't, and she was trying the best she could to keep things paced with him, to keep him calm and all right . . . until the colored lights went off behind her eyes and she had to concentrate on breathing and not making a sound for a while.

"Oh, God," she said, finally, and put an arm out into the cold air and hugged him. He let out a breath and just got heavier for a moment, relaxed on top of her because there was no room for him to do anything else.

"You're all right," she said, hand on his side, not wanting him to move. "You're all right, Ramey. Let me tell you, you got a couple friends on this ship. At least."

He drew a sharp, sudden breath, another one, as if the air had gone thin – or his sanity had.

She rubbed his shoulders, a little scared at that, kept doing it while he got his breathing straightened out again. "How'd you get here?" she asked, to chase the silence away and keep him thinking. "How'd you get on this ship?"

No answer. But NG was like that.

"You free-spacer, Ramey? Just a hire-on? – Or are you a Family merchanter? What's your real name?"

He shook his head, slowly, against her shoulder.

"Ramey a first name?"

Another shake of his head, just refusal to answer, she thought.

"Doesn't make any difference," she said. "You just got the moves, Ramey, just got the way about you. I don't care. Want to know about me?"

No answer.

"What I thought. – Well, me, I'm a hire-on, Pell, Thule, wherever. Seen a lot. Some of it not too pretty. They tell where Fitch got me?"

A few deep breaths. Quieter now. "They say."

"What d' they say?"

"Say you cut up a couple of people."

It caught her grimly funny, somehow, him with cause to worry about *her*, all along; and not funny: maybe they both had cause. She ruffled his hair. "Not habitual. Doesn't worry you, does it?"

"Don't care," he said.

Absolute truth, she thought, just flat, dead tired truth.

"Been that way too," she said, and felt the cold of Thule docks, remembered what the nights were like there when you were broke, – felt the cold of *Loki*'s deck through the blanket, chilling her backside; felt the cold chance that somebody could walk in and bring down the mofs on both of them. "But things change. I'm alive to tell you that."

"Can't," he said, "can't change," and he gave a long, deep breath that became a shiver, brushed his mouth past her ear. "Just a matter of time." A slow tremor started, like a shiver, got worse; and he started to get up in a hurry, but he banged the overhang of a girder and came down hard on her, smashed her with his elbow, shoved at her, but the space trapped them. "God!" he yelled, "God, – get *out* of here!"

No place to go: she knew a space-out when she saw one. She scrambled, blind for a second, blood in her mouth, fetched up against the icy metal of the can-track, got her knees up to protect herself, but he was just sitting there, bent double.

"Ramey," she said, shaking, trying to pull her clothes together.

He just curled over and tucked down, arm over his head.

She grabbed a blanket and got it around his shoulders.

"Go to hell," he said, between chattering teeth.

"Been there, too, you sum-bitch." She put back the blanket he shrugged off. "Should have kicked you good. Leave it, dammit!"

Long, long time he was like that, clenched up hard, shaking. She just sat there, leaned on his back and held the blanket around him, talked to him sometimes, wished she dared hit him with the trank she carried, but God knew if that was the right thing, or where he was, or when, out in some mental jump-space.

Finally he said: "Go 'way, Yeager. Get the hell out of here."

"You all right?"

"I'm all right."

"C'n you get up?"

He straightened up long enough to shove her away. "I said let me *alone*!"

She caught her balance squatting on her heels, put a hand down to steady herself, not a defenseless position. "You yell all you like, man. You want crew in here, you just yell your head off."

Silence from the shadow opposite her, a long, long time.

"Ramey."

"Get on back," he said without raising his head from his arms.

"Do what? Leave you to freeze your ass off? Get up. Come on."

No answer.

"Ramey, dammit."

Still no answer.

She pushed up to her feet, stiff, half-frozen, caught herself on the wall. "I'm going after Bernstein."

"No!"

"Then get on your *feet*, Ramey, hear me?"

He moved. He started getting his clothes together, hands

shaking. He didn't look up, and she squatted down again and blotted her lip.

"Sonuvabitch," she said slowly, with a despairing shake of her head, and put out her hand to press his shoulder. He shook that off.

"You're being an ass," she said.

"General opinion," he said. "Let me be."

"That how you pay all your favors?"

He sank against the wall, hand over his eyes, turned his shoulder away from her, just beyond coping with her.

Her gut hurt. She was still shivering with adrenaline and her teeth were chattering, but some kinds of pain got to her, and a man with a reality problem was a hard one to sit through. A spacer who'd had done to him by another spacer what Fitch had done – that was hard even to think about.

What this crew had done, on the other hand –

– maybe just not knowing what to do with him . . . She didn't know what to do with him either, right now. She was ready just to give up and go away and let him pull himself out of this particular hole in his own time, man wouldn't do himself any hurt, he never had.

And maybe there was just nothing she could do but make him crazier.

He passed the hand over his face and leaned back against the wall, finally, bit of light falling on his jaw, on one eye.

"You all right?" she asked.

He nodded, exhausted-seeming.

"Musa said Fitch didn't give you your trank," she said. "That true?"

Second nod.

"Fitch shoved me in that damn locker during undock," she said. "I was scared he wouldn't."

The single visible eye flickered. Blinked, fast.

"Fitch is the crazy one," she said. " – You merchanter, Ramey?"

No answer.

"Ramey, you scared of me?"

No answer.

"I figure," she said quietly. "You got all you can handle. I can understand that. But I tell you something, Ramey, I don't need anybody either. Not going to lean on you, not going to doublecross you. I would appreciate it if you kind of watch where your elbows are going."

He reached across the gap between them and pressed her arm, once, gently.

She put her hand on his, held onto his fingers. "You want to go back to rec and buy me a beer? I'm still not sure my credit's in the bank."

He shook his head.

"Come on," she said. "Doesn't scare me."

Another shake of his head. His jaw showed knotted muscle.

"All right," she said. "I'll take your advice on it. But I tell you what. Someday you're going to do that."

"Fitch," he said. Cold straight shot. Damned sobering one. "Name's NG," he said, then, as if some obstruction in his throat had broken loose with that. "Don't make a case of it. Don't stand outside the rest."

"I understand you."

He lifted his hand and touched her jaw, gentle, gentle touch, and it brought back what he could be, either the crazy man or the sane one, she wasn't even sure which was which with him.

"You're going to give me a hell of a rep," she said. "I tell McKenzie I'm going off with a guy, I come back with a cut lip. – Where's the other holes on this ship, so I can explain where I was? A lot of them?"

"Galley stores. Services. Core lift-bay. Stowages."

"Mofs get upset?"

Shake of his head. "Most don't."

"But Fitch is looking."

"This is Orsini's watch. Fitch is mainday."

"Orsini an S.O.B.?"

"Different kind." NG ran a hand through his hair and leaned his forehead against it. "He – "

The door opened. Lights came up.

NG's hand reached hers in a flash, clenched it. She closed down hard, sat absolutely still while voices drifted back, woman's voice, man's sharp and angry.

A switch thumped, machinery whined, and the cans moved on the track. Bet snatched the blanket clear of the rail, where it could hang the track up, saw the can coming at her and pressed against NG for a moment as can after can cycled past, pushing against her with brutal force, shoving at her back and hip, enough to drive the breath out of her.

More machinery. NG's hand pressed her head close against his shoulder as a loader clanked.

And stopped.

Things quieted after a while. The voices were a dull murmur over the ship-noise. Then the lights went down and the door shut.

She sat there with her teeth chattering, the cold all the way through her.

"Gap's still there," NG said, of the way they had gotten back into this hole. "Always is."

"Good," she said, clench-jawed, because she'd been thinking about that, too shaken-up to look.

"You better go," he said. "Slip past the shop door. It could be open. That was Liu and Keane. Liu's a bitch."

She had to, that was all. She got her stiff limbs to work, she squeezed her body between the cans at the curve and got herself out and down the corridor, walking like she belonged there, with her knees weak and her gut gone to water.

She stopped around the line-of-sight from Ops, hung out near the lockers for a good few shivering, worried minutes until NG showed up.

Not expecting her. That was clear.

"It's late," she said. Somehow the crew was at fault for the whole damned mess, and for the aches and her cut lip. And for him. And she was mad enough now to be stubborn. "I tell you what, I want that beer. I go in, sit down, you just come in and make a move. All right?"

He nodded.

So she did that, came in and got the free tea the galley offered; and sipped it with a sore lip and hung around the counter with her back to two couples who were the only crew there.

So NG came trailing in after a little, and she went and sat down while he brought her the beer.

"Thanks," she said, and patted the place beside her on the bench.

But he went and got his and drank it standing at the counter, with his shoulder to her.

# Chapter 12

"We got a water-leak in galley," Musa said wearily, "Bernstein wants you to fix."

Then Musa stopped and looked at her twice. So did anyone who got up close.

"You caught hell," Musa said. "You got trouble from anybody?"

Bet shook her head. "In the shop," she said. "Tried to recoil some line, it snaked round and got me."

Best lie she could think of, that could account for a bruise on her head and a cut lip.

"Hey," Musa said, worried-looking, "you got to watch that stuff, Bet, don't pick any fights with it."

Like hell Musa believed that story.

"I'm all right," she said.

And got on the damned leaky coupling in the galley, a crawl through an access barely body-wide, and a nice flat-on-her-back and slightly over to the side reach next to a damned, noisy refrigeration compressor in a space that gave you barely enough room to get a wrench on the bastard. Bernstein, she figured, was well through the necessary jobs and into the real busywork scut.

"Sonuvabitch," she kept saying between her teeth, just to keep the breath moving, and other things, while hot water dripped in her face.

She got the line disconnected, got the failed coupling off and stuffed it, the work of the two fingers that could reach it, into one pocket, got the replacement out of the opposite and lay there blinking hot water drip and trying to get the damn line dried off to take the adhesive on the coupling.

Effin' plumbing. Effin' same effin' system since humans blasted out of atmosphere. Maybe before. Modern effin' starship and the effin' plumbing got stressed in the effin' expensive swing-section galley and cheap little effin' gaskets had to be seated or nothing worked.

And the drip never ran out. Ran over her face and into her eye and down her cheek into her hair, while the damn thing had to fit on just so, and the damn com was sputtering at her ear, the plug come loose and about to fall out where nobody human could get at it – *had* to wear the damn thing, reg-u-la-tion, when you were working in a hole like this.

"Yeager," it said, nattering at her personally this time.

"Yeah," she said, but the mike was out of reach too, the way she had to tilt her head to get the band-light to bear on what she was doing. "Yeah, I got my page – just a minute – "

Bernstein checking up on her.

"Yeager."

"I got my fuckin' hands full!" she yelled at it.

"Yeager! Check in!"

She held the line and the coupling with one hand, shaking head to foot, made a desperate reach to adjust the com. "Yeager here!" she yelled.

And heard Bernstein's voice. " – forty seconds to firing."

*Oh, my God.*

"Say again," she said. Like a fool she grabbed after the coupling and jammed it home on the snap-ring.

"This ship is moving, Yeager! Thirty seconds!"

She reached after the cut-off valve, screwed it open, a half-dozen fast turns. The coupling held.

"Yeager!"

She started eeling out of that access, using heels and hips and hands, fast as she could go.

The take-hold bell started ringing.

"You got hot water!" she yelled to the com. "Can't get your access-door!"

"Dammit, where are you, Yeager?"

She scrambled up and grabbed the E-belt, bright yellow D-ring, put her back to the galley wall and snapped the shoulder-hip restraint closed, put a hand behind her head, pulling her head down. "Clear!" she yelled. "Clear!"

*Loki* kicked, her neck-muscles strained, feet lost their footing and the whole galley-cylinder rumbled on its track, reorienting until the strain became weight on her feet, and the general com was yelling: *Going for jump. Move with caution.*

*You have time to secure doorways and stow hazards. Burn-rate will increase two hundred forty-five percent over the next three minutes. . . .*

She unclipped the E-belt and let it snap back into its housing, she knelt down, swung the access to and screwed the bolts tight by hand, fighting the drag that tried to tear her hand down.

Up, then, weighing near double, hauling that weight erect, hand back to pull the jumpseat down, straddle it, pull the yellow D-ring again, to haul it over, get the tab inserted.

Down the burn-deck, complete vacancy – crew had gone to whatever E-clips they could find, against solid surfaces, inside compartments, no time to rig the hammocks.

Hell and away more comfortable, flat on your back on the inside burn-deck, than upright on a jumpseat in a swing-section.

*This ship is approaching jump. . . .*

Got a problem, we got a problem, God, something's on our tail out there. . . .

I had to stop for the damn cut-off valve. God, I could've been stuck in there –

God, God, – we're really moving – got a hell of a push on this ship – where's my trank pack?

She fought for air, felt the drag at gut and joints, lifted a hand up after the trank pack in her breast-pocket, found it, got her fist around it and squeezed the trigger against her neck, only bare skin she could orient to.

We going to shoot at that sonuvabitch or what?

Where's NG? Musa and Bernstein?

Everybody all right?

Got hot tea when we get there.

Wherever. . . .

*. . . coming up again, siren blowing. . . .*
*Battle stations, condition red, condition red. . . .*
*This ship is now inertial. . . .*
*Stand by. . . .*

*Crew may attend emergencies with caution. . . .*
*Condition still red. . . .*
*Medical to 23. . . .*

Hell of a way to be first in line, she thought, helping Johnson the cook throw trank-packs and c-packs at crew who got themselves to the counter, handing out ten-packs for the scarcely mobile to carry back to friends a little wobblier, while the com thundered advisories at them –

"*A second jump is possible but not imminent. We are presently in transmission silence. . . .*

"*We have suffered one fatality. Scan-tech John Handel Thomas–*"

"Shit!" Johnson groaned.

"*– died instantly on impact. The captain expresses his personal regrets.*

"*Station-chiefs and area monitors, medical is attending two serious injuries: do not send minor injuries to sickbay. . . .*"

"Yeager," her personal com said, Bernstein alive and functioning.

"Yessir!" she said, never stopping the rhythm.

"*See me when we're stable.*"

"Yessir." That tone was trouble. Her stomach had a new reason for upset.

"*This is the captain speaking. A bogey of carrier-class entered system. Our exit at an opposed angle gives us a considerable lead time into this system, we hope enough to make finding us difficult. We are presently low-V and positional calculations are virtually complete. I'm allowing crew to stand down from battle stations on a condition yellow. Off-shift crew, rig for jump. We'll remain in condition yellow until further notice from command. . . .*"

"*We will manage a shift-change in five minutes,*" came the precise, clipped voice she'd learned as alterday command, Orsini, – via the general com, while she was having a sandwich, privilege of being stuck in rec with the mainday lot. "*Alterday crew prepare your lists.*"

"What do I do about shift-change?" she asked Bernstein via com.

Bernstein said, "Call it luck. I'll skin you next shift. Tell Jim Merrill get his butt up here on call."

"I got to tell him?" she protested. Merrill probably reckoned that her presence here in rec having a sandwich meant she'd been half-shift on a temp, and that Jim Merrill was therefore going to skip a little duty-time.

"He can bring your stuff up," Bernstein said.

So she had to go to Merrill, over on the bench contentedly having his sandwich, and say, "We're complete on the galley plumbing job. I got a call from Bernstein says tell you report on the change and bring the gear up."

"Shit!" Merrill said. She unbelted the tools, took off the com and turned it and the duty over to him.

But before she could get back to the counter she had Liu-the-bitch on her, telling her she was low man in Engineering and she was pleading off on Bernstein, getting special privileges like a half-shift and that sandwich and by implications too vague to prosecute, fraternizing with some unnamed officer to do it.

You didn't argue with Liu, the word was. Liu was senior on mainday Engineering, a small, almond-eyed, black-haired woman who carried a knife, at least on dockside. Bet looked down at the shoulder-high attack, Bet listened patiently to the high-decibel shouting, then said: "I got no quarrel with your worrying about it, mate. But I spent down to jump under that damn galley cabinet, and she's all fixed and you got hot water and the sandwich was free, so I'm not going to turn it down. Matter of fact, *I* was up there handing out packs and hauling out sandwiches with Cook, it being my shift. Don't tell me about lay-abouts."

Liu fumed. Merrill sulked. Other crew stared, a whole shift of people she didn't know — a scary lot of people she didn't know, who had themselves a shouting controversy to entertain them instead of the chance of a take-hold and another jump.

She got speculative stares, caught a little edge of a whisper to the effect that: "That's Yeager. Liu better watch herself. Want to lay a bet?"

The other man made the obvious pun.

She'd heard that one since she was eight. Funny, she thought.

– Like hell.

*"Shift-change! No loitering and no talking!"* Fitch's voice went straight to the bone. *"Inverse order of seniority, sign-off protocols are word of mouth! Go, go, go! . . ."*

Everybody made it, mainday to stations, alterday back to quarters, at least to the corridor where mainday had rigged the hammocks. She saw Musa and NG come in and she treated herself to a beer, since Cook said her credit had come through, and she bought them both one, no question about her being polite to her whole shift, and getting briefed while she was doing it. "Go on, sit down," she said, to both of them, while they were drawing the beers, "I can buy my mates a drink, f'God's sake, NG, you don't have to be such an effin' stand-off – " Innocent as could be, for the benefit of whoever was listening.

And: "Yeah, NG, sit down," Musa said. "Woman wants to buy you a beer, you better be polite about it."

NG sat down, worried-looking, on Musa's other side, in the crowded goings-on in rec, people so busy getting fed and settled, Bet thought, nobody was going to notice.

"Everything come through all right?" she asked.

"Damn press was running," Musa said, "and we got the master shut-down, but we got stuff stuck all over the mold. Mainday's going to bitch – "

Liu was Musa's opposite number. Bet grinned and sipped her beer.

And NG, quietly, never looking exactly at her while he ate: "Bernie couldn't raise you." With the implication of no little worry around Engineering.

"Damn compressor going in my ear," Bet said. "I never heard the bell. Bernstein wants to see me, I got an idea I'm going to catch hell."

"Well, lookit what we got," a tech named Linden jeered at NG's back, sitting down with a couple of his buddies, and NG heard it, Bet figured, since she did; but Musa leaned over to look past NG, and said, loudly:

"Is that Linden Hughes down there? H'lo, Lindy! How's it going?"

"How you doin', Musa?" the answer came back, man leaning to see who that was, a whole lot more polite.

"Not so bad." Musa leaned back again, and Linden Hughes leaned back, avoiding conversation. NG, between, swallowed a last gulp of his sandwich and washed it down, fast, finishing the beer.

"Going to my hammock," NG said. "Thanks."

"Damn mouth," Bet said. "NG, – "

"Let it go," Musa said, putting a hand on her knee; and NG just went to wash up and turn in.

"It's not damn right," she said.

"Shut *up*," Musa said.

So she shut up, Musa's advice generally seeming worth listening to.

# Chapter 13

Quiet night, all told. The morning bell went off and the com flooded announcements at them:

*This is the captain speaking. We've passed beyond our alert parameters without incident. I'm down-grading the alert to stand-by. We're remaining on passive-scan only. We've communicated our sighting to an allied ship which made jump during the last watch. . . .*

No different than in the Fleet, Bet thought. You got your information after the fact and if you got killed it was generally a surprise to you.

So the hammocks stayed rigged, but you could get back in quarters and get a shower, which was high priority after a jump right along with other things, your skin tending to shed a bit and whatever you were wearing tending to make its seams too well acquainted with your joints, not mentioning it smelled like old laundry. So she took a fast one, changed to sweater and pants and kited on out to breakfast, – no sign of Musa and NG, which meant she was running late or they were in the showers.

Chrono by the counter said a little late. So she put a little push on it, gulped her toast and tea and a cup of orange, and headed on to Engineering.

Musa was there. Musa gave her a jaw-down nod and a cut of the eyes toward Bernstein, and she wiped her hands off on her pants and went over to Bernstein's station.

"Sir."

Bernstein gave her a slow look. "You want to tell me about the com?"

"No, sir."

"You *tell* me about the com, Yeager."

"Yes, sir. Fell out of my ear, sir."

"Didn't hear the bell."

"No, sir. Thank you for the page, sir."

Bernstein looked at her a long few seconds.

"You stayed in there getting that fuckin' water on. You damn fool, if that line wasn't secure we could've emptied the damn tank all over rec-deck."

"Yessir. But I dunno heaters. Just pipes. Didn't want anything to blow. So I turned it on."

"That's the trouble with you damn big-ship trainees. You dunno heaters. You know pipes. Everybody's a fuckin' specialist."

"Yessir."

"What'd you *do* as a hire-on?"

"Sit watch, sir. Small repair. Never claimed I was more'n that when I hired on. Said I wouldn't muck with a system I didn't know, sir. But I didn't figure a galley heater was critical to the ship."

Bernstein stared at her like she was something he was thinking about stepping on.

"What condition was that line in when you got my page?"

"Just wasn't hooked on the clip-end, sir. I heard you, I hooked it up, I cut the water on, I moved, sir."

Long silence out of Bernstein. Long, deep breath. "Yeager?"

"Sir."

"You come on here with no papers, you got the spottiest damn training I ever worked with – I *ought* to chuck you right over to Orsini and let him put you in Services."

"Yessir."

"'Yessir.' 'Nossir.' – You got an *opinion*, Yeager?"

"Rather be in Engineering, sir."

"Tell me the truth, Yeager. Did you ever *have* papers?"

"Lost 'em in the War, sir."

"Don't lie to me."

"No, sir."

Another long silence. "Spottiest damn training I ever worked with," Bernstein said. "But you got the hands and you got the nerves. You know *anything* I can rely on, Yeager?"

"Hydraulics, sir. Electronics."

"What else?"

She thought fast and hard. "Small com systems. All small systems. Motors. Pumps."

Bernstein frowned. "Real specialist. What class freighters you been working on?"

"Small, sir. Some stationside work." She drew a breath, took the jump, because she *wanted* to establish her alibis. "Did a little stint in militia before this."

"Where?" Bernstein asked sharply.

"Pan-paris." Records were blown there. It was Union territory now. No way to check it. No way to check anything she claimed there.

"You ever worked with weapons-systems?"

"A little." The air felt too thin. She cleared her throat. "Much as a merchanter carries, sir. And station systems. Small stuff."

Bernstein sat looking at her. Looked at her up and down. Nodded slowly. "Tell you want I'm going to do, Yeager. I'm just going to keep this in mind. You just don't do any damn showoff stunt again."

"Yessir."

"Sign in."

"Yessir." The hand twitched. She didn't move it. She found her shoulders in a brace and gulped air and relaxed, walked over and did the sign-in, exchange with Jim Merrill, who was waiting with no great cheerfulness, with Ernst Freeman.

"Take your time," Merrill said.

"Sorry about that," she said.

"You got no continuances except the clean-up in shop."

"Right," she said. "Thanks, Merrill."

"Where's NG?" Freeman asked.

"I dunno," she said, and looked around, all the way around. Freeman was NG's mainday, Freeman was still standing here, not waiting on Merrill, Merrill having left. "I'll find out."

Her eye tracked to the clock. Fifteen minutes past. Her heart sped up. She went over to Musa, at the counter an aisle back. "Musa," she whispered, " – where's NG?"

Bernstein came walking from the other direction. "Either of you seen NG this morning?"

"No, sir," Bet said.

"Saw him in quarters," Musa said, frowning.

"Shit," Bernstein said, and yelled at Freeman: "Go on, you're relieved. I'll cover you myself."

Freeman left.

"Shit," Bernstein said again. "Musa, go look in the shop."

"Yessir," Musa said, and left.

Best they could do, Bet thought. Short shift, boards to be covered, NG missing and Musa off looking – that left herself and Bernstein.

So she grabbed the board and ran NG's checks, took down numbers and called Bernstein to look-see on a fluctuation. "Inside parameters," Bernstein said.

About that time Musa came back. "Not in the shop," Musa said.

"I'll check quarters," Bet said.

"He's not there," Bernstein said. "I already put in a call. Man's ducked into some hole, is what. *Shit!*"

"Let me try to find him," Musa said. "Sir."

"This department's got work to do, dammit! Get on that check, or we're going to have Orsini down here. – *Damn* that sonuvabitch!"

"Let me look," Bet said.

"You don't know *where* to look."

"I know a few places. I seen a few things on this ship. Sir. Please."

"If you find him – "

"If I can get him back here – "

"You got an hour," Bernstein said. "You try the core-access, you try the lockers, the stowages – "

Bernstein ticked off the places on his fingers, a few more than NG had named to her.

"Seen him last in quarters," Musa said. "He was dressing, nothing was wrong that I know."

"Nothing's ever wrong that anybody knows," Bernstein muttered. "Get the hell gone. Get him. Hit him over the head when you find him. Move, Yeager!"

She moved. She went back up to the shop-storage, she looked in the nook she knew to check. No luck.

Dammit.

*Nothing was wrong that I know* –

No way that you cut up into officers' territory, no damn way you even thought about that. There were the several accessways to core, but they were low-G and colder than a rock and no way in hell a man was going to hide out there unless he was desperate.

Lockers weren't NG's favorite place, considering, but they were the likeliest and they were on the way – past a fast check on the core-lift bay, no joy there either.

She just started opening doors, God knew what you were going to find at this hour, it being mainday's rec-time, and you hesitated to search them all the way to the back, but it was a case of desperation.

Locker one, locker two, locker three, all negative. She had a stitch in her side, caught her breath and decided a look-see in cleaning-stowage was worth it.

Dark in that slit of a place. Light came in from the open door, on somebody's legs. "Sorry," she started to say, then got the notion that somebody wasn't moving. She moved her shadow, reached and cut on the lights.

NG. Not asleep, not that twisted position.

"God. NG, – "

She got down and shook at his leg. "NG?" She was afraid to try to move him. She got his pulse at his ankle, slapped at him. "NG?"

There was a twitch, then, a little movement.

"NG, dammit!"

He drew the leg up, moved, slowly, until she could see the mess he was, his face all over blood, blood on the deck –

"Oh, my God." She took his arm, kept him from falling on his face. "Stay put. I'll get Bernstein."

"'M all right," he said, reaching for a locker-handle – grabbed her arm when she started to get up. "No! I'm all right!"

"What in hell, you're all right? Who did this?"

He shook his head, hauled himself up to his knees, just held onto the lockers a moment.

"I'm getting Bernstein," she said.

"No!"

"Bernstein's after your ass, dammit, I got to tell him, you just don't do anything stupid til I get back, hear me?"

"No!" He hauled himself to his feet and staggered. She grabbed him. "Can't go to the meds," NG said, grabbed a locker handle and held on. "Just go to Bernstein, tell him I'm going to clean up. I'll get there soon as I can."

"Hell, you will! Stay there!"

She ducked out, went to the first general com station and punched in Engineering. "Mr. Bernstein, sir, this is Yeager. I found him."

"*Where?*" the chief's voice came back instantly: he must be sitting over the com. Or wearing one.

"Supplies locker, sir. Somebody beat hell out of him."

"Get med on it."

"He doesn't want that."

"Get a med on it, Yeager, you going to be a problem?"

"He says – "

"I don't care what he says, Yeager. Do it!"

"Yessir. What's the number?"

Bernstein said, she keyed it, made the call, went back inside to find NG in the cleaning cabinet and trying to wash up at the utility sink. The water was running red.

"Med's coming," she said. "*Bernstein's* orders. I tried to talk him out of it."

"Shit," he said, and leaned on the sink.

"Who did this? Did you see them?"

NG shook his head.

"*Why'd* they do it? You start it?"

"Last night," he said thickly. "Tried to tell you."

"You mean your sitting with us?"

NG just shook his head. "Don't get into it."

"Was it Hughes?"

"Don't get into it! Don't get into it, how many times do I have to say it? Call medical, tell them it was a mistake, I just hit my head on a locker, for God's sake – "

"Bernstein won't have it. I tried."

"You were on general com," NG muttered slowly. "Dammit."

"Nothing broken," the med said to her, the other side of NG, NG on the table between them, with the med shining lights in NG's eyes, probing after places NG had as soon not have public; but the cubbyhole of a surgery offered no privacy but a sheet. "He's got a mild concussion. Locker door, was it?"

" 'S right," NG said.

"Hell of a locker," the med said. Fletcher was the name, older woman. A doctor, no less. "Don't argue with it again."

"Yes, ma'am," NG said. "Want to go back to duty."

"I can give you a medical."

"No, ma'am."

Fletcher frowned – her mouth was made for it – and ticked off some notes on a keypad. "You got a painkiller, muscle relaxer, pick it up in galley this evening, one with meals. I shot a little local into those spots, should carry you til then. No alcohol with the pills. Hear?"

"Yes, 'm," NG said, meekly, and slowly sat up, between her help and Fletcher's.

And stopped, frozen, looking toward the doorway.

Khaki shirt, command stripes. Not Fitch: a tall, black-haired man with a permanent beard-shadow.

"I hear we have an injury," the mof said: *Orsini*. The voice left no doubt.

"Sir," NG said, and slid off the table and kept his feet.

"How did that happen?" Orsini asked NG.

"Accident, sir."

"Are you a witness?" Orsini asked, looking at Bet.

"No, sir. Mr. Bernstein asked me bring him in, sir."

"Accident in Engineering, then."

"In stowage, sir," NG said. "Locker door sprung on me."

Long silence. "Any others victims of this door, Fletcher?"

"Not yet," Fletcher said.

Orsini nodded slowly, hands behind him. He walked around to the end of the table while NG pulled his bloody clothes together. "I'll want a copy of the write-up."

"Working on it," Fletcher said. "I'll send it over."

"Released to duty?"

"His request," Fletcher said.

Orsini looked NG's way. "You're dismissed. Go clean up. You too, Yeager."

"Yessir," NG said.

"Sir," Bet said; and NG walked on his own getting out of there, walked on his own in the corridor, still fastening up his jumpsuit.

"It's all right," Bet said. "It's going to be all right."

"It's not all right," NG said. "It's not going to be all right. Keep away from me. Hear me?"

"No way in hell, mister."

NG said nothing. He walked back to quarters, he slipped in, where mainday crew was asleep, he changed clothes while she waited by the door and he came back again.

So she walked with him.

All the way to Engineering.

"Hell," Bernstein said, getting a look at him, and shook his head.

Musa didn't say anything. Maybe Musa had told Bernstein, maybe Musa hadn't. She figured Musa would have done what was smart.

NG just checked in on the sheet, made no arguments when Bernstein put him to paperwork.

"Fill out your own damn accident report," Bernstein said. "It's not my job."

But Bernstein caught her apart and said: "Who did it?"

"I dunno, sir, I got my suspicions. Sir, – *Orsini* was up there, in sickbay."

"I got the call. Listen to me, Yeager. If somebody else comes into sickbay banged up, he's got a problem. Fighting's a serious charge on this ship. You hear me?"

"Know that, sir."

"How *much* do you know?"

"Musa filled me in. About NG. About what happened."

"You better be smart, Yeager. You better be damn smart. You better listen to Musa. – You better know what you're buying when you buy NG any beers, hear me? Because this crew knows what's new on this ship, this crew knows whose idea it is, and you're going to make trouble if you get independent ideas, Yeager, have you got the shape of that?"

"Yessir. I got it."

Bernstein took a deep breath. "You got it. I've been trying to save this man's life, Yeager, *and* keep him sane. Now this has happened. Worse can happen. This is friendly, compared to what can happen. All they have to do is lie. They can still do that. You understand? They can call it self-defense."

"I can lie, too, sir. This Hughes bastard jumped me, NG stepped in. Exactly how it happened, sir. If it has to."

"Don't be a fool!"

"Yessir."

"Was it Hughes?"

"Dunno, sir."

Bernstein gave her a long, cold look. "You armed, Yeager?"

"Not right now, sir."

"What's in your pockets?"

She fished up her card. And a fat bolt.

"What're you doing with that?"

"Going to put it up, sir."

"You do that. And you and Musa – just kind of walk behind him when he goes places. Not one of you. Both. Hear me?"

"Real clear, sir."

Bernstein walked off.

And talked to Musa.

She exhaled a long, shaky breath.

*Game I know, sir. Damn nasty one. But I do know the game, sir.*

# Chapter 14

"I got news for you," Bet said, leaning over NG's chair, putting her hand on his shoulder; NG flinched, mild attempt to get rid of her, but she was at an inconvenient angle. "Musa and I are walking you out of here tonight – "

"I got enough trouble."

"You haven't heard the rest of it. Musa and I are walking behind you in the morning, we're walking you to supper, we're walking you into quarters, anytime you move, you got us behind you."

"And how long does that last?" He swung the chair around, far as he could without bashing her knee. "Stay out of it."

"What's their names?"

"Not your damn business."

"Going to be. Mine and Musa's. We agreed."

"I said let me alone! You *trying* to get me on report?"

"For what? Walking down a corridor?"

"They'll find a way." NG wasn't doing well. He waved a shaking hand. "Just go to hell. I got enough trouble."

"What're you going to do next time?" She slid past his knee, into the seat next to his at the counter, facing it to him; leaned forward, arms on knees. "What're you going to do, merchanter-man, if they *aren't* through hitting on you?"

"That's my problem."

"Mnn." She stuck out her foot between his, against the circular foot-rest of his chair, stopping him from turning it. "No. It's Bernstein's orders. Bernstein's own idea. And I'm not stupid. Didn't come off any Family ship. Maybe I know this game, all right?"

"It's not just them – "

"Yeah, yeah, that's all fine. What're Musa and I going to do? You were drinking our beer. Bunch of skuzzes takes exception to that. So what do we do, just play stupid? Act like we're just too stupid to see how A fits with B? Or too stupid to know if you push a thing you got to be ready to back what you did? Lot of this crew isn't committed on this, lot of this crew don't care shit about you, lot of this crew doesn't give you two thoughts in a week — because you didn't *mean* shit, friend, til you got yourself beat up and now it looks like Musa's got to decide to ignore that or not. And I do, being the new guy. So you got yourself an *organization*, you see what I'm talking about?"

"Fitch'll kill you!"

"You're not listening, merchanter-man. You're not playing the game right."

"Shit."

He was turning away. She braced her foot and grabbed his arm.

"And that right there is one of the problems, friend."

"Get your hand off me before I break it."

"Mmmm-mmm. Won't put a mark on the guys that beat you up and now you're going to break my hand. Real smart."

He shook her off.

"Muller told me," she said, "you got this way of repaying what people do for you."

He shoved the chair the other way around this time, kicked her foot out of the way and got up.

Right face-on with Musa.

"Sit down," Musa said.

"Hell!"

"Looks like we got to beat shit out of him," Bet said to Musa. "Seems to be the only way he takes anybody seriously."

"Leave me alone!" NG shoved Musa out of his way, headed for the door.

"NG!" Bernstein shouted across the room.

NG took a couple of strides more toward the door. And stopped there, as if there was some kind of invisible line on him.

"It's my order," Bernstein said. "You damn well do what you're told."

NG shoved his hands into his pockets, made a move like a shiver, then turned around with that damned cocky set of his jaw, cut lip and all.

"Yessir," NG said.

NG left, they left – Bernstein having held all of them until all the mainday shift came on; NG walked into rec and got his pills and they got beers and sat –

"Dammit," NG said when they parked themselves one on either side of him.

Musa patted him on the knee. "Everything's fine. Doing just fine." And Musa looked at him, leaning a little outward on the bench. "That eye's going to turn all colors, isn't it?"

People stared as they came in. People minded their business, until they got what they fancied out of earshot, and then heads got together and not too furtive looks darted NG's direction – people naturally wondering what had happened to NG's face, and the business about NG having one more chance with Fitch being, as Musa put it, shipwide famous, there was certainly a little morbid speculation going on, damn right there was.

"You stay right here," Musa said, patting NG again on the knee. "I got to get me another beer."

But Musa got directly into a conversation with Muller before he got to the counter, – not without saying exactly what he wanted to say, Bet figured, sipping her beer and watching NG from the corner of her eye – watching whether he reacted to anybody in particular this evening.

Linden Hughes reacted – walking in, seeing him there.

Damn sure.

"That the man?" she asked NG without turning her head.

"I got enough help."

"Sure. Him. His friends. You got all sorts of help."

Silence out of NG.

"You got it wrong," she said. "You got it all backwards. *Friends* is the ones you help."

"You're a damn fool," he said, and got up and went off toward quarters.

So she went.

And caught up to him inside, in the dim light.

He stopped short. "Get off my tail," he snarled at her.

"Hey, fine," she said.

"Look," he said, and came back, hands open. "Look, Bernie's got this great idea, works just fine until some damn emergency comes up and Bernie's got to have Musa off over here, and you're off over there – "

"All you got to do is be halfway smart. Like you weren't."

"Musa's not going to put up with this past three days, Musa's going to duck out of it soon's Bernstein gives him the excuse, and that leaves you, you understand me, that leaves you in that damn locker. You like that?"

"Musa and I got this understanding, just this little arrangement – "

"What kind of arrangement?"

"What you think. Same's with you. Or–ga–ni–za–tion, merchanter-man. You understand Family? I'll bet you do. Same thing. Same thing."

NG looked as if she had hit him in the face.

And he walked off on her, down the aisle to his bunk.

A second later, Musa walked through the door.

"What's that?" Musa asked.

*Family merchanter, for sure*, she thought. *I bet you anything you like.*

But she said, staring after NG, arms folded: "Just getting something at his bunk."

Musa scratched his shoulder. "Not real happy, is he?" Musa said. "Didn't figure."

"I got to tell you," she said, "I been sleeping over with him."

"He all right?" Musa asked.

"Little nervous," she said. "Real sweet, sometimes."

Musa thought that over. "Been a long time," Musa said. "Long time for me, too. You're a pretty woman. Can't blame him."

She laughed a little. Felt a little nicer, at that. Nobody ever had said that but Bieji when he was drunk.

That was what you had to do, find yourself a niche and a couple or three you could trust. That was what was the matter with this ship, that there were so damned few you could, you could pick that up right out of the air. And she hadn't felt safe on this ship until she felt Musa put his arm around her.

Musa was all right in bed too, during the vid, when the bad guys and the good guys were noisily shooting hell out of each other on the screen at the end of the quarters, to the cheers of the drunks and heavy breathing from the couples behind the privacy screens.

NG was in neither category. NG was sleeping, if he could. More likely he was hurting, but at least he was safe – right next to the bed both of them were in, NG's being endmost toward the vid, Musa's being next over.

It was something Musa had bargained his way into at Bernstein's instigation, back when NG had first come onto alterday shift – Musa having a favored mid-quarters bunk that Muller had been all too glad to trade for, and nobody but Musa being on speaking terms with NG.

That was the way Musa explained it, anyway.

Which was how Musa with all his seniority ended up next to the vid, with cheering drunks sitting on the deck at the foot of the bunk he was sharing at the moment – good question now and again whether it was the vid they were cheering.

"Damn fools," Musa said between breaths.

"'S all right," Bet said, and laughed, because it was funny, laughed and got Musa to laughing, quietly, under the blankets they had thrown over themselves.

"You're a good woman," Musa said – Musa smelled of perfumed soap, no less, Musa had clean sheets, Musa had hauled out an old bottle of real honest-to-Mother-Earth whiskey and poured her a big hit on it. It was something she had only heard about, from *Africa* troopers old enough to remember it.

Where'd you get this? she had asked, and Musa, pleased, had said, Taste of home.

So Musa was from Earth. The Fleet had fought for Earth. *Africa* had gone back to fight there. It was kind of an obscure connection that formed, not even a friendly one most of the time, but it made her think what a tangled lot of things it took to get an *Africa* trooper and a man like Musa into the same bed.

Lot of places that led.

The vid reached a series of explosions, the drunks yelled. Musa voice-overed the next lines from memory, funnier than hell, at least drunk as she was getting, and poured her another drink.

The vid went quiet of a sudden. The drunks groaned into a disappointed silence.

"*This is the captain speaking,*" the com thundered out. "*This ship will make jump at 0600 mainday.*"

Then the vid started up again, but the talk was quiet then.

"Damn," Bet said, "gone again. Where now?"

"Easy to answer," Musa said.

"Where, then?"

"Wherever they got us put."

"Damn," she said, and hit him a gentle punch.

"Actually," Musa said, settling down to be comfortable a while, "not too hard to guess. The Fleet's got its ass kicked twice now, back at Earth, they popped out again, nobody knows where, – they say maybe old Beta Station – "

That could put a chill into you. There had always been rumors in the Fleet that Mazian had a hole-card, and the name of abandoned Beta, old Alpha Cent, had come up – the bad-luck station, second star humankind ever parked a pusher-can at and set up to live there – and, the story ran, it had just gone transmission-silent one day, the constant data-flow to other stations had just – stopped, no reason, no explanation, and not a scrap of a clue left behind when a ship finally got there – sublight – to investigate. Beta Station had systematically shut down, and the pusher-module that could have gotten the people off was gone –

But no wisp of wreckage or electronic ghost of a transmission ever told what had happened.

"They'd be fools," she said, and thought to herself it was the kind of rumor Mazian himself might have started, just to confuse things.

"They jumped to some point in that direction," Musa said. "That's what I hear."

"So maybe they know some point of mass nobody else does."

"Could be. Or maybe they just jumped out to old Beta and laid real quiet. Beta would be good for them, all that old mining and biomass gear, antiquated as hell, but if the dust ain't got it it's still there. Could be what he's done."

"Is that where we're going?"

"Not us. No."

"Then what are we doing?"

"Keeping the lanes open. Not letting that sum-bitch cut us off from Earth. Not letting him peel off the Hinder Stars. He could start the whole war up again, get Earth cut off, force Pell into Union or force Pell to deal with him, one way or the other. Sure as hell Pell can't hold out independent if Earth goes into his pocket. Sure as hell the Hinder Stars are nothing but a damn human warehouse. You found that out."

"Found that out," she said.

The vid never did get as noisy again, not what was going on-screen, not the crowd that was watching. A lot of people left to go out to rec and get a beer and talk, and a lot of people just sat around on bunks to drink and talk.

"I got to check on NG," she said, and leaned down off the edge of the bunk to put her head below the level of the privacy screen.

"He all right?" Musa asked.

"Looks to be asleep. 'Scuse."

She crawled out and ducked under, and sat down again on NG's bunk, beside him.

Half-asleep, all right. Pills had a kick to them. He gave her a bleary look.

"You hear that?" she said. "We got jump in the morning."

"Got to wake up," he muttered.

"No, you sleep. Musa and I'll pour you into your hammock in the morning. No problem. You can trust us." She squeezed his hand. "G'night. All right?"

No answer. The fingers didn't twitch. But he was all right. She and Musa had custody of the pills – in case. And if *Loki* was going somewhere tomorrow, wherever that was, then at least they were starting out in good order this time, no surprises.

She ducked back under, crawled back into Musa's bed, cold and shivering.

Man who didn't mind that was a gentleman, she thought.

# Chapter 15

Out of the bunks and off to duty stations, theirs being the lucky watch that drew duty through this particular jump: scant time for a dance through the shower, grab the trank-pack and the c-pack off the galley counter along with a Keis-and-biscuit and a hot drink while Services was stringing the hammocks for mainday. NG was barely functioning, limping around and definitely reluctant to leave the hot shower, but Musa was next in line, and she steered NG out to the breakfast line, bleary-eyed and sullen as he was.

"I'm saying get off me," he muttered while they were going through the door. "Watch doesn't mean hanging onto me."

"Hey, you're not put out about me and Musa, are you?"

"Hell!"

"So go on." She nudged him with her elbow. "Get your breakfast."

He looked bloody awful, one eye swollen, mouth swollen, and his expression this morning made no improvement. He muttered something for an answer, limped toward the line ahead of her.

Hughes and his friends. She saw it coming before NG did, a half a second before Hughes shouldered him and knocked him off his balance.

"Watch where you're going!" Hughes said.

"*You* watch where you're fucking going!" Bet hissed at Hughes, grabbing a fistful of sleeve. "You want an argument, mister, you got one."

Hughes grabbed for her wrist and ended up with nothing – not going to cut loose in a full-scale brawl, no, not here, not likely; but the whole rec-hall got quiet.

"You a friend of his?" Hughes said, and there was just ship-sound in the hall.

"May be," she said. "I dunno your quarrel with him, and I don't *care*, mister, but I'm on his tail on orders of the chief, who don't like his crew running into any locker door. Nothing personal."

"*Screwing* with him on the chief's orders too."

"*That's* personal and that's shit. Don't give me shit, mister. I'll give it back."

Real quiet.

"No fighting," NG said.

"That's fine," she said. "I ain't fighting. Man's just got a little problem. Probably glandular. You want to fuck with me, mister? Take you right down to that locker, soon's this ship clears jump. You *and* your two bedmates there. We can straighten everything out."

"Here, Lindy, – " Musa showed up, right through the audience, thank God, still damp from the shower, low-key as always. "We got a little problem?"

"Problem's your new girl," Hughes said. "Problem's this piece of garbage on our deck."

"*Problem* is," Bet said, loud and sharp, "we got some crossed lines here, this is the same skuz butted in yesterday while our shift was sitting down doing simple business over a beer; and beyond that I don't fucking *care* what his problem is, somebody took severe exception to that beer, in the dark and from the back, the way I see it. So I'm asking, was it you, Lindy Hughes?"

Lot of quiet, then. Some more mainday crew had strayed in from duty, and their voices got quiet too, more spectators.

"Somebody did this ship a favor," Hughes said.

"Hell if it did!" she said. "I hear all to hell and gone what NG did, but I see nothing but a damn good engineer at his post ever'day doing his own job and several others', and the only time he ever missed he was lying beat half to death in the supplies locker, so don't tell me about responsibility, mister, I seen more of it in NG Ramey than I seen in whatever fool beat up our Systems man when this ship is apt to go jump any damn minute – "

Slow, measured clap of the hands from somewhere around the fringe. That nettled Hughes. "You want to fuck with him?" Hughes asked, playing to the crew at large. He made a wide gesture. "Neo comes on here and tells us what a fine, upstanding man NG Ramey is. Shit!"

"Pull off, Lindy," Musa said.

"Fucking neo."

"I said, pull off! Bernstein's orders. Somebody beat up our Systems man, and we got orders to keep him in one piece, it ain't a question of preferences, mine or hers."

"I ain't taking shit from her!"

"Shut it *down*, Lindy."

Long silence. Then Hughes shouldered past, and so did his friends.

"Sorry about that," Bet said under her breath. "He shoved NG in line."

Musa put a hand on her shoulder and pushed her in the direction of the counter. NG was still standing there, in whatever frame of mind she didn't care to figure at the moment. She got her packs and her breakfast. Johnson the cook was there, galley staff working fast to set up for after the jump. Johnson gave her an under-the-brows look.

"You're crazy," Johnson said, which she took for a friendly warning.

"May be," she said. "But I go with what I see."

She got NG's two packs too, and collected a second breakfast and brought it back to him.

NG took them, no expression, no look directly at her, he just tucked the packs under an arm and gulped the biscuit and the tea. She swallowed hers, too much adrenaline coursing her bloodstream to afford any appetite, her stomach in a knot, but you took food when you could get it, hell with Lindy Hughes.

A couple of mainday Engineering were there, Walden and Farley having come in, maybe having been there through the ruckus. She didn't spot Hughes any longer.

Damn stupid, she thought, with her mouth full of biscuit. She was catching more attention from little confabs here and there in rec-hall than was good for anybody.

— Yeager, you've done it good and proper. You've just picked yourself a fight you can die in.

— Better'n some, though. . . .

— Spent all my grown life fighting Earth's fight, and look

at how they paid us. None so bad to take on one that *I* pick, none so bad to go out that way, if I got to.

Just give me targets, that's what Teo would say.

She looked over at NG standing there sipping tea with a sore mouth. Gave him a sort-of smile.

He glared at her like somebody cornered.

"You got a terrible attitude," she said and elbowed him in the ribs. "Cheer up, NG."

He walked off on his own, to throw the cup in the bin and head off for work. But she was on his track and she caught Musa's eye and Musa came, still gulping the last of his breakfast.

So they trailed him around to Engineering, NG half a dozen strides in the lead, Musa and herself behind, herself walking with hands in pockets and a kind of unreasonable cheerfulness while NG looked mad as hell.

But they got there the way Bernstein said, no time at all that NG was ever out of their sight: they got in, checked systems with their opposite numbers; and Bernstein came in to take over from Smith – off a general briefing for the mofs, one could guess.

Bernstein and Smith talked a moment, in the privacy ship-sound afforded, while they were going through the routine shift-change checks, she saw that out of the corner of her eye, and she felt the sweating nervousness start –

Calm down, calm down, she kept telling herself. No firefight on the other side, just another sit. It's the way this ship works, it's all she does. . . .

But the hands wanted to shake and the gut kept tightening up, just anxiousness to get it done.

Damn, I'm not up to this, they got NG on the boards, and he's crazy and they got me and I'm not an engineer; and besides us they got just Musa and they got Bernstein, and what in hell kind of way is that to run a ship?

Can't be a firefight, she thought, no way they'd put alterday crew up when there was a shooting match coming.

Bernstein finished with Smith, walked over to take the stats from NG. The take-hold started ringing, the advisement of the coming engine-start. "So where are we?" she asked, being curious. "Where're we going?"

"Classified," Bernstein said.

A body tried.

"We don't fight," Bernstein said. "We just stay ready to run. That's all."

"Yessir," she said.

"No different than we've been doing," Bernstein said. "We got a half hour. Burn's about to go. Take the number three chair. – How're you doing, NG?"

"No problem," NG said, cold and preoccupied, flipping switches.

She was the one with the upset at her stomach as she settled into her place and set herself up, trank-pack and c-pack and earplug and all, nothing else to do, since mainday had been good enough to sign the shop sealed and secure.

The burn cut in, an authoritative shove of the engines that built fast and hard. The deck shook and the whole swing-section of Engineering command rumbled on its tracks as it reoriented, a quiver deep in bones and nerves.

*Here we go.*

"You watch this readout," Bernstein said over the complug in her ear, and brought the station three screens live. "You got the panic button there and you push it if any display starts flashing, you push the panic button and the system will route it to me and Musa, you got it, Yeager?"

"Yessir."

"You know the parameters on the containment?"

Her heart jumped. "Yessir."

"That's your number one, there. On your right. If you get a sudden trend in the numbers you don't like, you push your number one red button and the panic button together. That sends it to me, got it?"

"I got it, sir, but f'God's sake tell me I'm not the only one on that."

"You're not. I like more than one pair of eyes on it. Watch your screens, Yeager, and don't bother me, I got my hands full. – We're on count now. Start your trank."

She grabbed the pack and squeezed it, felt the sting in her hand and the old tension in her gut. She could see NG's station from where she sat, she could see NG reach after the trank and take his. His face was still calm, but sweat stained his jumpsuit and beaded on his skin.

*Hard* push now.

"Five minutes," Bernstein said.

Her thoughts wanted to scatter. Hughes; and NG; and Musa last night; and the containment readouts and the numbers; and the chance of trouble otherside.

Watch the damn numbers.

Only time for so much.

*Is NG all right?*

*How long's it been since he sat station on a jump?*

Flash of the space behind the cans in the stowage; NG tripping wild, hand in the middle of her, hand bashing her lip –

*He do that often?*

And she thought, just as the final bell rang and they were bound for jump:

*Does Bernstein know what he's doing putting a load on NG? Expecting him to work in jump?*

*Man could kill all of us –*

Down again. She heard electronic chatter in her ear.

She tried to focus, sorted after the numbers in her recollection, remembered to watch the rate on number one. Saw the numbers falling away.

My God.

She hit the buttons, heart pounding.

"Got that," Bernstein said, "got it. She does that."

Sweat poured. She slumped, feeling the flutter in her muscles head to foot.

NG said: "Doing all right, Bet. Little slippage in one of the arms."

She felt like fainting. Breath came short for a little and she felt a cramp in her gut she hadn't felt in years, like maybe the treatment was wearing off.

Or it was advancing age, maybe.

*V*-dump, then. She felt the pulse through the ebbing trank, felt them come down again.

She fumbled after the c-pack, kept her eye on the screens while she pulled the tube out and got a sip.

Second dump, *hard*, God – hard. . . .

The numbers –

"We got that drift again!" She had the button punched.

"Got it, got it," Musa said.

*God!*

She wiped sweat and took another sip, reminded herself they were used to doing this with one fewer. Old game of Scare the neo. Never a time that they weren't onto that system. But, *damn!* it was all tekkie problems, it was all garble, she didn't know what damn arm NG was talking about or what it had to do with the magnetics or what in hell somebody was doing just then that pulled the numbers back to safety.

The ship just *worked*, dammit, tekkies made it work, you never thought about the ship just blowing up or losing its braking because of some damn numbers on a screen.

She was shaking. She wanted a drink. She wanted a shower. She wanted to get to the head. She sat there watching numbers til her eyes ached. And NG just talked back and forth with Musa and Bernstein, calm and cold, until Bernstein said, "Bridge is giving us an all-clear to unbelt. Yeager, you want to take a five minute break?"

"Yessir." She had to pry herself out of the chair. She headed straight for the outside and the E-section head, between Engineering and the purser's office, not half scared about the ship changing its mind and moving, and making a Yeager-shaped dent in the paneling – not half the scare those damn numbers put in her, flowing away like the ship was bleeding to death right through her fingers and she didn't have a patch for it.

Damn, *damn*, if everybody else could sit there like that, so cold, if NG could sit there like that, just pick up and go on working with the shakes and all –

Damned if she couldn't.

Thirty-seven years old and starting over as a neo. So she got the shakes.

That was just adrenaline you didn't know what to do with. But you learned, damned if you didn't, you learned what to do with that charge-up nature gave you, and you got your head to working and you just did it, that was all, whatever it was. Bernstein wasn't going to hand her a damn thing real without checking her on it, and at least nobody was shooting at her while she was learning it.

Please God he wasn't going to hand her anything real and on her own.

*What do I say if he does? I don't know what the hell you're talking about?*

Questions about her papers, all the way to the captain's office, that was what honesty got her. They might forgive her being stupid, might just put her on plain scutwork; but then Bernstein could tell the captain she was too damn good at some things and too damn stupid at others and things didn't add up right, that was where it could go once the questions started.

You *learned*, was all you could do, and you said *no* when you had to, and you never agreed to anything you couldn't fix.

"Shakes?" Bernstein asked her, stopping by.

"Nossir," she said.

He patted the top of the chair. "Did all right. We just got a little play in a servo, always wanders a little when we drop out. You know why?"

She gave him a desperate look.

"Nossir."

"Suggest you ask somebody real soon, Yeager."

"Yessir," she said. "Thank you, sir."

Bernstein patted the chair back again and walked off on his business, and she just sat there a second.

While her heart settled.

# Chapter 16

Quiet evening in rec, vid going in the quarters, a lot of the shift just collapsed in their bunks.

There was a large run on beers in rec, but just quiet drinking: lot of headaches for tomorrow.

And their own little group of three collected at the end of the bench next the galley, nobody bothering them, while two good Systems engineers drew diagrams on a slate and tried to get what they knew through a dumb skut's head.

It made half sense. "Why's it do that?" she asked.

"God does it," NG said, exasperated. "Just believe it happens."

"No, no," Musa said, "fair answer, now."

NG erased the slate and started re-drawing his schematic of little labeled circles, patiently, meticulously.

"Boy's damn smart," Musa said, hunkering closer. "Never did get this part myself."

"The hell," NG muttered, giving Musa a dirty look, and went through it again, how and why the flare-off worked when a ship dumped *V*.

It made her sick at her stomach when she started figuring it in terms of what could go wrong. Or of what that number-drain was and what could happen if things just failed to go right.

"Well, are we going to *fix* that damn thing?"

"First chance we get."

"We got to put in for a fill soon," she said.

"Where we put in," Musa said, "they got no facilities. And we can't afford the sit."

"We can't afford to lose the – "

Musa shushed her. "Business, business don't go in rec. Drink your beer."

She took a sip. NG took a big one.

And seeing the look on NG's face she wished she hadn't said that about losing the ship in hyperspace.

Seeing the look on his face —

And beyond it, where Lindy Hughes and his couple of friends were sitting, talking, momentarily staring this way.

"Hughes is down there," she said with a second cold chill in her stomach.

"Hughes is on this shift," Musa said. "He's got a right."

"He's shit." She picked up the slate, she cleared it off and she gave it to Musa, thinking that if it wasn't so traceable and so likely to land on NG, a simple accident could account for Lindy Hughes.

"He's damn stupid," Musa said. "Bernstein's over all the techs. Man's got a real problem. If he's real damn smart he'll transfer."

NG just sat there.

"Going to take this man to bed," she said to Musa, putting her hand on NG's knee.

"No," NG said, and got up and went and threw his cup in the bin.

And went to the quarters by himself, past Hughes' stare.

"Man's upset," she said.

"Yeah," Musa said.

"I got to see to him," she said, worried about NG, worried about Musa, – damn, she'd had enough crazy men. But Musa turned his callused hand up and took hers, and squeezed it.

"You be careful of Hughes. Hear? Some things I can't pull you out of."

"Yeah."

"Get."

She got. She tossed the cup, walked back to the dim quarters, heard a little catcall from Hughes' company, and found herself face to face with McKenzie in the doorway.

Shit! she thought, and flinched when McKenzie grabbed her arm, pulled her inside, and said he had to talk to her.

"I got business."

"You got trouble," McKenzie said, and his hand hurt her arm. "You got major trouble." He shoved her over against the first privacy screen, right by the door. "Listen here."

"That's my arm, mister."

The grip lightened up. He was standing close, pushing her into the corner. "NG the appointment you were talking about?"

"What if it was?"

"You'd be damn stupid. *Damn* stupid." Another jerk when she started to move. "Listen to me! The man's going to get you killed. People are trying to warn you – "

"You in with Hughes?"

"I didn't have a damn thing to do with it. I'm trying to warn a fool. You don't know this ship."

She pulled to get her arm free. He eased up again, and she might get all the way loose, but there was a note of something honest in the things McKenzie was saying.

"I got my orders," she said.

"That include sleeping with him?"

"Is *that* your problem?"

"Go to hell," he said, and shoved her loose. "Go straight to hell if you're set on it."

She grabbed his arm then, before he could get out the door. "McKenzie. You heard anything?"

"I'm telling you there's ways things get done on this ship and ways things come back at you on this ship and you're being a damn fool, woman. Don't be playing games."

"Appreciated," she said, quietly. "Appreciated. What's your percentage?"

No answer.

"Yeah," she said.

"Don't be stupid. I'm telling you, I'm just telling you, is all. You can take it any way you like."

The man confused her. Bad feelings to start with, man suddenly coming at her like this –

"Damn few women on this ship," McKenzie said reasonably. "Hell of a waste, Yeager."

"Me with him?"

"That too."

She suddenly liked McKenzie a lot better than she had – a little too eager to start with, maybe, but saner than she had looked for. She touched him on the arm with the back of her hand. "I tell you," she said, "you might be all right, Gabe. I hope so."

He put his hand on her hip. *God!* she thought, nettled. He

said, "I'm telling you – you go around making cases where everything was quiet and things can happen to you."

"That a threat?"

"No." He took the hand back. "Damn, I told you – "

"You made me nervous as hell, friend. I'll tell you that. But I could have been wrong."

"Wrong about what?"

"About you being in with Hughes."

"Damn, I'm not!"

"What's Hughes' game?"

"He's a sum-bitch," McKenzie said. "Just a plain sum-bitch, no percentage in it. Got his little clique. He may be under Bernstein, but he's got ties on the bridge. He's got Goddard on his side. Navcomp. Goddard's a poker partner of Kusan's and Orsini's, you follow?"

"I know Orsini."

"Goddard's a – " McKenzie shut it down. "You just watch it. I'm giving you good advice."

"I'm listening."

"That's all. Just get clear of it. Figi and Park and me, and Rossi and Meech, we just stay the hell out of it."

"You scared of Hughes? You got the same pull, topside, what about the scan-ops?"

"I'm not scared of Hughes. I'm just not interested in borrowing somebody else's trouble. I'm telling you get clear of it before you mark yourself with this, you already got people talking."

"Saying what?"

"Saying you're a damn fool. Come in here, cross the lines, stir up the whole damn watch on old business – I don't know what Musa's game is, maybe you got him going the same as you got half the men in this watch – but I don't say I don't believe it about Bernstein – he hauled NG's ass out of the cold or he wouldn't be here. And maybe there's people on this ship don't like what happened to him, but that won't buy a thing. They won't be there when it comes head-on against you."

"You?"

"I'm not a fool either. I'm telling you, you're setting yourself up for some bad hurt. I don't like to see that. Damn, I don't like to see that."

"I appreciate it. I do." She patted him on the arm. "You got yourself on my good list for that. Tell you what you *can* do cheap, that's be eyes for me and Musa where we can't."

McKenzie scowled. "What percentage?"

"Favor-points with me. Maybe with Bernstein, who knows?"

"Bernie's favor-points don't spend on mainday bridge, I'm telling you. You go on, you're in for it."

"I got you clear. I got you absolutely clear."

Fitch.

"Just so you do." He came up close against her, gave her a nice little pass of the hands she didn't mind at all. "Damn," he said, and she said,

"You know where I bunk? Got a bottle, got some picture-stuff. Make free of it. Anytime. You and Park and Figi."

"What else comes with it?"

"Lot else might. You want to party? I bring my mates."

Long silence.

"You're buying trouble."

"Get a few other guys. Get some bottles. We got no push on us, we got no likelihood of an alert I know of – What d'you think?"

"Dammit – "

"Nice pictures. Got a viewer too. Tell you what, I get NG up there for about half an hour, then you just happen by, everybody else happens by – one at a time – "

"You're crazy as he is."

"Vodka."

"Damn. All right."

She grinned, gave Gabe a peck on the cheek and a pat on the backside and took out down the aisle.

# Chapter 17

"We got a little trouble," was what she told NG when she caught up to him, in the dim light down by his bunk, down by the vid. "Don't ask questions. Come on. Fast."

And when she got him as far as the ladder to the loft: "Come on, it's all right."

"Dammit," he said, confused-sounding.

But he went in front of her up the ladder – a lot of trust, she figured, from a man who had lately been ambushed.

She caught him up, grabbed him by the arm and steered him right for her bunk – got him that far and then he started pulling back.

"Where's Musa?" he asked.

"Musa's right where he needs to be. Just shut up, stay put, don't make me trouble." She edged between him and the privacy screen, tilted up her bunk in the dim light and pulled out a bottle, the viewer, and Ritterman's pictures, and set them on the floor. She let the bunk down then, said, "Sit down. Don't be so damn conspicuous," and when NG did that, sat down beside him, reached after the bottle, uncapped it and took a drink. "Here."

He took one. She took one. He took a second; she snuggled up close, swung around on one knee on the bunk and settled with a leg in his lap. "Dammit," he said, catching on. He made to give her the bottle back and get up, she got her knee in the way, got her arms around his neck and said very close to his ear:

"Didn't say we couldn't entertain ourselves. Just keep it quiet, all right, and don't spill my bottle."

He stayed put. In half a dozen seconds he was warming up a lot, went back on the bunk, she did, and somehow they managed not to spill the vodka.

"Where's Musa?" he asked while clothes were coming askew.

"Oh, I dunno," she said. "He's taking care of stuff. I'm just keeping you where you can't get into trouble."

"Dammit, dammit, – " he mumbled, and after that not much.

Man always did have a primary problem with sex and priorities, or maybe life just got cheap. So he was occupied when McKenzie showed up, McKenzie with a "Mind?"

"Help yourself," she said, and held onto NG, while NG was trying to scramble up off the bunk. "It's all right, McKenzie was going to borrow the viewer."

"Hell!" NG said.

"It's all right," McKenzie said, and got the viewer and sat down on the bed. "That vodka you got?"

"Sure."

"Excuse me," NG said, gone all cold, but Bet snagged him with an arm before he could escape.

"No, no," she said, "NG, Gabe's a friend."

"Dammitall!"

"No problem," McKenzie said, all easy, and Bet hooked a knee over NG's to keep him sitting. McKenzie thumbed the power on the hand-viewer, popped a fiche in and took a look.

"What d'you think?"

"Shee-it," McKenzie said, "that's something."

"Let's see." She reached, while NG sat there in stony silence. She took a look, passed it to NG.

"Not interested."

"Don't be a lump." She reached after the vodka and traded Gabe back the viewer. "Here."

"Where's Musa?" NG asked in a flat voice, refusing the drink.

"Musa's just fine. Have a drink."

"I'm getting the hell out of here."

"You want to walk down there and get into trouble?"

"Trouble's here."

"No trouble." She pushed the drink on him. "Come on. Gabe's just sitting look-out."

Sullen silence. But he stayed put.

"How you doin', Gabe?" While she kept her arm tight around NG.

"Fine," McKenzie said, and took another drink and passed it back.

Then Park and Figi showed up in the aisle, mostly shadow, from past the privacy screen. "H'lo," Park said.

"Oh, damn," NG said. "What is this?"

"Party," Bet said, holding onto him. "You're invited. Stay put."

"The hell!"

"Keep it quiet. Everything's fine. Have a drink. Gabe's a friend of mine, these are friends of his."

"What are you doing?" he asked, real quiet. "Bet, what're you doing?"

"Just be polite. Friends of mine dropped by after some stuff, it's no big problem. Everybody knows everybody, just sit back, take a drink – "

"I want out of here," he said in that same tone. His muscles were all hard. His voice was just over the edge of calm. "Bet, I'm leaving."

"No, you're not. Musa'd skin you. Sit still."

As Park and Figi added their heft to the load on the bunk, and the mattress slanted a little.

"Hey, vodka," Figi said; and Bet put her arms around NG's middle, and her legs to front and back of him, and got familiar again.

"Stop it," he said under his breath.

"Just be nice," she said, but she didn't push him, just took the bottle in her turn and gave it to him, and he took a big drink of it, while the viewer passed around and Park and Figi made appreciative noises. NG was tense as drawn cable, just ready to snap, but she got another drink into him, got him to take a desultory look at the viewer, which did him no good at all.

Then Rossi and Meech showed up with their own bottle, and sat down on the floor in what space there was, right in the escape aisle. And a couple other strays came in, so the viewer was going wide circles now.

And NG was just sort of back in the corner of things with her, up against the wall, trapped, and relaxing a little when nobody turned out to notice him – and since she curled herself around him and got her hand in his and just kept things secure and friendly awhile.

"What in hell?" Musa asked, coming up from around the curtain, and NG tensed up all over.

"I got him," Bet said, and:

"Have a drink," McKenzie said, offering Musa the bottle.

"Shit," Musa said, but he stood there and took his drink.

"See?" Bet said into NG's ear. "Ever'thing's fine."

No word out of him, not a thing, just a shiver, NG tucking up against the wall and staying real quiet.

So she worked at relaxing him.

"Let me alone," he said.

"Come on," she said. "It's friends."

"*Dammit, let me alone!*" he yelled, and shoved her and started through, but she tackled him from the back and yelled, "Gabe, stop 'im!"

NG stepped on Meech and got tangled up, with her holding around his neck and Gabe getting him from the front and Meech and Rossi impeding him from below.

He went crazy then, swinging on them, twisting to get loose –

"Where d'you want 'im?" Gabe called out, no soberer than he had to be, and: "*God, let me alone!*" NG was yelling, fighting to get loose, while the whole mass dumped itself generally back on the bed.

"You want us to hold 'im for you?" Park asked.

"Man's crazy," Rossi said. "Told you he was crazy."

And Musa didn't say a thing about it: Musa was one of those holding onto NG til he was half-smothered and gasping after breath.

"Give the man a drink," Bet said. "NG ain't crazy, he's just a little nervous. Careful, there! Sit him up!"

Because they were a little gone, having a damn good time, but gone, and NG was gone too, out-there, deep-spaced and having trouble breathing.

"Ease off," Musa snapped, and let go to fend Rossi off pouring vodka down NG, and shoved her hard. "Ease off, Bet, dammit!"

"Man's all right." She didn't take the shove for serious, just slipped in again and got her hand on NG's shoulder while everything was quiet and everybody was catching their breaths. "NG? Nobody going to hurt you. Nobody going to hurt you."

"Go to hell," he said, teeth chattering.

"Hey, let up, let up," she said, and disengaged Rossi and McKenzie and Figi, and Musa, one by one, everything staying quiet. God! if it got out of hand and some drunk sod decided *he* was common property along with the bottles –

She got the bottle from Rossi, offered it, shaking-scared NG was going to blow up and blow everything to hell. "Come on," she said. Like coaxing a kid out of a hidey-hole. "NG?"

He just stared at her. Musa patted him on the shoulder, telling him it was all right, telling him get his breath.

"You got a mate talking to you," McKenzie said, drunk and expansive. He shook at NG's knee. "You hear 'im? Mates trying to help you, you sum-bitch. Take a drink."

"Let me go," NG yelled, between gasps after air. "Let me *go*!"

"Let 'im loose," Musa said. "Let Bet have 'im."

"Get 'im drunker," somebody advised from the periphery, who else had come up to kibitz Bet had no idea. There was a crowd gathering, – dangerous, damn, the whole thing was getting out of limits and what could happen next –

"I got 'im," she said. "Gimme the bottle."

Rossi gave it; she took a drink herself, said, "Relax," and offered a swig to NG.

He took a deep one, drank twice between gasps for breath, and she took it back, took another one, and peeled her suit down and got down on the bunk with NG while the bottle went round and by-standers cheered.

He stopped fighting. He wasn't good for much, but he shivered and then relaxed. After a minute or so he got a little buzz out of it, and put his arms around her while she said into his ear, the air between them fumed with alcohol:

"You're doing fine, merchanter-man."

Damn if he didn't about manage it then, witnesses and all, when some fool started to unhook the privacy screen on the next bunk, that was Mel Jason's, Jason being nowhere to be found, and all Jason's pin-ups in danger of folding. "Hey, careful with her stuff!" Bet yelled. "That's my neighbor."

"Let that be!" Musa yelled, and McKenzie and Park and Meech got it stopped, while NG just struggled up on his arm to see what was going on and went out like that, thump, curled onto his side.

Somehow there had turned up far more people in on this than she had brought in, there were a couple more bottles going around, – had to be, or the first couple were bottomless – and she pulled her clothes together and just leaned against NG with her head spinning and her ears buzzing while Musa and McKenzie and his mates controlled the booze and the drunks and started up a dice game.

So it wasn't so exciting anymore, except the viewer was going the rounds to howls and comments, the bottle kept passing, and somebody was saying Mel Jason was mad as hell about the crowd in the loft.

But the crowd had kept growing, it was noisy, and she figured then she could be in real trouble, so she kept faking her drinks after that when the bottle came her way, and sobered a bit, leaning there at the head of her bunk on a body she finally figured out was NG, and insulated on the left by Figi's broad rump. So she was all right back there, behind a wall of friends, NG was safe where he was.

But it all settled down, Musa was drunk as a docksider while he played his mates out of their credits, all the while spinning some incredible tale about serving on *Gloriana*.

On *Gloriana*, for God's sake – a sublighter.

Man was old enough, maybe.

She felt a shiver in her bones, like meeting God, figuring how old Musa *could* be, because if time-dilation got to spacers nowadays, it was nothing to what the old sublighters had gotten, and although they were all changed and FTL'ed now – the several of those nine original ships that still survived – *crew* could still be alive –

Musa had a bottle of real whiskey in his bag –

Musa had learned his engineering the patchy way, knew practical because-it-works things, but not the technical words for it, like somebody grown up in FTL ships.

Musa had seen Earth –

The curfew-bell rang quietly. "Party's over," somebody said, and people groaned and wondered if they could negotiate the ladder.

"Want us to leave him?" Musa came to her to ask.

"Yeah," she said; and gave Musa a bleary hug and a kiss,

and a sloppy, passionate kiss to Gabe McKenzie, too. "See you later," she said with his hands all over her. "Owe you one."

"*Major* one," he said.

"I got to get my stuff," she said, remembering that. But people had been halfway considerate, piling fiches and viewer on the bunk, taking their empties with them, so she grabbed up the fiches and stuck them in her patch-pocket and she grabbed up the viewer and she shoved that deep into her bedding.

Then she just collapsed with NG for a pillow, struggled and worked one-armed to get the safety mesh across both of them, sort of, and clipped it in.

And passed out.

"What in hell – " NG mumbled sometime during the night, and stirred and lashed out with his arm, or he had been doing that and that was why her shoulder hurt.

"'S all right. I got you. Go to sleep."

"Hell!" He flailed out again, kneed her good, trying to straighten himself out, and then he got the safety mesh clip undone and that spring-wound itself back across her while she was trying to get her arms around him and reason with him.

"You're all right. You're in my bunk, settle down – "

"Shut *up*!" came a female voice from next door.

"Shhhsssh," she whispered, trying to hold onto him the while. "Curfew's long gone. Lie still."

"Going to my bunk," NG muttered, shoving his legs off and tearing loose from her.

"You're in the *loft*," she hissed, fast, while he could still hear her, because in his condition she wasn't sure he wouldn't walk right into the net or right off the ladder.

He left. She got up and she followed him, staggering and reeling herself, saw he got down the ladder all right before she went back to her bunk and fell in, doing the netting on autopilot, that was all she had left in her.

Mel Jason was pissed, no question about that. Mel stormed past her when she was dimly taking account of the fact she didn't have to put on yesterday's jumpsuit to make the showers, she was still wearing it.

So, well, Jason was always pissed.

She ran her hand through her hair, got up, staggered over to the edge of the balcony and hung there on the safety netting to get her eyes in focus and see that Musa was up and Musa had NG in view, NG already up and looking like he had been through the showers ahead of the wake-up, his clothes being unrumpled. So she went back and made her bunk – the lump she found doing that was the viewer, that had to be stowed underneath; and her thigh-pocket was full of fiches, but they were all still flat. Everything seemed to have come through all right, except she had a headache.

Except when she got downside she was running late, NG and Musa were already out at breakfast, she supposed: almost everybody was ahead of her.

And that *almost* was Lindy Hughes.

Didn't mind being in line for the head in front of that man; *didn't* like being in the showers with him damn near the last in quarters.

But you didn't shy off.

So she just went on ahead in when a guy came out, meaning there was a stall free; and she went in, stripped down for a quick rinse and a dry, – mind your own damn business, Yeager, she was telling herself, soaping up.

The door opened. Hughes was standing there.

"I hear you'll do it for anybody," he said.

"Want to find out?" she said. "Or you want to keep what little you got?"

He made a grab for her. She just grabbed his coveralls and went with the grab, and Lindy Hughes kept going, right into the wall and the shower toggle.

"My God!" she yelled, bashed the back of his head with her elbow, his face with her knee, and let him hit the floor, then when he stirred, smashed down on his head with her bare foot, again and a second time when he kept trying to move. Then she stepped out past his body and looked at Davies from Cargo, who was out in the aisle, naked as she was; so was Gypsy Muller. "I tell you, that damn fool came charging right into the wall, hit his head something terrible. Somebody better call infirmary."

"Shee-it," Davies said, and grabbed his clothes; "Shit for

sure," Gypsy said, looking at her and Hughes' clothed legs lying across the shower threshold.

As Hughes' friend Presley showed up in the doorway.

"Better call infirmary," she said. "Your friend slipped."

"You damn bitch!" Presley said.

"Hey, it ain't *my* fault." She edged past Davies in the body-wide aisle. "God, I got soap all over. 'Scuse, please."

"Damn bitch!"

"You got trouble," Davies warned her.

"Yeah."

Presley was picking Hughes up, Hughes was coming around, sitting up bleeding from the forehead. *Nasty* cut.

"Be nice," she said to Hughes. "And *I* won't say it was rape."

Hughes looked at her with murder on his face.

"We was just doing an exotic in the shower," she said. "You just hit the soap. Right?"

Man added it up – two witnesses and Presley.

"You damn whore," he said.

"You want you and me to go up to the captain's office? I'm for it, – or you want to go up to infirmary and just tell 'em how you hit some soap and slipped? *I'll* save your ass for you. You can owe me one."

Maybe Davies and Gypsy would back her. Maybe they'd side with Hughes. But she *didn't* think so in Gypsy's case.

"Son of a *bitch!*" Hughes said, blotting his forehead.

Not a sound from anybody then, except Presley helped Hughes get up.

And Gypsy said, after Hughes was on his feet: "Looked like a slip to me. Nobody needs any damn *trouble*, Lindy."

"Yeah," Davies said.

Hughes glowered, blotted his forehead with the back of his hand – he was dripping red on the tiles.

And he shoved Presley out ahead of him and left.

Bet let go her breath.

"Thanks," she said; and looked at them – Gypsy who stood there in the altogether and Davies who was grabbing after his towel.

"Late," Davies said. "Damn, we're going to be late."

Gypsy just stared at her. Then he nodded, once, decisively, and didn't look unhappy.

She went and rinsed the soap off before it ate her skin, washed the blood off the shower floor, grabbed her clean clothes and tossed the old ones in the bin.

Not a drop of blood on those.

Mainday crewman opened the outside door, first of the incoming shift. "Evenin'," she said, uncomfortable in his staring at her.

But about half a dozen mainday crew were out there, and she got more than one stare on her way out, felt them uncomfortably close against her backbone from there to the door and out.

# Chapter 18

Late for sure. She came kiting into Engineering, said, "I'm here, sir," to Bernstein, and Bernstein gave her a moment's glowering attention that upset her stomach.

"Everybody gets one," he said.

"Yessir," she said, fast and sharp, and went to check the duty board.

Not to socialize for a while, NG and Musa both being on the rounds and on the reports: no shop-jobs, no fix-ups, a real conspicuous shortage of fix-ups lately on alterday shift, mainday doing the scut-work, since it had three times the personnel. Bernstein's list under her name was short: Calibrations Check Assist: see Musa.

So she did.

"He *ain't* happy," Musa said, meaning, she thought, *not* Bernstein.

"Yeah, well," she said, with this little sinking feeling, then got down to ship business, figuring NG could keep and Bernstein's good will was real important just then. "Calibrations Check Assist. List says that's you."

"Show you," Musa said, and bringing her over to station three boards: "Man's mad," Musa said under his breath. "I tried to talk to him, he's not talking, *not* real reasonable. Bernie's onto it that something happened, I said give me some room with it – Bernie said all right, but he give me this look, understand, I dunno how long he's good for."

"I got you," Bet said, and: "Hughes grabbed at me in the showers, man had an accident this morning."

"Damn."

"Nothing broke. Gypsy was there, and Davies. Ever'body says he must've hit some soap and fell."

"Going to stick by that?"

"Dunno how he couldn't. I was stark naked, he was

dressed, we got three stalls, we was four in there, me and him and Gypsy and Davies. Even mofs can count."

Damn. *Wish* she hadn't used that word. For a moment Musa was looking at her real funny.

"Yeah," Musa said. "I'll talk to Gypsy tonight."

Musa showed her the routine, mostly computer-stuff: you just got the *Calibrations* program up and you told it which system and it ran checks for a few minutes and then told you if it found things outside pre-set parameters.

That was all as easy as filter-changes.

Except NG was walking around like he had murder on his mind and he wasn't looking at anybody.

And Hughes was off in infirmary telling whatever damn lies Hughes could think up.

And she could hear Orsini asking the chief med, that morning when it was NG getting patched up, *Anybody else have trouble with that door?* And the med saying, with a deadpan face, *Not yet*.

So she got the CCA run, because mainday was busy with the shop-scut and the plain maintenance – and the core-crawl and the sync-check and the dozen other nasty jobs for reason of which mainday had to be wanting to cut their throats about now –

– while a dumb skut whose only real expertise was field-stripping arms and armor was trying to learn which board was which, never mind qualifying for a license. Bernie wasn't pushing *anybody* on his understaffed shift, wasn't having anyone on alterday turn a hand on anything but at-the-boards Engineering Ops and absolute on-deck or in-shop maintenance – and damn sure wasn't doing anything that could send one of his crew out alone and unwatched.

Which told you something, she was afraid, first because the ship just might not be *tending* to routine maintenance in any major way, which could have any of several reasons, like being close to a docking; or like being in chancy space.

Or maybe Bernie had a deal with Smith on mainday, because Bernie didn't want any more accidents like NG's.

Til when? she wondered. How long is Bernie going to keep this up? How long *can* he? And she remembered what NG had said – that sooner or later Bernie was going to get pressed or Musa was going to get tired of shepherding him around, and Hughes or somebody was going to get him.

But NG didn't know what had happened to Hughes this morning and he needed to know that. So she found an excuse, seeing NG was over to the end of the main console, where there was a nook, while Bernstein and Musa were talking urgently about something – which, she had this uncomfortable feeling, could be Musa explaining something other than readouts.

To a mof. But a mof you could trust – one you'd better trust, if that mof really, actually *wanted* to know what had happened in the showers.

"Musa says you're mad at me," she said coming up on NG. She reached out to his arm and he twitched her hand off, instantly.

"Hell, no," he said. "Why should I be?"

She had meant to warn him about Hughes right off. It didn't seem the moment. "You got along *fine*."

He had trouble breathing for a second. Then he shoved her hard with his elbow, turning away, but she got in front of him and it was a wonder with a look like that, that he didn't swing on her.

"You were *all right* last night," she hissed, under the white noise of the ship. "Everybody took it all right, everybody saw *you* take it all right, more's the point. You were downright human last night."

Didn't go well, no. He got this absolutely crazy look, and he was going to shove past her or hit her, she was set for it.

But he didn't. He just stood there until his breaths came wider and slower. "Yeah," he said, "well, I'm glad."

"You don't figure it," she said.

He couldn't talk, then, she saw it, he didn't want to crack with her and he couldn't get himself together to talk about what had happened; and that hurt look of his got her in the gut.

"People were doing fine with you last night, you understand me?"

No, he didn't, he didn't understand a damned thing, – embarrassed, she thought, more than the offended merchanter sensibilities he knew he couldn't afford on this ship; he knew and if he was getting eetee about that, she wasn't even going to acknowledge it.

No, what was bothering him was a damn sight more than that, she thought, recalling how he'd spooked-out for a minute last night, just gone, complete panic; and he didn't ever want people to see him like that.

But, dammit, they *had* to see that, that was part of it, people had to see what was going on with him and most important, they had to see him recover and handle things. She couldn't fix that part of it. She didn't want to.

"I *got* to talk to you," she said, and moved him – she wasn't sure he was going to move – into that corner where there was about a meter square of privacy from where Bernstein and Musa were. "You got a *problem* with what happened?"

No answer.

"You were *all right*," she said. "Wasn't anybody made any trouble, people were saying something just being there, you understand me? McKenzie and Park and Figi, they were *all right* with you, they come in on my cue, they were there all the time, and they were real solid from the start, or I'd've stopped it cold before it got where it did, trust me I got some sense. There was McKenzie and there was Park and Figi and there was Musa, wasn't anybody got past them, wasn't anybody even tried, they just drank the booze and looked at the pictures, – they *ain't* a half-bad lot, NG, I imagine it was Gypsy and maybe Davies and six, eight others up there. I told McKenzie ask a few friends, and McKenzie knew you were going to be there when he asked 'em, so people knew, or if they didn't, you can damn well bet they found out; and they stayed anyhow. So there was five mates, all the time, between you and anybody who started trouble. All the time. You think I'm fool enough to start a thing like that without knowing my parameters?"

He just stood there.

"NG, you were *all right*, you did fine last night."

It was still like everything was garble to him. At least he looked confused as well as upset. At least he seemed to know he wasn't understanding.

Or maybe, at bottom, he just didn't remember who there had been and how many; or he was scared thinking of what could have happened: he'd been out cold, no question; and he'd been isolated too long to trust himself drunk with anybody, even somebody he halfway trusted when he was sober. "Didn't let anybody touch you," she said. "Wouldn't do that. Promise you."

He gave back against the wall, looked at her a moment like she was some kind of eetee, then leaned his head back, turned his face away and stared into nowhere a second or two, all the wild temper gone. He just looked hurt and tired and quietly, heart-deep, mad at something. A muscle worked in his jaw. "I have work to do," he said. Distant voice, a little wobbly and a little nowhere. And he straightened up and made to do that, but she blocked him.

"That's not all!" she said, fast, while he was listening to anything at all. "Hughes come at me this morning. Hear me? I set him back some."

He was focussed tight on her then. Scared.

"*Don't* do anything stupid," she said. "*Don't* go out of sight, for God's sake. You can be mad at me, just don't do anything that's going to put you where there aren't any witnesses."

"You're a damned fool," he said. "Bet, they're going to kill you."

"Mmmn, no, they aren't. Don't you worry."

"*Fitch* – " He got his voice down, under the ship-sound, and if Bernie and Musa were through talking over there across the consoles, they were letting them both alone for the moment. "I told you from the start. You're going to get killed."

No, – no, not good for a man's pride to say she had sent Hughes to infirmary, after Hughes had sent *him* there – even if it had been Hughes and two friends and a no-fighting rule that got him, even if it had been a supply locker Hughes had caught him in, and NG had a lot of real spookiness when it came to being boxed in and trapped.

"I been on ships like this all my life," she said, reasonably, – a lie, but the important part was true. "I told you, there's ways to get at people without laying a hand on 'em, and there's a time you can do it and get away. I know Hughes' game, damn if I don't. You can trust me, NG, you can *trust* me. I know what I'm doing."

That was a real hard thing for him. But he thought about

it. She saw the figuring going on in his eyes, saw him scared and upset, and shying off from the obvious conclusion.

Couldn't. Couldn't make it that far. And he was at least straight enough with her to let her see it.

"I been there," she said. "I been there more'n once, man. Like letting a knife against your gut. But you got to take a chance on it now while you *got* a chance. You got a handful of guys come up to a party you was at and they give you a little haze about it, but *friendly*, you understand that? You got to say good mornin' now and don't take it hard. They got their pride too, and they come a long way, a *long* way last night. You got to come at least that far to them."

"The hell I do."

That made her fit to hit him. But she said, calmly and quietly, "Dunno how you feel about them or why. But I sure know what you owe me, mister, and if you slap them in the face after all I've done you make *me* a fool. You're the one'll get me killed."

That got through, how deep, she couldn't tell, but it hit, and he shut up and just looked mad, the way he would when he was cornered.

While she had the shakes like a neo, fighting with a damn merchanter who had been no more than a kid when she had signed onto *Africa*.

*And* learned the lessons he had yet to figure out.

*Damn* him!

*I can fuckin' see why you make so many friends on this ship, mister. . . .*

She didn't say that. She just walked off and left him, too mad to think straight, but Bernstein had been patient, and Bernstein deserved a calm face and a clear head.

So she went over to number three station and checked comp to see what her next-up job was.

*See me,* it said.

She shut down and turned to go do that – but there was a bridge officer in the doorway, and her heart did a little tick-over.

Orsini . . . *not* just sightseeing, damn sure.

Orsini did his little courtesy to Bernstein, Bernstein caught her eye and beckoned.

So she walked over and Musa melted off sideways, finding business to attend to.

"Yeager," Orsini said.

"Yessir?"

"There was an accident in the showers this morning."

"Yessir."

"You were a witness?"

"Yessir."

"What happened?"

Hope to God Hughes took the cue she'd handed him and *hadn't* gotten elaborate. Or didn't want to go up on counter-charges.

"Wasn't a line outside, I guess Lindy just figured there might be a stall free, and he come in just as I was drying off – opened the door, he scared me, I guess I scared him; anyway, he must've hit a wet spot."

"He slipped."

"I guess he slipped, sir."

Long silence from Orsini. A dead-black stare, while the sweat ran down her sides.

Then Orsini wrote something down on the TranSlate he was carrying, something more than a sentence, said, "That'll be all, Yeager," and she said: "Sir," while he walked off.

She didn't want to look at Bernstein. But you didn't walk off from a mof without a courtesy either, and Bernstein waited.

"Sorry, sir," she said, then.

"What'd he do?"

"Made a grab," she said. Bernstein didn't look like he was going to kill her, so she added, "At a soapy woman. And him dressed. Must've lost his grip, sir."

"Yeager, – " Bernstein drew a breath. "You watch it. *Dammit*, you watch it."

"Yessir." She was shaking. That was twice this morning.

"You got a finish-up on a system over in the shop. You want to see to that? Ought to take you about an hour. This afternoon you got sims on three, long as you can stand it."

Simulations. Engineering sims. It didn't help her stomach at all.

A close brush with Orsini, Hughes and his friends were damn sure going to be smarter coming at her now, Musa thought she was a fool, NG was ready to kill her, and Bernie wanted an unlicensed machinist running the boards on a jury-rig like *Loki*.

Sure.

She went and started the electronics job, flipped through the manual and found out it was out of the helm-engineering interface.

God.

Do-it-in-your-sleep stuff – if you didn't know where it was going back to. She triple-checked everything, went to Bernie to ask if there was an install or if she just left it, and he said, "That's the backup to the backup now, but there's some reason it blew. Mainday's still looking for it."

Makes you real confident.

Damn ship's falling apart.


NG still wasn't speaking much by shift-change – as if every word cost him money – but he was civil, at least, and subdued, – the NG who sat the boards, mostly, just business.

"You got to help me some more," she said to him, "with this stuff with the boards. Bernie's on me about it."

And he just nodded, nothing really engaged and nothing really to fight with, not actually looking at her.

She was sure Musa read him just fine, she was sure Musa was mad about NG's acting up, but NG wasn't going to give either one of them a handle to grab, just a not-there, don't-care, do-what-you-like.

It made you want to back him up against a wall, that was what it did; but you couldn't, NG would do about what he'd done with Hughes and his friends, she reckoned.

So he just wandered on around the rim on his own with them behind him, and he walked up on the end of the supper-line in rec and didn't speak to anybody, didn't look at anybody, even when people looked at him to see what kind of mind he was in.

And she and Musa got in line behind him and he didn't turn around, didn't come alive at all.

Damn him.

What in hell d'you do with him?

Knock him across the deck if he was on *Africa*, damn right somebody would.

But he wouldn't've lived, there.

She remembered the flash, the shock, the smell of burned flesh. And the skut with the grenade.

Remembered guys that just stopped ducking.

*Man's bent on suicide. Not even that. He's just left, just gone away. Won't fight. Won't fight til somebody pushes him.*

*Dangerous as hell is what he is.*

*At the boards.*

*Or anywhere else critical.*

"What're they having?" she asked NG. Elbowed him in the back when he ignored her, and was ready to duck. "Huh?"

He didn't react at first. Then he said, calmly, "Think it's meatloaf."

"Meat, hell," Musa said, "it's got fins."

NG sort of looked at him, she said: "We got to be close to port, it's getting worse," and NG halfway woke up a little – just was *there* again.

"Haven't got to the stew yet," he said, "that's the worst."

Like, God help them, NG was trying.

"Stew or that egg-and-ham stuff," Musa said. "Let me tell you, I remember pork that was a pig."

*She* remembered, once in her life – eating what used to be warmblooded and walking around, instead of tank-stuff. She wrinkled her nose, a little queasy. "Had it once. Flavor's fine. Dunno about the feel of it."

They moved up in line.

"Where'd you get it?" Musa asked. Not suspicious-like. Interested.

"Crewmate got it off this dark-point trade," she said.

That was where *Africa* had got it, all right, except they hadn't paid for it, out in the dark between the stars – where ships met in realspace and the carriers had taken what they wanted.

Blood all over a wall. AP's didn't leave much of a man's middle. First time she'd been with the boarding-team.

Pork that night. Galley did it up in little pieces for the whole ship's company. Except you could bet your ass the bridge crew got slices.

The line moved up. "Fish," Musa was saying. "Told you it was fishcake."

NG shrugged. He stood there ahead of her with his hands in his pockets, looking down again at the floor like he was going away again and she just reached out and tweaked his sleeve.

"You all right?"

He looked at her very odd for a moment – scared, maybe, worried, but *there*, thank God.

"Don't slip on me," she said.

He didn't say anything. He just stared until the line moved and Musa bumped both of them and got them to close it up.

NG looked back at her a second time, like he was trying to figure something just outside his reach.

"Hey," she said, "I *ain't* the enemy, you know."

And that came out funny, kind of a chill going through her gut.

"Go on," somebody yelled from behind, "do it in the locker."

Their turn. They got the meatloaf. Musa did. It was pale, pale gray and it smelled fishy right past the flavor-stuff and the sauces cookie put on it, it crunched with bones you tried not to notice.

Tried not to notice the way people kind of looked toward them while they were eating either, how heads got together and voices were quiet and Hughes was at the other side of the rec-benches, down at the opposite end – Hughes with a patched-up mess in the middle of his forehead and a lot of looks their direction. Hughes and his two mates; and Mel Jason sitting with Kate and a couple of the other women, all of them with their heads together –

There was a kind of a gap between her and NG and Musa and everybody else – not a big one, but they were a three-set, no mistaking it, on the end of the bench – until McKenzie and Park and Figi got through the line and took that spot. Deliberately.

*Man*, she thought, looking at McKenzie, *I do owe you.*

"Hughes isn't happy," McKenzie said for openers, and took a big drink of his beer.

"Pity," Musa said.

NG was wound tight as a spring. She felt that. "What's he saying?" she asked Gabe McKenzie.

"Says he'll settle accounts," McKenzie said.

"You're taking a chance, then."

"Yeah," McKenzie said.

She thought about that, thought about what she owed and where, and how NG was likely to react to company, damn him anyway; but she was about to take the chance when Musa said, "Got to arrange a get-together, you and us."

Musa having manners *and* sense, God save him.

"Might," McKenzie said.

"Yeah," she said, and nudged NG with her knee. "All right?"

NG nodded and mumbled, "Fine."

So they got a card-game together at McKenzie's and Park's bunk, the two being next to each other. They did a little drinking, a little talking – NG and Park being about equally conversational, but Figi was a card-artist, no question, the moment you saw him shuffle, and Figi gave a kind of shy grin and proved there was a real brain in there, the kind that could remember what had turned up in a deck.

NG wasn't bad at it either, come to find out; and Musa was sharp as you'd expect when a guy had spent long, long realspace voyages with very little rec aboard.

"You can get skinned in this company," she complained, figuring up it was two and a half beers she had lost to Figi by now.

"That's how he got so healthy," McKenzie said. "All those beers."

Figi just grinned, and sipped the one he had.

About which time the vid died and the lights came up full in the quarters, bright as morning, and a voice yelled out, via the intercom:

"*Inspection!*"

"Good God," McKenzie said in annoyance.

And: "What in hell's that?" Park said. "We ain't touched a port."

"*Go immediately to the center aisle where you are. No talking. No delays to secure materials. If you're drinking or eating, hold it; if you're doing anything else, leave it. No talking, no discussion, no walking around. Move now!*"

"Shit," NG muttered, and sent a twitch through Bet's nerves.

"Shut *up*," she hissed, scared for reasons she couldn't exactly pin anything on, except when NG took a notion to be an ass he could do it up in ribbons, and she didn't like that attitude. She took her beer and she took herself to the aisle, leaving everything the way the mofs said, all six of them standing out there. Musa went on sipping his beer, other people did, so she figured it must be all right, while the mof search squad came in and started at the other end of the quarters.

God, when they pulled a check in the troop-deck, you didn't sip any beers, you swallowed it to keep the ship move-ready, you threw everything loose into the mesh bag that hung by your bunk, you stood in that aisle at attention and you didn't *think* about drinking any beers while the mofs were going through your stuff and writing down every frigging thing that wasn't inspection-ready, God *help* you if you had drugs or unregistered armament in your locker.

People did talk, under their breaths, shifted around a little to do it, where the mofs weren't right at hand, you could hear the little muttering under the ship-noise.

Then two more mofs walked in, Orsini *and* Fitch together.

"Oh, God," somebody said.

She slid a glance toward NG, saw the set of his jaw, saw him take a deliberate slow drink of the beer he was holding and stare murder in Fitch's direction.

They just stood there, and talk died down entirely in the area.

Fitch was in his own morning rounds and Orsini was on duty during his rec-period, both, you could figure, because they were searching *all* the bunks and all the stuff, what belonged to mainday as well as what belonged to alterday.

The search had started near the vid, four junior officers she'd never laid eyes on, but that could include a whole lot of the bridge crew, even those that were alterday. Bunks got turned up, the storages underneath inspected, everything got a general lookover, but it went pretty fast.

Hell of a time to start looking for drugs, Park was right. No sense to start searching now for what they could have brought aboard. Probably some damn thing had gone missing, maybe they'd lost a bottle or two out of the officers' mess, maybe the captain had lost his watch or something. Probably *was* a stolen-goods check, if they *were* finally headed into port, to make sure something didn't get carried offship and bartered for booze. That was probably what was going on.

But it sure as hell made you start tallying up what you had brought aboard and re-checking the regs in your mind to see if you had anything you weren't supposed to.

No prohibition on anything she had, she was sure of that: she'd read that list *real* careful. And they were already past NG's bunk, thank God, with no problems evident.

The search got to them, they stood quietly, all six of them, while the mofs turned up McKenzie's bunk and then Park's and Figi's, and the guys' across the aisle, and worked all the way down to the bulkhead.

Up to the loft then.

Nothing I got's illegal. Please God.

She sipped her own beer, feeling odd about it, telling herself this ship was hell and away looser about a whole lot of things. But you couldn't help worrying – particularly when you knew you had enemies, and particularly when you'd had the message delivered that same day that some sum-bitch with bridge-level connections was out to get even.

"*Yeager,*" the intercom called out. "*Come to your bunk area.*"

Oh, *shit*!

She took a deep breath and started to excuse herself past, felt somebody pat her back, another take her arm.

One was Musa, the one who held her arm was NG. She looked at him and gave a shrug. "Probably the viewer," she said: at the moment she hoped to hell it was.

He let her go, she went and climbed the ladder, and somebody else was coming up after her, which she had a very clear idea was the two watch-officers. She didn't look over her shoulder, she walked on to where the four inspectors had gathered – where her bunk was standing on its side and they had the underneath storage open to view.

Their sniffer-box was going crazy, the red light was flashing, and a plastic packet of capsules was lying on top of her stuff, right there in front of God and everybody.

"This your bunk?" one asked.

"Yessir," she said. "But I didn't put that there."

About the time Orsini and Fitch showed up and the inspection crew said how they'd found it – of course – in her stowage, and she said, when Orsini asked her whether she had a prescription, "Nossir, but that's not mine."

"Whose is it?"

"Lindy Hughes', sir. He said he had something for my headache, said he'd leave it at my bunk."

"You consider going to the pharmacy, Yeager?"

"Didn't know it was prescription, sir, must've got it this morning, he had an accident, you know, figure he didn't think it was strong enough to worry over."

Orsini took the packet in his fingers. "Remains to be seen if this is prescription."

"Yessir."

"Find out where Hughes's been," Fitch said.

*Wasn't* a presence-sniffer they had, then, just a basic job, no way to track where anybody was – more the pity.

"I'd like to point out, sir, if I was running contraband, I'd do it in a better container."

"You want me to note that down, Yeager?"

"Yessir. I know the ways stuff gets past. And how it doesn't. Plain plastic bag isn't going to get past anybody."

"You want to tell us anything else?" Orsini asked.

"Don't mind to take a test, sir. Nothing in my system except the last trank dose."

Fitch picked up the viewer and shoved a fiche in. He was quiet a moment. Looking. Then Fitch turned the viewer off and gave her a cold, measuring stare.

"Think you'd better come to Administrative, Yeager."

"Yessir," she said, and went where Fitch and Orsini indicated, back down the aisle, down the ladder, a couple of steps ahead of them.

There was a gossipy murmuring in the crew. It got quieter in her immediate vicinity. She saw NG close up, saw him with a panicked look on his face – not waiting where he was supposed to be, not him, not Musa either, who had a firm grip on his arm. What NG might do scared her, so she just gave him a straight I-don't-know-you stare and kept walking to the door, calmly as she could, because Fitch was there, Fitch was likely to pick up on any communication she made with anybody and write *that* into his report.

They got through to the door, they walked out into rec and general com started calling Lindy Hughes to report to Orsini's office.

That gave her a little satisfaction, at least. If she was going down, if this was going to start with little questions and get to the ones she didn't want asked — then it didn't matter as much who had done it as she just wanted to take a few shots that counted, and take out the ones that did matter.

They had her stop by infirmary and do the tests: she was real glad about that – "Nothing but the last trank-down in my system," she told the med. "That's all you're going to find."

"Hope so," Fletcher said.

She was confident about that. She wasn't, about the interview in the office.

Except Bernstein showed up as they were going in, said, "What in hell, Yeager?" And she said, "Wish I knew, sir," – figuring that saying more than that right then, just outside Orsini's office, while Orsini was opening the door to let her in, was going to annoy him seriously.

Civ procedures. Civ mofs ran all over each other's prerogatives, and talked to each other in ways that made her nervous, but having Bernstein waiting out there was a comfort, even if she figured it could set Orsini off.

So she walked in, stood quietly at informal rest while Orsini came in and sat down at his desk. He pushed a button on the console.

"We're recording."

"Yessir."

"You maintain the pills belong to Hughes."

"I've got every reason to think so, sir."

"Why?"

"Man promised me."

"After his accident with the door."

"Shower head, sir."

"*Don't* be flip with me."

"Yessir."

"Friend of yours?"

"Nossir, not much. But if he tells me he's going to do something, I won't doubt him."

Orsini made a note on his TranSlate, looked up under his eyebrows. "You're a smartass, Yeager."

"Sorry, sir."

"You *like* Hughes? Got anything personal with him?"

"If he set me up I got something personal with him, yessir, but I haven't had that proved yet."

"You insist he promised you pills for a headache."

"I stick by what I said, sir."

"You come onto this ship, you pick fights, you create dissension in *my watch*, Yeager, you just make trouble all up and down the line, don't you?"

"Nossir. No fighting, sir."

"Lindy Hughes just slipped."

"I was all over soap, sir. Probably he was joking around, I take it that way, sir."

Another quiet note onto the TranSlate. A shift of black eyes upward again. "God, I hate smartasses."

Didn't seem the time to say anything. She waited, hands tucked behind her.

"You tell me, Yeager . . . *are* you smart, or just smartass?"

"Hope I'm smart, sir."

"You know what they call you on the bridge?"

"Nossir."

"Spit 'n polish, – Shit won't stick to you, is that it?"

"I try not to get into it, sir."

"Smartass again."

"Sorry, sir."

Orsini rocked his chair back, hands folded across his middle, and stared up at her a long time. "You come on this ship with papers by the grace of your last captain, you *haven't* got the rating you claim, have you?"

"Machinist, sir."

Long, long stare of those black eyes. "Hughes make a grab at you?"

She felt the sweat running. "Wouldn't venture to say, sir."

The com beeped. Orsini took it private, using the earpiece, listened while he watched her.

"Thanks," he said to whoever. And to her: "Headache, is it?"

"Yessir."

"It's not Hughes' prescription. It's dust. You know that word?"

Worse than she figured, then. "Yessir."

"You still think it's Hughes."

She thought about that, with Orsini staring up at her and her heart thumping hard. "I think if that was what he meant he's no friend of mine."

"You ever thought about the diplomatic branch?"

"Nossir." She hated round-the-corner attacks. Orsini was that kind.

"Are you clean?"

"Yes, sir."

"Where do you suppose it came from?"

"Somebody who wanted me in a lot of trouble, sir."

Long silence again.

"Why?"

"I don't know, sir."

"Spit 'n polish, where'd you learn your manners?"

"Lot of ships, sir." She made herself shift weight on her feet, stand easier, civ-like. "And station militia. Pan-paris."

He might believe it. He might not. He said, one brow lifting: "*Militia*, was it?"

"Yessir."

"What rank?"

"Specialist."

"In what?"

"Weapons tech, sir."

He thought about that, rocking his chair. Finally he said, "What kind?"

"Whatever we could get."

*Too* much truth, in the last years, the losing years. Her pulse skittered and fluttered while Orsini kept up that gentle rocking.

"You can wait outside."

There was no indication how it was going. No figuring anything with Orsini. "Yessir," she said, and she went and opened the door.

"Send Hughes in."

Hughes was out there, sitting on the bench along the wall. So was Bernstein out there, standing talking with Fitch. "Your turn," she said to Hughes.

Hughes got up, scowling as they passed each other, and she sat down on the bench in Hughes' place, while Bernstein and Fitch went on talking, Bernstein just as calm and reasonable as if it was the supper menu they were talking about, instead of NG Ramey.

". . . no question," Bernie was saying, to Fitch's objections, "he's steadied down a lot, no sick-reports, no problems. . . ."

"The man's always the center of something. I'm not surprised to find him in the middle of whatever's going on." Fitch made a move of his hand and pulled Bernstein over out of earshot. Voices dropped, Fitch's face stayed angry, Bernstein's worried.

Had to be coming up on alterdark, thirty minutes or so, and that meant the alterday evening/maindawn lapover ended. So did Orsini's optional jurisdiction, unless Orsini planned to stay up around the clock, and small chance Orsini intended to do that.

Small chance that Bernstein *could*, counting he had one of his shift under arrest and NG under consideration for arrest – God *knew* for what . . . but Bernie might have his hands full tomorrow, working the boards himself unless he pulled somebody off mainday right now and put him back to bed, or unless Orsini was going to let him work somebody twenty four hours solid at the boards –

And Fitch was just warming up, just starting to ask questions.

Like about NG.

*What in hell can he have done?*

*God, are they on him because of me?*

*If they have, if Fitch corners him – God knows what he'll do, he'll go out on Fitch, he'll do one of those eetee spells with Fitch watching and they'll jerk him off the boards, they'll lock him up – it'd kill him, it'll finish him –*

*If he doesn't go for Fitch's throat . . .*

*If Fitch doesn't goad him into it . . .*

*And Fitch would.*

She sat there staring at the wall while a couple of the bridge crew and a mainday tech on business walked through. She listened to the few words she could catch from Fitch and Bernstein. Bernstein was looking worried, from what she

could catch out of the corner of her eye; and she reckoned
Bernstein didn't even have the right to stay there, once the
curfew rang and the watch passed to Fitch, Fitch could order
him out of it, Fitch could order any damn thing he wanted
with anybody in his way – except maybe Orsini.

*Oh, God! let Orsini stay on the case.*

Bernstein and Fitch stopped talking. Bernstein just stood
there looking upset, but Fitch walked off a little up the rim
and gave some order on his pocket com, with his back
turned, so she couldn't hear what he was saying, or read
lips for it.

Bernstein walked back to her and said: "The packet was
dust."

"Yessir, I heard – "

"They're pulling half of main Engineering, putting them
on alterday."

"What are they going to do?" She felt the panic rise and
fought it. No use for the adrenaline rush, nothing to fight,
and it sure as hell didn't help a body think. "They didn't
plant anything on NG – "

"Musa's rep is clean, and that's a given. Just keep calm.
You've got a witness."

"They arrested NG?"

"He's up for questioning. Just questions."

*God.* Like someone had hit her in the gut. She couldn't
breathe for a second. But the mind went on working, thinking about him and small spaces, about him and his temper
and Fitch getting him in his office – and she thought about
how to stop that and the answer came up the only way she
could sort it out.

"What's the log if I tell Orsini it's mine?"

Bernie frowned, quick and hard; and she thought in the
same second that *log* wasn't a civ word, and that Bernie hadn't
missed it and that Bernie was adding that up, somewhere in
the muddle of everything else going on, Bernie was upset as
hell and ready to kill Hughes with his bare hands.

Because they were in a trap and *she* should have broken
Hughes' damn neck, hell with the chance of getting caught
at it – the chance of Lindy Hughes coming back at her was
a hundred percent, and she'd *known* that, dammit, known it
right in the gut and she'd pulled back from what she should

have done til Gypsy and Davies and Presley were in on it and everything was too damn late.

So when you screw up you cover it, Bet Yeager. Same as under fire.

"It's a detention offense," Bernstein said, quiet and fast, under the ship-noise. "If you're lucky. You don't sign off this ship. There *isn't* any discharge, you understand me? You've got no priors, you've got a good work record – but you *know* what happened to NG – "

"I'll live. I'll *get* Hughes – someday. I'll pay him."

She was saying that to a mof. But Bernie understood her, Bernie was somebody you could say that to and Bernie would keep his mouth shut when Hughes had a real bad accident someday.

"Think I better talk to Orsini," she said, "before curfew goes."

"Dammit," Bernstein said. "Dammit to hell, – "

"Yeah," she said, took a deep breath and felt halfway better. "But little spaces don't spook me." She motioned with her eyes toward the door. "I got to talk to him. How much time do we got?"

Bernstein did a fast, covert check of his watch. "Three minutes."

"God!"

Bernstein went to the office door, hesitated a bare half-second.

"Mr. Bernstein," Fitch said from behind them.

Bernstein pushed the button.

Door was locked. Sure as hell.

"Mr. Bernstein."

As the bell rang.

Stupid as hell, she thought. Power games at the top of the whole damn command. But it was valid, it was past alterday's shift, and Bernie looked Fitch's direction the way he had to and said with a deliberate slowness, "Yes, Mr. Fitch."

"Yeager," Fitch said, and invited her with a move of his hand. You didn't say no. Even Bernstein couldn't – twice over Bernstein couldn't do anything with Orsini refusing to open his door and armed Security a little way down the corridor just watching everything that happened – two of

them, probably Fitch's own pick of the docks. Or wherever.

Probably Orsini thought it was Fitch at his door, and
Orsini wasn't about to unlock and talk. More damn power
games between the watch officers, no word from Wolfe, the
whole command busy with its own politics and a skuz like
Hughes had favor-points with the tekkie sum-bitch bridge
officer he was probably in bed with, enough to get away
with murder.

Or Fitch had been hunting something on Bernstein himself
for a long, long time, and everything else was just Fitch's way
of getting the leverage.

So she said, mildly, "Yessir," got up from the bench and
went where Fitch indicated, trusting Bernie to do as much
as he could.

Fitch's office, it happened, being the next over.

# Chapter 19

"Wasn't mine, sir," she said, one more time through the drill.

"Are you thinking I'm a fool?" Fitch asked.

"I'd never think so, sir."

"Seems to me you do, seems to me you think everybody on this ship must be fools. *I pulled you out of the fuckin' brig, Yeager, I signed you on this ship, and you haven't been a fuckin' thing but a pain in the ass, you know that?*"

"I don't think so, sir."

"You don't *think* so, you don't fuckin' *think* so! You're calling me a *liar*, Yeager. Are you calling me a liar?"

"I don't admit the charges, sir."

They were recording, she was sure; and if they were they weren't going to get a damned thing Fitch could edit into something else.

And maybe Fitch was just crazy or maybe he was better in control than he looked and he was trying to get her to react. He left his desk, he prowled the office while he yelled at her, he bent down and he yelled in her face.

She thought, *Better than you have tried*, and she retreated into null-mode, just the same as standing at attention with old Junker Phillips yelling at you, just focus on the questions and keep twisting right back to your basic position, no matter where the son of a bitch tried to lead you. If you didn't say anything different they couldn't get anywhere, and they got mad and then they got bored and then they just logged you what they could and gave up and maybe eventually forgot about it.

Yessir, nossir, nossir, I don't admit the charges.

And if the son of a bitch couldn't scare you he might want you to hit him; might just push you far enough that you could, if you were a fool, but you weren't, so you didn't.

Nossir.

Keep at it all day if you want, mof. Keep at it til shift-change and Orsini's watch starts. I got the time.

At least NG's not in here.

"*You hear me?*"

"Yessir."

Fitch grabbed the front of her jumpsuit and jerked her hard, and she just gave with it, just went limp.

"Gave you a chance. Hauled you out of one brig and here you are trying to get in another. Hauled you out of there and you were carrying contraband. *Weren't you?*"

"Nossir."

She figured Fitch would hit her. He jerked her hard, leaned into her face and said, "I have other sources, Yeager, I know where the trouble comes from on this ship and I know where to go when something's wrong and nobody in lowerdecks wants to talk."

Man's crazy, man's absolute crazy, she thought; and thought, He's talking about NG.

"You want to think it over?" Fitch asked her. "You want to think about it?" He jerked her up to her feet, pulled her off balance and she didn't do the natural thing, didn't grab at him or hit him, just got her feet under her and bashed her leg against the transit-braced chair. He hit her, jerked her and hit her along the side of the head.

Won't show, she thought while her brain was ringing. Bruises won't show there.

So she brought her knee up.

He hit her, about twice before she went flying backward into the wall and hit it full length, thought she was going to stand up, but she bounced off it and the floor came up.

Hazy for a second, then. She moved to tuck up and protect herself, and she had a view of Fitch's boots, figuring he was mad enough to kick hell out of her.

Plenty of bruises, damn sure.

"Get up," he said. She lay there, he grabbed her and jerked her up by the collar and hauled her to her feet.

She stared him in the eyes, thinking, Got you, you sum-bitch.

Got you, if you got any regs on this ship.

He pulled her over to the chair, he sat her down, he went

over and set his rump on the corner of his desk, just looking
at her.

She sucked the cut lip and kept staring at him.

"You're asking for it," Fitch said.

She didn't say a thing.

"Catch your breath," Fitch said calmly. "You want a
drink?"

"Nossir."

Fitch cut the recorder off, ran it back a minute or so.

Didn't restart it. And she worried then.

"I keep the records," Fitch said. "See what smart gets you?
Come onto this ship, go right for the troublemakers – You've
been damned useful, Yeager. You think you're smart. But I
don't need a thing out of you – now we're off the record. I
just need you to exist. Bitch."

She figured she was in for it, then, figured Fitch had plain
revenge in mind and a whole lot of things could have been
a bad mistake.

"Now," Fitch said, "I want you to think about something.
I want you to think how you can save your own ass, because
this is the chance you've got. I want you to think about how
you can go on being useful to me, and I'm going to help you
think about that, you hear me?"

"Yessir."

*Damn! No simple son of a bitch. . . .*

*Going to hurt for this one, Yeager. . . .*

*So you lie. But what's he want?*

"All you have to do is get along with me."

"Yessir."

He got off the edge of the desk, he came and took hold of
her the way he had and she flinched, mad that she did that,
but the nerves remembered, the body wanted to protect itself
and if you did that they'd space you sure.

He slapped her across the face, once, twice, three times,
and he stopped, but he was still holding onto her and her
bones hurt and her ears rang and her vision fuzzed . . . and
hit her the way he could, and her obliged to take it . . .

He shook her, one neck-popping snap. "You want more?"

"Nossir."

"Those drugs yours?"

"Nossir."

He hit her again. "Are you any use to me?"

"Dunno, sir." Talking made a bubbling feeling, now. Blood, maybe. "I try."

Fitch said, "How's that?"

"Try, sir. Real cooperative."

"I think you're lying, Yeager. Would you lie to me?"

"Nossir."

The grip on her clothes let up. She tensed up, expecting a sneak blow, but he let her sit there.

"You want your friends to be all right, is that right?"

"Yessir."

"There's a washroom back there. You go clean up. Then you can go."

She stared at him.

"You understand me," Fitch said. "Report on the drugs is inconclusive. – I sure as hell better not catch you in any more trouble, Yeager. You *or* your friends, you hear me?"

"Yessir," she said. She got up, the way he said, wobbling, she managed to focus enough to see the door, and she went back into the cubby with the sink and toilet and turned on the cold water. The mirror showed a face better than she expected, the blood from her nose and mouth went with a couple of handfuls of cold water. The red on the sides of her face didn't.

She blotted dry with the towel, she looked up and Fitch was mirrored in the doorway.

Her gut clenched up. She couldn't help it, and couldn't help it when she had to turn around and face him, and pass him when he moved back ever so little to let her brush past him. – Dammit, she knew what he was doing, wasn't half surprised when he put a light hand on her shoulder, enough to make her stomach heave.

"You do better in future," he said. "And we'll get along just fine. Hear?"

"Yessir."

He motioned her toward the door. She went, opened it herself, walked out into a vacant corridor. The cold of the water was going. Her bones ached, her vision still kept blurring, and she had to walk around the rim and get some rest and get up, she supposed, at alterdawn – back on duty; but she realized numbly that she had no idea where NG and

Musa were, or what had happened to them or whether NG was next in Fitch's office.

She grayed out for a second, found herself in rec, walking up to the quarters door, got just about that far before she got dizzy and had to hang there a second. Then she shoved off and walked into the dark, past sleeping crewmates, down as far as Musa's bunk and NG's, and they were both empty.

God.

She had to sit. She picked Musa's bunk, and sat down and after a moment lay down, in the idea that if either of them came back the way she had, they'd come here, and she didn't think she could make the loft, she was too dizzy and too sick.

The dizziness got better after a few minutes of lying down. But the fear didn't.

Exactly what Fitch had done to NG.

Exactly.

Except it could get worse. Except you toed the line with Fitch or he'd see you had accidents, and he had his hand-picked skuz aboard to see you got up on charges – no damn wonder Hughes and his bridge connections were so solid –

Goddard. Goddard, over nav, Hughes' operator.

Friend of Fitch's.

Fitch picked the personnel.

Got himself a skut who carved up two people on Thule, just out of the goodness of his heart and his faith in humanity hauled her aboard and let her loose –

Like hell.

Like hell Fitch didn't run this ship. . . .

Or intend to.

Bernstein had to be a pain in the ass to him. Bernstein had been on mainday until he got a bellyful of Fitch and transferred to alterday –

– like anybody else who could manage it.

*Alterday* was where you went if you couldn't get along with Fitch and you had a little pull – like Bernie had gotten NG and Musa to his shift; or you got there by being Fitch's hand-picked damn spies –

– like Lindy Hughes.

*Should've killed that skuz.*

*Will.*

Except – the facts were real clear now, what the real rules were on this ship – that meant you went head to head with Fitch, and that meant –

Fitch had just given her a preview of what it meant.

And Fitch had NG in there by now, another locker-door accident, that was all. A lot more valuable alive –

You didn't make martyrs, you just beat hell out of 'em and you turned 'em back into the 'decks to start the rest of the campaign –

– like little accidents to your stuff, and then little accidents to you, so you knew if you fought back you were going to be in Fitch's office, and maybe in the brig when the ship went jump –

– like little accidents to your friends. And your "friends" would pull off and leave trouble alone, if they were smart.

Or just human.

You always gave your enemies an out, right in the direction you wanted 'em to go. That was what the Old Man used to say. That was what Fitch was doing. And he shouldn't make her scared, old Phillips had belted her across a hallway once; but Junker Phillips wasn't trying to kill you, he was just trying to keep you alive.

*Fitch* was trying to kill you. Or Fitch was trying to break you. And those were the two choices you had. Crew like this had to have an example. Like NG.

But NG was too crazy to break and too valuable to kill.

Not when NG was a way to Bernstein's gut.

And Fitch didn't damn well need her now – except as another way to put the screws to NG.

Who wasn't as crazy as seemed, not *half* as crazy as seemed, if he was still alive and Bernstein was.

Man named Cassel wasn't.

Man named Cassel had had a fatal accident. In Engineering.

And NG Ramey took the shit for it.

Cassel had been a *friend* of NG's. And Bernstein's.

She found her hands in fists, tasted blood and swallowed it; and knew if Fitch so much as stopped her in the corridor after this she was going to be shaking head to foot.

*Shake like hell suiting up*, she thought, flashing on what it felt like, with your body cased in ceramics, with the servos whining when you moved and the pressure of the bands on your body that told the suit what the body wanted. And the damn servos got confused as hell if you started shaking and everybody knew it, because they stuttered and chattered –

Embarrassing as hell. So you developed a sense of humor about it, since you did it every damn time –

Adrenaline charge. Stutter and rattle.

Smell of oil and metal and plastics. Human sweat and your own breath inside the helmet.

You were machine, then. Human gut inside a human-shaped machine. And it took a damn lucky shot to damage you.

Sure missed that rig, sometimes. Sure hated to leave it, in that corridor on Pell.

Shakes stopped after you got going. Servos smoothed out and you floated, like nothing was effort, and nothing could stop you.

But armor's got no thinking brain, armor's got no guts. – *That's you, skut, you're the Operating System. It'll walk after you're dead, but it don't fight worth shit in that condition. You're the brain and the guts. Remember it.*

*Damn right, Junker Phillips.*


Somebody bumped the bed. She woke up with her heart thumping, knew right off that she was in quarters, and in Musa's bunk, waiting on her mates, and that there were two men, shadowed against the night-glow, one with Musa's shape and Musa's smell, and one with NG's, touching her, gathering her up when she tried to move, hugging her so everything hurt.

"I'm all right," she said. "You?"

"Fine," NG said, or something like that, and she just held onto them awhile, not caring that it hurt. NG felt over her face, and the way his fingers stopped at her lip and her right cheek, and the way the spots were both sore and a little numb from swelling she got a mental picture the same as he had to, what she had to look like.

He didn't say a thing. And NG was dangerous when he didn't.

She grabbed his hand. Hard. "You listen to me," she

whispered. "You listen good. Not going to talk, here. But craziness is what Fitch wants. *Hear* me?"

NG didn't say anything. He tensed his hand just enough to keep the bones from grinding.

"Going to bed," Musa said, putting a hand on her back, giving her a little shove. "His bunk. Hear?"

"Yeah," she said, feeling a little tightness in the throat. She leaned over and pressed her mouth against Musa's stubbled cheek. "Love you," she said. "Love you, man."

Musa shoved her again, and she crawled out after NG, to follow him.

NG grabbed her and held her at arm's length. "He'll kill you," NG hissed at her. "He'll kill you, you understand me?"

She wobbled on her feet and hung onto him and left him nothing to do with her but get her to his bed, and get in with her, and hold onto her, clothes and all.

"I got him figured," she said into his ear, fainter than anything was likely to pick it up. But you never knew. Fitch could even bug the damn pillow. She wrapped a leg over him, snuggled body against body until they fit together, which was the only way to be comfortable sleeping double in a bunk. Her back hurt. Her head was pounding. She said, wishing Fitch could hear, "I seen skuz before. Nothing new. Shush, they could have bugs in bed with us." She moved against him, gentle as she could, figuring he could have sore spots too, and that was one of them. But he didn't seem hurt, didn't seem interested that way either, he just kissed her face and made that kind of love to her, just real gentle, real careful, not even sex, but she liked it.

Liked it and found herself scared the way she'd never been scared for anybody in her life. You served with guys, you knew people got killed, and partners did, like Teo, sometimes real hard ways. But none of them she had lost had been her fault, and none of them had ever had to risk what NG was risking for her.

She drowsed what felt like a few minutes before the morning bell went off, before it was time to move and go up and get a change of clothes, and face stares at her face and hear the whispers behind her back.

Face NG and Musa too, with the lights on. "Pretty bad?"

she asked them: Musa grimaced and shook his head, and NG said, "Damn him to hell."

She had to face Lindy Hughes, too, and Presley and Gibbs, who gave her dark stares and snickered about her looks.

"Hey, Yeager," Hughes yelled out, "your man been beating on you?"

"Hell, no," she yelled back, "Fitch did. Wanted me to kiss his boots for him. Which end did he make you kiss?"

Real quiet in the quarters, just then. A lot of stares.

"You got a mouth, bitch."

"You're *all* mouth, skuz. You dropped the drugs in my bunk. Or one of your skutty friends did. Funny thing, I *thought* I smelled you up there."

Deathly quiet.

"You'll get yours, bitch."

"Yeah, from the back. Same as you got NG. Tried it on me in the showers and you got your head busted, didn't you? Damn shower-crawling skuz. Looking up the stalls. That the only thing that does it for you?"

Nasty cut on Hughes' forehead. And one eye was turning black. Didn't improve his looks any at all.

A few people were walking around, going to showers, trying to ignore the shouting match.

But one of the bystanders was Gabe McKenzie, who shouldered past the gawkers and came and stood by her and NG and Musa with his hands in his pockets.

And another was Gypsy Muller, who strolled into the middle and said, "You got what you deserved, Hughes. Swallow it and choke."

Park and Figi came in, then, right beside Gabe McKenzie, and then Meech and Rossi; and Moon and Zilner, Gypsy's mates, and then, God, one of the women, Kate Williams, out of Cargo, just planted herself at the edge and stood there with her arms folded.

Nobody was moving now. Until Hughes said, "Fuck you," under his breath, shoved one and the other of his mates into motion and walked out.

"Good riddance," McKenzie said.

*Not* Fitch's plan. Damn sure.

There were new faces in the quarters, Freeman and Walden and Battista and Slovak from mainday Engineering, Weider and Keane, too, she recognized them on the fringes of the commotion. She saw everybody staring at her and her mates and McKenzie and his, and everything still real quiet, so quiet you could hear the rumble of the ship.

"Sorry," she said, to everybody in general, "damn sorry. I hate a fight."

It was like the whole quarters drew a breath then. People moved. People discovered they were behind schedule and the shower-line wasn't full.

"Thanks," she said to a few in particular, and then she found herself with a slight case of the shakes. "Damn!"

"Time we got rid of that skuz," Park said.

Bad news for a man when people on his watch got that opinion of him. Hughes had to figure it, Hughes wasn't stupid, at least not in that department.

"Hell of a mess," Gabe McKenzie said, looking at her. She put a knuckle to her cheek, which was so swollen it pulled the eyelid.

"Yeah," she said, and figured he meant her face. She was cold sober for a second and scared . . . and that wasn't the mess she was thinking of.

"He's likely headed straight for Fitch," Musa said, "and he won't even stop for breakfast."

You couldn't stand in the middle of the quarters and yell out warnings about the mofs. The regs had a name for that kind of activity, and you didn't want to be the ringleader. But she wanted it passed, and she wanted it spread it fast. "If they got the quarters bugged," she said, looking down at the deck and muttering, "he's already onto it."

They hadn't thought. They hadn't expected. There were traditions and there were rights and even with all the evidence of what was going on the crew hadn't thought of that – not even Musa had, and he was damned sharp.

"I got to talk," she said, "but not here and not now."

And after showers, out in rec in the fast-moving breakfast line, where the noise made specific pickup a lot less likely, she got NG and Musa up close and said, "Listen. Listen fast. Hughes isn't what's going on last night. It may have been. But it's Fitch now. I think he's *trying* to make a blow-up, and not just with us."

"Bernie?" Musa wasn't slow at all.

"I think it is. He wants one of us to blow up, NG, you hear me? I pushed Hughes and I pushed Fitch some last night, and he's pushing me, trying to spook me, same as he tries to spook you. What'd he *do* last night?"

NG hesitated, his mouth not working real well; Musa said, "Called us in for questions. Kept us sitting in Ops for a couple hours. Asked questions."

"You and him together?" She hoped to hell it was together, that Fitch *hadn't* put all the pressure on he could.

NG nodded. Musa did, and she drew an easier breath.

"So I'm supposed to spook," she said, "and he's not going to lay a hand on you, he wants you to blow and do something stupid, and then Bernie might."

Musa's eyes went thinking-sharp on that. NG said, a ragged, hoarse whisper: "He'll put you in that damn locker, Bet, that's the next step. . . ."

She felt a chill, knew he was flashing on that place, that time, knew McKenzie behind them and Williams in front of them had to be hearing it, even if some bug wasn't. "I know that. Know it real clear. But we got no choice, Fitch isn't going to give us a choice, we just got to keep our heads clear. He could grab any one of us. He can do it any time he can set us up, and that pressures Bernie, you hear? Skuts like us don't matter topside, you and me don't cross Fitch's mind one day out of thirty, it's a Bernie-Fitch fight going on. I don't know a damn thing else, but I pick that up real clear. Some of alterday bridge crew has got to be transferees like Bernie, them that want clear of Fitch; others has got to be Fitch's pets. Same as the 'decks. Hear? And Lindy Hughes is on the way out of here, but if Fitch doesn't own anybody down here now, he's going to find somebody he can spook or buy. Isn't he?"

They didn't say anything, they were thinking; Williams snatched up her biscuit and tea and it was their turn, over against the wall to gulp a few bites and put things together.

"He's fouling up Engineering," Musa said, "hauling in people off their shift, – messing up Bernie's operations, forced transfers into his shift – but not us. Mad people, lot of heat and no outlet."

"We got to be nice to them," she said, and washed down a fast gulp of breakfast, hot tea stinging her lip. She nudged NG with her elbow. "We got to be 'specially nice. Even if they get skutty with us, – they been put upon, seriously put upon, and we got to make things easy as we can."

"They got an earful," Musa said, "and they may've come in mad, but there's no fools in that bunch. *They* got contacts back into mainday. I got to talk to Freeman."

NG nodded, calmer now. He had pocketed his biscuit, was only drinking his tea – upset stomach, she thought, no appetite; but he was following everything, she was sure of it. And sure of him, in spite of the fact his hands were shaking.

"I got two fast questions else," she said. "Where's Orsini this morning and where's the captain last night?"

"Good question," Musa said after a breath.

"What in hell does Wolfe *do* on this ship? Does Fitch run everything?"

Scary question, possibly a mutinous question. And she thought about the chance of it getting past the three of them.

Musa said, in the lowest possible voice, "He ain't a real activist."

"Shit!" she whispered, disgusted, irritated, and, God! missing *Africa*. Porey might be a bastard and a bitch, but you never had any doubt somebody was in charge up there.

*Scary*, to know what *was* going on in *Loki* command; and she tried to put it together with the slight, cold man she had met, once, in the downside office.

Not a stupid man. Not a man who'd cower in his cabin. Not a man who'd give a damn about shooting you in cold blood, either.

Damn good captain, at least as far as keeping a ship like *Loki* alive through the war years. But you didn't know how many sides he'd played, or even what side he was playing now.

Spook ship captain and a spook top to bottom, evidently, and she didn't like it.

It was real odd not to be the only ones headed into Engineering, – Freeman and Walden and Battista and the rest headed around the rim in the direction opposite to what they were usually going, and checking in with Liu and her crew under Smith – Liu with dark looks and a sullen, short manner, and Mr. Smith a little down in the mouth, over talking with Bernstein like most mornings.

But Bernstein saw them check in and came straight over, mad and upset even before he got a look at the damage.

"Damn," Bernstein said then.

"Little argument with a wall," Bet said. "Can I talk with you, sir? Private?"

"Five minutes," Bernstein said, and went back to Smith to settle something, while they sorted themselves out and Musa got Freeman and Battista and the rest of the transfers over in the corner. Fast, hard talking was going on over there.

And NG . . . NG just put his hand on her shoulder and squeezed ever so gently.

"Don't you think about anything stupid," she said. "Hear me?"

Because he was capable of it, capable of just walking into Fitch's office and killing him. *She* thought about the same thing, if it got down to being shoved in any locker with no trank. Take out the main problem and leave the ship to Orsini. There was a chance for everybody with Orsini.

And you could start figuring like that, if you were good as dead already.

"Hear me?"

He nodded, made a struggling little noise like a yes, as if everything in him was so dammed up that nothing could get out, and he didn't know how to talk to people anymore without being crazy.

"Team-play," she said. He got a breath and nodded as if he meant it, then grabbed up his data-board and went off to do his work. Alone. Like always.

"Sir," she said, when Bernstein got back to her and they got off in the corner, "has Fitch got something in for you?"

It wasn't what Bernstein had looked to hear. It was impertinent, and maybe it wasn't information he wanted to hand out to whoever asked.

"He indicate that?"

"I just got this feeling," she said.

"What happened?" he asked.

"Hauled me in, asked me about the drugs, knocked me around and let me go. And I got this bad feeling it's not finished. I got this feeling it didn't have a damn thing to do with Hughes. I get this *feeling*," she said on a deep breath, "he's got it in for this shift, and it's not NG. — And I don't ask to know, except to tell you that's what we think, and we're watching out for it. — I tell you another thing, sir, — it's no secret in quarters what happened last night and there's a lot who don't like Hughes, and a lot I don't think like Mr. Fitch very damn much, sir. Begging your pardon, but a lot of people don't think we got fair shift and they think crew's being pushed."

Bernstein was upset. Not mad. Upset. Finally he said, "Musa keeps me updated."

Not surprising, no.

"You being a fool, Yeager?"

"Nossir."

Bernstein passed a hand over the back of his neck. "The lid needs to stay on."

"Yessir," she said, "you want it, you got it."

He gave her a long, long stare then. "Where'd they get you?"

"Sir?"

"Spit 'n polish. Where'd they get you?"

"Thule, sir." Her heart started thumping, painfully hard. "You know that."

"One of Fitch's picks."

"I signed with the captain, sir, at least, I asked *him* for a berth."

"Fitch picked you out of the station brig."

"Got arrested after I talked to the captain. I had some trouble on Thule. I'm *not* in the habit of knifing people, sir."

"Knifing people. That's not what I hear."

"Man asked for it, sir."

"Asked for what you did?"

There was a lot of the upstanding merchanter in Bernstein. A lot of sensibilities. Like Nan and Ely, back on Thule. She tried to put that in perspective, tried to see how a man like Bernie would even think, if she told him what Ritterman was.

"Yessir," she said, and stopped it there. "He did."

Bernstein was quiet a few seconds. Then he said, "Must've. Must've. So the captain signed you. Personally."

"Yessir," she said, puzzled because it puzzled Bernstein. "At least verbal. I ran into Mr. Fitch first out of the ship, I says, is there a berth? See the captain, he says. So I came aboard and I saw him and he said report. But they arrested me first."

Bernstein rested his thumbs in his waist-loops, looked at the deck a moment, then at her. "And Fitch came after you."

"Yessir." She felt more and more cornered, wondered if she ought to explain more than she had, or whether that could only make it worse. "Got picked up on one charge and they pulled a search and they found this guy. . . ."

Bernstein wasn't paying attention to that, she realized. It wasn't her record and the murder, it was the Fitch connection Bernstein was worrying about, and who she was working for, even this deep in — especially this deep in, and this close to him. She shut up and waited for him to think everything out.

"You just be real smart," he said finally. "You tell me the truth, the whole truth. Are you Mallory's?"

That caught her so far to the flank her jaw dropped. "Nossir."

"Orsini wondered."

She felt herself shaking and trying not to show it, not to let a wobble into her voice. "This ship got some trouble with Mallory?"

"Orsini just wondered. Pan-paris militia, huh?"

"Yessir."

"You lying to me, Yeager?"

"Nossir." While the sweat ran on her chest and the air seemed thin and cold. "I been around a bit, I guess the habits just took."

"I think you *are* lying."

She stood looking Bernstein in the eye, desperate and thinking that there was no way back from what he was asking. If he spooked, she was dead, that was all.

"*Africa*," she said then, dry-mouthed. "*Africa*, sir. Separated from my ship at Pell."

Finally he said. "Crew?"

"Marine, sir."

The silence hung there.

"I don't mean anything against this ship," she said. "Truth, I just wanted off the stations." And in the long further silence: "I give you everything I got. You're a good officer. And you asked and I told you. All I know to do now, sir."

"Anybody else you've told?"

"Nossir."

Bernstein rubbed the back of his neck. Shook his head. Looked at her finally, sidelong. "You take orders?"

"Yessir. I take yours."

"Did you hit Fitch?"

"Just shook him up. Thought he'd leave some marks. Only defense I got, sir, let people know what he's doing, only thing I could think of, maybe to get it on record what he's doing. Dunno whether that was smart or not."

"It was smart," Bernstein said, "so far as it goes. Where it goes next . . . Dammit, be careful, Yeager. Be *damned* careful."

She drew a deep breath. "Yessir. I got that straight. All of us. — But there's others taking our side in this Hughes business. McKenzie and his shift. Williams. Gypsy Muller and his mates. Nobody in quarters is standing with Hughes now. So we got that, sir."

Bernstein digested that piece of news for a second. Then: "You check in with medical at all?"

"Nossir."

"Get the hell over there."

"I can — "

"Documentation."

"Yessir," she said, having it clear, then. "But what do I tell them happened?"

"Tell 'em the locker door that got NG got you. Musa and Freeman can walk you over. Keep you with witnesses."

"Musa — " she protested.

"NG's on duty, he's not going anywhere. I don't want *you* getting stopped."

"Yessir," she said, on a breath. "Thank you, sir."

But she was scared, deep down, about going to the meds, about leaving the situation with NG. She thought of a dozen things that could go wrong or get out of hand, the kind of superstitious unease that jump set into her. You left things at loose ends and they came back and got you, in ways you never planned.

Chance always got you. And if you left any string untied, it happened.

She stopped like a coward and looked back at Bernstein, wanting – God knew – to ask him what he thought, wanting reassurances. But that wasn't the most important thing. Bernstein outright deciding he couldn't trust her wasn't the worst thing that could happen.

Worst was the irrational stuff, the kind that went wrong just because you trusted it – and it killed you.

"Sir, – what I told you about me . . . I don't think NG'd feel at all comfortable to know that."

"I don't think so either," Bernie said.

# Chapter 20

They walked past the lockers, around the curve to rec, where alterday's breakfast was cleared away and mainday was having evening beers. "Just keep moving," Musa said, when they started through.

Damn right, Bet thought, conscious of her face and the reason for the stares. God, there was Liu-the-bitch, with Pearce, the senior Systems man, Freeman's yesterday mates – Liu and Pearce stared, Musa waved a hello and kept going, and Freeman undoubtedly looked back, – a man had to, when he had to walk by his former mates on alterday's duty, and miss the beers and the talk, the bed-sharing and the partnering and everything else the situation had yanked away from Engineering's mainday shift.

Like being kidnapped and raped in the bargain, it was, and small wonder if Liu and Pearce didn't look exactly cheerful seeing them kiting past on Bernstein's affairs.

Not a happy crew back there, not happy looks that came their way – mainday had been messed with, Engineering was far and away the largest command in the 'decks, and if mates had been transferred, if Mr. Smith was unhappy and Mr. Fitch was pissed, then it wasn't going to be a happy crew for some little while.

Freeman, poor sod, looked like he was bleeding a little; and she wished she could say she was sorry, but she didn't think Freeman wanted to hear it from her, most of all.

"Locker door, huh?"

"Yes'm," she said to Fletcher, while Musa and Freeman waited outside and she was sitting buck-naked on the surgery table letting Fletcher shine light in her eyes and look in her ears for blood or such.

"Not concussed, I think," Bet murmured, wanting the

exam over and her clothes back. The surgery was cold and Fletcher's hands felt colder. "I had that before. Doesn't feel like it."

"Happens you're right," Fletcher said, turning the light out, flipping the little scope other-end-to. Fletcher put a steadying hand on her shoulder.

And jabbed her in the back with the scope. Bet straightened up and swallowed down a *damn!* with a gulp of air, because breakfast nearly came up and her eyes watered.

"Just fine, aren't you?"

"Thing was cold," she said. With the cabinets and the counters shimmering through the water in her eyes and her nerves still jerking. Fletcher ran the probe lightly up and down her back.

"Should have been in here last night," Fletcher said. "I take it that's when this happened."

"Yes, ma'a – " Stars exploded. Her breath went short. " – 'am. Did."

God, she was going to pass out.

"So you went to sleep on it. Who with?"

"I just went to bed."

"Alone?" Fingers ran over the sore spots. "Hell, you *couldn't* come by after it happened. You have to wait and call me out of my rec time. . . ."

"I'm sorry."

"You ought to be." Fletcher went over to the cabinet, looked at the scan-images again, made notes with lines going to this part and that, then started searching the shelves, in that way that inevitably meant medicine. Hopeful sign. Prescriptions meant there was a pill to fix it.

Fletcher said, "Must've been just after I saw you last night."

"Yes'm."

"When?"

She didn't like that kind of question. *Documentation*, Bernie had said. It was a damn Q & A about what kind of story she was spreading about Fitch, that was what it was turning into, and she wanted off the edge of the table, wanted to get her feet on the floor and take the strain off her back. Most of all she wanted to get to Musa outside and get back to Engineering, where, God knew, if somebody called Bernstein out to the bridge or somewhere, NG was all alone with a half dozen mad as hell transfers.

Fletcher found what she wanted and picked up a hypo. Popped the cylinder in.

"I don't need any shot," Bet said. She thought about Fitch, about maybe Fletcher putting her out, Fletcher working with Fitch –

You signed on a ship and you were subject to the meds, that was the way it was. Like God. You got walked into sickbay for a simple lookover and a pill and not even Bernstein could keep Fletcher from giving her that damn hypo. . . .

Fletcher knew it, of course. "I'll do the prescribing, Ms. Yeager. And that means following orders. No core-crawling for the next couple of weeks. No deck-mopping. No bending work. No lifting. That's an order. I'm writing it on your record."

After which Fletcher shot her first in the shoulder, then in three excruciatingly painful spots in the back, and told her, while she was close to throwing up, that she was going to check her into sickbay for forty-eight hours.

God!

"I got duty –"

"You've got a strained back, is what you've got, Ms. Yeager, not mentioning the bruises."

"Ma'am, I've got orders, I can sit station. The department's short, we've got new transfers – "

Fletcher turned her back and searched the drug cabinet again.

God, maybe she *was* in with Fitch.

"Dr. Fletcher, I swear to you, I don't need any sickbay. – Look, look, I'll sit. Won't walk around at all."

Fletcher unwrapped a packet and started making notes of some kind. "All right, I'll make a deal with you. None of the things I named. No using the arms. Sit and watch, period, or I'll put you in here and I'll trank you down and see you rest."

"Yes'm," she said.

*Documentation, hell. God, Bernie, what did you do to me?*

*But, shit, any damn thing could go on if I get stuck in sickbay, NG's back there alone with those guys, and in quarters, all it takes is somebody distracting Musa, Musa turning his head, NG just*

*getting out of sight half a minute, near Hughes or his friends —*
*Showers or somewhere —*

"Your drug test was negative," Fletcher said, handing her two different pills and a cup of water. And after she had swallowed them: "It won't be now. Hear me?"

She stared at Fletcher a moment, replaying that, trying to figure out what Fletcher was telling her, whether it was a set-up or a rescue —

No way in hell they could get a valid drug test now — in case there was any reason to try again. . . .

"You steady enough?"

"Yes'm." She hauled herself off the table, determined not to flinch, and started pulling her clothes on, fast, because the jolt started a sweat, and she was afraid Fletcher was going to take that for an excuse to hold her after all.

*Just get me the hell out of here —*

Scan. Reading the scan. Hypos. Pills. The longer this took, the longer Musa was standing out there in the hall.

And the longer Bernie and NG had no help.

Fletcher gave her a paper and two packs of pills. "You stay out of trouble," Fletcher said. "Follow directions. You've got a written order there, exempts you from certain duties. Carry it. Call me if the pain gets worse. And don't ignore it, dammit."

"Yes'm."

"One of those pill-packs is NG's. Fool didn't pick up his refill. Make sure he stays on it. *Hear*?"

Fletcher was one of the friendlies, she suddenly knew that. She suddenly knew what Fletcher was doing with her papers and her shots and her pills and she suddenly knew why NG might not have been a useful target in any trumped-up drug-search.

"Yes, *ma'am*," she said

Fletcher didn't say anything, Fletcher just dismissed her with a back-handed wave of the hand and kept writing.

Go. Be smart. Keep your head down.

Damn right, she thought, and she went, light-headed with relief, out into the corridor to pick up Musa and Freeman.

*Not* just Musa and Freeman.

Liu was out there.

Bet stopped cold, off-balance and thinking, Oh, God. . . .

"All right?" Musa asked her.

"Gave me some pills," she said, clutching the packets and the paper Fletcher had given her, while the corridor went tilted and her head floated. Liu, senior mainday, gave her a head-to-foot sidelong stare and said to Musa, finishing something or another: "Much as we can, anyway."

Secrets. The whole corridor drifted and steadied on Liu's sullen face, before Musa took her by the arm and steered her down-rim toward the galley-section.

"What's going on?" she asked.

"It's all right," Musa said, and let her go at the step-up, where the deck narrowed.

Through the galley-cylinder to rec, in among others, not fast, just walking.

Liu was behind them until then, Liu dropped off at the galley counter and Freeman stayed with her a second, then caught them up again.

Place smelled of beer, the quarters had that same damned vid playing again, she could lip-synch the words. It could have been alterday rec, you could expect McKenzie and Gypsy and the rest to be here, but they were all the wrong faces, the faces that arrived in the morning and left in the evening, they were the bodies that just filled the beds during alterday, and they were standing, watching, conversation fallen off in this uncanny quiet.

Maybe it was just Fletcher's damned pill that made things seem so unnatural and so dangerous. Maybe it was the shots that still hurt and made her a little sick and shocked.

Maybe everybody *was* looking at her and her company, and the rumor had gotten to mainday that there was the fool that had taken on Fitch and made all the trouble.

She wasn't navigating well when she got to Engineering. She did a fast scan to find out NG was there and safe, and that war didn't seem to have broken out – mumbled, "I got to sit, sir," when Bernstein asked what Fletcher had said, and then things were fairly fuzzed after that, except voices kept coming and going and things echoed.

"Think I'm sick," she said, not quite mad, not quite scared, she couldn't get that far, but she was sure now that she'd been

208 C. J. Cherryh

dosed, and that she wasn't in pain anymore, and the back
didn't hurt, and she could have worked, could have done
most anything including float around the section, except
Bernie came over, the skuz, and got her attention with a
hand on the shoulder and asked if she wanted lunch –

– meaning the cup of tea and the little Keis-rolls Services
brought you, the stuff that was about as appetizing as a
glue-stick. Usually she skipped it, but Bernie said it was
a good idea she eat it, and she couldn't find where she'd
misplaced her objections to pushy people who wanted her
to do things: so she did it.

Just absolutely zee'd, no question. She sat there with the
padded seat tilted a little back, watching and listening in
complete placidity, heard people talking around her.

And finally, a while after lunch, the voices started coming
clear and the boards in front of her came into a little clearer
focus.

She had to go to the head. She was aware of being spaced,
she sat there as long as she could stand it, until the discomfort
was more or less overcoming the fuzziness, and finally she
got up and walked.

Somebody grabbed her. It was NG. She blinked at him
and said, "I got a prescription for you, the doc give it to
me. . . ."

She felt damned embarrassed by mid-afternoon, cold sober
again and realizing, with a sudden snap to clarity, that she
was sitting in Engineering at station three, and that people
were talking near her seat, one of them being Freeman, one
being Musa, and one being Bernstein.

"Awake?" Bernstein stopped to ask her.

"Yessir." She reached after the arm of her seat and got up,
still wobbly and trying to remember how she had gotten
there. The whole day was a blank. Just gone. And Bernstein
hadn't thrown her out, just let her sleep it off in her chair.
"Damn," she muttered, "I hope to hell I didn't insult anybody."

Bernstein quirked an eyebrow at her and gave her a smile,
in a good mood, for God's sake, after all she had told
him, after everything that had happened. She leaned on the
seat-back and looked at everybody, at Walden, Slovak and

Keane, with their heads together – and NG over at station one, unscathed.

Hadn't taken Fletcher's pills, evidently.

"Been a real quiet day," Bernstein said then, and looked at Freeman. "Why don't you take off early?"

She might be zee'd. She *wasn't* stupid. She stood there holding to the seat-back, a little pain in her back, a general rubbery feeling about her legs that said a long walk wouldn't be a good idea – and figured it wasn't out of simple muddled priorities that Bernstein let an *Africa* trooper drug-case sit his boards all day and sent a healthy Systems man back to quarters.

There was some talking going on, dammit, stuff was flying between alterday Engineering and Liu's team, on one level and another – Musa had had a go at Liu, Freeman was going back early, it didn't look like there'd been any bar-brawls in Engineering during the shift, and Bernstein wasn't pissed at anything – she knew him when he was, and this wasn't that kind of day, not at all.

*Isn't what Fitch wanted*, she thought, and thought with a little sense of things delicately balanced, that Fitch being out asleep all their day, he was going to wake up and find out things that wouldn't make him happy.

Then they were going to go to sleep and Fitch was going to be awake thinking of ways to fix that.

Hell of a way to carry on a war, she thought, and stood there watching Freeman check out and head back to quarters, doubtless, where he was going to be in time for breakfast with his proper mates.

"Feeling any pain?" Bernstein asked her, as if she was all right with him, as if everything was.

"Not much," she said slowly, wondering what the hell Bernstein was up to. But Bernstein wasn't about to say and she wasn't going to upset things with questions, hell, no.

She sat down again, she didn't bother anything, mostly she ran the sims and watched the colored lights, still phasing out a little – still with a little numbness about the common sense and feeling that she ought to be more spooked than she was.

She wasn't too bad by rec time, all right enough to have a beer or two, sitting with the new guys on the bench, with

NG and Musa and McKenzie and Park and Figi; and NG wasn't too bad either, a little tranked and placid on Fletcher's stuff –

Fletcher had herself an official scan record of a back that justified the happy-stuff she had dosed her with, no matter it didn't halfway hurt until Fletcher started messing with it, and Fletcher had poured enough different kinds of stuff into her to make it real unlikely a test would prove a damned thing. Her *and* NG . . .

God, NG was kind of pitiful, relaxed as he was, sitting on the bench between her and Figi and leaning against the wall – eyes large-pupilled and this sort of happy look on his face, like he was finally just gone, people could do what they wanted with him, hell if he cared.

"You doing all right?" she asked him, and he mumbled that he was, and took another sip of beer.

Not much for him, in that condition. She was getting his drinks for him and no way was he getting any more alcohol, beyond the one, just soft drinks. Probably wouldn't notice. Didn't remember to drink very often.

They sat, they talked, people came by to meet Freeman and his mates and say a welcome-in, and to say how happy NG looked –

Meech, the son of a bitch, even went so far as to reach over and shake NG by the shoulder, with a "Pleasantest I ever saw 'im," at which NG, conscious, might have gone for him, but NG took it with a kind of bewildered look.

Never trust a prescription with just one pill in it.

"He all right?" Gypsy asked.

"Fletch give him a relaxer," Musa said. "Pre-scription."

No sight of Hughes and his pair of skuz since dinner. Watching the vid, maybe. Not so easy to transfer, when it was the whole effing alterday navcomp tekkie crew asking: that was what Musa said – bridge tekkies got used to their operators and vice versa, and mainday was higher rank than alterday, and there was no way in hell the mainday operators were going to take Hughes and crew and no way they were going to shift-trade with alterday just because Lindy Hughes went and pulled a skutty trick.

So Lindy Hughes was somewhere being real quiet this

evening, and it was absolutely amazing how nice people were being, just absolutely amazing, people like Liu and Freeman and all, having every right to be mad, being so friendly it could give you a sugar overload –

Because – it didn't take much brains to figure it – alterday had been hassled, alterday had been rousted and the mofs had come busting into quarters on what just had to be a tip –

– and beat hell out of somebody they couldn't prove a damned thing on.

And *that*, in the humble estimation of the 'decks, was just a step too far.

*Now, I'm not saying what would be illegal to say,* Musa's line had been, she heard him in action, *but I do say if somebody's got the idea to roust us or any one of us we got to take a real firm position on that problem . . . nothing against the rules, no, but we ain't just the machinery on this ship, that you can kick and cuss, and maybe we got to make that clear for people that've gotten a little far from that fact –*

So the Lius and the Musas and the McKenzies and the Gypsy Mullers of the 'decks were smiling and telling their mates to smile and be nice, and Bernie was being nice to Freeman and just bending double and twisting sideways to welcome them in, ditto Musa, and the beers were being bought and people were just walking around being deliberately, cussedly po-lite with each other. So it *was* funny, people *started* having a good time and being in a good mood, like it was a joke going around – and NG being as tranked as he was, people came by just to look at him.

NG being as tranked as he was, he was going from bewildered to having a tolerably good time, especially when a delegation headed by Meech and Rossi bought him the second beer, the one she wasn't going to let him have. Rossi put it into his hands, got his attention with a little pop on the side of the face and said he looked like he needed another beer and a bunch of the bridge techs had gotten together and decided he should have one on them.

NG just stared at Rossi open-mouthed, Rossi walked off, and finally NG started drinking that one, totally glazed.

"Hey," she said, "sips."

She took it down a bit, enough to keep him from passing out where he sat, maybe, and Figi was on his other side – if he fell that way, Figi was built like a rock, probably wouldn't even notice.

You couldn't sit on the rec-deck. You could squat. In case somebody needed through in a hurry. Meech and Rossi and some guys brought some dice, and they squatted and they gambled for cred-points, dece a round.

Damn, even Freeman and his mates were in it, beyond loose, all the way to blown – Battista and Keane headed off to bunks or a locker party, God knew, it was all getting noisy enough in rec nobody heard the first mof-alert.

But the noise fell off fast – real fast, when bridge crew showed up, small, dark fellow, and the squatters stood up and cleared the through-way.

"Kusan," Musa said under his breath.

Helm 2 himself, alterday command.

Kusan looked around him, Kusan scanned faces and said: "Yeager."

It was real, real quiet of a sudden, just noise from down at the end of rec and out of the quarters where the vid was going.

And there was damn-all to do but hand the rest of her beer to Musa and nudge NG over upright so he wouldn't look as crashed as he was, and get up and say, "Yessir, I'm Yeager."

"Ms. Yeager," Helm 2 said, beckoning her to come, and to everybody at large: "As you were."

There wasn't a sound. Not a sound, except of a sudden NG said, "What's going on?" and tried to get up, except Musa grabbed onto him.

"Shut it down!" Musa had to say, too loud.

"Isn't any problem," Bet said.

She wished not. It was Fitch's watch, the tail end of Orsini's. Again.

And she hoped Musa could get a call through to Bernstein, or someone could.

"Bet!" NG yelled, mad as hell, crazy-sounding. Trying to get himself in trouble, that was what he was doing. But people must have shut him up. She was afraid to look back to see.

# Chapter 21

She was still a little out-there while she was walking the corridors beside Kusan, too much beer and one of Fletcher's smaller pain-killers, which combination let her feel no real pain, but she remembered what pain was and who could cause it; and while there was certainly no reg against the 'decks drinking and gambling in rec, there damn sure was a reg against drunk and disorderly. She sneaked a tug at her jumpsuit, a rake of the fingers through her hair, a quick roll-down and snap of the safety-tuck on her sleeves, duty-like. The beer-smell and the wide spill on her knee she couldn't do anything about, and there were probably three and four charges Fitch could think of, just looking at her.

Like beer and pills. Like spitting on the main-deck if Fitch said she'd done it, or a drunk and disorderly – real easy.

But it wasn't Fitch waiting at the step-up to the bridge, it was Orsini – and Orsini was clearly where Kusan was delivering her.

"Are you drunk, Yeager?"

"Not sober, sir, to tell God's truth." She was halfway upset – having gotten one set of ideas arranged in her head and then coming up against Orsini, who was being a fool if he thought it was safe to pull her in at this hour, where what had happened last night could happen again.

If Orsini cared about that.

Orsini looked her up and down. "Spent a lot of today in that condition, haven't you?"

*What d'we got, a damn morals charge?*

*But it was Fletcher did it, Fletcher's Bernstein's friend – isn't she?*

"Yessir, I apologize, sir."

"Come along," Orsini said, and led the way through the bridge-cylinders, past mainday ops, past Helm, past –

Fitch stood on the bridge watching them go past. He didn't

challenge Orsini. She wasn't sure if he followed them, then.
She couldn't hear, in the general racket two sets of footsteps
made on the hollow deck, in the whisper of multiple cooling
and circulation fans and other people moving around on
business. She just stayed with Orsini, wondering what in
hell he was after, telling herself it was all right, Bernstein
hadn't acted overly upset with what she had told him —

*Like they'd known already that something was wrong about me,
and Bernie was still on my side* —

*But Orsini thought I was Mallory's. . . .*

She did take a fast look back, to see where Fitch was.
Not behind them . . . but Fitch undoubtedly knew where
they were going, and maybe Fitch was just waiting for the
shift-change, knowing that when Orsini was through, it was
always his turn.

*Hope to hell you got a smart notion how to stop that, Mr.
Orsini, sir.*

*Hope to hell you got some concern about that.*

*Hope to hell you and Bernie came to some understanding about
whatever's going on. . . .*

Orsini passed right by his own office, passed by Fitch's.

*Where're we going?* she thought. And: *Oh, God . . .*

They stopped in front of a door with a stencilled: *Wolfe, J.*
and no more designation than Fitch's office or Orsini's had.

Orsini pushed the button, the door opened on the office
and the man inside, and Orsini said: "Yeager, sir."

Fancy place, carpet, panels, a big black desk and the captain
sitting there waiting for her — blond, slight man in khaki.
Pale eyes that didn't care shit what your excuse was for
existing, just what you were doing that crossed his path for
five minutes and annoyed him.

The door shut behind her. Orsini left her. Wolfe rocked
his chair back, folded his arms.

Wolfe said, "Machinist, are you?"

She felt distanced from everything around her. Nothing
added, except that everything she had told Bernie had spread,
Orsini knew, now Wolfe knew. She thought, between one
heavy heartbeat and the next: *Bernie, damn you, well, you had
to, didn't you?*

She said, "I worked as that, sir. On *Ernestine*."

"Rank."

"M-Sgt. Elizabeth A. Yeager, sir." And she added, because she was a damn smartass fool, and she hated being crowded: "Retired."

Wolfe wasn't amused, Wolfe sat there looking up at her, with no expression at all.

"*Africa*, is it?"

"Yes, sir. Was." Nothing else to say. Bernie'd evidently said it all.

Damn sure.

And she'd had this dumb dim hope that Bernie didn't think she was a threat and that maybe all the way to top command, a ship that got its crew out of station brigs didn't give shit what it raked in for crew –

Except she'd all along discounted Wolfe.

Damn dumb, Yeager, damn dumb. So who do they think you're working for if you aren't Mallory's?

Effin' obvious, Yeager.

"You lied to me," Wolfe said.

"Nossir. Everything the way I said. Crew slot is all I wanted, it's all I want right now."

Long silence. Wolfe never had any expression. She stood there, just went away a little inside, figured past a certain point they were going to do whatever they wanted to do and if command had made up their minds to freight her off to Pell and Mallory or space her inside the hour, there was damn-all she could do about it.

But this man could. *Could* help her, if he would, if what happened in the 'decks ever concerned him at all, if he didn't just leave crew to suffer Fitch and Orsini's private war and their maneuvering for power –

There were ships like that, in the Fleet.

"When did you leave your ship?"

"Pell, sir. When the Fleet pulled away, I was on dockside." She added, uninvited, hammering away at what she wasn't sure Wolfe had heard the first and the second time: "Not my ship now, sir. This is."

She wasn't sure Wolfe wasn't outright crazy. She wasn't sure she ought to take one course or the other with him. Or maybe nobody was loyal to this ship, and Wolfe just didn't figure her. He had that kind of look, just the least doubt in that cold, ice-blue stare.

Maybe he would just throw her back to Fitch and Orsini and let them fight it out.

*What in hell does Wolfe do on this ship?* she had asked Musa. And Musa, uncomfortable in the question: *He ain't a real activist. . . .*

Man had to be aware too, that he wasn't totally safe, if she wanted to commit suicide and take him with her.

But he sat there. He rocked back in his chair and looked at her a long time and said, "What's the last contact you had with the Fleet?"

That was the question. That was the big one. "Last was my com breaking up. On Pell. Nothing since." She could see him saying to Fitch: Find out what she knows. She said, quietly: "'Decks never knew anything, no more than here, sir."

Long, long silence, Wolfe just sitting there.

"Master sergeant, was it?"

"Yessir."

"Mechanic?"

"On my own rig, sir. Some of us were."

"Tactical."

"Tac-squad, sir."

"Where before that?"

"Came aboard at sixteen, sir. Born on a miner-ship."

Wolfe pushed his chair back on its track, got up, walked to the side of the desk. He wasn't armed. She'd thought he might be.

He walked to the side of her, walked around to her back. She didn't know what a civ would do under the circumstance, gone straight from dumb smartass kid to shipboard manners a skut better have to survive in the 'decks. And those said stand still and keep your mouth shut when a mof wanted to think what he was going to do about you.

*Anything you say, sir.*

*Til you prove you're a fool, sir.*

*Til I know I got no percentage in anything, sir. Then I'll take a few.*

*But —*

*God, what'd they do with NG then? What'd NG do, himself?*

Wolfe walked over to the low table and the cushion-chairs at the side of the office, meddled with something as if he'd forgotten her.

Maybe he had. Maybe he was just slightly crazy. Maybe he was going to see how long a skut could stand there without panicking and doing something stupid.

Indefinitely. Sir.

"Sit down," Wolfe said. She looked at him. He was offering her a chair at the office table.

That spooked her, when yelling wouldn't have. "Yessir," she said, and came and started to sit down, and then thought about her work-clothes and the chance of beer-spills, deck-dust or worse on that pretty white upholstery. She dusted off, for what good that would do, but Wolfe having sat down, she sat, opposite him, and watched him open the little box there.

Chess set. Real one, not just a sim. Real board, real pieces, God knew how old.

"You play?" he asked.

"Some," she said. In the 'decks you played anything and everything.

"Black or white?"

God, he was crazy, she was sitting here in the hands of a crazy man. "Your pick, sir."

He turned the box, gave her white.

So the first mmoove had to be hers.

She frustrated him a couple of times, which he took with that same dead-cold, appraising look at the board that he gave to her while she answered his questions . . . long, long after the shift-change bell.

What mining-ship?

What's Porey like?

Finally: How much elapsed-time on Tripoint-Pell?

Question that could kill a ship. Kill everyone she'd served with – if she was tekkie enough to know that answer down to a hair, what *Africa*'s running-cap was.

But you had to know how much mass she'd been hauling.

Wolfe asked that too. And she honestly didn't know. The elapsed-time down to a half hour, but not a thing about the mass. . . .

"Made many runs in the Hinder Stars?"

"A couple. Mostly Pell–Mariner–Pan-paris. Wyatt's. Viking."

You'd remember *that*, sir. Remember it damn well, if you were a spook during the war.

While his fine-boned fingers moved a piece to threaten a knight, and a rook, some moves down.

"You remember the *Gull*?"

Name ought to mean something. There'd been a lot of names. They'd taken the *Gull*, a little ship, hell if she could sort out whether that was the one they'd blown or one of the ships that had decel'ed and taken boarders when they were operating at Tripoint.

Ship-corridors through the mask, past the green readout glow. Scared faces. Mostly scared faces.

Except the fools who tried to make a fight of it, locked body to body with a rider-ship, with marines on their deck.

"Dunno, sir, we took it. Tripoint. I recall the name."

*Something to do with you, sir? Or this ship?*

Wolfe didn't say more than that.

She took a pawn, worrying was she supposed to do that. Wolfe was a better player. Wolfe was moves ahead, and he set you up a route he wanted you to take.

Did it this time.

"Shee – " she started to say, and swallowed it in time.

"Tac-squad," Wolfe said, moving a pawn. "Boarding party. Stations or ships."

"Yessir."

"Know what you're doing with docking equipment?"

"Yessir."

"Weapons systems?"

"Yessir."

She lost a pawn. Was going to lose a knight. She saw it. Moved the rook.

Damn.

"Armor?"

"Yessir."

"What do you think about this ship, Sgt. Yeager?"

"I'm not a sergeant anymore, sir."

"What do you think about this ship?"

"I got friends aboard."

"On *Africa* too."

That was a hard thought; and damned clear what he was asking. "Yessir. But no way this ship could take her, and if she could, that's the way it is, got friends there, got friends on board here." She moved the threatened knight. "Don't even know who's alive anymore. Here I do. Me, for one."

"If you weren't on board?"

She honestly thought about that, put herself back on *Africa*, with *Loki* for a target. Her hand hovered over a pawn and she lost her focus. Saw herself up on charges, old Junker Phillips' face –

"Have to shoot me," she said, and made the move, giving up the pawn. "I dunno, dunno I could ever get to that, sir. But I got people here – got a lot of people on this ship."

"So I've heard."

Heard about me and NG. God, I got him in trouble, maybe Musa, too, if Musa wasn't what he is.

McKenzie – Park and Figi – all those guys –

Maybe Bernstein, too.

Wolfe took the pawn. She took his knight.

She saw it coming, then. Rook took queen in four moves. Check and mate.

She bit her lip, surveyed the board.

Knew Wolfe was several moves ahead in the other game, too.

"You can go," Wolfe said.

"Thank you, sir." She got up carefully, as if the whole place was rigged with explosives. She was sweating. She only half-felt the pain in her back.

*What do I say? Enjoyed the game, sir?*

Wolfe let her walk to the door, let her open it, let her walk out into the restricted section by herself.

She walked through to the bridge, through Fitch's territory to the med-area corridor, through the galley to rec and the darkened quarters.

0258 alterday.

She went to Musa, told Musa she was back. Musa was wide awake, asked her: "You all right, Bet?"

"Fine," she whispered back, only then getting a bad case of the shakes. She went right on over to NG's bunk, but Musa followed her. Musa said, "He's sleeping one off."

Sleeping one off, hell. He was tied to the damn bunk, out cold. "Dammit," she said, popped him a light one on the cheek and started working at the knot, shaking so badly she could hardly work the cord through, especially when NG came to a little and started pulling. "What'd you give him?"

"Figi's sleeper hold, for starters. – He's all right. I've been watching him."

"Hell! – Hold still!"

"Bet, . . ."

He wasn't crazy. Not half as crazy as where she'd been. She got him loose, he hugged her til he hurt her back, but she didn't mind that. She had sore muscles and he had a bitch of a hangover, evidently, because he made a miserable sound and held his head.

"Fitch?" he asked.

"Wolfe," she said.

He dropped his hands. Musa said, beside her, "What happened?"

"Captain wanted a chess partner," she said, and almost spilled what Wolfe had been asking her for three hours, she was so aching tired and so rattled. She got it together, remembering nobody in the 'decks knew what the mofs knew about her. Most of all NG didn't know. And she didn't know how long that would last or what he would do when he found out.

Merchanter, lost from his ship. And there was one way, in the War, that that would have happened.

"That was all," she said. "We played chess."

# Chapter 22

"What happened?" was a question she got too damned often in the shower-line and at breakfast, everybody from McKenzie to Masad out of Cargo, people coming up to her, and then putting their heads together to whisper the business elsewhere.

The first time she was caught a little off-balance, and hesitated, and said, "The captain asked into it," as if it was the Fitch business, which was a damn lie, at bottom, and she wished she'd never been so stupid – like a challenge to Fitch, and using Wolfe's name for a weapon. It might get back to Fitch. It might make him think twice. It might also make him talk to the captain about it, and that wasn't the outcome she wanted, damn sure.

So she wished she could take that back. She changed it as far as she could the next time she was asked – said, "Captain wanted to ask me some questions, said keep my mouth shut."

Damn stupid, Yeager. That mouth's going to kill you someday.

She ate her breakfast with her mates, and they were worrying about Fitch, they were thinking about Wolfe and trying to reckon whether Wolfe was going to come down on her side, that was all they understood about it.

"I'd be gone," NG had said quietly, in the dark, before the little sleep she had gotten, "except for Wolfe. I don't know why. Favor to Bernie, I guess. I don't understand it."

Most she'd ever gotten out of NG on that topic, that dozen or so words.

And when she thought about it this morning, she thought Fitch had to be worried right now, damn worried, and that she ought to be happy about that situation, ought to thank God Wolfe had stepped in, and ought to be a whole lot more cheerful than she was.

Except Fitch just meant to kill her. Wolfe seemed to have decided something last night, Wolfe had let her go, Wolfe had written her down as a liability or an asset, she didn't know which.

In either case, — expendable.

Hell, she thought, sipping her morning tea, tail back in the fire. What's different than it ever was?

She had that answered until she saw NG looking at people this morning, looking around him, looking at her and Musa and paying attention to human beings the way he could those damn boards, saner this morning than she'd ever seen him.

He'd gotten drunk with friends last night, people had cared enough to sit on him and knock him stupid to save him, and she'd gotten back safe, God in the person of Wolfe had intervened to stop Fitch from killing her, and maybe things weren't going to be the hell they'd been for three years.

Yeah.

*Nothing could hurt him before this. Not even Fitch. He wasn't sane enough to hurt, when I came aboard, and look at all I've done for him. Helped him no end, haven't I?*

*Man'd have died for me last night, all he could've done, but he'd have done it.*

*Maybe he's got some crazy notion my trouble is his fault. Maybe he thinks he's responsible for me, the same as for Cassel.*

*If he ever was responsible for Cassel.*

*Can't prove it, can't ever prove it, can't even do that much for him.*

*And what when he learns what he's been sleeping with?*

Dealing with NG in a social situation was like handling a live grenade — you really had to pay attention, all the time, to the little things — like how he'd jump like he was wired if somebody touched him unexpected, he'd tense up when people came up on him, he'd do this little subtle flinch when he knew people were going to speak to him. You had to know him to know it was a flinch, but he was just on-alert all the time, schiz as hell, trying so damned hard, and sane enough to be scared, himself, that somebody was going to startle him and he was going to blow up — he held onto her and Musa like they were his lifeline, that was what he was doing at breakfast, with people asking him how he was doing, how's the head, NG?

Hughes had just made himself scarce. Headed off to work early, thank God.

And NG was doing all right, so far, with social acceptability cold sober, doing all right and once, with Freeman, even managing a thin, tentative grin . . . not the smartass one, the real, wide-open one.

Doing just fine until they got to Engineering and Bernstein met them with: "Yeager, Mr. Orsini wants to see you."

"It's all right," she said to NG, and touched his arm. "I know what about. No problem."

"What?" NG asked her point-blank, delaying her at the door. "Fitch?"

"They're just trying to figure out some things." Best lie she could manage. "Fitch won't lay a hand on me. You can believe it."

So she checked out of Engineering before she'd even checked in, didn't say a thing to Bernstein about last night, and Bernstein didn't say anything to her.

Probably Bernstein and Orsini had talked. Orsini and the captain would have. Maybe the captain and Fitch – last night, his day, after she had left.

So she went up-rim to Orsini's office, she sat down and she got what she thought she would, question after question, while Orsini took notes on the TranSlate.

Nossir, nossir, yessir, nossir, I don't know anything about ops, sir.

At least Orsini didn't act as if *he* was out to kill her.

"You have a problem with Mr. Fitch," Orsini said.

"I hope not, sir."

"You have a problem," Orsini said.

"Yessir."

"I trust you won't be stupid about it."

"I don't plan to be, sir."

Orsini gave her a long, long look. And started asking other questions, the kind she didn't want to answer.

Specific detail, on *Africa*, on her cap, what she carried, how many she carried –

I don't know, she said sometimes. Sometimes she shied off, inside, but she couldn't do that – had to make the jump, finally, and be *Loki*'s, or not, and talk or not.

*What can I tell them that Mallory couldn't? Hell, they got a renegade Fleet captain giving them any cap they ask. What's anything I know worth, against that?*

So she answered, sat there telling things that might help kill her ship, one little detail and the other and deeper and deeper – far as a belowdecks skut could betray her ship, she did that –

Because here was here, that was what she kept telling herself. Because the war was lost, whatever it had ever been for, and Teo was dead, and the ship she was on was all that had to matter anymore –

Nothing to go back to. Pirates, people called the Fleet now. Maybe that was so.

"War's over," Orsini said. "There's nothing Mazian can win. Not in the long run. Just pointless destruction. Just more casualties. Best thing Mazian could do for his people is come in, sign the armistice – take what he's got coming and save the poor sods on his ships. But he won't do that."

She saw the docks again, being stationside, permanently, doing station scut, if they didn't do a wipe on you and leave you too schiz to defend yourself. Or there was Thule, maybe, one damn great hole they could dump all Alliance's problems into, same as they'd dumped Q-zone.

Hell if they'd come in. Hell if they would.

"Let's get specific again," Orsini said, and she didn't want to, didn't want to talk for a while, kept thinking about Teo and wondering if Bieji was still alive on *Africa*.

Bieji'd give her one of his black looks and tell her no hard feelings, but he'd try to blow her ass away.

Stay alive, Junker Phillips used to yell, *stay alive, you stupid-ass bastards, I got too much invested in you –*

"Yeager?"

"Yessir," she said. Here and now again. This ship, these mates.

Nothing personal, Bieji.

She sat there finally, throat sore from talking, Orsini note-taking again.

She thought, What I've done, there's no halfway, is there? Can't betray these mates, *and* them.

She wanted to go somewhere and take a pill for her back and her head, she wanted to have a bath and see NG's face and Musa's and be back in rec with her shift, and remember why she wanted this ship. Right now she couldn't, right now she couldn't remember anything but *Africa*, couldn't see anything but Bieji and Teo and how it had been –

But those had been the good years. Those were the years before she'd lived off *Africa*, before she'd seen *Ernestine*, been from Pell to Thule and wherever they were now –

– older, maybe. Tired. Maybe just taking any out better luck might give her. She wasn't sure, unless she could feel what she felt on this ship again and shake the devils Orsini called up.

Orsini put down the stylus and got up from his desk, going to send her back down to Engineering, she thought: there was still time enough before the shift change.

God, she had to go back and go on pretending there was nothing wrong . . .

Had to tell NG somehow – before he found it out from somebody else.

"I want to show you something," Orsini said, motioning to the door.

"Sir?"

He didn't answer that. He showed her out, up-rim toward the bridge, to a stowage locker. He opened the door and turned on the lights.

Like so many corpses, pale, fire-scarred body-shapes stood belted to the left wall.

Armor.

*Africa*, one stencil said. *Europe*, the other. And names.

*Walid, – M. Walid.*

Memory of a small, dark man, grinning. Always with the jokes.

God . . .

Orsini was looking at her. She walked into the locker, laid a hand on the one rig. "Knew this man," she said. And then, afraid Orsini would read a threat into that: "Acquaintance, anyway."

"Collected it at Pell," Orsini said.

"You could've got mine," she said. "Left it there."

"Maybe your friend was lucky."

She shook her head.

"They're not in good shape," Orsini said. "Figured to

use them in emergencies: figured they were free, why turn them down? Lifesupport halfway works, most of the servos operate on that one, – it'll move, at any rate, but nobody's got time to fix it."

"Not real comfortable," she said, thinking, God, the damn fools, with a gut-deep memory of what a human joint felt like with a servo pushing it just a little past reasonable, wondering if Mallory who must've let them have the rigs had ever provided the manuals. She touched the surfaces, tried the tension in the arm, felt her stomach upset at what was going on in her brain, all the old information coming up like pieces of a disaster – parameters, connections, –

– her hands were close to shaking. It was *Africa*'s gut, the armor-shop, the voices she hadn't been able to recall, the smells and the sounds.

"Fixable?" Orsini asked.

"Yessir," she said, and looked at him, trying to see the white plastic lockers and Orsini's face, not the gray, echoing space she remembered. She said, knowing nobody gave a damn, "But I don't want to."

"Why?"

*I don't want to handle this stuff again. I don't want to think about it –*

She said, realizing she had stirred suspicion, "Thought I was through with rigs like this." Then another reason hit her, in the gut. "And I don't want people to know where I come from."

Orsini said, quietly: "Can you get these things working right?"

"Yessir, probably."

Man wasn't paying attention, man didn't care. She didn't expect otherwise.

"No need to have it general knowledge," Orsini said. "We're insystem, slow rate, going to dock here and fill. You can make it back and forth up the lift. You've got enough level deck here."

She looked at the L by the entry, thought about what she could get to in the shop. "Yessir." Without enthusiasm. It was in-dock work he meant and no liberty. But she hadn't really expected one, under the circumstances. "Not real easy. But I could do that."

"Not all crew gets liberty," Orsini said. "Takes five years' seniority. And the captain's approval."

"Yessir."

"You might eventually get a posting out of it," Orsini said. "If you have the right attitude."

She stood there thinking, *Right attitude. Hell.* And thinking that the mofs could think they owned these rigs, but you didn't just suit up and have everything work. She didn't say, *Who am I supposed to fit this for?* and explain that part of it; or think she had to say something if Orsini didn't.

Maybe Orsini would call that a bad attitude.

She just said, "I'll see what I can do, sir."

# Chapter 23

The news about their heading into dock was on general com when she headed back for Engineering, forty-odd minutes to shift-change.

"Everything all right?" Bernie asked, asking more than that, she reckoned, and she frowned at him, just not able to come back from it and knowing she had to – had to put a decent face on things and not do anything that could make Bernstein wonder about her, because Bernie was watching, Bernie was going to be making regular reports to Orsini and Wolfe and maybe Fitch, and she knew it. You asked a body to be a turncoat and you'd better keep an eye on them, if you had any respect at all for them.

Damn right, sir.

Nor trust them if they smiled at you.

She said, "Wasn't a real good time, sir."

Bernie looked sad at that. But at least he didn't frown back at her.

"Anything the matter?" NG said – NG the first one to come up to her, on his own, when you never used to get NG out front on anything.

She said, thinking fast, "Looks like I don't get a liberty."

It wasn't what NG had worried about, for sure. He looked upset, touched her arm. "Hell, I never have had. *I'll* be here."

Got her right in the heart. She couldn't think for a second, couldn't remember what she'd decided two beats ago her story was, or put any organization in her thoughts.

*NG'll be on board. Him and me. God.*

"You didn't expect it," Musa said, from beside her.

"Dunno, didn't think, til they made the announcement; and Orsini told me it was five years. Shit, Musa, – "

She didn't want to think about months and years. A week

was hard enough, NG bound to ask what she was doing topside while they were in dock, or why Orsini had her out of main Engineering, going back and forth between the shop and topside.

Damn!

Musa gave her a hug around the shoulders, friendly. Bernie didn't mind a little PDA, NG didn't say anything else, back in his habit of no-comment, and she tried to cheer up, which she reckoned made it a tolerably good act.

Damn, damn, and damn.

They did a burn before shift-change, they started doing others, after.

"*We'll be docking at Thule Station . . .*" Wolfe said on general address.

She felt sick at her stomach.

*Wonder if Nan and Ely are still there. How long've we been out, realtime?*

She counted jumps they had made, figured maybe as much as a year, stationside.

She stowed everything she wouldn't need, stuffed a duffle with things she would, same as those who were going stationside – "Hard luck, Bet," people dropped by to say, and some few of them, McKenzie included, were cheeky enough to say, "Yeah, well, but you and NG got free bunks and all the beer aboard. – Want me to buy you anything?"

She checked with the purser's office and found out she could draw on her liberty money even being held aboard, and that NG was downright affluent, never having used his liberty credits except for on-board beers.

"Vodka," she said to McKenzie, trusting him with a sizeable draft on her account. "Walford's is cheap, Green dock, listen, I got some incidentals I need, stand you three bottles if you hit supply for me."

"Hell," McKenzie said, "give us a list. Nobody's in port but us, we got to make do with dockers, and you know Figi's going to be in a damn card game from the time he hits – Park and me can go shopping, buy you anything you want."

"You're a love," she said, feeling better for the moment, and took McKenzie off in the corner and exchanged about twenty concentrated minutes of accumulated favor-points.

Real special, this time, rushed as it was – hard to know what it was, maybe that they were both in a desperate hurry, and taking time to be mutually polite, maybe just that they'd gotten beyond acquainted and all the way over to looking out for each other.

She wanted that right now, wanted somebody it just wasn't complicated with, who cared about her; and she hurt her back doing it and didn't regret it later, when the take-hold was sounding and she hauled thirty kilos of hammock and duffle down to the stowage area to clip in and hang on with the rest of alterday and most of mainday.

Not the mofs. Mofs and a few of the mainday tekkies got to ride the lift down from the bridge to the airlock, of course – except for the lucky few who drew duty part or all of the port-call.

*I hope to hell Fitch gets a long liberty. Hope the sonuvabitch gets laid at least once. Might help his disposition.*

Mostly she worried about Hughes and his friends being out there with Musa and her and NG not being. "Keep an eye on him," she'd asked McKenzie, and McKenzie'd sworn he would.

They made a tolerably soft dock, no teeth cracked, no bruises, and crew stood in harness waiting for permission to move about, laying grandiose plans for the bars they were going to hit – *yeah, sure, mates, on Thule.* . . .

They got the permission, they unclipped, they milled or they settled down on their duffles and checked through their cred-slips.

Johnny Walters had left his kit. There was usually some poor sod. There was always a volunteer who'd get it down by shift-change. "Yeah," Bet said. "NG or I, one. Who else? Make a list."

Damn list always grew when people found out there was a quarters-run going. "Shit. Write it down! I got a year's worth of favor-points coming from you guys. . . ."

Except Dussad, out of mainday Cargo, who muttered something about having NG into his stuff –

"You want a favor?" Bet asked, swinging around, read the

name on the pocket and said, "Dussad? You want a favor or you got a problem with me and my mate?"

"You got lousy taste," Dussad said, and of all people, Liu said, "Take it easy." And McKenzie said, "Nothing wrong with NG. He just doesn't talk too good."

"Ask Cassel," a mainday woman said.

God, they couldn't move, they were here til they got orders. NG just stood there, nobody could go anywhere or do anything.

Gypsy said, "Man's got by that. Man's stood his watches, took his shit for it, long enough."

And Musa:

"Damn valve blew, Ann, you get your head in the way of it and it *happens*, it don't matter if you got a mate there. The rest of it's hell and away too old to track."

"He got an opinion?"

"Let him the hell alone," Bet said, and threw NG a look, couldn't not; NG was just staring somewhere else, jaw clenched – God, he couldn't talk, just damn couldn't, out-there for the moment. "Let him alone."

"I know what his mates are saying. I want to hear what he's got to say about it, all right? There's a lot of trouble going on. I want to know what the guy has to say."

McKenzie said, "I'll buy you a drink, Dussad. We'll talk about it."

Quiet for a second or two, real tense. The lift clanked and whined, high up on the rim – mofs doing their business with dockside.

"Drop it," Liu said. "Drop it. Dussad. Later. All right?"

"What about my kit?" Walters asked, in the silence after. "Is somebody going to go after it?"

They finished the fetch-downs list, mofs went out and did customs, lot of noise from the lift and the airlock; and they waited and talked, and bitched, –

Prime bitch coming, if you drew duty, if you had to get up and wish everybody Drink one for me, while the captain got on the general com and told everybody clear out and when the board-call was. "I got a couple of old friends here," Bet said to Musa. "Drop in by the Registry, wish Nan Jodree and Dan Ely g'day for me. Stand 'em a drink if they got the time."

Depressing, when everybody cleared out in a noisy rush and left the downside corridor all to the two of them – and NG paying attention again, but down-faced, quiet. Damn that Dussad.

"Well?" she said, looking at NG, and sighed and picked up the duffle and the hammock. "Where d'we put it?"

NG looked at the corridor and looked up and down the curves in either direction, and finally sighed and said, in all that awful quiet of shutdown: "Locker's all right."

They got Walters' kit down, a matter of climbing up the curve using the safety clips, also stuff for Bala and Gausen and Cierra, – and for Dussad, NG did that, did all the climbing around, the dangerous part, where you could take a long, long fall if you got careless clambering through the quarters. "You'll hurt your back," he told her. "I'll do the climbing, you just stay down here and catch it."

He acted all right. She wished she knew what to say about Dussad and mainday shift, that had been NG's – and Cassel's. She wished she knew what was going on in his head and she wished she had Musa here, to talk to NG, if nothing else. Or Bernstein. Bernie could get through to him. She wasn't sure she could, she wasn't sure she wanted to get into the topic with him at all.

*Damn* Dussad. Hughes had stayed out of it, Hughes had to be taking all of it in and wanting to say something – and there was no doubt he would be saying something, in the bars and up and down dockside for five days, causing as much damage as he could, dropping stuff in ears he knew would be receptive, and in a liberty, down to the last day, the shifts mixed.

*Damn*, she wanted to be out there. Most of all she wanted NG out there in Musa's keeping, not on-ship, brooding on things, working alone while his partner was off doing what she couldn't let him know –

She ought to tell NG, *had* to tell him sooner or later what was going on, and alone on the alterday watch might have been a decent time to do it, except for Dussad and that damn woman from mainday, – Thomas, she thought it was, Ann Thomas, navcomp, *Hughes'* opposite. Alterday *and* mainday nav both were a pain in the ass, she decided – must be

something in the mindset; while Dussad, out of Cargo, was
a hard-nosed hard-sell sonuvabitch, but you couldn't fault
him too much, – just want to bust his damn thick skull,
was all.

"Eyes up!" NG yelled from overhead. "Fragiles!"

They weren't the only crew missing liberty: Parker and
Merrill were on mainday duty in Engineering, and Dussad
and Hassan just had a partial, going out to the suppliers' and
dealing for the ship, with whatever spare time they were
efficient enough to gain; while Wayland and Williams were
on a three-day pass, having to come back and supervise the
supply loading, and a lucky handful of bridge crew, rotating
off-ship for sleep and whatever rec-time they could squeeze
in, was responsible for the fill, indicator-watching, mostly,
and communication with Thule Central – an ops routine she
knew, for once, the intricacies of cables and hoses, the names
of the lines and what the hazards were – learned it because
you'd always had to worry about sabotage, in the war, and
when *Africa* was in dock, the squad was always out there in
full kit, checking the hook-ups, posting guard –

Dammit.

She kept remembering. She didn't want to. There were
those dead rigs topside, waiting for her, like ghosts –

And NG was going to ask questions, NG had a natural
right to ask questions about where she was going every day,
and why.

They had the night, at least. "I'm not making love in any
hammock," she said to NG, setting up, having consulted
Parker and Merrill via com on what was going to be quarters
for four people, alternately, in the main stowage, – so they
just spread their two hammocks down for padding on the
stowage deck, and, it turned out during the set-up, got
themselves a brand-new bottle of vodka when Walters and
some of the guys showed up to pay off the fetch-downs.

"You sure ain't missing much," Walters delayed to say to
them. "Place is *dead*, places are closed up, about two bars and
a skuzzy sleepover still open, and that's it. Nothing alive out
there but echoes. . . ."

Made her feel sad, for some odd reason, maybe just that

it was a slice out of her life, however miserable, maybe that there was something spooky about it now, knowing a piece of humankind was dying, the dark was coming just like they'd said, taking the first bases humans had made leaving Sol System.

Like those names in the restroom they just painted over. *Polaris*, and *Golden Hind*. God, Musa could probably remember Thule in its heyday.

And came back, a crewman on an FTL, to see it die.

"Bet?" NG asked her, nudged her arm, when the lock-door had shut, when Johnny Walters was away to the docks, and she thought, for no reason, *Everything we ever did, – the War, and all, they'll paint right over, like it never was, like none of us ever died –*

*Mazian doesn't see it. Still fighting the war –*

*Hell. What's winning? What's winning, when everything's changing so fast nobody can predict what's going to be worth anything?*

She felt NG's hand on her shoulder. She kept seeing Thule docks, Ritterman's apartment, the Registry –

The nuclear heat of Thule's dim star.

Curfew rang.

Walters' vodka, bed, privacy, all the beer they could reasonably drink and all the frozen sandwiches they could reasonably eat, out of Services, next door.

Wasn't too bad, she decided, putting tomorrow out of her mind, the way she had learned to do. Just take the night, get her and NG fuzzed real good –

Tell him later. The man deserved a little time without grief.

So they ate the sandwiches with a beer, chased them with vodka, made love.

Didn't need the pictures. Didn't need anything. NG was civilized, terribly careful of her back –

Not worth worrying about, she said. And got rowdy and showed him a trick they used to do down in the 'decks, her and Bieji.

"God," he said. He ran his hand over the back of her neck.

Nobody else had that touch. Nobody else ever made her shiver like that. Nobody else, ever.

*He* was the one who got claustrophobic . . . but for a second she couldn't breathe.

Here and now, Yeager. This ship.

This man. This partner.

"You all right?" he asked.

"Fine," she said, and caught the breath, heavy sigh. "I just can't get stuff out of my mind."

He worked on that problem. Did tolerably good at it after a minute or two, til she was doing real deep breathing and thinking real near-term. – One thing with NG, he didn't question much, and he knew the willies on a first-name basis. Knew what could cure them for a while, too.

She said, somewhere after, when she found the courage: "Bernstein just left me this nasty little list of stuff, topside, seems I'm the mechanic and you got the boards." She tried to say what it was. And had another attack of pure, despicable cowardice. Couldn't trust it. Couldn't predict what he'd do. Didn't want a blow-up til she'd gotten a day or so alone with him, softened him up, got an idea what was going on with him. "I hate it like hell. You're going to be alone down there."

"Been alone before," he said. "Been alone on port-calls for years."

He didn't ask what the work was. She told herself that if he had asked she would have gone ahead and spilled it right then. But he didn't. Wasn't even curious.

Thank God.

# Chapter 24

"Ms. Yeager," Wolfe said, when she arrived on the bridge and looked around for the mof-in-charge. The captain was not who she was looking to find. "Sir," she said, and by way of explanation: "Mr. Orsini –" Wolfe nodded. "Go to it, Ms. Yeager."

"Thank you, sir." She gave a bob of the head and took herself and her tool-kit to the number one topside stowage, where she could draw an easier breath.

It wasn't Fitch in charge, thank God, thank God.

Not Fitch in charge anywhere else on the ship, she hoped, but there was no way to find that out without asking, and she didn't figure asking was real politic. Mofs were handling the matter, mofs had their ways of saving face, and if Fitch *was* on board he was going to be twice touchy if they had him under any hands-off orders regarding her.

Couldn't push it. Didn't even dare worry about it.

So she got down to work, clambered up the inset rungs to set a 200 kilo expansion track between two locker uprights, hooked a pulley in, ran a cable and a couple of hooks into the service rings of the better of the two rigs, and hauled the thing up where she could work without fighting it.

You could figure how Walid might have died – considering there was no conspicuous damage to the rig, no penetration at first glance that ought to have killed him – but those that got blown out into space had been low-priority on rescue. Nobody in authority on Pell had much cared about the survival of any trooper, and the air only held you for six hours.

Six hours – floating in the dark of space or the hellish light of Pell's star.

Arms wouldn't work far enough to reach the toggles. Couldn't even suicide. The rig had caught some kind of an impact – when it was blown out Pell's gaping wounds into vacuum, maybe; it had survived the impact, but it was shock enough to throw play into every joint it owned –

– and spring a circulation seal in the right wrist and a pressure seal in the same shoulder. Scratch the six hours. You could lose a wrist seal and live without a hand, but when you lost a main body seal, you just hoped you froze fast instead of boiled slow, – and which happened then depended on how much of you was exposed to a nearby sun.

"Helluva way, Walid." With a pat on the vacant shell. "You should've ducked."

*Lousy sensahumor, Bet,* –

Walid's voice. Clank of pulleys, skuts bitching up and down the aisles while they suited up, the smell of that godawful stuff they sprayed the insides with. . . .

A whiff of it came when she took a look at the seals. Even after a guy died in the damn thing, even after the rig had been standing months and years in a chilled-down storage locker, the inside still smelled like lavatory soap.

She took inventory on the *Europe* rig, real simple c.o.d., a lousy big puncture in the gut, right under the groin-seal. Big guy, name of W. Graham, *Europe*'s tac-squad B-team – Willie, she remembered, strong as any two guys, but no chance at all against a squeeze or an impact powerful enough to punch right through quadplex Flexyne.

God.

So, well, if you wanted to see how bad the joints were, the easiest way was just to strip down and start building the rig around you joint by joint, freezing not only your ass off, but various other sensitive spots, because the internal heater wouldn't work until the rig was powered up, and you didn't want the power on while you were making tension adjustments. You messed around with lousy little pin-sized wrenches and screwdrivers and tried not to chatter your teeth loose while you were getting the wrench or the screwdriver seated in little inconspicuous holes, about three to five of them a joint, and you fussed and you messed with one turn against another, and you tried the tension in this and that joint, til it felt right.

While your nose ran.

But you warmed up, joint by joint. Joint by joint, starting

with the boots, the rig cased you in and linked up, joint with joint and contact with contact, heavy as sin and about all you could do to lift a knee and test the flex, clear up to the body-armor.

Tension-straps between two layers of the ceramic, each with their little access caps, and their nasty little adjustment screws on the action, too, four or five a segment, that pulled the sensor contacts up against bare skin, contacts that were going to carry signals to the hydraulics – all those had to be tightened or loosened, so they'd all loosen up to the right degree when you pulled the release to get out of the armor, and go right back to the proper configuration when you got inside and threw the master switch: you could feel all those little contact-points, and they shouldn't press hard, but they shouldn't lose contact either, and the padding that kept you from bumping up against those contacts too hard in spots had to be tightened down or loosened up with another lot of fussy little spring-screws.

Some damned fool had just got in and powered up. Probably fallen on his ass or sprained something just trying to stand up.

She hoped to hell it had been Fitch.

Maybe it was that thought that brought him.

The door opened. And she was sitting there on the deck half-naked and half-suited, with Fitch standing in a warm draft from the door.

Fitch looked at her, she looked at Fitch with her heart pounding. Dammit. The man still panicked her.

"Yessir," she said. "Excuse me if I don't get up, got no power at the moment."

"How's it going?" Fitch asked.

Plain question. She rested an armor-heavy wrist on an armored knee. "Thing's a mess," she said. "Fixable. Take me a little while. Few days on this one."

Silence, then. "Tac-squad, huh?"

"Yessir."

If you had a quarrel with a mof, you for God's sake didn't act up and you didn't get snide, you just kept your face innocent and your voice calm and all professional, no matter what you were thinking.

"Is that insubordination, Ms. Yeager?"

"Nossir."

"Hard feelings, Ms. Yeager?"

"I've had worse than you give, sir."

Fitch took that and seemed to think about it a minute.

Stupid, Yeager, real stupid, *watch* that mouth of yours.

"Smartass again, Yeager?"

"Nossir, no intention of being."

"Are you quite sure of that, Ms. Yeager?"

"Twenty years on *Africa*, sir, I was never insubordinate."

"That's good, Ms. Yeager. That's real good."

After which, Fitch walked out and shut the door.

*Dammit*, Yeager, that was bright.

God, NG's working alone down there. Where's Wolfe? Who else is on watch?

She threw the four manual latches on the gauntlet, slid it off; threw latches on the body-armor and on the chisses and boots. Fast. And scrambled up and put clip-lines on the scattered pieces and grabbed her clothes.

"Got to check supply," was the excuse she handed the bridge when she went through. "Be back soon as I can."

Down the lift, all the way to downside, and up the curving downside deck in as much hurry as she could, past the deserted lowerdeck ops, up-rim toward the shop.

And naturally she popped into Engineering on the way. "H'lo," she called out at NG's back, over the noise of working pumps, and startled NG out of his next dozen heartbeats.

"God," he said.

"Fitch," she said. "Just thought I'd warn you."

He leaned back against the counter. She stepped up onto the first of the gimbaled sections that turned Engineering into a stairstep puzzle-board. "No particular trouble," she said, and raised a thumb toward the topside, casual. "Captain's up there too, what I saw."

"They come and they go," NG said. Worried, she thought. "Captain may have gone dockside. Don't get off in places with no witnesses."

"I'm working right next the – "

The lift was operating, audible over the heartbeat-thump of the fueling pumps.

" – bridge. I better get to the shop. I'm picking up some stuff, if Fitch asks."

"He'll ask," NG said, sober-faced, and she started back to the corridor and stopped again, with this terrible fear that Fitch intended something, that Fitch could, for firsts, spill everything.

"I got something I got to talk to you about," she said. "NG, – "

He looked scared. She was. Maybe they caught it off each other. And the lift had passed the core, had made that little catch it did when it passed through.

"He'll try to hurt us," she said. "Whatever he says, that's what he's intending to do. Whatever happens, don't believe anything til you ask me, – hear me? You hear me, NG? You got to trust me."

"What's going on?"

"I – " She heard the lift stop, downside. There wasn't time, wasn't time to do anything but mess things up if she threw it out cold. The way Fitch might. "Just for God's sake – He's trying to get to us. Whatever he does, whatever he says, remember what the game is. All right?"

He stared at her.

She eeled past and out the door again, ducked fast into the machine-shop entry, hitting the lights on the way.

Cold, God, your breath frosted. You got the cold right through your boots, off the tilting deck-plates, and the air bit bare skin and clothed parts alike. She cut the heat on, cursing the sum-bitches who'd decided to powersave, and hurried, grabbed a few extra clip-lines, typed, *Flexyne?* on the terminal, and got inventory and location of tubing and sheets.

*Flexbond?*

Location of that, too. She blew on her fingers, entered six clip-lines and wondered what was going on next door, wondered whether she just ought to walk back in, whether it was Fitch at all, whether he was next door with NG, what in hell was going on over there. . . .

God knew what she'd babbled, sounded like a fool, or worse. . . .

*You got to trust me –*

*God! If that won't make a man check his pockets –*

She took her lip between her teeth and stood there shivering a second, then made up her mind and ducked out into the corridor again, down the curve past Engineering. The door was open and Fitch *was* there, all right, she saw him talking to NG, NG standing there paying all his attention, the way you better do with Fitch –

She couldn't hear anything, couldn't read lips: NG wasn't saying anything and she couldn't see Fitch's face. She just went on past, down to the lift and up again the long ride to the bridge.

Her coming up here got a bare turn of the head from the officer on duty – not even sure who it was. She had a momentary, desperate thought about going straight to the captain and telling him how Fitch was pushing them – but that might not be a good idea.

She stopped, turned, took a deep breath.

"'Scuse, sir, is Mr. Bernstein or Mr. Orsini aboard?"

"Not at the moment," the officer said.

"Would you mind, sir, putting out a call? I've got a problem with the fix."

"Mr. Fitch is on duty."

"Yessir, but Mr. Orsini said call him specifically."

"I'll advise Mr. Fitch of that."

Shit.

She said, "Thank you, sir," restrained the hand from a salute, and walked off very politely, down to the locker.

Not real smart to try to talk to Wolfe, right after the man had said a solid no. Better get back to work, long enough to make it look like she did have a problem, then try to get downside again.

No probability that Wolfe was aboard, unless he had been in downside ops and just not advertising the fact. But the stowage and sickbay were the only topside areas that were swing-sectioned like the bridge, only places you could get to up here, only places you'd *want* to get to up here, the mofs' quarters being all upside down or sideways as long as the ship was in dock and the ring was locked down, which meant ordinary doors were upside down and a step beyond the swing sections would put your foot on the overhead. Wolfe might have a cot downside, in ops or the purser's office, captains not tending to stay in dockside sleepovers like ordinary mortals, captains usually spending their dock time in places like the Station Residency, where service was fancy and the high and the mighty didn't have to rub up against their crews on liberty.

And if Wolfe was on his own liberty-tour, off having pork and real whiskey or whatever captains ate that the 'decks never saw, well, hell if that cold bastard was going to want to hear that Bet Yeager had the willies about Mr. Fitch.

*Dammit, Orsini knows Fitch is on-ship right now, Bernie's got to know — Bernie's got to care. . . . Bernie's got to be smart enough to figure what can happen. . . .*

*Probably a stupid panic, Fitch never pushes anything that'll get shit on him, he's smarter than that, that's always the trouble. If Bernie was smart enough to get a hands-off and a no-talk order down from Wolfe, then Fitch won't dare open his mouth to NG —*

*Please God.*

She shut the locker door again, attached the clips to the nearest ring, and sat down to work on the damn rig again, familiar feel, familiar smell that set off memories just handling it, waked up old ways of dealing with things — fond thoughts of how Fitch could just turn up dead somewhere, — except, dammit, ask anybody on the ship who'd have most reason to want Fitch dead and the answer would always come up NG Ramey; and even if nobody gave a damn about Fitch taking a long fall, you couldn't axe somebody that high up unless you could really make it credibly an accident that just couldn't be anything else.

*God, isn't Fitch going to come back topside?*

*What's going on down there?*

While she sat there adjusting little damn tension screws . . .

And hell if that sonuvabitch mof on the bridge had ever called Orsini, just count herself lucky if maybe he wouldn't even bother to call Fitch.

*Oh, God, Bernie, check back in, you know Fitch is out for blood — get your ass back on this ship, get Orsini back here —*

Nothing. Just nothing, while she adjusted screws and took pieces off and put them on again, sick at her stomach, thinking and thinking of ways to get at Fitch.

*Get him to hit her, maybe, get him somewhere near the safety limit in the corridor out there —*

*Sorry, captain, he was shoving me and I just moved —*
*What if he didn't die?*

She heard the lift work again, heard it reach topside, and sat and patiently adjusted screws and thought, *I got to have the Flexyne, shop's got to be warmer now, I can go down there and get some tubing, get a chance to talk to NG — no knowing if it was Fitch just come up, but he can't be still talking down there. . . .*

*Damn, if I go down there I got to tell NG everything. . . .*

*Got to find him in a decent mood, I got to —*

*God, I hope he didn't hit Fitch.*

She hooked the left gauntlet up with the left arm, flexed the fingers — whole arm exhausted just from the resistance in the damn thing.

*If I try to make up what I'm going to say I'll just screw it up — I just got to tell him, is all, whether or not Fitch's done anything, either patch it up or head it off —*

She safety-clipped the sleeve, closed the lid on the toolkit.

The door opened. She looked up at Fitch, Fitch walked in and looked over what she was doing, the scattered pieces of the rig.

"Having a problem, Ms. Yeager?"

The airlock opened, distant echo through the ship. She tried to collect herself and remember what exactly she'd said to the mof out there, said, "Mr. Orsini didn't indicate whether he wanted a patch or a fix, sir."

"How's it coming, so far?"

From Fitch, a quiet and civil question. It rattled her. She made a second try after scattered wits, got a breath. "I dunno, sir, nothing particularly wrong with the rig, except it must've hit something pretty hard, probably — "

"How much to go on this one?"

"I dunno, sir, depends on whether I go for a clean fix or a dirty one."

"How well's a dirty one hold?"

"'Bout the same. Just a matter of — "

"How long?"

*Doing it right*, she had been about to say. *Pride.* Something like that. Fitch's attitude pissed her. But she said, "On this one, . . . maybe eighty, a hundred hours. I want to get into the pumps, check — "

"What about the other one?"

"I dunno, sir. Longer than that."

"You need some help?"

"I don't think we got it," she said. "You know or you don't know, you go to fuckin' around with the joint screws, you can get everything out. You ever *had* it in adjustment, you got a chance; you ever had somebody messing with the screws, you got no starting point to depend on, you got a real mess. Sir."

Muscle in her knee started twitching from the angle she was sitting at; one in her arm was trying. Or it was the cold. Or it was Fitch standing there staring at her.

"I want this one working," Fitch said, "tonight. I want the other one working – tomorrow. Do you need any help, Ms. Yeager?"

*Listen to me, you son of a bitch.* . . .

But you didn't say that.

"I can't do that, sir. Can't promise that."

"I don't care how you do it, Ms. Yeager. I want this equipment fixed, I want it fixed dirty and working, I want both working by tomorrow, you understand me, Ms. Yeager?"

"Can't do it."

"We're not talking about your getting any sleep, Ms. Yeager. Or taking any breaks. *I want this thing fixed, and I want it now, Ms. Yeager.*"

"I don't know if the other one *can* work, I don't know if any of these damn pumps aren't blown, I don't know how many of the circulation lines ruptured when that rig took a hole, I got *no* notion whether all the motors work, or whether we got some of those damn little screws stripped out, in which case that rig may not *go* into adjustment, sir, until I machine something and take the damn seating apart – "

"Just *do* it, Yeager."

She sat there on the floor staring up at him, too mad to shake at the moment, wondering was he after getting her logged with something, was he just being a sonuvabitch, or . . .

"There some kind of problem, sir?"

"Not your worry, Yeager. Say we've got a little difference of opinion with station management."

Scratch the notion of just quietly screwing it up.

"Say we've got a real problem here," Fitch said between

his teeth. "Say we need that equipment, Ms. Yeager. We need it, and we *may* need it to work."

Pulse steadied into a slow, heavy beat, trouble-sense working on more than Fitch of a sudden.

"Mind to say, sir?"

Fitch stared at her like she was a spot on the deck. She stared back, jaw set, with this notion, this sudden notion, that she might be real important to Fitch . . . and that Fitch didn't like that and didn't like her and didn't like anything about it, but she was what he had.

"You *fond* of people in this crew, Ms. Yeager?"

"Some."

"You sleeping with Ramey, Ms. Yeager?"

She gave Fitch the long, cold stare, thinking, *God, what's he after?* "Happens so," she said. "Yessir."

"Make you a deal, Ms. Yeager. You get me what I want, by tomorrow, we clear the file on Mr. Ramey. Do you like that idea?"

*The man's an absolute crazy.*

"How do you feel about that, Ms. Yeager?"

"I'd say that was a takeable deal, sir, except I'm going to need that help. I could need a good machinist, maybe just somebody to put me together a four-ply of Flexyne, to order . . ." Lying, because that was what the man wanted to hear. She started ticking off the items on her fingers, thinking desperately, the while, *Can I believe this sonuvabitch? Can I believe a thing he says? What's he up to and what's he trying to do?*

*Or what's wrong out there?*

"You got Merrill."

". . . plus a live body." With a gesture toward the *Europe* rig. "For that. Sir."

"Custom fit."

"Only way it works." She opened up the tool-kit again and rammed her hand into the gauntlet, threw the manual toggle. Made a fist. "Precision fit. Or you fall on your ass or throw something. Sir. – Who's supposed to wear it?"

Long moment of quiet in the locker, just the distant heartbeat of the fueling pump.

Fitch said, "You and me, Yeager."

Pieces and facts just went off, out of reach. She looked

up at him and didn't see anything but Fitch being outright crazy.

"Yessir," she said, then, with this terrible feeling that belonged with the smell and the feel of the rigs. Different than the shells you wore on ordinary business. Damn different. Didn't have to make sense why the mofs ordered it. Didn't have to make sense why this one did. They told you go kill some sons of bitches and you went and did that, before they got you first. You didn't ask why. You didn't ask who. You just did it.

*But I got friends on this station –*

Crewmates out there, too, with their asses on the line.

NG downside, no knowing what Fitch had said –

"Does NG know?" she asked Fitch. "Did you tell him where I come from?"

Fitch gave her a cold stare. "Like that, would he?"

"What did you tell him?"

"That if he wants to stay alive he's going to sit that station hours on and hours off. We've got six people left on this ship and *everybody's* on, twenty-four solid. Or this ship's going to die here. He is. Your friends out there. And you. Hear me?

"Yessir," she said. "I got you clear."

"Then get it the hell *fixed*, Yeager."

Fitch went out the door, Fitch shut it, and she grabbed the gauntlet and the forearm and started mating up lines and shoving in push-clips, thinking how the back hurt, thinking how the back was going to hurt a damn lot more, –

Wishing that was all there was to think about.

*Damn it, damn it, damn it, going to die in this one, Yeager, this whole thing's got the taste of it, everybody in one big fuckin' hurry, where in hell is everybody, what kind of mess has station got us in and why is the fuckin' pump still running if we got station troubles so bad?*

*Fitch is lying. Fitch is fuckin' lying, when did the man ever do anything but what served Fitch?*

*Going to die in this one, going to die, going to die, and what in hell's NG going to think about it?*

*Think I screwed him over, that's what, what else is he going to think?*

*Dammit.*

She safety-clipped the finished arm, got herself up on her knee and hauled herself up to her feet, headed out the door and through the bridge pulling her sleeve to rights.

"Yeager!" Fitch yelled at her back.

She got to the lift, pushed the button and looked back at him coming her direction. She held up five fingers. "Five minutes. Five minutes downside. You want that fuckin' rig fixed, *sir*, you stay off me, stay off my friends."

While the door opened.

She walked in, she faced about. Fitch stood there with his face turning red.

The door shut and the lift engaged.

He could stop it from the bridge, she reckoned. There were a lot of things he could do from the bridge.

One of them wasn't to get those rigs operational, not by any finagle in hell.

# Chapter 25

She hit the downside corridor running, sprinted the up-curving deck, dived into Engineering and came up onto the stairstep deck-plates with a clatter that brought NG face-about and frightened-looking before she got to him.

"I got five minutes," she said, holding up the same hand. "Fitch gave me that much. I got to tell you – Fitch is saying the ship's in trouble, they need me to fix this stuff – "

Damn, it wasn't getting to the point. She stalled, dead, and he stood there staring at her . . .

Scared for her, she thought, and she halfway choked on that thought.

"Fitch give me this deal," she started to say. But that wasn't it either.

"They got this job. . . ."

Third bad try.

"NG . . . I dunno if you got any notion . . . Hell, I'm not merchanter, you understand me?"

*Militia* came to her tongue, last desperate lie. But she didn't say it. Make a man a fool once. Not twice. Not and ever expect him to forgive you.

". . . I was with Mazian."

She wanted some cue where to go next, and he didn't react, he just had this glazed-over, scared look.

She said, "Never wanted to lie to you, never wanted to load it on you, what I come from. I figure you're the most likely on this ship to want my hide, probably with good reason . . ."

Maybe he'd gone away, gone out-there again. Maybe he wasn't even listening anymore. He didn't look mad, just numb.

She reached out and touched his hand. It was cold and hard as the counter it rested on. "Want you to know," she said, "I never lied to you about anything else, never did anything I thought would hurt you. I never would, hear me?" She shook at his arm. "NG. Hear me?"

Maybe he did, maybe he didn't. He pulled his hand and looked away from her.

She could have said her ship-name too. It had been a point of pride all her adult life. But *Africa* had a rep with the merchant trade, a bad one. She'd learned that, on Pell docks. And maybe he didn't need to know that yet, maybe he just would rather not know.

He didn't say anything, didn't look at anything in particular for a second, then discovered the slate in his left hand and studied it as if he was going to find some answer there.

Logical as anything. Some things had to rattle around awhile before you could even start to think.

So she figured it was just a case of walking out quietly, letting him alone and letting it settle as much as it ever could – Merrill was coming in, Merrill and Parker both were going to be working down here, he wasn't going to be alone, thank God.

But he caught her arm as she was going. She stopped, wanted to grab onto him – but he didn't invite that, just put his hand on her shoulder, just a quiet "don't hate you, Bet. . . ."

But it had as well be a 'not sure I can say anything beyond that, either.'

He let her go. She looked back when she got to the door.

She said, because she didn't want to leave him in all that quiet, "Is Merrill up? Fitch was going to call him."

"Fitch said there was shop-work, said we're going twenty-four on."

She nodded. So he could be civilized, get the job done, shove the personal stuff over til the mind could cope. It was a relief, of a kind.

"What's happening out there?" he asked.

"Dunno," she said. "They got these busted-up armor-rigs, they got some damn problem they think they need this stuff, real fast – Fitch says. Not everything Fitch says is making sense – "

You hearing me, man?

" – Fitch says there's trouble onstation, Fitch says there's just six guys on this ship, everybody else is off. I got this terrible feeling it's no accident who's left aboard."

His face had that scared look again.

"Do what Fitch says," she said. The adrenaline was running out. She was getting the shakes, feeling sick at her stomach. "I got to go. Fitch gave me five minutes down here. I got to go back. Stay out of trouble. I *need* you, understand me? For God's sake, I need you."

"What *deal*?" he asked, suddenly getting words out.

Then he *had* been tracking, sharper than she thought. Her heart thumped over a beat. She started to lie . . .

Remembered in time what she'd just said about lies.

"Clean slate," she said on autopilot, gone numb herself, while her brain was trying to figure out how much he'd understood, *what* he understood, whether there was anything she could say in two seconds that could make any difference. "You and me, clean slate. Fitch says. Says it's station trouble. – But if we got station trouble – why in hell is the *pump* still going?"

"*Yeager!*" Fitch's voice rang out over the general com.

She saw NG's face, cold and shocked, as she spun around and ran out the door, headed down the corridor as fast as she could.

*He could've heard, God, I think he heard that –*

"*Ten* minutes," Fitch said when she got topside.

"Sorry, sir. But we got some stuff straight. NG's straight with it. He's all right. Promise you."

Fitch just gave her the eye a second. Then: "Twenty-four hours, Yeager."

"*Yes*, sir."

She moved. She got to the locker and she moved double-time – dirty job, Fitch wanted.

So you did any damn thing that luck might let hold six hours.

Which was as long as you could last anyway, without a reserve pack.

And they didn't come with any.

One of the circulation pumps was blown, she'd expected that, thank God the next valve on the line had shut before it froze.

Jim Merrill had that one to fix – wide, hard stare from Merrill when he opened the door on number one topside stowage and found out exactly *what* the Flexyne was for, and where the pump he was supposed to fix came from.

"Shit," he said. "They expect us to fix *these* things?"

So nobody'd briefed Merrill, at least. Maybe a lot of crew had known what was in the topside locker, maybe for years. Maybe just for this run. She didn't know. He gave her what he'd brought, she got up and gave him the dead pump. "Fast as you can turn it around," she said; and she had to ask: "How's NG doing down there?"

"Being a sum-bitch, what's he ever doing?"

"Shit."

"He said – " Merrill sounded as if he wasn't sure what he was walking into. "Said – ask you what in *hell's* going on up here."

She looked at Merrill with this sudden dumb-ass hope for the situation and wished she had an answer. But NG'd asked, dammit, he was at least talking to Merrill, he was still working down there.

"Tell him," she said, " – tell him he knows everything I do. Tell him keep his head down. Tell him I got no notion whatsoever of dying in this place."

"*What's* going on?" Merrill asked.

"Fitch says station trouble. You figure it. Fitch still out there?"

"On the bridge," Merrill said. "Outside. – What kind of trouble, f'God's sake?"

"Dunno. Got *no* idea. Captain's missing since morning, crew's been sent off – "

"Crazy," Merrill said. "Whole thing's crazy."

And when she didn't say anything else, Merrill left. She heard the lift go downside while she was measuring the new line.

Thule's pump was still running, Thule was still pouring her small tanks into *Loki*'s, fast as the antique machinery could push it. Thump. Thump. Thump.

*Nobody's been back to the ship. You'd expect crew to come aboard and stow stuff they'd bought, if there wasn't something wrong . . . You could get robbed on Thule docks. You didn't carry stuff around, more than just your necessary cred-slips.*

Trouble, Fitch said, and station was still going on with the fill, like it wasn't anything to do with that department of station affairs –

*Maybe somebody bashed somebody, maybe we got law trouble here, going to try to strongarm somebody out of station lockup. Loki wouldn't take any shit off station-law, not in any skuz place like this –*

*But why's it only Fitch aboard, where'd that other officer go, where's the captain, why in hell'd Fitch send everybody off-ship but me and NG and Parker and Merrill, just Engineering types –*

*Just us that ain't exactly his good-list . . .*

*Send everybody out for a show of force on the docks, maybe?*

*Who ever said Fitch is telling even half the truth?*

She got the line fixed, the seal in, the pump seated, one she'd borrowed out of the *Europe* rig, working on the notion of getting at least one rig test-ready. She powered-on the plastron section, tested the valves at the seal-points, and the systems stood it.

Bet your life it would.

– Trooper joke.


Merrill brought her a sandwich up. She ate it, stuffing her mouth occasionally, chewing while she worked. She caught a little sleep, unintentional, just enough to bump her nose on the helmet she was holding, and to wonder where in hell she was and what she was doing half-frozen with a helmet in her lap.

She wasn't counting hours, just working as fast as she could without making problems – she had this grease-pencil tally written on the deck, of systems checked and to-be-checked, a skut's memory in place of the computerized tick-off on a slate with built-in prompts, had a lot of cobbled-together, hand-made pieces because supply didn't have them, had one tension-screw slipping on the right shoulder, so she borrowed one out of the left hip; a couple in the right elbow, so she borrowed them out of the left.

Trades like that.

She went out and asked Mr. Fitch for a hot tea and another tube of Flexbond. Fitch looked around from his station at the boards, snarled at her, told her get her ass back to work, but the tea showed up anyway, Merrill brought it.

One favor out of Fitch, she thought.

Merrill brought something else, too, said quickly, in a low voice, leaning close to her, "Fitch's keeping systems live," and handed her a little dozen-times-smeared note in grease-pencil.

It said: *Malfunction not minor. Take any chance get out. Ask Merrill.*

It also said: *The other thing — Mostly I think I knew. Ok.*
*— NG*

She looked at Merrill, cold inside as well as out.

"What's he talking about?" she whispered.

Merrill put his mouth up against her ear. "Systems has been telling command all along we got a problem. Systems is saying this ship's going to blow clear to hell if we go on running like this. Now we got a five-day fill here. *Hell* of a lot of mass we're taking into that tank. What in hell's the captain doing, that's what we're trying to figure. . . ."

*Wasn't* minor, *wasn't* minor, what happened coming in. . . .

"But what else can we do? I know we got a problem. But they can't fix it here."

"We don't need a full tank to get to Pell! They were supposed to do a partial here and get us on to Pell with a light load, where we can get a fix on that damn thing, that's what Mike understood, that's what Smitty and Bernstein understood. What's this five days crap, that's what mainday Systems is asking. Why've they got the ship cleared, and what's this stuff about armor? They put the whole crew off, like they don't know out there that that fill's still going? D' they think Systems won't talk, or Engineering doesn't have to know what mass we're hauling? Systems says — not sure who's in charge here. Command's gone crazy. Systems says — maybe jam the airlock. Get us off this ship. . . ."

She got this colder and colder feeling. She wiped the bit of plastic to a smear, twice, to be sure. You could die for what was written there.

She whispered, "Don't know, don't know. Tell NG — tell him twenty-four hours. Tell him for God's sake *wait*. Trust me. I'll find out."

Merrill caught a mouthful of air. "I'll tell him," Merrill said. And opened the door to go.

Face-on with Fitch.

"We got a problem, Mr. Merrill? Ms. Yeager?"

"Nossir," Merrill said, and ducked out.

"We got a clear run on number one," Bet said, fast, before Fitch thought of a second question. "I got the patch on number two there, going to run the rough adjustments off me, far as I can, save you some standing, sir. Then I got to have the body that's going to wear it – about two hours to fit it. Best I can do."

Fitch stood there looking at her. She wondered if guilty thoughts showed that much.

"You sure you don't have a problem, Ms. Yeager?"

"Nossir," she said. Her voice was going. It cracked when she was trying to keep it steadiest. "Nossir, everything's fine."

"You sure Engineering doesn't have a problem?"

"Nossir. Not any problem."

"We're running *behind*," Fitch said. "You understand me, Ms. Yeager?"

Time-sense was gone. "Yessir," she said, thinking, *I got to sleep. I got to sleep, I can't think like this –*

She was shaking when Fitch shut the door. She drank the tea and slopped it.

*Lying to me. Man's lying.*

*What in hell's he want out of me, why in hell'd Wolfe hand me to Fitch and leave?*

*Going to make a damn mistake, like to make one with Fitch, like to adjust that rig for him, damn, I would . . .*

She had crazed thoughts, like Fitch pulling a gun, like Fitch just killing her outright once she was through and taking the rig for one of his cronies –

*Who's my size, that'd stand for Fitch?*

*Kill him first. I could. This thing could. Just walk out there, do everybody a favor –*

*But the captain put me here. Captain knows about that wobble NG's talking about –*

*Damn. Damn! What's the hurry-up on these rigs? What changed, since we made dock?*

*Who'd risk blowing the ship, if all he's got to do is break Wolfe's neck, promote his own faction, and cruise on into Pell?*

# Chapter 26

She slept again, just a sprawl on the deck while she waited for Merrill to bring a finished job up, lay down with her cheek against the icy deck-surface and went out cold a precious quarter, maybe half-hour, because except that, it was done.

It was a mistake, maybe, because she came awake with Merrill shaking her, and couldn't remember for a couple of beats where she was, couldn't get her arms to work to get herself off her face, because her back wouldn't take her weight. Just dead, gone. And the back hurt and the joints hurt and the cold had made her stiff.

"You all right?" Merrill was asking her. "You all right, Yeager?"

After a while you got from being afraid you were going to die to wanting to get it over with. She crawled up off her nose, butt-high, elbows on the deck and just rested there a second while Merrill told her how NG was all right with waiting, NG and Mike Parker both, but on an in-case, they were going downside to work on the outside lock controls, two Systems guys used to throwing around giga-numbers out there trying to hotwire a security circuit –

God. "Fitch'll *know*," she hissed at Merrill, scared somehow Fitch had the place bugged, Fitch was right outside. "Dammit, where's the captain?" Merrill was downside, Engineering was right alongside ops, right down there next to the lock, they'd hear it if anybody came or went.

"No news," Merrill whispered. "Nothing. Like there wasn't anybody *out* there . . ."

"Crew's got to know they got the ship closed up, dammit, aren't they going to wonder? Aren't they going to ask? What the fuck are they doing out there?"

"Nobody knows," Merrill said. "We've called the bridge,

Mike asked to get a call out, tried that. No go. Two on the bridge and us."

"Fitch out there?"

"Goddard."

Hughes' operator. "Shit." She sat up, crashed back against the wall, banged her head. "Fitch's *sleeping*! Screw *that*! Tell 'im I need 'im, tell Goddard get him up, it's time to do that body-fit."

You stripped down to fit the rig, you started with the boots and you built up from there, and it was cold, damn, it was, no locker on the ship had good vents.

Gave her a good deal of satisfaction, Fitch standing there in his underwear – not bad scenery, either, even if he was a sonuvabitch, kept himself right in shape bouncing crew off the walls. Few scars, real good one on the ribs, probably a knife in some sleepover, probably deserved it, she thought, tightening up little screws.

Put a little black crud on the braces inside the boot, clamp the boot shut and adjust until all three braces left a stain on the skin. Not neat, gugged up the suit-surfaces something awful, but if you had to fit a neo it was easier than asking did it touch: it always felt like it touched, til you knew better.

Besides, it was Fitch.

Left boot, right boot, left shin, right shin, knees and chisses.

While Fitch stood there with a com-plug in his ear listening to stuff she'd have given a deal to hear.

And with a damnable lack of attention to the discomfort, like what he was hearing was a hell of a lot more real to him.

Lower body. She flat had to sit down in a minute and take a break. Her hands were shaking so her fingers couldn't keep the driver in the damn little invisible slots.

And of a sudden Fitch moved, knocked the fragile driver out of her fingers, *hurt*, dammit, so she sat down hard on her backside, not sure for a second he wasn't coming past her.

But you couldn't walk fast in that weight. Fitch activated his com, said, "No answer," to whoever was listening, and repeated it, louder: "No answer, dammit, do what I said. . . ."

She picked herself up, rapped on the armor-leg to get his attention, started to work again – flex here, turn there, sir, *hold* it there, sir. . . .

*Push* it, sir, or it'll stop you there. . . .

Damn, she'd like to set it about one tick looser.

But give Fitch one thing, Fitch had his mind on business and you told him to hold and he held, no twitches, no complaints. *Fitch* wasn't real rested either, eyes looked like hell.

"Think this thing's going to work," she confided in him, what little voice she had left. "Ran a systems-check, it didn't blow . . ." And jumped to the question she was after. "We prepping for fire, hard vacuum, – what?"

"Anything," Fitch said. "Anything it has to."

"You ever stood up in one of these, sir?"

Dead silence.

"Power goes on, you got to relax. That's the main knack to it. Minute you tense up, you got the rig taking orders, you twitch, like you're going to fall, rig's going to over-react and you'll lose it. Some like it set real loose, some want a hair-trigger react-time, you got your choice, sir – this one's set fast, I can take it down half."

"I'll take your judgment on it," Fitch said, downright civil.

"How much time you got to try this?"

"I don't know," Fitch said. He never looked at her while she was working, she never took liberties with the situation. "Maybe none." Fitch took a breath and let it go, said, into the com, "I got that."

"We got a weapons interface," she said. "We can patch right into the rig's systems, if you got a gun with an I/O plug, ranging, tracking, auto-fire, anything you got."

Pure smartass arrogance. Lucky if the ship *carried* sidearms that good.

Hell if Fitch was going to let her near anything of the kind if they did.

"We got plain sidearms," Fitch said after a moment, "be lucky if we get a target."

Different Fitch than she'd ever heard . . . tired man, mostly civil man, with a muscle tic in his right arm and skin cold as a corpse right now.

Hell of a pair they made, Fitch complaining, finally, hoarsely, "What the fuck you *doing*, Yeager?" when she was shaking so bad she couldn't get the screwdriver seated. "Sorry, sir," she said. She was shaking, he was shivering, the thing kept slipping, Fitch being turned at a godawful angle at the time, while she was trying to get the main body joints to max-set.

Somehow, she was mostly on auto by then, she got the plastron put together, got the right sleeve and gauntlet on, and she bit her lip and did little screws until Fitch himself made a com-call to Goddard for hot coca and sandwiches.

Breakfast or supper, she didn't even remember. Mike Parker brought it up, didn't say anything. She remembered dimly that Parker and NG were down there committing an act of mutiny, that all Fitch had to do was discover that somebody'd screwed with the lock downside . . .

Five quick guesses who'd go up on charges.

She didn't have any appetite left. She just chewed and swallowed big lumps, washed them down with coca and wished it was beer.

Wished it was a good stiff drink of the vodka down in their makeshift quarters, most of all. But if alcohol hit her system right now she'd just be gone, out, zee'd in ten seconds.

Something came in that Fitch didn't like. She watched him listening to Goddard or whoever-it-was, frowning, shaking his head a little.

"I got that," he said to Goddard, which was as much as he had ever said.

"What's going on, sir?" she finally asked, just to have tried.

Fitch gave her a cold look, said, finally, "Just an on-going problem. — Let's get the rest of it. Promise you, if this thing runs, you get a sleep break."

*If this thing doesn't run*, she thought, thinking about pumps and servos blowing, filters going, all over the rig, *I'd rather shoot myself.*

"Let's get it then," she said, and checked the right sleeve, to mate it up.

All those little joints, all those little screws, right down the elbow and wrist and finger-joints.

She was half-blind when she finished. She really thought

about powering Fitch on without a warning, because Fitch was shaky-wobbly himself, and she had this vision what Fitch could do when the wobbles hit the body sensors.

But she didn't – didn't want to start a war where one wasn't, right now, didn't want to take a halfway civil Fitch and make a fool out of him.

"Tell you, sir," she said, in the croak of a voice she had, "you been standing long enough, if we got time, you better get some rest. If you power on when you got the shakes it'll throw you, don't want it to pitch you on your ass."

"Where's the switch?"

She showed him. He threw it, threw it back off damn quick, because it rattled.

"It runs," she said. "Wobbles is you." And being diplomatic, as Teo would say: "Most take a fall, straight off. Rather you didn't, sir. Better you get some sleep."

"When it runs," Fitch said. "Runs means when it *works*, Yeager. *Works* means when it works for me, so you show me the switches, you show me the technicalities, you show me the systems, so we both know it works, then we'll both talk about getting some sleep. *Hear me?*"

Damn you, I do, sir.

"Yessir, I hear you."

First thing you did, if you were instructing somebody, you put your own rig on. Fitch objected. "No need," he said; and she said, "There is, sir. Or I can call out the instructions from outside this locker til you got that rig under control. Sir."

Do him credit, Fitch did get the idea what she was talking about. And Fitch listened when she said Relax, and stood there watching while she stripped down and got into her own rig the right way.

She rattled and chattered too, when she powered on. She damped it down. "That's your adjustment, number three switch, sensitivity on the pickups. If you get the chatters you just screw it tighter til it stops. If you rattle loud enough you can draw fire."

Fitch didn't think that was funny.

"You got gyros that keep your balance," she said, no missed beat. Fitch was a helmeted, faceless form, bracketed in green-glowing readouts from her faceplate display, 360°

vision compressed and projected in a green shadow band on the top and bottom of her faceplate – Fitch's slight movement getting his hand and alternately his body bracketed in a stutter of yellow, his sounds amped up with a decibel readout ticking and flashing in her lower left. She took his hand and guided it to the first of the controls under the collar.

"You can see your hand, bottom 360 display, you got to get used to the distortion. This is lock, this is gyros, this is free-movement, three position switch, first over, see the blinking display, right corner of your screen, tells you that's switch two, position B, that's stabilizing on, A is lock, C is free. Got that?"

"A is lock, B is gyros, C is free."

"Rig tends to feel like it's out of balance. Different center of gravity, but don't forget those big boots under you. Put it on B, the gyros keep your balance and you got to really fight it to kneel or fall down. I'd advise you keep it on B awhile. Switch three's your sensitivity. I'd put it 85%. It's going to wear on you some, but better that than falling down. I keep mine at 150 amp to the rig's max at 300, but I been using these things twenty years. You don't need switch four, we got no base station, so that's no good. – Feel steadier at 85?"

"Cumbersome," Fitch said. "Stiff."

"You can designate sections for different amps, but it's overall sloppy. Put three up to 90, just up a point or two as you feel like it, but be careful when you start passing the hundred mark. Higher you set that amp-switch, that's the way the rig reads all your muscle twitches. At a hundred it'll move that much faster, hit that much harder, grip that much tighter. It's incremental. At 150, a guy can break a gunstock with a squeeze, and most guys never set the total rig over 250. You move gentle, handle everything like it was blown glass, don't jerk. Everything you do is amplified. Mass is more. When you get moving, you got to allow more to stop. Running stride's a float, light as you can, max-set walk's a lot the same. You got to be light on your feet. If you fall, don't fight it, don't jerk, fall won't hurt you, just take it and get back up. – Going to take the gyros off, now. Relax. Just stand. Lift the arm. Gently."

"Damn!" Fitch said, when the rig hummed and flexed. A

little jerk. Her arm and his crashed together and he broke a locker handle stumbling backward and forward.

She caught him, steadied him. She could hear the breathing, heavy gasps over the helmet-com.

Man not used to not being in control.

Man exhausted, mad as hell, and maybe a little scared.

He jerked, a rattle and stutter all up and down the joints, he lurched free and swung the arm further than he wanted, but he caught himself.

"That's pretty good," she said. "If you swing like that, you got to brace back harder than you would. Mass again. – Who're we supposed to use these on, you mind to say, sir?"

He didn't say anything for a minute. But she could hear the breathing.

"Suppose you just do your job," Fitch said, "explain the rest of these switches and stick to business."

"I got no problem with that, sir, except we got hundreds of switches, I take it our time is limited, and if I knew precisely what we got to deal with, I could figure out what functions you better know. Sir."

Silence. Then: "Suppose you don't be a smartass, Yeager, and you got a notion to stay alive. Let's just learn to move this thing."

"Yessir," she said hoarsely, with the wobbles in her joints and the readouts blurring and a real tight grip on her temper. "You got a good initial balance on your switches. Let's try walking."

He managed it fine at 95 and 100, upped it to 110 and did tolerably well – managed to stand the first time at 110 with the gyros when she hit him in the gut; didn't fare so well on the second try without – hit the lockers, but he didn't hit her hands hard when he bounced forward on the recovery.

"You got a real aptitude, sir." She adjusted her amp, shoved him at 130. He hit the lockers, bounced forward, she bounced him back, he got better at staying on his feet.

"You want to find out about the targeting, sir? Question of weapons?"

She kept after him, put her suit on lock finally and just rested, drilled him on the basics, droned through the standard new-skut lecture, sometimes with her eyes closed, but he couldn't know that.

"You got four settings, one's for right-handers, one's for left, some don't care, number one's autofire, skip that, we ain't got it, set it to 2, see the yellow bracket pop up on your foot there, sir, that's a fiber-optics in your right glove, gives you a fair idea what you got your gun generally pointed at. You can adjust the focus, rig understands spoken commands, you say Program On, Target, Manual, you say Cancel to stop it – " Flutter of grid and markers across her own rig's faceplate, that stopped with Cancel. "You can tell it left/right, up/down, tell it Set when you're happy – "

"Got it," Fitch said. Fitch wasn't sounding real focused himself.

"Think we got the basics," she said. She hoped. "Give you the verbals next try if I got time. Toggles are more reliable, some voices the pickup just doesn't get a hundred percent, don't know why somebody can't make a programmable that can tell sit from shit. – You want to get out of that thing, now, sir?" She didn't wait for a confirmation, she didn't want to hear no, she just came up and guided his hand to the master release. "There's your tension-straps. Left is on, right is off, you let 'em up and you unlatch, ever'thing just exactly like a hard-suit, once she's built and mated, same direction on the latches – sleeves first, top, boots and breeches – hold on, there, let me get the hanging-hooks, sir."

She unscrewed the sleeve-rings, helped him unmate the right one, he got the left, got his own top-section off, helmet and all, once she had it hooked, and he ducked out of it, sweat and grease to the waist, while she got her own joints unscrewed and unmated, and her own hooks on the shoulder-rings.

Fitch looked like he was going to fall on his face, white and sweating and wobbly as he wiped off and started to get his clothes on.

No sympathy, you sum-bitch. Her back reminded her of old debts, and oh, God, she wanted a beer.

Fitch was mopping his face, standing there with his clothes half together while she was putting hers on. "All right, Yeager, you're off. You got maybe six hours."

She blinked, too stupid to find the catch in that.

"Get!" he said.

She zipped up. "Can I draw a beer, sir?"

"Screw any skuz you want, drink, *get some sleep*, any way you can, long as you can get your ass up here cold sober when I want you. Hear me?"

"Yessir! Thank you, sir."

"*Get!*"

She shoved her feet into her boots, wobbled her way out onto the bridge where Goddard was still on watch, got into the lift, propped herself against the wall and leaned there with her head pounding and her knees trying to melt under her.

She didn't even go to the locker where their quarters was set up, she went staggering on up the curve, into Engineering, up to where NG was working, and startled hell out of him.

"Got a six-hour," she said. "We got Fitch's sweet goodnight. How you doing?"

# Chapter 27

S he wasn't navigating well, was just about fit to lie there in the seat at number three boards, breaking a half-dozen regs –

*Bernie'd die*, she thought, sipping a cold beer NG had gotten her out of Services, beer and not the vodka, because beer seemed more like food and there was more of it. Her hands would hurt if she weren't halfway numb, her back did hurt, she was afraid to take one of Fletcher's pills, as tired as she was, and she had the feeling a lot of things were going to hurt, if she sat still any time at all.

But NG was there. That was what she wanted most. NG was still speaking to her, he was standing there against the counter-edge with this desperate look, like he'd earnestly like things to make sense more than they did.

There was that lock downside, that *was* an option, one he'd risked his neck on. – "We've got a way out," he'd whispered to her, before he went down to Services for the beer. "It'll work."

And she'd said, not sure she wasn't wrong: "Not yet."

"When? When you're stuck topside?"

"Don't do it," she'd said. "*Don't do it.* It's not that simple. Something's wrong out there. Something *is* wrong, I got it listening to com up there."

NG didn't look happy. But he listened to her. He leaned against the counter now and said, "Better?"

"Lot," she said, and he just stood there. Waiting.

Because she said so.

*Man, you never asked, did you, what ship I come from, what I've done, where I been? You never said about yourself, either.*

*So what're you thinking? That you can throw all that away? But past is never past, man, past is, that's all; all you can ever get at is now and will-be.*

*You find that so, out there, where you been?*

*I damn sure have.*

She found the beer hard to hold onto: it took concentration to keep her fingers closed on the cup, she was that close to going out.

Crew was going to find out what she was, and there had to be a few with old grudges – on a spook ship, probably a lot of them. Terribly dirty trick, bringing NG out of his hole, getting him halfway acceptable, and then having it turn out she'd lied to everybody –

*Where's that leave him? God, –*

But NG waited, he sat there on this ship that saner crew like Parker and Merrill were complaining about and ready to duck out on, the whole crew ready to mutiny if they hadn't done it already out there – and they were sitting still on her say-so, too, she didn't know why. *They* might be worried about the consequences of guessing wrong, but if NG decided to go eetee he didn't always think five minutes down the line, damn sure he didn't play team with anybody –

– didn't used to, at least.

Cup slipped. She clamped down numb fingers, got it to her mouth, drank off the last couple of mouthfuls of it and let her arm rest then, just staring at him.

*Didn't ask me what I'm going to do.*

*Can't tell me anything either – what's going on out there, where crew is. . . .*

"*Merrill and Parker,*" Goddard's voice said over general com. "*Report to dockside.*"

She jerked awake, running that through her hearing again. Merrill and Parker were hauling themselves up from their pile of blankets over in the corner, scared-looking.

"What in hell?" Mike Parker asked, looking in her direction as if she might be holding some secret.

"Dunno," she said, trying to get the chair tilted forward, trying to get up, with NG's help.

But Parker went to the com over at the entry station and tried to ask Goddard why and what-for and just what in hell was going on, anyway.

Goddard just repeated the order, told them get their stuff, get, go.

"What about Yeager and NG?" Parker asked, God save

him, mad and keeping after it. "Do they get a relief, sir? – Have we got some kind of problem on this ship?"

"*They keep to stations*," the answer came back.

Parker kept trying. Goddard just shut him down. Parker looked at both of them, said, "Son of a bitch!"

She held onto NG's shoulder, feet and hands so numb she couldn't stand up, except NG was providing the balance-sense.

"I'm going to ask questions when I get out there," Mike Parker said.

But she stood there thinking, *Questions don't matter, then, what crew thinks doesn't matter, or they wouldn't turn Merrill and Parker out, now that they're through with them, they know too much what's going on in here –*

She thought, *We're the last, aren't we? Fitch's personal favorites . . .*

As Parker and Merrill got themselves out the door before somebody changed the orders. Footsteps outside got lost in the noise of the pumps. In a minute or less the lock cycled, and they were alone in *Loki*'s downside.

"We can still get out of here," NG said, holding onto her.

"They'd kill us," she said. That was the only sense she knew. "We got no defense for running. I don't know what the hell's going on out there, but something is, something is dead wrong – "

Bad choice of words. NG got her to a chair arm, got her to sit down. She put her arms around his neck, he put his arms around her and she hung there with her head spinning.

"I tell you," she said, "they're all crazy."

But she wasn't as scared as she ought to be for a second or two, wasn't half as scared as made sense, maybe because she'd seen more than made sense, topside, and it was all still rattling around –

*Fitch*, being civil –

*Fitch*, saying to Goddard, one supposed, *No answer* –

Goddard, sending one of their two Systems engineers and their only bona fide on-duty machinist out onto the docks to whatever trouble was supposedly going on out there, and leaving the ship their two gold-plated problems. . . .

*Three*, counting Fitch –

Four, if you threw in that sonuvabitch Goddard. A Systems man, the navcomp chief, an ex-Marine tac-squad sergeant and the mainday first officer –

"Goddard's *navcomp*," she mumbled, against NG's shoulder, then looked up, looked him in the face. "But that's all scan-stuff, isn't it? – They got ever' damn board on that end lit."

NG understood her, she thought.

He looked scared. He ought to be.

"If we get a warning," she said, "you get the hell off this ship. You hear me? We got two armor-rigs up there, working just fine. You got those hard-suits in that locker out there. Get one in here. If we get an alert you get it on and if we get a strike warning you get the hell off this ship, off the dockside, period, you don't stop to think. At that point, nobody's going to care. *Fitch* won't care. Things'll be too busy."

Black of space, gaping behind a seal-window. Whirling paper, whirling debris, trail of dust and freezing air going out a hole so fast you didn't even see most of it, just –

– felt the explosion, felt it in the dark, felt it when you shut your eyes at night, when you got too tired and you were by yourself and you started remembering –

"You think it *is* a ship?" NG said.

"I damn well think it's a ship. They want that armor fixed, that's why I'm here, and they don't trust me worth shit. There never was any problem with station. That's why Fitch can talk about six hours, twenty-four hours, they know it's out there, they know how fast it's coming. Fitch was talking to somebody, saying Don't answer. We sit at this dock like a merchanter with a problem, not saying a thing. Spook tactic long as I've known anything."

"Til they get a clear look at us. And that's damn far out. We're a sitting target and they won't care about the fact there's a thousand-odd innocent people out there – "

"You don't think we can run. You think the ship absolutely can't do it."

"Fifty/fifty," NG said. There was this look in his eyes, man remembering, maybe, what human beings tranked down to forget in jump. "Don't know. I've worked on it til I'm blind and I don't know. You get a deformation when you drop out, we've tried to write a program that goes back to the boards to tell the difference, but fifty/fifty the sensors are just screwed up. We told Wolfe, no guarantees, run low mass, minimal stress – "

Detail just muddled up in her skull, the whole room kept turning around, she only knew he was scared, and she was, and beyond her not knowing any answer, there might not *be* any answer.

Couldn't bluff, NG was right, couldn't depend on any Fleet ship not firing on them only because they were sitting at a station dock, – because they weren't dealing with anybody on either side who had an overwhelming lot to lose. The Fleet didn't: couldn't hold a place like Thule, just didn't have the ships. Even the Alliance didn't care about Thule except as metal that had to be junked; and the people were all Q-zone refugees Alliance wished it didn't have. Only some Pell lawyer was likely to complain if Thule got blown, but it didn't help them after the fact.

Antique station. Nothing to hold onto.

"One damn pump," she remembered suddenly. Thule dock. Cheese puffs. Ritterman. Herself and Nan Jodree standing in the Registry watching the screen. "One pump at this station that can handle a starship. We're sitting at it. More than that – our tank can drain this station dry and it takes the skimmers weeks to refill it. If that's what's going on out there, if there is a ship, if its tanks are low as ours and they blow us – they've blown the pump, they've blown what we've drunk down, they're stuck here – it's more than forcing us out, they've got to *take* this ship."

*That bastard Wolfe knew our chances when he brought us in here. Tanks nearly dry. Major mechanical with the drive. No way to run.*

*So you pull into station, you drink down all the available fuel and you defy the sonuvabitch on your track to come after you and take it back.*

*We're supposed to stop a station boarding with two armor-rigs and Loki's guns, dead broadside?*

*Fuckin' hell!*

# Chapter 28

She slept awhile, she didn't even remember lying down. She just woke up in a back-tilted chair with a blanket over her, staring at the lights.

Remembered too much, then, twisted over to see where NG was, and found him folded over at the next station counter, taking a nap of his own, probably with the auto-alarm set. He'd put her kit and a change of clothes on the counter by her: she got up carefully, stiff and sore as hell – and made her trip to the head. Not easy to do a thorough scrub in that cubby, from a recessed tap, but it helped.

NG had set her stuff up for her, took care of her, NG, who never took two thoughts beyond his own necessities –

Maybe, she thought, maybe he was more upset than he showed, and he was putting everybody off their guard so he could do something stupid like go after Fitch –

But a man with his thinking in a muddle didn't steady down the way he had, didn't suddenly start tracking on his job the way he'd been doing, now, she added it up, ever since he'd found out he couldn't shake her or Musa or Bernie off his tail.

Like he'd been drifting in his private space until he got this beacon – *Somebody else out here, man, somebody solid – pay attention, now – I got information for you –*

Maybe it'd been like that for her, she thought, the last several years. Maybe that was what made him impossible for her to let alone: he was the voice in her dark too, saying *I know what you've seen. You don't have to make sense. You don't have to explain a thing. It's not a requirement here. . . .*

Hell of a time to figure things out, Yeager.

She came back into Engineering with that thought, she came and bent over his chair with the intention of waking him up, telling him that, telling him at least how she felt –

But it was too embarrassing, and she went muddle-headed when she thought about talking to him like that. Maybe he didn't feel like that, maybe what he felt was something crazier, or saner, and it wasn't fair to push personal stuff on him. People opened their mouths and put personal loads on each other, and embarrassed each other beyond anything they could ever patch, was all they were likely to do, when everything was already all right and it could go along forever as long as people didn't say stupid things to each other.

*So keep your mouth shut, Yeager, just wake him up and be nice, you got to leave pretty soon. Last thing you can do is duck out on him without a goodbye.*

She bent down, blew on the hair at his temple, moved back when he woke up, to save her jaw.

"Was going to give you a nice wake-up," she said, "but you move too quick."

He rubbed a stubbled face. He looked like hell. He muttered something, dragged himself up, patted her on the shoulder, and went to gather up his own kit by the door, headed for a wash-up.

So she sat by herself, she watched the little numbers on the screens until he came back, which wasn't long. He hadn't shaved, just washed up a bit, and he got them a couple of soft drinks and a couple sandwiches out of the locker at station one.

She drank. She couldn't face eating. She tucked the sandwich in her pocket.

"I'll keep it for later," she said, and deliberately didn't look at the time.

*Take care of yourself*, she wanted to say. But that sounded too much like goodbye. She wanted to go over things with him, to make sure he was agreeing with her, but that was her nerves it was for, no good for his.

"Yeager," com said. "*Report topside. Five minutes.*"

"Damn," she said.

NG reached out and grabbed her hand. Held on a second.

"Got to answer that," she said, and stood up and pulled away before she did something, said something, they didn't have the time to deal with. "I got to get Fitch settled – "

"Don't trust him. *Don't* trust him."

"*Yeager! Battle ready! No fuckin' time, Yeager!*"

"Oh, shee-it!" Her heart jumped, the body did, she left the chair-arm and turned around and grabbed him, hard, said: "That's it, that's all of it – *get off this ship!*"

The siren started. She tore away and ran, banged the edge of the doorway, jumped for the corridor deck and sprinted for the lift.

Didn't tell him goodbye, didn't even look back until it was too late and she was headed around the curve, and only a fool would ignore that siren and delay for a backward glance.

She wanted to tell him to suit up, wanted to stand over him and be sure he did. He could be a fool, damn him, she'd told him too much –

God, the clock by ops showed less than six hours, there could be something loose scan hadn't counted, hadn't spotted, hadn't anticipated –

Damn Goddard! Damn Fitch! You dealt with the Fleet, you dealt with carriers and rider-ships, too many pieces loose in any situation to take chances with –

She hit the lift, she hit the button and after that it moved at its own rate, nothing you could *do* but stand there while it climbed and lurched past the core . . .

Thump, thump, thump of the fueling pump, louder than the siren for a few seconds, whole floor of the lift shaking –

*If that bastard Fitch is conning me, if he just wants me to move –*

The ship rang and shook as if a hammer had hit it. She grabbed for the safety-rail and white-knuckled it, taste of blood in her mouth where she had bitten her lip.

*God! Have we been hit, or was that fire?*

*Little ship, pinned to station, could be us doing the firing –*

*Could be –*

The lift stopped at the top, opened on the bridge. She headed out as the siren quit, passed Goddard yelling at her, Goddard sitting at his post, a khaki blur to her as she ran. It was the topside locker she was headed for, and that was standing open. Fitch was in there already suiting up.

"What was it?" she said, jerked the zip open and started peeling, fast.

Fitch said: "Friends of yours."

"The hell! – Is it *Africa*?"

"They've used every ID in the book. We don't know a hundred percent who it is. – Shit!"

"Easy, back it up – you're going to strip those damn ring-seals." She grabbed after Fitch's problem, but he got it, shoved her off, and she stepped into her own armor-breeches, threw the lever that seated it solidly around her, rammed her feet down into the boots and worked her toes into those while she came up under the hanging top-section and wriggled her arms and her body up into it, helmet and all.

Solid mate. Throw the latches. Sleeves last, mating at the mid-shoulder, left and right, tension engaged, screw the rings tight and not too tight.

She beat Fitch by a second, seals and all. She heard her own breathing and Fitch's, felt a shock rock the ship and saw the audio reading jump.

She muttered: "Was that them firing or us?"

"Us." Fitch turned, flat-footed the way a neo learned to move, powered-on and lurched after balance.

Firing every time the station's rotation gave them a target.

"We're assuming they *want* the fuel we're holding?"

"Say it's a good assumption."

"What've we got on us? Rider, carrier, or both?"

"Suppose, Yeager, you just leave the thinking to somebody else."

"What they're going to do, sir, they're going to knock hell out of this station, leave us with a major problem, like a couple thousand people with no fuckin' *life-support*, sir – "

"That hasn't bothered you before now, has it, Sgt. Yeager?"

She got a breath, kept her body loose, kept on the track. "They're going to chaff our fire, sir, after which they're going to punch a major hole in Thule Station, after which there's none of our guns any fuckin' *use*, sir."

"We understand the situation, Yeager, trust us we know our options – "

"Twenty years on *Africa*, tac-squad sergeant, *sir*, I ran these operations from the other side. You got yourself a boarding situation, *sir*, and my advice – "

"Twenty years on this ship, out-fighting you and your

murdering friends – and you can take your advice to *hell*, Yeager!"

"My *advice*, sir, is get ready to blow the tanks they want *and* the pump, let 'em know that, and get ourselves out on that dock and get ourselves some room, sir, because they got *no* trouble getting into this ship, from inside or outside, I can swear to *that*, sir."

Just the breathing. Then finally: "Ship out there is probably *India*. It's using a merchanter ID. That's a rider-ship in-bound. Maybe two of them."

"It's *Ganges* or it's *Tigris*, we got two AP's and two rigs and either of them's got at least thirty, at least one whole tac-squad with the weapons-sync we haven't got, and they aren't fools. They can use an insystemer dock, they'll get their squad on station, core or rim – rim, if they know Thule, they'll punch right through the section-seals, and meanwhile we may have the other rider coming up under us and a second squad coming right through our hull into Personnel with another thirty guys, that's what."

Fitch didn't like that. Didn't say a thing.

"So you give the orders, sir, whatever you want from here."

Two little blips on station-scan, other side of station, one more on long-scan, only the best-guess of position. Absolutely. Goddard didn't like having her standing behind him, Goddard probably didn't like being there himself. "We're going to dockside," Fitch told him, on outside-speaker. "You're on your own. Tanks go at your discretion."

"Yessir," Goddard said, and glanced away for a second to flip a switch. "Good luck, sir."

Hadn't heard the lock cycle. Usually you heard the hydraulics work, it even got through the pump-noise, and she hadn't heard a sound. She kept thinking, *He's waiting, we're still firing, he's waiting to the last minute –*

*God, God, NG, get out –*

"Where's crew?" she asked Fitch when they got into the lift. "Station shelter?"

"Deep as we can get them." The lift started down. "Holding Central at gunpoint. We got some faint hearts. You ought to be right at home with that situation."

"As happens," she said, calm and quiet. "Yessir." She fired a shot of her own. "You volunteer for this?"

"I got my pick of crew," Fitch said.

"Tanks are rigged?"

"Tanks are rigged. Goddard's got that business."

"Goddard going to get clear?"

Silence.

Son of a *bitch*, she thought. And didn't say anything. Couldn't say anything.

The lift touched bottom. She kept thinking, walking out behind Fitch, *I could kill this bastard*.

Take him apart.

Joint by joint.

"You going to order Goddard clear, sir?"

"Goddard's in command up there. It's his choice." Fitch opened up the weapons-stowage. "This is what we've got."

AP 200's, shells, caps, remotes. She picked up a remote and a roll of fine wire, spotted a box of Gibbs-caps and reached for it. Fitch got his hand in the way and took charge of the remote.

"We got heavy demolitions? Station's got to have, sir, miner-supplies."

Fitch didn't answer her. Fitch passed her an AP and a handful of slings of shells.

"Demolitions," she repeated. "Sir. Where?"

"We're taking care of that."

"Dammit, sir, you *trying* to commit suicide, or what?"

Fitch shifted around, looked her direction. Clumsy. And she wasn't. Damn right she wasn't. Maybe Fitch was thinking about that. Likely Fitch was thinking all along about that.

"Do these rigs have a direct comlink with theirs?"

Reasonable question. "Yes, sir, they *can* have. Riders are probably trying to pick up *Loki*'s internal stuff. Might get a bit of it. Just keep to channel B, between us. They probably haven't got the 'ears they'd need for that, not on a rider-ship."

"Can you get into their comlink?"

Second reasonable question. "Can't mimic their ID, sir. I can talk to 'em, I can hear 'em, but I'll show up as another number on their board the second I go onto Fleet-com, and I'll show as *Africa*. They thought of that a *long* time ago."

"Don't think they'd welcome you?"

"Nossir. My codes aren't current and they'll blow me to hell on a special priority. That relieve your mind, sir?"

"No end," Fitch said, picked up his stuff, laid a hand on her shoulder and pushed. "Out."

She moved, slung her AP and her shells over her left shoulder, tucked the wire and the caps in a third shell-sling and headed for the lock, thinking right then that there *was* an outside chance, she could go onto *India*-com, she knew names, lot of old drinking-buddies on *India* and they knew her and they knew Teo and Bieji Hager. They might at least wait-see, damn, she could go on that band and Fitch wouldn't know –

Tell them watch out for a schiz Systems man and get him out alive –

On *India*. Take NG into the 'decks.

Sure, he'd thank her for that.

She followed Fitch out the lock, down the ramp, onto docks she had bad dreams about.

Section-seals were in place, like walls at either end of the section. Personnel access to get through those was down at the coreward edge of the seals, airlock passage in the arch of the seal-doorways. Four section-seals on Thule, to sep the docks and keep a decompression from going station-wide. Up above, she could see the constant yellow flash of movement in the hoses, the pump still shoving its load into *Loki*'s gut.

They said Mazian still had ways of supplying himself, said he had some deep base, maybe old Beta Station itself, where nobody in his right mind would go – but supply lines only went so far, and Fitch said *India* was that desperate. That meant *India* was likely being shoved, run, pushed off her regular supply points, off in the deep – and that meant Alliance ships able to keep her from moving on stations.

Little *Loki* could have gone on as she was, sat silent while *India* refueled and provisioned herself off Thule – and *Loki* instead put herself in the way of trouble. Chance was, *Loki* hadn't known *India* was coming in, just had the bad luck to be going into dock, leaving a heat-trail *India* could pick up like a beacon, and *Loki* couldn't run.

But chance also was that Wolfe *had* known *India* was in

the game. Chance was, when they'd dodged out-system in a hurry that had killed a man, when Wolfe had been on the general com after that, saying they'd had a carrier-class bogey – Wolfe had known what he was playing tag with.

They'd talked with some Alliance ship, Wolfe had said that much. They'd traded information, after which Loki had jumped to Thule.

Old spook, her systems chancy to the point of suicide – mostly-stripped station due for demolition –

Easy equation, the way high commands did math.

"Know something?" she said to Fitch. "We were supposed to have help here. And we sit out there waiting. But we got to have fuel, we don't get this ship out of here without it, so we decide to move on our own, we were going to go in, raid that fuckin' tank, blow the pump and get out, hell with the stationers. But it wasn't our support showed up, it was *India*, – am I right?"

No answer from Fitch, she thought. Then:

"Half-right. We come in on inertial approach, close and quiet as we can. We could've blown that pump, could've ordered station to do it. If we could get that fuckin' carrier out of the equation our last rendezvous could have spared us enough to get us to 'Dorado, but it wasn't and they couldn't. So we come in here with a problem, Ms. Yeager, and it hasn't gotten anything but worse. Right now, we got those riders sepped off at low $V$. The way they're acting, the speed they used getting here, we're right and they're that low, *no* mass in those tanks to speak of. So we're playing dumb little merchanter – like they can move in here real fast and easy and make a little ship like us spit it up again. Only by now they've got a look at us up close, now they know they got a real problem unless they can *take* us, and they know it's a trap that's going to close. That what you want to know?"

Made sense. For the first time she got the feeling Fitch was on the level.

"Meaning we got help possible?"

"Meaning we've caught ourselves a Fleet carrier. Meaning that sonuvabitch Keu is dead $V$ at this star and we're blowing every skimmer Thule's got, disabling the section-seals. We're going to take out that pump, and we're sitting here throwing missiles at those rider-ships they can't throw back, because they don't want to blow the pump or our tanks. We've been getting amnesty-offers for the last half hour."

Fitch surprised her. You got him started and the man could talk.

"Keu won't keep his word," she said. "Kreshov might, he's one captain in the Fleet that might, but not Keu. — You trusting Mallory, by any chance?"

"Not by choice," Fitch said.

Funny as hell. Spook officer and an *Afriker* with the same opinion. She almost appreciated Fitch for that half-second.

"Don't trust you, either," Fitch said then. "But you've got Ramey to think about. Ship blowing up's not the worst thing that could happen to Mr. Ramey — not with his particular problem. Boy can't take orders. How long do you think he'd last, on *India*?"

She didn't say anything. Didn't think it called for it.

"Just insurance," Fitch said. They got to the seal-door airlock, likeliest access with the giant seal-doors disabled from Central. Fitch waved a hand in the general direction of the lock, invited a fool to go ahead, try to open it. "You want to critique the job, Yeager, you go right ahead."

"Hell, no, sir, if Mr. Bernstein or Mr. Smith had anything to do with those airlock controls, I got every confidence. I just want to do me some basic wiring, if you don't mind, sir, a half-dozen AP rounds, just put their caps in and peel their backsides off."

Fitch hitched his shell-slings up on his shoulder. "You want to do that, I'm going to take me a little walk over there."

She halfway grinned. "Know what mof stands for, — sir?"

"Yeah," he said, and walked off. The com said: "It stands for, I stand over here, and you wire it, Yeager."

# Chapter 29

Something blew, you could feel it through the deck-plates, and a nervous skut with a glove off, that being faster, doing wiring on a job like this one – really *hated* to hear sounds like that.

But the air stayed.

Thank God for favors.

In spite of which, she had her tether-hook fastened to the nearest metal strut, because decompression was a real likelihood, and there was an equally good chance of something like a missile coming right up through the deckplates or the blast-wall, a hello from *India*'s number two rider that they knew was out there.

Touchy little job, Fitch was right, you called it a grape-cluster, nobody remembered why – a little group of AP shells with their back ends peeled off and bare wire stuck under their end-seals, right over the little black dot where the contact was. You twisted the tails together for good contact all the way down the bunch, finished it off with a little Gibbs-cap in the middle of the wires, then you just bent the twist-tail of the cluster and hooked it over something convenient.

Mostly you hung them head-high, on girders and such. And in this case, made extra-long twist-tails and a good solid knot in those tails to make sure they held fast.

Another explosion, off in some other section.

She kept at it, with the bare hand freezing, because Thule's power was down, and bitter cold air coming through the vents on the rig, because they had six hours, longer if they didn't ask anything out of the circulation, and longer, too, because she wasn't asking anything out of the armor while she was sitting here making fussy little wire-tails and worrying more about static charges than she was about the booms and blow-ups around the rim.

At least Fitch wasn't a nag, man sat down and shut up

and just watched the way he said, saving it too, faceplate up, talking back and forth to Goddard, maybe clear to Central and Wolfe or Orsini, on *Loki*'s sealed-line phone, there at the pump-station.

She took another cap, turned its tiny edge-dial, set it as number three, was wrapping it in when the dock quaked and Fitch stumbled up to his feet.

She wound the tail, laid it down, unclipped her safety and jammed her right glove on, then grabbed up her gun and the rest of the shells. "Program," she said, "vent seal, amp 220, gyros."

Second blast as she was standing up. Readout said this one came from dead ahead. *Loki*'s berth – either *Loki* or the station wall around it.

Dammit!

She ran for Fitch's position behind the main pump housing, came in heavy-footed and needing the gyros on the stop. "They're in, sir, that was the ship took that hit – Get Goddard and NG off, tell them get down here!"

"I just did," Fitch said. "Goddard's on his way out. Your damn merchanter-boy isn't answering his com, Yeager."

"Shit!"

"There's the phone. You're patched into general com up there, *you* tell him get his ass out here."

She grabbed the phone, unplugged the line and shoved the plug into the com-patch. "NG? NG, it's Bet. Answer your damn page!"

The deck shook. Readout said behind her. Airlock, then. She saw Fitch ducked down behind the pump-housing, figured if the tac-squad was worth anything they'd probed the airlock before they sent anybody through, and they were just going to blast through the layers, one after the other. Took a minute or so more. "NG? Never mind answering, just get suited and get the hell moving! Come *on*, dammit!"

Flicker of bracketing on the ramp, somebody in a hardsuit.

She hoped it was NG, she didn't think it was.

Goddard's voice said, "I can't raise the son of a bitch."

Could've ducked out before this, maybe nobody was paying attention. Maybe he was *on* the docks and scared to answer . . .

Maybe he was gone-out, ducked into some hole on the ship – not tracking on here and now –

That damn hole in back of the storage-rack –

God!

"*NG, get out of the ship!*"

Flutter of bracketing as Goddard got into cover with Fitch, Goddard carrying an AP and a couple of shell-slings, give him credit for that much, the son of a bitch –

She wanted to kill him.

"NG!"

Wanted her hands on NG at the moment, wanted to shake him til he rattled, *damn* it, damn his spook ways –

"*NG! Get out here!*"

More shocks in the readout, marker-dot flashing on the airlock at her back. You didn't need to face a thing in a rig. But she kept looking toward the ramp, hoping for a damned fool to show up.

Dot still flashing, sound-reading coming up, secondary dot intermittent with brackets as Goddard was trying to get his gun loaded –

No more time to spend, no more. She unplugged the line, squatted down with Fitch and Goddard, pulled her safety-clip and attached to the buffer-skirt support on the pump-housing, only thing she could see that might hold. Fitch followed suit, got Goddard clipped.

*NG, dammit!*

Puff of fire at the airlock, sudden vapor following that –

"God!" Fitch's voice.

Air freezing as it met hard vacuum.

As the dockside blew out the airlock.

She got a grip on the buffer herself, as dust and junk flew past, as the rig's pickups registered a whistling howl of escaping air –

"You got to get them when they show," she said to Fitch and Goddard. "Got *Loki* at our backs, another damn squad coming behind us – "

Things left the ground and flew, stuff hit the seal-wall and stuck under the wind-pressure, stuff skidded and rolled across the decking, a couple of shipping cans flew like so much foil-scrap, and lights started going out, old-fashioned floods popping in the vacuum, other things started exploding, less and less audible as the air went away.

No way the tac-squad was standing in the path of that storm. They were hooked in, tucked down, never in the rigged airlock when it blew, just out there waiting for Thule to bleed to death.

Same as they were.

Coming through the first instant it was safe, and she had the remote, Fitch and Goddard had the AP's, and when the *India* team came through they met a barrage and started handing it back, firing as they went for the cover of girders on either side.

She let them. She hit .001 on the keypad, and the clusters blew, head-high, about the time wave two came in, straight into the AP fire, and the three-team came through –

002, 003.

Didn't want to look at what it did.

Faceplates were where you didn't want to get it.

"We *got* 'em," Goddard gasped.

She said, "We got 'em up our ass, dammit!" She unclipped, grabbed up the shell-slings and her gun and stood up. "We got one ship down there to deal with, we got more of 'em coming up our backsides – they breached the ship, they got to come *here*, dammit – "

She didn't care where Fitch and Goddard were going, she heard Fitch's, "Wait, Yeager," and she didn't stop to argue, she ordered the rig to max and headed up the ramp for *Loki*'s airlock.

Airlock blew out, all of *Loki*'s air hit her like a fist, knocked her down, the gyros brought her up and she rode the limb-movements, synched with them and had the rifle up before the rest of her was, was halfway up when vibration on the ramp told her something heavy had hit it running –

Gut told her it was armor, brain didn't have time to debate it: hands knew where to put the shell and the conscious brain got the fact a target was bracketed before it knew it had already pulled the trigger.

Conscious brain wondered was it a hardsuit or armor before the explosion went off in the guy's face.

Before she knew a shell had hit her and knocked her flat

and the rig was bouncing her up again, headed for *Loki*'s insides. . . .

Didn't stop for grace.

Didn't stop when she came face-on in the airlock with half a tac-team who maybe for a couple of critical ticks didn't reckon an oncoming rig belonged to a spook ship – til she got another one and took a shell from him, and yelled *Program-gyros-off*, while she was wondering if that leg was breached, it wasn't moving right.

She fired up as her opposition came up on gyros, got him in the groin and blew him out the inner door, as his AP tore hell out of the bulkhead and you couldn't see anything for smoke.

Spatter and soot all over her faceplate. She was still moving, leg still worked, loose, but it worked, she felt cold there and maybe the autoseal was working, didn't know, heard Fitch panting and gasping, "Goddard's dead – "

She walked *Loki*'s downside deck, she had a rattle in her armor, wasn't sure whether that tension screw in the left shoulder hadn't gone, wasn't sure that leg wasn't freezing in vacuum, she was getting that body-display that meant armor problems, whole left leg blinking red, shoulder blinking yellow . . .

They got to the lift shaft. The door was open, the car wasn't there, just lines hanging in the dark of the shaft, the kind troopers used for a fast drop. "Core," she said to Fitch, "they got in from the ship core."

She wanted, dammit, to stop and get on ship-com, see if she could raise Engineering, but there wasn't time, was a chance of any damn thing happening –

Explosion somewhere. The ship quaked.

"That might be the tanks," Fitch said.

"Shit!" She grabbed one of the hanging lines, pulled up the latch-down on her left shoulder, clamped it on the cable. "Going to the core – " She pulled Fitch a line close, threaded his hoist, wrapped her line under her right leg, pulled the lever down and held it.

Teeth slipped a little on the cable, scary as hell when you were halfway up.

Scary as hell when you thought about somebody getting into that shaft above or below and potshotting you on that cable. Had to use the night-glows, no way to see in the dark and cold what they were doing or where they were going, and it was help enough for somebody waiting at the core-access with a rifle –

Fitch was coming up all right, she saw the other cable tight, saw the cable attachments coming up fast above her on the support struts for the core-access bulkhead, good clear attachment, no gymnastics needed: she ordered the gyros, swung her feet up and planted her boots on the lip, leaned forward and made it, facing into absolute dark past the dim edges of the open access.

Graffiti on the wall, something painted –

Fitch bumped her, went back off the edge as she grabbed him, damn good thing she was holding the support. Her rig complained, the left arm slipped, but it hauled him up and his gyros got him steady.

Lot of dark. No sound except their own breathing, nothing from the pickups. Total vacuum.

The core access was standing wide open. Somebody had to have used an emergency crank to get both doors like that – big white circle and slash spray-painted across the lock controls –

– where you could see it only coming from *this* direction.

Fitch grabbed her arm, sudden shock of rig against rig.

*Goddard's sign-off, maybe, when they rigged the tanks to blow? Warning* Loki *crew out?*

No pump, she thought. No vibration through the deck. It had stopped.

The core went straight back from here, whole length of the spine, long, dark void. The glows and the night-sight got just the beginning of the conduits, the start of the grid that was the in-dock walkway along the downside.

She stood still, spooked. Fitch wasn't moving either.

Shaft of light came into the core. Floods from the ridership, she thought for a heart-pounding second, then she realized it was sunlight coming through a wound in *Loki's* shielding, blaze of light and glare bouncing off surfaces down the walk, glancing and dazzling off ice, so that the display and the readouts struggled to cope with contrast. The light made huge shadows out of the two giant conduit-bundles as

Thule's rotation carried the sun past their zenith. Moving bars of light and shadow touched the walkway and showed blazing white shapes lying on it, the walkway itself showed bent and melted – and iced . . .

Eyes wouldn't make sense out of it.

The glare from the star passed, moved up the wall, glare dimming to twilight.

She jerked a metal utility clip off her rig, threw it onto the grid.

No sparks . . .

Fitch caught her arm, no force against her amped rig, nothing but noise, a scrape of ceramics. "Yeager, we got nothing to do here, let it be, we got two rider-ships and a fuckin' carrier unaccounted for, come *on*, Yeager!"

You couldn't yell out to anybody, to see if anybody was still alive in here, you couldn't do anything, there wasn't any air to carry the sound, and the whole core was a trap, whole tac-squad wiped out – except the point-men that had gotten through and gone down the lines –

Not Goddard's work, couldn't be Goddard's work –

Power on that scale – Hell of a job. Cable from *Loki*'s whole damn electrical system, run right to that grid.

"Yeager!"

"Program," she said to the rig. "Fleet-com."

She got sputter back, got the hiss of distant voices, not the clear transmission of a rider-ship com close by:

"*Number one? Number one?*"

Some poor skut was lost out there, distant across station. She heard, more distant still, full of breakup, ". . . *Charlie niner one, that's forty.*"

And after a few seconds: "*We copy forty –* "

She cut back to channel B on manual, said to Fitch, "Just dropped into Fleet-com. They're 'lagged from each other, they're moving."

On the retreat. Fast.

Standard ops. Rider-captain's standing orders, always – cover your carrier. If a situation goes to hell, tac-squads are on their own, cover your carrier –

*No way out for them now. They're trapped. They know it. Carrier's stuck in system.*

"Time to get ourselves deep in station," Fitch said. "We're

going to hear from that carrier, round-trip, damn soon. Keu's not going to take this real passive. — Come on, Yeager, dammit. . . ."

She ignored the pull on her arm, muttered, "Go to hell. Sir." And tried to think, tried to remember where you could detach the main cables, and figure how you could set up that kind of a trap and spring it without being where you could see when to throw a switch, and you could, from Engineering — but not without monitoring the core didn't have and there hadn't been time to set up. So it had to be the dirty way — a hands-on job, where you could see your targets, get them all where you wanted them. Then throw the power on. And maybe go with it.

She walked out on the grid, turned her helmet light on, heard, "Damn fool," out of Fitch, and just kept walking, sweating, hoping like hell the cable had burned itself away, which, by all she could figure, it had —

She scanned the shadows, sweeping her light from side to side, scared to keep to the grid, which might be melted through and loose, a broken connection that she might accidentally bridge with a step — scared of that and scared to step off the walkway and risk running into that cable in the dark.

Sun swept slowly past again, threw light and shadow onto the wreckage of the core: gridwork and pipe and the glare of sun on ice where a conduit had sprayed surfaces, ice-glare on bodies, ice coating white armor —

Long hanging shapes from one core-bundle, pieces of burned hose —

Or free-hanging power cable.

Surfaces glazed in ice, bodies embedded in it, shadow again as the sun passed the area.

She looked around, swept her light past the ominous shape of cables, saw motion bracketed, spun around with the AP in hand, fire-bracket and motion-bracket overlapped as her hand centered —

Civ hardsuit! God!

Shot slammed into her, knocked her down, smoke hanging in a cloud as she came up again, motion in the smoke, smoke from her shot, smoke from his —

She froze with the gun aimed up, he froze with his level, a

nerve-twitch off, that was all that had missed him – figure up against the forward bulkhead, man with a rifle and no lights, just sun-bounce shining off the girders, off his suit-surfaces, a hard suit that never would have survived a direct hit.

He had to have figured it out, then, or he was out of shells: he wasn't firing again, was just wedged in there, into what cover the bulkhead and the shadow of the struts afforded.

"NG?" She tried *Loki*'s frequency. She wasn't sure he could hear, wasn't sure NG was hearing anything or seeing anything that wasn't years back, some other boarding –

People in armor –

She let her gun down, lifted her left hand, walked back along the grid with a stutter in her motion, shaking in every joint –

Signed to him, Come out.

She saw him lift the gun again.

And stop.

She beckoned again. Slowly NG started hauling himself up under the hardsuit's stationside weight.

Her motion-sensor suddenly bracketed something else – Fitch standing in the core access doorway, she hoped to hell it was Fitch.

NG staggered as far as the walk. She got his arm, helped him up onto the grid, patted his shoulder as she steered him toward the door.

Fitch said, "Get our asses out of here, dammit."

Fact was, she suddenly realized, Fitch didn't know the reverse toggle on the cable-grip.

Fact was, Fitch was mad as hell about it.

Til they got downside and halfway across the docks and had sudden contact with Orsini coming in on their com, telling them that something big had just dropped into system, using Mallory's ID.

She grabbed NG, brought his helmet into contact with hers, yelled it at him til he understood it, "*Norway*'s dropped into system! Riders deployed! We got help, understand? *India*'s low-*V*, Keu hasn't got a chance."

First time, maybe, NG was really sure which of them was which.

He damn sure wouldn't have put his arms around Fitch.

# Chapter 30

Lines of refugees again, scared people, headed out into the patch-together tube that crossed Green dock, waiting, with their meager belongings, line moving only now and again, but you couldn't tell them to wait anywhere else, people had a ship waiting out there that could take them, and people wouldn't follow instructions and take numbers and wait for the next shuttle out, they just jammed up and made their line and wouldn't leave it.

It was worth a riot to argue with it. Wolfe said let 'em, Neihart, whose ship was the biggest that had come in, said let 'em, Mallory was God knew where.

The jam-up in the corridor played hob with ship's personnel trying to get back and forth, you had to bust people out of their priorities, which meant upset, panicky stationers, but people got out of the way of *Loki* crew, figuring, Bet supposed, they were about one jump worse than Mallory's bunch and only one better than Keu's.

They got out of her way when she went down to the docks, they moved their baggage over and gave her a clear path.

But she stopped when she recognized a man in line and recognized the woman next on.

Man looked up, worried-looking.

"Mr. Ely," she said. She didn't put out her hand til he did: a lot of stationers weren't anxious to be friends.

"Ms. Yeager," he said, and: "My wife, Hally Kyle."

"Ms. Kyle, pleased to meet you." She saw Nan Jodree offer her hand, too, at her left, turned and took a cold-as-ice, still steady grip.

"Good to see you," Nan said. "*Good* to see you, Bet."

"Tried to find you," she said. "Mate of mine said he'd seen you on the list, but things were pretty scrambled."

"Going out again," Nan said.

"I got to bust ahead of you," she said. "I do apologize, I

got to be on this one. Going back to Pell, too, they're going to ferry us, at least our front end. All that matters of a ship, anyhow . . . You all right?"

"We will be," Ely said. "You? We were *worried* about you, Bet."

"I'm fine," she said. They were sounding the board-call. "Damn, I got to get down there – See you at Pell! – Nice meeting you, Ms. Kyle."

Bernstein was upset, patches all over, jury-rigged messes patched into the can-hauler's hull, three weeks to do that link-up, and Smith said it was all right, Bernie said it was a hell of a mess, Musa said he'd seen worse –

Mostly, she figured, it was better than they'd been going to do, on their own.

Better than they *had* done, getting into Thule.

Lot of the boards were shut down. Systems was mostly dark. Most of the ship just wasn't there, her tail-section due to take a ride into Thule's sun, along with Thule Station.

Piece of history going away.

She walked up to NG, said, "How's it going?"

NG made this little frustrated shrug, said, "What I *got's* fine . . ."

That'd been the strange thing, NG'd had his chance, Neihart had heard what he'd done, offered him a berth, Bernie'd said. On *Finity's End*.

NG'd said, "No. Thanks."

Bernie'd been a little off-put, Neihart's trying to steal his Systems man, but Bernie had said to her and Musa, "I don't understand him."

NG didn't explain himself, to her or to Musa, never mentioned it.

She said, now, finally, because her conscience hurt her, "Heard you had an offer."

He said, shaking his head, "Bernie outbid them."